D1523891

BEST
SCIENCE FICTION STORIES
OF THE YEAR
Ninth Annual Collection

ABOUT THE EDITOR

Gardner Dozois was born and raised in Salem, Massachusetts, and has been writing and editing science fiction for over ten years. His short fiction has appeared in most of the leading SF magazines and anthologies, and he has been a Nebula Award finalist six times, a Hugo Award finalist four times, and a Jupiter Award finalist twice. He is the editor of a number of anthologies, among them *A Day in the Life, Future Power* (with Jack Dann), *Another World,* and *Beyond the Golden Age.* His most recent books are the Nebula Award finalist *Strangers,* a novel; *The Visible Man,* a collection of his short fiction; *Aliens!,* an anthology edited with Jack Dann; and *The Fiction of James Tiptree, Jr.,* a critical chapbook. He is also co-author, with George Alec Effinger, of the novel *Nightmare Blue* and is currently at work on another novel. He is a member of the Science Fiction Writers of America, the SFWA Speakers' Bureau, and the Professional Advisory Committee to the Special Collections Department of the Paley Library at Temple University. Mr. Dozois lives in Philadelphia.

BEST
SCIENCE FICTION
STORIES
OF THE YEAR
Ninth Annual Collection

Edited by
GARDNER DOZOIS

E. P. Dutton I New York

Acknowledgment is made for permission to print the following material:

"Sandkings," by George R. R. Martin. Copyright © 1979 by Omni International Ltd. First published in *Omni*, August 1979. Reprinted by permission of the author.

"Bloodsisters," by Joe Haldeman. Copyright © 1979 by Playboy. First published in *Playboy*, July 1979. Reprinted by permission of the author and the author's agent, Kirby McCauley.

"Camps," by Jack Dann. Copyright © 1979 by Mercury Press, Inc. First published in *The Magazine of Fantasy and Science Fiction*, May 1979. Reprinted by permission of the author.

"giANTS," by Edward Bryant. Copyright © 1979 by Condé Nast Publications, Inc. First published in *Analog Science Fiction/Science Fact*, August 1979. Reprinted by permission of the author.

"Down and Out on Ellfive Prime," by Dean Ing. Copyright © 1979 by Omni International Ltd. First published in *Omni*, March 1979. Reprinted by permission of the author.

"Redeemer," by Gregory Benford. Copyright © 1979 by Condé Nast Publications, Inc. First published in *Analog Science Fiction/Science Fact*, April 1979.

"In Trophonius's Cave," by James P. Girard. Copyright © 1979 by Mercury Press, Inc. First published in *The Magazine of Fantasy and Science Fiction*, May 1979. Reprinted by permission of the author.

"The Ancient Mind at Work," by Suzy McKee Charnas. Copyright © 1979 by Suzy McKee Charnas. First published in *Omni*, February 1979. Reprinted by permission of the author and the author's agent, Virginia Kidd.

"Vernalfest Morning," by Michael Bishop. Copyright © 1979 by Michael Bishop. First published in *Chrysalis 3* (Zebra). Reprinted by permission of the author and the author's agent, Virginia Kidd.

"The Way of Cross and Dragon," by George R. R. Martin. Copyright © 1979 by Omni International Ltd. First published in *Omni*, June 1979. Reprinted by permission of the author.

"The Battle of the Abaco Reefs," by Hilbert Schenck. Copyright © 1979 by Hilbert Schenck. First published in *The Magazine of Fantasy and Science Fiction*, June 1979. Reprinted by permission of the author and the author's agent, Virginia Kidd.

For information contact:
Elsevier-Dutton Publishing Co., Inc., 2 Park Avenue, New York, N.Y 10016

Library of Congress Catalog Card Number: 77-190700
ISBN: 0–525–06498–2

Published simultaneously in Canada by
Clarke, Irwin & Company Limited, Toronto and Vancouver

10 9 8 7 6 5 4 3 2 1

First Edition

For
Janet and Ricky Kagan

CONTENTS

ACKNOWLEDGMENTS

The editor would like to thank the following people for their help and support:

Michael Swanwick, Jack Dann, Susan Casper, Marianne Porter, Virginia Kidd, Jim Frenkel, David G. Hartwell, John Douglas, Pat LoBrutto, Victoria Schochet, John Silbersack, Kirby McCauley, Charles L. Grant, Sharon Jarvis, Steve Roos, George R. R. Martin, Charles C. Ryan, Stuart Shiff, Ed Ferman, Roy Torgeson, Andrew Porter, Edward Bryant, Terry Carr, David Axler, Tom Purdom, Geo. W. Proctor, James Baen, Howard Waldrop, Lois Wickstrom, Gregory Benford, Dean Ing, Patricia Cadigan, Arnold Fenner, Fred Fisher of the Hourglass SF Bookstore in Philadelphia, and special thanks to my editor, Jo Alford.

Thanks are also due to Charles N. Brown, whose excellent newzine *Locus* (P.O. Box 3938, San Francisco, CA 94119—$12 for twelve issues) was used as a reference source throughout the Summation.

INTRODUCTION

Summation: 1979

The big SF boom of the late seventies did not bust and collapse in 1979—not quite. For the first time, though, there were definite signs that the end of the boom may be at hand, and if the wave of success that had been building for the past four years did not quite shatter and fall in 1979, the guess of most observers is that it has at least crested. The question now seems to be not "can the boom keep on booming?"—that seems fairly well settled: It cannot, at least at anything like its former headlong pace—but "can SF as a genre hold on to some of its new prosperity and popularity, hold on to at least some of the new high ground it gained during the boom?" If it cannot, we may soon see the collapse and disastrous retrenchment long predicted by some critics, and the next few years may be bleak ones for SF.

So far, at the beginning of the eighties, the outlook is not sanguine. According to the SF newsmagazine *Locus*, the results of a sales survey by the Association of American Publishers show that sales of mass-market paperbacks declined 10 to 15 percent for the period January to May 1979 as compared to sales a year ago—the first downturn in paperback sales since World War II; January through May hardcover sales were also off 15 percent from a year ago. This is an industry-wide phenomenon, of course, affecting all of the American publishing world. It stems from causes such as inflation, recession, and the skyrocketing prices of both hardcover and softcover books (caused in turn by the skyrocketing costs of paper, labor, and so forth). Nevertheless, SF seemed particularly hard-hit, perhaps because it has been overextending itself in the past few years (glutted markets mean falling sales), or perhaps because, in a coherent and cohesive genre, the effects were more recognizable.

The slowdown in sales that put a damper on British SF last year hit the American SF scene with a vengeance this year: All SF magazines, with the exception of *Omni*, were down somewhat in sales in 1979. Ace, Dell, Berkley/Putnam, Harper & Row, and several other publishing houses made cutbacks in their SF lines this year, some of the cutbacks severe. All over the SF world, money is tight, editors are buying more cautiously, publishers are less willing to back their editors, books that are considered to be less than surefire commercially have been postponed, shelved, or dropped outright, and rumors persist that at least two major paperback SF lines are in danger of being dropped entirely by their publishers. Risk-taking is way down in the short-story markets, and dozens of writers have had stories rejected for being "too far out," "too risky," "too literary," "not enough like Star Wars," and so forth. Corporate publishing, with its emphasis on bulk sales and uniformity, is strengthening its hold on the genre. And as sales become riskier, advances go down: Robert Silverberg's novel *Lord Valentine's Castle*, which sold to *hardcover* at the height of the boom for a reputed $127,500, sold to paperback this year for "only" a reputed $75,000—still a big advance, certainly, but not a patch on the half-million-dollar paperback sale observers were predicting for the book last year.

And yet, in spite of all these evil portents, I am not willing to scatter ashes over my head and conclude that All Is Lost. A touch of historical perspective is needed. SF has survived periods of collapse and disastrous retrenchment before, and can—and will—survive such a period again. I don't think things will get that bad, that fast, and I have (what seems to me to be) sound historical reasons for a constrained and cautious optimism about SF's future.

One: It has been pointed out, I think with a good deal of justification, that every boom-and-bust cycle has left the habitual SF-reading audience *larger than it was before the boom began.* SF is, at the moment, an enormous genre. More SF was published in 1979 than ever before, more than one hundred books a month, according to *Locus*, with more than half of those books new titles (a record that is likely to stand for some time). Even if cuts a good deal more substantial than any so far announced are made, the "retrenched" genre will probably still be larger than the genre *as a whole* was prior to the start of the late seventies' boom. Things may get a lot tougher and tighter, a great deal of the present fat may eventually be trimmed away, but even so, I seriously doubt that SF will ever go back to pre-1974 levels of readership or advances or sales.

Two: There *are* counterentropic trends visible: The enormous success of *Omni*. Dave Hartwell's renovation of Pocket Books, and the fine new hardcover line he's putting together for Simon and Schuster. The success, to date, of the hardcover line from St. Martin's Press. The slow but steady improvement in the Doubleday SF line under Pat LoBrutto. The commercial stability of the Del Rey SF line. The new SF line being started at Playboy Press, and the assignment of Page Cuddy as Avon's new editor. The fact that, in spite of cutbacks, Dell, Ace, Berkley/Putnam, and Harper & Row have continued to keep strong SF lines alive. The fact that "quality" publishers like Knopf are dabbling in SF, with, so far, a measure of success. And the fact that, in spite of the SF books that don't sell, many SF books *do* sell very well indeed, both in hardcover and paperback—and some sell phenomenally well.

Three: There are more good writers, of many diverse types, producing now than at any time during the history of the genre, including the so-called "Golden Age" of the forties. Golden Age (and earlier) writers like Asimov, Heinlein, Sturgeon, Leiber, Simak, and Williamson are still writing, as are postwar big names like Anderson, Knight, Pohl, Budrys, Dickson, Harrison, Herbert, Clement, Clarke, Vance, Aldiss, Ellison, Sheckley, Dick, and Silverberg. The new writers of the sixties—Delany, Zelazny, Niven, Moorcock, Malzberg, Wilhelm, Lafferty, Russ, Spinrad, Bova, Le Guin, Disch, Roberts, Tiptree, Wolfe—became the big names of the seventies, and are still creating as vigorously as ever. And those writers who were unknown at the beginning of the seventies have established a reputation base, are now beginning to produce work a quantum jump better than any they've produced before, and are well on their way to becoming the big names of the eighties: Michael Bishop, Joe Haldeman, Gregory Benford, John Varley, Jack Dann, Howard Waldrop, George R. R. Martin, Phyllis Eisenstein, Ian Watson, Christopher Priest, Vonda N. McIntyre, Edward Bryant, Lisa Tuttle, George Alec Effinger, Elizabeth A. Lynn, Marta Randall, Charles L. Grant, Joan D. Vinge, Pamela Sargent, Robert Thurston, and easily a half-dozen others. Surely *some* of this amazing spectrum of writers will survive any possible period of retrenchment.

Four—and possibly the most important reason of all—: Good new writers continue to come into the field in a steady stream, and as long as there are good new writers coming along, there is hope for the future of SF. Recent years have seen promising debuts by James P. Girard, John Crowley, Hilbert Schenck, Dean Ing, Greg Bear, Michael Shea, Jane Yolen, Tony Sarowitz, Paul David Novitski, Mildred Downey Broxon, Carter Scholz, Charles Sheffield, Connie Willis, Bruce Sterling, Jake Saunders, Donald Kingsbury, Cynthia Felice, David Drake, A. A. Attanasio, Lee Killough, Alan Ryan, Somtow Sucharitkul, Bob Leman, James Patrick Kelly, John Kessel, Juleen Brantingham, and a dozen others. A bit farther down the road are writers like Michael Swanwick,

Eileen Gunn, Leigh Kennedy and Beverly Evans, who are just making
their first few sales at the beginning of the eighties (with Swanwick in
particular already starting to acquire a reputation among insiders): behind
them is yet another rank of hopefuls. Many of the above writers will falter
and fall by the wayside, some will turn out to be minor writers or
occasional writers (not necessarily the same thing), but some of them will
be among the big names of the nineties.

My own forecast, then, for the state of SF in the eighties is that we
can expect tough times, belt-tightening, and a general loss of creative
energy in the early eighties (as was also true in the early seventies), but
that if we can somehow hang on to artistic diversity in the face of the
homogenizing pressures of corporate publishing (if SF is not mashed
down into as rigidly standardized a mold as, say, gothics or regency
romances), and if commercially "marginal" but artistically vital story
markets like *The Magazine of Fantasy and Science Fiction* survive, then
we can expect to see a return of energy and prosperity in the mid-to-late
eighties.

Only time will tell if I'm right—or dramatically wrong.

Again this year most of the action was in the magazine field, in spite
of sagging midsummer sales, and most of 1979's good short fiction
appeared in one magazine or another.

Although conservative critics continued to predict *Omni*'s imminent
demise throughout much of 1979, that magazine not only survived but
prospered. With a circulation of roughly 800,000 newsstand sales per
issue, plus a subscription list of 100,000, and with major advertisers like
General Motors locked into long-term contracts, *Omni*'s survival for at
least the next few years seems assured. Meanwhile, it is the most widely
distributed of any SF magazine (carried by most newsstands, drugstores,
supermarkets, etc.), people can be seen reading it in laundromats and on
buses and subways and commuter trains, and many observers have
recognized it as one of the major publishing success stories of the past ten
years. Somewhat more surprisingly, *Omni* has proved to be an artistic as
well as a commercial success; after a moderately slow start last year,
Omni published more first-rate short SF in 1979 than any other magazine,
with the perennial exception of *The Magazine of Fantasy and Science
Fiction*. Excellent work by George R. R. Martin, Suzy McKee Charnas,
Dean Ing, Gregory Benford, and Gene Wolfe appeared in *Omni* this year,
along with good stories by Juleen Brantingham, Jack C. Haldeman II, Joe
Haldeman, Alfred Bester, Ben Bova, Rick Gauger, Spider Robinson,
Robert Haisty, and Roger Zelazny.

Toward the end of the year, former fiction editor Ben Bova moved
up to replace Frank Kendig as *Omni*'s executive editor, assuming responsibility for the total editorial content of the magazine. Bova was in

turn replaced as *Omni* fiction editor by SF writer Robert Sheckley. Certainly much of the dramatic improvement in the overall quality of *Omni*'s fiction this year can be attributed to Bova's work as fiction editor, and it will be interesting to see what sort of effect the appointment of Sheckley will have—Bova and Sheckley are very different as writers, and I would surmise that their literary tastes differ widely as well. Sheckley, for instance, is usually thought of as a writer with an anti-technology slant, but if he therefore bars "hard" SF from *Omni*, stuff like the Benford and Ing stories, he might well be making a serious mistake. As yet, of course, no one knows what changes Sheckley actually *will* make, or in what direction those changes will point. Whatever does happen, it is to be hoped that the quality of the fiction in *Omni* will remain up to this year's high standard.

Over at *Analog*, new editor Stanley Schmidt is also competing against Ben Bova's track record (Bova was editor of *Analog* for seven years before moving to *Omni* late in 1978), and he so far has not quite measured up to it. Under Schmidt's first full year as editor, *Analog*'s cover art has improved dramatically, but the overall quality of the fiction has gone down. Many of *Analog*'s most popular series of recent years—particularly Spider Robinson's "Callahan's Bar" stories and Sam Nicholson's "Captain Schuster" stories—have followed Bova to *Omni*, and *Omni* also published many individual stories this year by people like Joe Haldeman, George R. R. Martin, Orson Scott Card, Dean Ing, Gregory Benford, and Spider Robinson that almost certainly would have appeared in *Analog* if they'd been written a couple of years ago. Many of the above writers were developed by Bova during his long tenure as *Analog* editor, and their de facto desertion to *Omni* has drained a lot of the life from *Analog*. So far Schmidt has not succeeded in developing new writers exciting enough to adequately replace them. Good stories by Edward Bryant, Gregory Benford, Robert Thurston, Donald Kingsbury, Michael McCollum, and a few others did appear in *Analog* during 1979, but on the whole the short fiction this year was gray, dull, and overly familiar, a fact that is perhaps partially accountable for the continued slow dwindling of *Analog*'s circulation (below the 100,000 copy-per-issue mark now, according to *Locus*). In fairness to Schmidt, it should be said that even Bova and John W. Campbell himself were unable to immediately impress their editorial personalities upon the magazine—it took both of them a couple of years to really hit the top of their editorial stride, and such may well be the case with Schmidt. Certainly it is too early to count Schmidt out; if he is willing to take a few more risks, widen his scope, and accept stories that lean away from the *Analog* formula (as Bova did in his time by pushing stories like Haldeman's "Hero" and Pohl's "The Gold at the Starbow's End" in front of an initially hostile readership), then he may be able to reverse what now looks like a gradual downward trend.

Isaac Asimov's Science Fiction Magazine also had a somewhat dull year fictionally, and also suffered a slight overall loss in circulation. Again, at least part of the blame may perhaps be placed on a formula that may be becoming overly familiar—there was a uniformity of style, subject matter, and treatment to many of the stories *IASFM* published this year, something that was noticed and commented upon by several other critics; there is a slight but distinct "juvenile" feeling to much of *IASFM*'s fiction, as if the magazine is being surreptitiously aimed at an audience of teenagers. And, although it is an admirable thing to encourage new writers, *IASFM* may be relying *too* heavily on them—material by new writers has sometimes taken up 80 percent or more of the magazine, and one uneven new writer has frequently had two or three different stories in the same issue under various pseudonyms. Whatever the cause, *IASFM* remains a remarkably uneven magazine; it probably publishes a higher percentage of good solid second-string material than any other magazine in the field, but rarely publishes anything of really first-rank quality. Good stories by Isaac Asimov, Randall Garrett (Garrett's "Lord Darcy" series also seems to have deserted *Analog*, appearing now in *IASFM*), Nancy Kress, Tony Sarowitz, Paul Novitski, Bill Earls, John M. Ford, Tanith Lee, Gene Wolfe, Milton Rothman, and others appeared in *IASFM* during 1979, but the only really first-rate material to appear there this year was the de facto serialization of Frederik Pohl's novel *The Cool War*, broken up into several novellas that ran throughout the year.

Asimov's SF Adventure Magazine, *IASFM*'s new companion magazine, suffers from most of the same faults as *IASFM*, but in exaggerated form—*ASFA* seems to be selling poorly, and was reported to be in financial trouble by the end of the year. After a poor start in 1978, *ASFA* picked up slightly with this year's summer issue, which contained good stories by Samuel R. Delany and Roger Zelazny, only to drop sharply in quality again with the next issue. No other issues have yet appeared. The official word is that *ASFA* is "on hold," awaiting more detailed sales returns, but most genre insiders are betting that *ASFA* is dead.

Galileo gave up its status as a subscription-only magazine this year, and became widely available on newsstands for the first time, distributed by Dell. *Galileo*'s publishers were initially optimistic about the change-over, announcing that they expected "to reach a circulation of more or less 100,000. By the end of the year, however, rumors were flying that the *Galileo* management was disappointed by the newsstand sales (averaging only 20 to 30 percent of distributed copies, according to *Locus*, out of a 150,000 copy-per-issue press run), and by the beginning of 1980 they had announced tentative plans to drop newsstand distribution and return to a subscription-only policy. (Just in case, *Galileo*'s subscription address is: 339 Newbury St., Boston, MA 02115; $7.50 for six issues;

$12 for twelve issues.) Fictionally, *Galileo* pulled off a real coup this year with the serialization of Larry Niven's long-awaited novel *Ringworld Engineers*, and with the upcoming serialization of Joe Haldeman's new novel *Worlds*, but its fiction at the shorter lengths could still use a good deal of improvement—although some excellent work by Connie Willis did appear here this year, along with good work by M. Lucie Chin, Cynthia Felice, and John Kessel.

At year's end it was also announced that *Galileo* is purchasing the faltering *Galaxy* magazine, which published a few issues of negligible quality at odd times throughout the year, and turning it into a companion magazine for *Galileo*. *Galaxy* will be published bimonthly, alternating with *Galileo*. *Galaxy*'s new editor (the third in two years) will be *Galileo*'s present review editor, Floyd Kemske.

Once again in 1979, *The Magazine of Fantasy and Science Fiction* was the most consistently excellent of all the SF magazines. Despite the higher sales and circulations of other magazines, *F&SF* is and has been for years the genre's most important magazine, unrivaled in its artistic leadership, with only *Omni* coming even anywhere *close* to it this year in quality and consistency. Excellent fiction by Jack Dann, James P. Girard, Vonda N. McIntyre, Hilbert Schenck, Michael Shea, Christopher Priest, Gary Jennings, Phyllis Eisenstein, Marta Randall, Bob Leman, Barry N. Malzberg, Bill Pronzini, Andrew Weiner, Jane Yolen, Lee Killough, John Morressey, James Patrick Kelly, John Kessel, Joanna Russ, and a host of others appeared in *F&SF* in 1979. In spite of its many excellences, *F&SF*'s circulation remains dangerously low, and I urge everyone reading these words who cares about the future of SF to subscribe to this magazine; it is difficult to find on most newsstands anyway, and to miss it is to miss the cream of the crop of magazine SF. (*F&SF*'s subscription address is: Mercury Press, Inc., P.O. Box 56, Cornwall, CT 06753; $15 for one year, twelve issues.) Certainly if you are going to subscribe to any SF magazine, *F&SF* should be first—support of *F&SF* is the one place where the expenditure of a few dollars of your money could help to ensure the survival of quality SF through the potentially turbulent times ahead.

Two non-newsstand, subscription-only magazines deserve mention: *Whispers*, edited by Stuart David Schiff, and *Shayol*, edited by Patricia Cadigan and Arnold Fenner. *Whispers* features the work of supernatural-horror and sword-and-sorcery writers, and published an especially good novella by Fritz Leiber this year in *Whispers 13-14*. *Shayol* is one of the most handsomely produced magazines in SF, featuring graphics, poetry, and SF and fantasy by a host of bright young talents. This year's *Shayol 3* was particularly attractive, featuring fine fiction by Steve Utley, Howard Waldrop, Michael Bishop, Lisa Tuttle, C. J. Cherryh, and the late Tom Reamy. (*Whispers*: P.O. Box 1492W,

Azalea St., Browns Mills, NJ 08015; $7 for a four-issue subscription. *Shayol*: Flight Unlimited, Inc., 1100 Countyline Road, Bldg. 8, #29, Kansas City, KS 66103; $10 for a four-issue subscription.)

UNEARTH, another subscription-only magazine, may have died this year; nobody seems to know for sure, but I haven't seen an issue in a while, and mail sent to them is coming back as undeliverable.

The original anthology market was weak again this year. Of the former "Big Three" hardcover anthology series, now reduced to the "Big Two" by the demise of Damon Knight's *Orbit* series, the best in overall quality was Robert Silverberg's *New Dimensions 9* (Harper & Row), which contained excellent material by Ursula K. Le Guin and Tony Sarowitz, and good work by Peter Alterman, Jeff Hecht, Timothy Robert Sullivan, and Felix C. Gotschalk. There was, however, a similarity of tone and mood to many of the stories in *New Dimensions 9* that made the overall mood of the anthology too homogeneous. Many of the stories here might have shown up to better effect if they had been set off against different types of material. Last year I reported that *New Dimensions* was tottering on the brink of oblivion; this year I'm delighted to be able to report that the series has, at the last moment, been given a new lease on life. Although Harper & Row *has* dropped the series (they will bring out one more volume already in preparation), it has been picked up and continued by Pocket Books, who will publish *New Dimensions 11* as a paperback original in the summer of 1980. The paperback *New Dimensions* series will be coedited by SF writer Marta Randall, starting with #11; Silverberg has announced his intention of slowly phasing out of control of the series over the span of the next few volumes, ultimately leaving Randall as sole editor. The other Big Two anthology, Terry Carr's *Universe 9* (Doubleday), was somewhat bland this year, although it did contain good stories by Greg Bear, Paul David Novitski, and Gregory Benford, and an intriguing but flawed novelette by John Varley.

Of the newer anthology series, James Baen's *Destinies* (Ace) and Roy Torgeson's *Chrysalis* (Zebra) seem to have most firmly established themselves—four volumes of the *Destinies* series appeared this year, and three volumes of *Chrysalis*. Of the two series, *Destinies* is the more solid, featuring good work this year by Haldeman, Benford, Ing, David Drake, Larry Niven, and Charles Sheffield. My only real complaint is that the stories here are too homogeneous in subject and style, and some of them too heavy-handedly preachy in behalf of the cause of space industrialization and colonization (Baen himself has, only partially in jest, referred to *Destinies* as "a tool of the Space Industrialization Conspiracy, a self-appointed organ of agitprop for high technology and space exploration"). If Baen can open *Destinies* up to different kinds of material, and can get his writers to downplay the heavy polemics (agitprop, however well-intentioned, is the fatal enemy of art), then *Destinies* may well become a lasting and important anthology series. *Chrysalis*, on the other hand, while it does not seem to be grinding any particular political ax, is also much more uneven in literary quality. Good material did appear in *Chrysalis* this year—by Michael Bishop, Karl Hansen, and Charles L. Grant in *Chrysalis 3*; by Robert Thurston and Alan Ryan in *Chrysalis 4*; and by Hilbert Schenck in *Chrysalis 5*—but the bulk of each volume was taken up by bad or mediocre stories, some of which should not have seen professional print at all. Torgeson seems to be more open to experimentalism and diverse types of story material than Baen, a quality to be sincerely applauded in these days of minimum-risk taking, but he needs to sharpen up his editorial discretion and flail away a great deal of the chaff here if *Chrysalis* is ever to become a really important series. It might help to decrease the frequency of publication—the three *Chrysalis* volumes produced this year could and probably should have been boiled down into one fairly good anthology. It might also help to use fewer vignettes; there are very few decent vignettes written during any one year, and yet *Chrysalis* published dozens of them this year, most of them execrable. Torgeson also started a fantasy anthology series called *Other Worlds* (Zebra) this year, about which most of the same remarks could be made.

George R. R. Martin's *New Voices 2* (Avon) featured first-rate work by Lisa Tuttle and Thomas F. Monteleone, and interesting though flawed material by Spider Robinson and Gary Snider. Charles L. Grant's *Shadows 2* reinforced this series' reputation as a showplace for sophisticated, well-written horror stories, featuring first-rate work by Elizabeth A. Lynn, Jack Dann, and Michael Bishop, and good fiction by Peter A. Pautz and T. E. D. Klein.

No editions of the *Andromeda, Stellar*, or *Analog Yearbook* series appeared this year.

One-shot original anthologies were also scarce in 1979, unlike last year. The best one-shot anthology of the year was Charles L. Grant's *Nightmares* (Playboy Press), similar in tone and quality to Grant's *Shadows* series, and containing good original work by Beverly Evans, Steven Edward McDonald, Chelsea Quinn Yarbro, Geo. W. Proctor and J. C. Green, as well as good reprint stuff by Jack Dann, Stephen King, Avram Davidson, and others. The stories in Lee Harding's *The Rooms of Paradise* (St. Martin's Press) are full of original and speculatively exciting ideas, but are often poorly or indifferently executed, making for an interesting but uneven book; Michael Bishop, Ian Watson, and Gene Wolfe contribute the anthology's best stories, with Brian W. Aldiss, Cherry Wilder, Philippa C. Maddern, and George Turner also doing good work. Also interesting were *Amazons!*, edited by Jessica Amanda Salmonson (DAW), and *Thieves' World* (Ace), edited by Robert Asprin.

Many good reprint anthologies appeared in 1979, marking the

apparent resurgence of this market. Among the best were: Robert Silverberg's *The Best of New Dimensions* (Pocket Books), which belongs in every SF library, alongside 1976's *The Best From Orbit*; Terry Carr's *The Year's Finest Fantasy Vol. 2* (Berkley); Isaac Asimov, Martin Harry Greenberg, and Charles G. Waugh's *The 13 Crimes of Science Fiction* (Doubleday); Barry N. Malzberg and Bill Pronzini's *The Fifties* (Baronet); Martin Harry Greenberg and Joseph Olander's *Science Fiction of the 50s* (Avon); Robert Silverberg, Martin Harry Greenberg, and Joseph Olander's *Car Sinister* (Avon); Isaac Asimov, Martin Harry Greenberg, and Charles G. Waugh's *The Science Fictional Solar System* (Harper & Row); and Jerry Pournelle's *The Endless Frontier* (Ace).

None of 1979's novels thrust itself forth as obviously and unmistakably the year's best—as had Le Guin's *The Left Hand of Darkness*, Haldeman's *The Forever War*, or Pohl's *Gateway* in their respective years—but the year was nevertheless a good one, seeing a large crop of strong and speculatively exciting novels published across a wide spectrum of style, subject matter, and taste.

My own personal favorite was Len Deighton's *SS–GB* (Knopf/Del Rey), a dark horse candidate many will consider to be on the periphery of the field. My opinion is that this brilliantly executed book, an "alternate worlds" novel about the Nazi occupation of England, is as valid as SF as any book about spaceships and black holes—and in the quality of its characterization and prose, and its grasp of historical milieu and complex political and psychological realities, it is head-and-shoulders (unfortunately) above the genre average. One SF writer, though, who loses nothing to Deighton in either psychological sophistication or technical expertise is Thomas M. Disch, who with the superbly written *On Wings of Song* (St. Martin's Press) has produced a novel that may well cross genre boundaries to gain Disch the wider audience he deserves. Although parts of Disch's *334* and *Camp Concentration* were perhaps superior in some respects to *Song*, *Song* is a more even and sustained overall performance; there is hardly a false step in the book, and Disch's elegant prose, dark wit, and razor-edged irony have never worked to better effect. As effective in a totally different way is Arthur C. Clarke's *The Fountains of Paradise* (Harcourt Brace/Del Rey), one of Clarke's best novels, perhaps *his* most balanced and evenhanded literary performance to date. Although not a stylist of Disch's sophistication, Clarke's prose is clear, flowing and precise, and occasionally poetic in a register that even Disch is deaf to—that poetry, the celebration of the transcendence of technological man, is what makes the book (as it makes all of Clarke's best work), along with the vast scope and awesome originality of the engineering project that is the book's ostensible subject, and the ring of authenticity he brings to its description. Although smaller than the backdrop they move against, Clarke's characters are adequately complex in their dry and understated English way, to balance the book, and add the human interest large-scale technological SF novels often lack. My only real quibble with *Fountains* is that Clarke's civilized, war-free One World Utopia seems to me completely unreachable; I can't see how we could possibly get there from here, and Clarke, maintaining a discreet silence, makes no real attempt in the novel to show us how we supposedly did.

Another novel that operates on a vast technological scale, if somewhat less successfully, is John Varley's *Titan* (Putnam). *Titan* deals with a concept even larger and more mind-boggling than that of the Clarke novel and the technological/physical stuff is worked out in ingenious and fascinating detail; but the book lacks the tension, unity, and grace of *Fountains*, and ultimately gives the impression of having done less with its own material than it might have done. *Titan* has much to recommend it, but an episodic plot and an abrupt and unconvincing ending make *Titan* "merely" a good SF novel, instead of the great one it might have been. Yet another novel of grand scope that ultimately fails because of poor execution (and fails a great deal harder than *Titan*) is George Zebrowski's *Macrolife* (Harper & Row): Zebrowski comes up with some intriguing conceptualization here, and the book's time scale is certainly vast enough to suit the most cosmic-minded of fans, but the book's characters also lecture at each other for page after unbroken page of stiff dialogue in true Gernsbackian fashion and as a novel *Macrolife* is didactic, static, sociologically naive, and dull. Old pro Frederik Pohl effortlessly steers his new novel *Jem* (St. Martin's Press) past many of the problems that threaten to founder *Titan* and *Macrolife*, and yet in spite of the suppleness and expertise Pohl brings to its execution, *Jem* ultimately feels to me like minor Pohl (which would, of course, be very good indeed for most other writers). Like Pohl's award-winning *Gateway*, the writing is excellent, and many of the incidental concepts marvelous; unlike *Gateway*, the underlying satiric structure is too obvious (the three political Blocs from Earth, each matched with/satirized by one of the three intelligent native races on the planet Jem), and the characterization lacks the deeply felt empathy of *Gateway*, leaning away from human complexity toward caricature in its portrayal of unsympathetic characters. In structure, in its emphasis on satire, and even in its terminology ("the Greasies," "the Peeps"), *Jem* is more reminiscent of the *Galaxy*-era Pohl of the fifties, the Pohl of *The Space Merchants* and "The Midas Plague" than the Post-New Wave Pohl of *Gateway* and "The Merchants of Venus," and I can't help wondering if this book wasn't originally started in the fifties or early sixties and only finished or refurbished recently. Published originally as a series of stories over an eight-year span, Michael Bishop's *Catacomb Years* (Berkley/Putnam), a "novel of stories" all sharing a common background in a domed Atlanta of the future, is also somewhat uneven: The Bishop of 1970's "If a Flower Can Eclipse" is just not as good a writer as the Bishop of 1977's "The Samurai and the Willows" or 1978's "Old Folks at Home." Overall, however, the book is excellent, certainly one of the year's best, and is a valid, though necessarily episodic, novel—the writing and characterization range from good to superb, and the mosaic picture set forth of city life in the future is bizarre, fascinating, and of almost Byzantine complexity. Michael Bishop's *Transfigurations* (Berkley/Putnam), expanded from Bishop's famous story "Death and Designation Among the Asadi," is another major novel, excellent in its evocation of truly *alien* aliens and their strange and intricate interface with humanity. Also first-rate is Kate Wilhelm's *Juniper Time* (Harper & Row), an intense, psychologically complex, and all too plausible picture of one woman's life in a brutalized future of "diminished expectations"; only the slight murkiness of the ending keeps the book from being as strong as Wilhelm's award-winning novel *Where Late the Sweet Birds Sang*.

John Crowley's *Engine Summer* (Doubleday) is a thoughtful and literate book, detailing the intricate lifeways of one of the stranger and more interesting Utopias of recent SF; Crowley's book will be too slowly paced for some, but rewards close and careful reading. Samuel R. Delany's *Tales of Neveryon* (Bantam) is being marketed as a sword-and-sorcery book, complete with a cover painting of a sword-wielding hero confronting a dragon, but the reader who picks up this intelligent and unusual fantasy in search of another *Conan* rehash will be disappointed and perhaps dismayed. Like Crowley, Delany is concerned primarily with the lifeways and social motivations of his characters (the description of palace politics and intrigues in the book's first section is particularly fine), with special emphasis on the ways that economics, linguistics, and sexual mores affect society. Throughout the novel, Delany plays with stock fantasy cliches in a way that will outrage many sword-and-sorcery fans—the muscular barbarian hero, for instance, turns out to be a bondage freak and homosexual pederast. Decadence is also the key word in Michael Moorcock's lush and sophisticated novel *Gloriana* (Avon), a beautifully crafted, slyly witty, and, yes, decadent book that is probably the best novel Moorcock has produced in a long and often uneven career. Stylish fantasy of another sort is provided in Elizabeth A. Lynn's *Watchtower* (Putnam). Last year I referred to Lynn as a "promising first novelist," and with *Watchtower* she had fullfilled a good deal of that promise, producing a strong, lyrical, and compassionate novel peopled with finely drawn characters. Lynn's *The Dancers of Arun* (Berkley/Putnam), a sequel to *Watchtower*, is also first-rate, although it lacks some of the powerful personality contrasts and conflicts that are at the heart of the other book. Richard Cowper's *The Road to Corlay* (Pocket Books) and Phyllis Eisenstein's *Shadow of Earth* (Dell) were among the other books this year that were reminiscent of fantasy in trappings and atmosphere while remaining valid SF—*The Road to Corlay* is an evocative "Post-Holocaust" novel reminiscent of Pangborn's *Davy; Shadow of Earth* is a gripping alternate worlds novel featuring an unusually strong and vividly portrayed protagonist.

Stephen King is another writer who has been working with good effect at the shadowy borderland between SF and fantasy. Although he is best known as a writer of supernatural horror fiction, King has been drawing closer and closer to SF with each book, providing interesting hybrids of SF, fantasy, and horror fiction along the way. His closest approach to SF yet is to be found in his engrossing new novel *The Dead Zone* (Viking). Conceptually, *The Dead Zone* is old hat, concerning a man who gains clairvoyant powers, and the affect those powers have upon his life. In execution, however, *The Dead Zone* is terrific; King is a tremendous storyteller, a lively and effective prose stylist reminiscent of John D. MacDonald, and a writer able to create paper characters who live and breathe and bleed—all this makes *The Dead Zone* one of the best handlings of the ESP theme in many years, although there's not even a close approach to a new idea in the book. King's *The Stand* (Signet—a very expensive book available now for the first time in a mass-market edition) also breathes new life into old, worn-out SF material, and succeeds in making an 816-page "Just-After-the-Holocaust" novel not only interesting but riveting, something I would have thought impossible this many years after *On the Beach*. Here there *is* a new idea, and a honey, as King audaciously blends the post-Holocaust subgenre with a Tolkienesque fantasy of the ultimate confrontation between Good and Evil that takes place, appropriately enough, in modern-day Las Vegas. King maintains control of this immense and multilayered book almost all the way to the end (there is a feeling toward the end that he is just trying to get it all *over with*), and ounce for ounce *The Stand* is probably the best reading bargain of the year. Another master of science-fantasy, this one a veteran who has been conjuring up marvels for thirty years or more, is Jack Vance, present this year with *The Face* (DAW), the long-awaited (for over ten years) fourth novel in Vance's "Demon Princes" series, started in 1965 with his famous novel *The Star King*. Vance fans will need to know no more than that. For those not familiar with Vance, *The Face*, although not quite up to the level of *The Star King*, is a prime example of what Vance does best: fast-paced action and galactic intrigue set against a marvelously evocative background of strange alien worlds and cultures, all laced with Vance's dour irony and deadpan wit.

Also worthwhile were Tim Powers's *The Drawing of the Dark* (Del Rey), George Alec Effinger's *Heroics* (Doubleday), Michael de Larrabeiti's *The Borribles* (Ace), Michael Connor's *I Am Not the Other Houdini* (Perennial Library), Roger Zelazny's *Roadmarks* (Del Rey),

Octavia E. Butler's *Kindred* (Doubleday), Greg Bear's *Hegira* (Dell), D. G. Compton's *Windows* (Berkley/Putnam), Pamela Sargent's *The Sudden Star* (Fawcett), Ben Bova's *Kinsman* (Dial Press), George Turner's *Beloved Son* (Pocket Books), Phyllis Eisenstein's *Sorcerer's Son* (Del Rey), Poul Anderson and Mildred Downey Broxon's *The Demon of Scattery* (Ace), Robert Anton Wilson's *Schrodinger's Cat* (Pocket Books), Dean Ing's *Soft Targets* (Ace), Poul Anderson's *The Merman's Children* (Berkley/Putnam), Spider and Jeanne Robinson's *Stardance* (Dial Press/Dell), and a reprint of Algis Budrys's *Some Will Not Die* (Dell), a long-unavailable novel whose first section has interesting parallels with King's *The Stand*. SF readers may also be interested in Ursula K. Le Guin's *Malafrena* (Putnam), although it is neither SF nor fantasy, but rather a mainstream novel set in the imaginary eastern European country that was the location of Le Guin's *Orsinian Tales*.

Worthwhile short-story collections also appeared in large numbers in 1979, although there were not quite as many of them as last year.

Michael Bishop's *Catacomb Years* (Berkley/Putnam), if counted as a collection rather than as a "novel of stories," would probably be the year's best, containing as it does some of the most memorable SF stories to be published during the seventies. If *Catacomb Years* is discounted, then Vonda N. McIntyre's *Fireflood and Other Stories* (Houghton Mifflin) is the best collection of the year, a strong and elegant collection of literate and thoughtful SF by one of the genre's best new writers. Also excellent is Christopher Priest's *An Infinite Summer* (Scribner's); Priest is one of the most prominent members, along with Ian Watson, of what I suppose must be called "The New British New Wave," for lack of a less clumsy term, and in *An Infinite Summer* he provides memorable examples of just how effective and fever-dream vivid that type of writing can be. One of the best reading buys of the year is to be found in Damon Knight's *Rule Golden and Other Stories* (Avon), a collection of five superb novellas, among them the hard-to-find (and magnificent) "The Earth Quarter"; highly recommended. Also highly recommended are *The Best of Avram Davidson* (Doubleday) and Stephen King's *Night Shift* (Avon). Davidson is the underappreciated master of sly, richly strange, and subtly hilarious SF and fantasy, and King's collection will send chills up the spine of the most jaded and hardened readers. Ian Watson's *The Very Slow Time Machine* (Ace) is worthwhile but uneven: Watson is an idea man, and comes up here with some of the most outrageous and imaginative concepts of recent times, but his execution of those ideas is sometimes sloppy and indifferently good. Norman Spinrad is also an uneven writer, but *The Star-Spangled Future* (Ace) is probably his best collection to date; there are a few mediocre stories here, but heavily on the plus side are "Lost Continents" and the classic "The Big Flash," among others. New writers

Joan D. Vinge and Charles Sheffield occasionally show the unevenness of development, but make strong debuts in, respectively, *Eyes of Amber* (Signet) and *Vectors* (Ace); note particularly "Tin Soldier," and "View from a Height," the Hugo-winning title story in the Vinge collection, and "Fixed Price War" and "The Treasure of Oderiex" in the Sheffield.

The year's other good collections were: *The Best of Hal Clement* (Del Rey), *The Best of James Blish* (Del Rey), Randall Garrett's *Murder and Magic* (Ace), Philip José Farmer's *Riverworld and Other Stories* (Berkley), Theodore Sturgeon's *The Stars Are the Styx* (Dell), Cordwainer Smith's *The Instrumentality of Mankind* (Del Rey), Brian Aldiss's *New Arrivals, Old Encounters* (Harper & Row), and C. L. Moore's *Judgement Night* (Dell).

The best SF reference book of the year, and probably the best of the decade (rivaled only by last year's *Index to Science Fiction Anthologies and Collections*), was *The Encyclopedia of Science Fiction* (Doubleday), edited by Peter Nicholls. Unlike the other books of recent years that have claimed to be SF encyclopedias (for instance, Brian Ash's confusing and error-riddled *Visual Encyclopedia of Science Fiction*), Nicholls's huge volume is a true encyclopedia, alphabetized, cross-referenced, the individual entries concise and well-researched, as up to date and as error-free as it is possible for such a compendium to be. There is a slight inevitable bias here toward the British New Wave, but on the whole the book is admirably balanced in its consideration of difficult and often partisan issues. *The Encyclopedia of Science Fiction* is an indispensable reference work and research tool for anyone interested in SF; if you have room for only one book *about* SF in your library, make this the one. Also monumental was Isaac Asimov's 732-page autobiography *In Memory Yet Green* (Doubleday). Actually, huge as it is, *In Memory Yet Green* is only *half* of Asimov's autobiography, covering his life up to 1954; the other half, *In Joy Still Felt*, is due sometime in 1980. I have heard people complain that *In Memory Yet Green* is boring, and in truth, Asimov himself readily admits that "nothing of any importance has ever happened to me," so that we have pages devoted to such things as Asimov taking a driving test or Asimov passing a gallstone. Such material seems unpromising, yet such is Asimov's skill as a nonfiction writer, and such the charm he manages to project even while dealing with everyday mundanities, that I found the book absorbing, with only a few dull spots in its vast length. Asimov fans will, of course, be interested; for others, the book is worthwhile—if for nothing else—for the detailed picture it paints of what it was like to be a struggling young would-be SF writer in the New York of the depression years, a milieu so different from the present that Asimov might just as well be writing about life on an alien planet. In ironic contrast to Asimov, Samuel R. Delany has led a life many would consider exotic and fascinating (member of a rock band, world traveller, shrimp-boat fisherman, et cetera), and yet in *Heavenly Breakfast* (Bantam) he has produced a slender little volume of autobiography not a sixth of the size of *In Memory Yet Green*. In truth, though, *Heavenly Breakfast* is only a partial autobiography, dealing with one memorable winter (the winter of 1967—the "Winter of Love," as Delany puts it) Delany spent in a hippie commune in the East Village. If, indeed, it should be considered an autobiography at all: Delany calls it an "essay," and admits to changing the sequence of events to suit himself and either combining several persons to make a single character or "atomizing" single persons to make several. A fictionalized autobiography? A heavily autobiographical novel? Whatever it is, this look into an alternate life-style is fascinating, as lean and eclectic as anything Delany has written in years; good enough, in fact, to whet my appetite for the full-length autobiography I hope Delany will turn his hand to one day. Ursula K. Le Guin's collection of critical essays, *The Language of the Night* (Putnam), edited by Susan Wood, is a little *too* eclectic; although the major essays here are clearheaded, incisive, and wise, there is also too much minor material included (brief introductions to other people's books, award acceptance speeches, even a fanzine semi-interview), and the effect is inevitably one of padding. If Le Guin did not have enough serious critical material available to fill up a book, the editor might have been better advised to wait until she did. As it stands, this is a book that should be in libraries, and that will repay close attention by serious readers and scholars, but its indiscriminate inclusiveness somewhat diminishes its overall effect. No excuses can be made for *A Reader's Guide to Science Fiction* (Avon), edited by Baird Searles, Martin Last, Beth Meacham, and Michael Franklin—it is simply a bad job, riddled with factual errors and omissions, confusingly organized, and disappointingly shallow in much of its historical/critical perspective; I had expected better of Searles. *Starlog's Science Fiction Yearbook* (Starlog Press) covers much the same ground as Searles's *Reader's Guide*, but a good deal more successfully. Edited by David Gerrold and compiled by David Truesdale, this is a worthwhile and fairly complete overview of the year in SF, particularly valuable for its coverage of the often-ignored SF magazine field. "Opinionated" is probably the word that most typifies Lester del Rey's *The World of Science Fiction* (Del Rey); Lester has never hesitated to tell anyone his position on anything, and he sets his opinions on SF here in unequivocal form. Whether you agree with those opinions or not will probably determine *your* opinion of the book. Since I disagree with many of those opinions, particularly those concerning the significance of the last fifteen or so years in SF, I can't really recommend it; it is, however, full of interesting historic detail of the early days of the genre.

None of this year's SF movies managed to generate the excitement of 1977's *Star Wars*, although several of them were large box-office successes, and a couple of them were even worth watching. The year's best SF movie was *Alien*, which succeeds in spite of several serious flaws, including numerous scientific errors and a plot riddled with logical inconsistencies. *Alien* rises above these drawbacks by some extremely good production values (uniquely, more in the areas of set design and dressing than in the "space hardware" special effects that have become a stock cliché of recent SF movies), and by the simple fact that it is *scary*—a suspenseful and riveting two hours, *Alien* is in fact one of the scariest movies ever made, thanks in part to intelligent direction, and in large part to H. R. Giger's obscene and surrealistic "monster" (the alien of the title), certainly the most effective movie menace ever put on the screen. Giger is also responsible for the eerie interior of the alien space-ship, enormously more persuasive in its sense of utter *strangeness* than the alien artifacts in most SF movies, which usually rely on dry-ice smoke and colored filters to evoke "alienness." The cast turns in a number of good performances, outstanding among which is that of Sigourney Weaver as the only one aboard with sufficient guts and brains to take on the marauding alien. If for nothing else, *Alien* would be worthwhile as the first SF/horror movie where the heroine doesn't scream and faint when confronted with the monster. Another offbeat SF movie was *Time after Time*, in which H. G. Wells matches wits with Jack the Ripper in modern San Francisco. The movie's writers have no real understanding of the intricate mechanics of time paradox, and again the plot is marred by logical inconsistencies, but as a film *Time after Time* is witty and fast-paced and the performances are good, particularly that of Malcolm McDowell as the befuddled and idealistic H. G. Wells. The long-awaited *Star Trek: The Motion Picture*, perhaps the year's most relentlessly hyped SF movie, struck me as adequate, although again scientific boners and lapses in plot logic abounded. When you consider, though, that $40 million was spent on making *Star Trek: The Motion Picture*, more than the entire budget of *all* the television *Star Trek* episodes combined, you begin to wonder if "adequate" is really good enough—certainly the movie is no better than some of the individual television episodes, and, with its draggingly slow pace, worse than many. The much-touted special effects ranged from good (the cosmic cloud) to amazingly poor (the obviously painted-on backdrop of San Francisco, with most of the bustling spaceport crowd in the foreground also painted on!)—$40 million. My, my, my! Mediocre as *Star Trek* was, Disney Studio's *The Black Hole* made it look like a masterpiece. Grindingly, unrelentingly bad, *The Black Hole* is one of the most dumbly plotted, ineptly acted, and scientifically illiterate movies I've *ever* seen. It is also terminally cute, with the seemingly mandatory "cute robots" so *sickeningly* cute that they make *Star Wars*'s R2D2 look plain and bluff by comparison; you could also see the wires that enabled them to ''fly'' in at least two scenes. A bad job all around.

Maybe *The Empire Strikes Back (Star Wars II)* will be better. (Maybe.)

The 37th World Science Fiction Convention, SeaCon, was held in Brighton, England, over the Labor Day weekend, and drew an attendance of 3,200 people. The 1978 Hugo awards, presented at SeaCon, were: Best Novel, *Dreamsnake*, by Vonda N. McIntyre; Best Novella, ''The Persistence of Vision,'' by John Varley; Best Novelette, ''Hunter's Moon,'' by Poul Anderson; Best Short Story, ''Cassandra,'' by C. J. Cherryh; Best Editor, Ben Bova; Best Professional Artist, Vincent Di Fate; Best Dramatic Presentation, *Superman*; Best Fan Artist, Bill Rotsler; Best Fan Writer, Bob Shaw; Best Fanzine, *Science Fiction Review*; plus the Gandalf Award for Best Fantasy Novel to *The White Dragon*, by Anne McCaffrey; and the Grandmaster of Fantasy Award to Ursula K. Le Guin.

The 1978 Nebula awards were: Best Novel, *Dreamsnake*, by Vonda N. McIntyre; Best Novella, ''The Persistence of Vision,'' by John Varley; Best Novelette, ''A Glow of Candles, A Unicorn's Eye,'' by Charles L. Grant; Best Short Story, ''Stone,'' by Edward Bryant; plus a Grandmaster Award to L. Sprague De Camp.

The Fifth Annual World Fantasy Awards were: Best Novel, *Gloriana*, by Michael Moorcock; Best Collection, *Shadows*, edited by Charles L. Grant; Best Short Fiction, ''Naples,'' by Avram Davidson; Best Artist, Alicia Austin and Dale Enzenbacher (tie); Special Award (professional), Edward L. Ferman; Special Award (nonprofessional), Donald H. Tuck; plus a Life Achievement Award to Jorge Luis Borges.

The John W. Campbell Memorial Award was won for *Gloriana*, by Michael Moorcock.

Dead in 1979 were: Robert Bruce Montgomery, who as ''Edmund Crispen'' was one of the best-known British SF critics and anthologists; Ed Earl Repp, one of the early SF writers who worked for Gernsback's *Amazing, Science Wonder Stories*, and other pulp magazines; Richard C. Meredith, author of *We All Died at Breakaway Station* and six other novels; John Barry, British film designer for such SF movies as *Star Wars* and *Superman*; Wilbur Scott Peacock, former editor of *Planet Stories*; Dr. Christopher Evans, computer scientist and one-time science editor for *New Worlds*; Walter H. Gillings, former editor of the British *Tales of Wonder*; Theodora Kroeber-Quinn, author of the classic anthropological study *Ishi in Two Worlds* and mother of SF writer Ursula K. Le Guin; and Immanuel Velikovsky, whose book *Worlds in Collision* outraged an entire generation of scientists.

BEST
SCIENCE FICTION STORIES
OF THE YEAR
Ninth Annual Collection

If you ever owned an ant farm when you were a kid, you know how fascinating it was to stare through that thin pane of glass at the scuttling alien creatures beyond. It might have been even more fascinating—and alarming—if the creatures on the other side of the glass had been capable of watching you in return . . . of watching you with unwinking insectile fixity . . . of watching you even while you slept . . . of watching you and laying plans. . . .

Few SF stories have ever been genuinely frightening, but the shocker that follows—certainly one of the most suspenseful and just plain scary *stories of recent years—should provoke a crawling sensation along the spines of even the most hardened readers.*

Born in Bayonne, New Jersey, George R. R. Martin made his first sale in 1971, and soon established himself as one of the most popular writers of the seventies, winning a Hugo award in 1975 for his novella ''A Song for Lya.'' His books include the novel The Dying of the Light *(Pocket Books), two collections,* A Song for Lya *(Avon) and* Songs of Stars and Shadows *(Pocket Books), and, as editor, the* New Voices *series of anthologies, now up to* New Voices 2 *(Avon). Upcoming from Pocket Books is a collaborative novel with Lisa Tuttle,* Windhaven. *His story ''Bitterblooms'' was in our* Seventh Annual Collection. *Martin presently lives in Santa Fe, New Mexico.*

GEORGE R. R. MARTIN
Sandkings

Simon Kress lived alone in a sprawling manor house among dry, rocky hills fifty kilometers from the city. So, when he was called away unexpectedly on business, he had no neighbors he could conveniently impose on to take his pets. The carrion hawk was no problem; it roosted in the unused belfry and customarily fed itself anyway. The shambler Kress simply shooed outside and left to fend for itself. The little monster would gorge on slugs and birds and rockjocks. But the fish tank, stocked with genuine earth piranha, posed a difficulty. Finally Kress just threw a haunch of beef into the huge tank. The piranha could always eat one another if he were detained longer than expected. They'd done it before. It amused him.

Unfortunately, he was detained *much* longer than expected this time. When he finally returned, all the fish were dead. So was the carrion hawk. The shambler had climbed up to the belfry and eaten it. Kress was vexed.

The next day he flew his skimmer to Asgard, a journey of some two hundred kilometers. Asgard was Baldur's largest city and boasted the oldest and largest starport as well. Kress liked to impress his friends with animals that were unusual, entertaining, and expensive. Asgard was the place to buy them.

This time, though, he had poor luck. Xenopets had closed its doors. L'Etherane the petseller tried to foist another carrion hawk off on him, and Strange Waters offered nothing more exotic than piranha, glow-sharks, and spider squids. Kress had had all those; he wanted something new, something that would stand out.

Near dusk he found himself walking down Rainbow Boulevard, looking for places he had not patronized before. So close to the starport, the street was lined by importers' marts. The big corporate emporiums had impressive long windows, in which rare and costly alien artifacts reposed on felt cushions against dark drapes that made the interiors of the stores a mystery. Between them were the junk shops—narrow, nasty little places whose display areas were crammed with all manner of offworld bric-a-brac. Kress tried both kinds of shops, with equal dissatisfaction.

Then he came across a store that was different.

It was very near the port. Kress had never been there before. The shop occupied a small, single-story building of moderate size, set between a euphoria bar and a temple brothel of the Secret Sisterhood. Down this far, Rainbow Boulevard grew tacky. The shop itself was unusual. Arresting.

The windows were full of mist—now a pale red, now the gray of true fog, now sparkling and golden. The mist swirled and eddied and glowed faintly from within. Kress glimpsed objects in the window—machines, pieces of art, other things he could not recognize—but he could not get a good look at any of them. The mists flowed sensuously around them, displaying a bit of first one thing and then another, then cloaking all. It was intriguing.

As he watched, the mist began to form letters. One word at a time. Kress stood and read.

WO. AND. SHADE. IMPORTERS. ARTIFACTS. ART. LIFE-FORMS. AND. MISC.

The letters stopped. Through the fog Kress saw something moving. That was enough for him, that and the LIFEFORMS in their advertisement. He swept his walking cloak over his shoulder and entered the store.

Inside, Kress felt disoriented. The interior seemed vast, much larger than he would have guessed from the relatively modest frontage. It was dimly lit, peaceful. The ceiling was a starscape, complete with spiral nebulas, very dark and realistic, very nice. All the counters shone faintly to better display the merchandise within. The aisles were carpeted with ground fog. It came almost to his knees in places and swirled about his feet as he walked.

"Can I help you?"

She almost seemed to have risen from the fog. Tall and gaunt and pale, she wore a practical gray jumpsuit and a strange little cap that rested well back on her head.

"Are you Wo or Shade?" Kress asked. "Or only sales help?"

"Jala Wo, ready to serve you," she replied. "Shade does not see customers. We have no sales help."

"You have quite a large establishment," Kress said. "Odd that I have never heard of you before."

"We have only just opened this shop on Baldur," the woman said. "We have franchises on a number of other worlds, however. What can I sell you? Art, perhaps? You have the look of a collector. We have some fine Nor T'alush crystal carvings."

"No," Kress said. "I own all the crystal carvings I desire. I came to see about a pet."

"A lifeform?"

"Yes."

"Alien?"

"Of course."

"We have a mimic in stock. From Cella's World. A clever little simian. Not only will it learn to speak, but eventually it will mimic your voice, inflections, gestures, even facial expressions."

"Cute," said Kress. "And common. I have no use for either, Wo. I want something exotic. Unusual. And not cute. I detest cute animals. At the moment I own a shambler. Imported from Cotho, at no mean expense. From time to time I feed him a litter of unwanted kittens. That is what I think of *cute*. Do I make myself understood?"

Wo smiled enigmatically. "Have you ever owned an animal that worshipped you?" she asked.

Kress grinned. "Oh, now and again. But I don't require worship, Wo. Just entertainment."

"You misunderstand me," Wo said, still wearing her strange smile. "I meant *worship* literally."

"What are you talking about?"

"I think I have just the thing for you," Wo said. "Follow me."

She led him between the radiant counters and down a long, fog-shrouded aisle beneath false starlight. They passed through a wall of mist into another section of the store, then stopped in front of a large plastic tank. An aquarium, Kress thought.

Wo beckoned. He stepped closer and saw that he was wrong. It was a terrarium. Within lay a miniature desert about two meters square. Pale sand tinted scarlet by wan red light. Rocks: basalt and quartz and granite. In each corner of the tank stood a castle.

Kress blinked and peered and corrected himself, actually, there were only three castles standing. The fourth leaned, a crumbled, broken ruin. The three others were crude but intact, carved of stone and sand. Over their battlements and through their rounded porticoes tiny creatures climbed and scrambled. Kress pressed his face against the plastic. "Insects?" he asked.

"No," Wo replied. "A much more complex lifeform. More intelligent as well. Smarter than your shambler by a considerable amount. They are called sandkings."

"Insects," Kress said, drawing back from the tank. "I don't care how complex they are. He frowned. "And kindly don't try to gull me with this talk of intelligence. These things are far too small to have anything but the most rudimentary brains."

"They share hiveminds," Wo said. "Castle minds, in this case. There are only three organisms in the tank actually. The fourth died. You see how her castle has fallen."

Kress looked back at the tank. "Hiveminds, eh? Interesting." He frowned again. "Still, it is only an oversized ant farm. I'd hoped for something better."

"They fight wars."

"Wars? Hmmm." Kress looked again.

"Note the colors, if you will," Wo said. She pointed to the creatures that swarmed over the nearest castle. One was scrabbling at the tank wall. Kress studied it. To his eyes, it still looked like an insect. Barely as long as his fingernail, six-limbed, with six tiny eyes set all around its body. A wicked set of mandibles clacked visibly, while two long, fine antennae wove patterns in the air. Antennae, mandibles, eyes, and legs were sooty black, but the dominant color was the burnt orange of its armor plating. "It's an insect," Kress repeated.

"It is not an insect," Wo insisted calmly. "The armored exoskeleton is shed when the sandking grows larger. *If* it grows larger. In a tank this size, it won't." She took Kress by the elbow and led him around the tank to the next castle. "Look at the colors here."

He did. They were different. Here the sandkings had bright red armor; antennae, mandibles, eyes, and legs were yellow. Kress glanced across the tank. The denizens of the third live castle were off-white, with red trim. "Hmmm," he said.

"They war, as I said," Wo told him. "They even have truces and alliances. It was an alliance that destroyed the fourth castle in this tank. The blacks were becoming too numerous, and so the others joined forces to destroy them."

Kress remained unconvinced. "Amusing, no doubt. But insects fight wars, too."

"Insects do not worship," Wo said.

"Eh?"

Wo smiled and pointed at the castle. Kress stared. A face had been carved into the wall of the highest tower. He recognized it. It was Jala Wo's face. "How . . .?"

"I projected a hologram of my face into the tank, then kept it there for a few days. The face of god, you see? I feed them. I am always close. The sandkings have a rudimentary psionic sense. Proximity telepathy. They sense me and worship me by using my face to decorate their buildings. All the castles have them, see?" They did.

On the castle, the face of Jala Wo was serene, peaceful, and very lifelike. Kress marveled at the workmanship. "How do they do it?"

"The foremost legs double as arms. They even have fingers of a sort, three small, flexible tendrils. And they cooperate well, both in building and in battle. Remember, all the mobiles of one color share a single mind."

"Tell me more," Kress requested.

Wo smiled. "The maw lives in the castle. Maw is my name for her—a pun, if you will. The thing is mother and stomach both. Female, large as your fist, immobile. Actually, *sandking* is a bit of a misnomer. The mobiles are peasants and warriors. The real ruler is a queen. But that analogy is faulty as well. Considered as a whole, each castle is a single hermaphroditic creature."

"What do they eat?"

"The mobiles eat pap, predigested food obtained inside the castle. They get if from the maw after she has worked on it for several days. Their stomachs can't handle anything else. If the maw dies, they soon die as well. The maw . . . the maw eats anything. You'll have no special expense there. Table scraps will do excellently."

"Live food?" Kress asked.

Wo shrugged. "Each maw eats mobiles from the other castles, yes."

"I am intrigued," he admitted. "If only they weren't so small."

"Yours can be larger. These sandkings are small because their tank is small. They seem to limit their growth to fit available space. If I moved these to a larger tank, they'd start growing again."

"Hmmm. My piranha tank is twice this size and vacant. It could be cleaned out, filled with sand . . ."

"Wo and Shade would take care of the installation. It would be our pleasure."

"Of course," Kress said. "I would expect four intact castles."

"Certainly," Wo said.

They began to haggle about the price.

Three days later Jala Wo arrived at Simon Kress's estate, with dormant sandkings and a work crew to take charge of the installation.

Wo's assistants were aliens unlike any Kress was familiar with—squat, broad bipeds with four arms and bulging, multifaceted eyes. Their skin was thick and leathery and twisted into horns and spines and protrusions at odd places upon their bodies. But they were very strong, and good workers. Wo ordered them about in a musical tongue that Kress had never heard before.

In a day it was done. They moved his piranha tank to the center of his spacious living room, arranged couches on either side of it for better viewing, scrubbed it clean, and filled it two-thirds of the way up with sand and rock. Then they installed a special lighting system, both to provide the dim red illumination the sandkings preferred and to project holographic images into the tank. On top they mounted a sturdy plastic cover, with a feeder mechanism built in. "This way you can feed your sandkings without removing the top of the tank," Wo explained. "You would not want to take any chances on the mobiles escaping."

The cover also included climate-control devices, to condense just the right amount of moisture from the air. "You want it dry, but not too dry," Wo said.

Finally one of the four-armed workers climbed into the tank and dug deep pits in the four corners. One of his companions handed the dormant maws over to him, removing them, one by one, from their frosted cryonic traveling cases.

They were nothing to look at. Kress decided they resembled nothing so much as mottled, half-spoiled chunks of raw meat. Each with a mouth.

The alien buried them, one in each corner of the tank. Then the work party sealed it all up and took their leave.

"The heat will bring the maws out of dormancy," Wo said. "In less than a week mobiles will begin to hatch and burrow up to the surface. Be certain to give them plenty of food. They will need all their strength until they are well established. I would estimate that you will have castles rising in about three weeks."

"And my face? When will they carve my face?"

"Turn on the hologram after about a month," she advised him "and be patient. If you have any questions, please call. Wo and Shade are at your service." She bowed and left.

Kress wandered back to the tank and lit a joy stick. The desert was still and empty. He drummed his fingers impatiently against the plastic and frowned.

On the fourth day Kress thought he glimpsed motion beneath the sand—subtle subterranean stirrings.

On the fifth day he saw his first mobile, a lone white.

On the sixth day he counted a dozen of them, whites and reds and blacks. The oranges were tardy. He cycled through a bowl of half-decayed table scraps. The mobiles sensed it at once, rushed to it, and began to drag pieces back to their respective corners. Each color group was highly organized. They did not fight. Kress was a bit disappointed, but he decided to give them time.

The oranges made their appearance on the eighth day. By then the other sandkings had begun carrying small stones and erecting crude fortifications. They still did not war. At the moment they were only half the size of those he had seen at Wo and Shade's, but Kress thought they were growing rapidly.

The castles began to rise midway through the second week. Organized battalions of mobiles dragged heavy chunks of sandstone and granite back to their corners, where other mobiles were pushing sand into place with mandibles and tendrils. Kress had purchased a pair of magnifying goggles so that he could watch them work wherever they might go in the tank. He wandered around and around the tall plastic walls, observing. It was fascinating.

The castles were a bit plainer than Kress would have liked, but he had an idea about that. The next day he cycled through some obsidian and flakes of colored glass along with the food. Within hours they had been incorporated into the castle walls.

The black castle was the first completed, followed by the white and red fortresses. The oranges were last, as usual. Kress took his meals into the living room and ate, seated on the couch so he could watch. He expected the first war to break out any hour now.

He was disappointed. Days passed, the castles grew taller and more grand, and Kress seldom left the tank except to attend to his sanitary needs and to answer critical business calls. But the sandkings did not war. He was getting upset.

Finally he stopped feeding them.

Two days after the table scraps had ceased to fall from their desert sky, four black mobiles surrounded an orange and dragged it back to their maw. They maimed it first, ripping off its mandibles and antennae and limbs, and carried it through the shadowed main gate of their miniature castle. It never emerged. Within an hour more than forty orange mobiles marched across the sand and attacked the blacks' corner. They were outnumbered by the blacks that came rushing up from the depths. When the fighting was over, the attackers had been slaughtered. The dead and dying were taken down to feed the black maw.

Kress, delighted, congratulated himself on his genius.

When he put food into the tank the following day, a three-cornered battle broke out over its possession. The whites were the big winners.

After that, war followed war.

Almost a month to the day after Jala Wo had delivered the sandkings, Kress turned on the holographic projector, and his face materialized in the tank. It turned, slowly, around and around, so that his gaze fell on all four castles equally. Kress thought it rather a good likeness; it had his impish grin, wide mouth, full cheeks. His blue eyes sparkled, his gray hair was carefully arrayed in a fashionable sidesweep, his eyebrows were thin and sophisticated.

Soon enough the sandkings set to work. Kress fed them lavishly while his image beamed down at them from their sky. Temporarily the wars stopped. All activity was directed toward worship.

His face emerged on the castle walls.

At first all four carvings looked alike to him, but as the work continued and Kress studied the reproductions, he began to detect subtle differences in technique and execution. The reds were the most creative, using tiny flakes of slate to put the gray in his hair. The white idol seemed young and mischievous to him, while the face shaped by the blacks— although virtually the same, line for line—struck him as wise and benevolent. The orange sandkings, as usual, were last and least. The wars had not gone well for them, and their castle was sad compared to those of the others. The image they carved was crude and cartoonish, and they seemed to intend to leave it this way. When they stopped work on the face, Kress grew quite piqued with them, but there really was nothing he could do.

When all of the sandkings had finished their Kress faces, he turned off the projector and decided that it was time to have a party. His friends would be impressed. He could even stage a war for them, he thought. Humming happily to himself, he began drawing up a guest list.

The party was a wild success.

Kress invited thirty people, a handful of close friends who shared his amusements, a few former lovers, and a collection of business and social rivals who could not afford to ignore his summons. He knew some of them would be discomfited and even offended by his sandkings. He counted on it. He customarily considered his parties a failure unless at least one guest walked out in high dudgeon.

On impulse he added Jala Wo's name to his list. "Bring Shade if you like," he added when he dictated the invitation to her.

Her acceptance surprised him just a bit. "Shade, alas, will be unable to attend. He does not go to social functions. As for myself, I look forward to the chance to see how your sandkings are doing.''

Kress ordered a sumptuous meal. And when at last the conversation had died down and most of his guests had gotten silly on wine and joy sticks, he shocked them by personally scraping their table leavings into a large bowl. "Come, all of you," he commanded. "I want to introduce you to my newest pets.'' Carrying the bowl, he conducted them into his living room.

The sandkings lived up to his fondest expectations. He had starved them for two days in preparation, and they were in a fighting mood. While the guests ringed the tank, looking through the magnifying glasses that Kress had thoughtfully provided, the sandkings waged a glorious battle over the scraps. He counted almost sixty dead mobiles when the struggle was over. The reds and whites, which had recently formed an alliance, came off with most of the food.

"Kress, you're disgusting," Cath m'Lane told him. She had lived with him for a short time two years before, until her soppy sentimentality almost drove him mad. "I was a fool to come back here. I thought perhaps you'd changed and wanted to apologize." She had never forgiven him for the time his shambler had eaten an excessively cute puppy of which she had been fond. "Don't ever invite me here again, Simon." She strode out, accompanied by her current lover, to a chorus of laughter.

Kress's other guests were full of questions.

Where did the sandkings come from? they wanted to know. "From Wo and Shade, Importers," he replied, with a polite gesture toward Jala Wo, who had remained quiet and apart throughout most of the evening.

Why did they decorate their castles with his likeness? "Because I am the source of all good things. Surely you know that?" This retort brought a round of chuckles.

Will they fight again? "Of course, but not tonight. Don't worry. There will be other parties."

Jad Rakkis, who was an amateur xenologist, began talking about other social insects and the wars they fought. "These sandkings are amusing, but nothing really. You ought to read about Terran soldier ants, for instance."

"Sandkings are not insects," Jala Wo said sharply, but Jad was off and running, and no one paid her the slightest attention. Kress smiled at her and shrugged.

Malada Blane suggested they have a betting pool the next time they got together to watch a war, and everyone was taken with the idea. An animated discussion about rules and odds ensued. It lasted for almost an hour. Finally the guests began to take their leave.

Jala Wo was the last to depart. "So," Kress said to her when they were alone, "it appears my sandkings are a hit."

"They are doing well," Wo said. "Already they are larger than my own."

"Yes," Kress said, "except for the oranges."

"I had noticed that," Wo replied. "They seem few in number, and their castle is shabby."

"Well, someone must lose," Kress said. "The oranges were late to emerge and get established. They have suffered for it."

"Pardon," said Wo, "but might I ask if you are feeding your sandkings sufficiently?"

Kress shrugged. "They diet from time to time. It makes them fiercer."

She frowned. "There is no need to starve them. Let them war in their own time, for their own reasons. It is their nature, and you will witness conflicts that are delightfully subtle and complex. The constant war brought on by hunger is artless and degrading."

Kress repaid Wo's frown with interest. "You are in my house. Wo, and here I am the judge of what is degrading. I fed the sandkings as you advised, and they did not fight."

"You must have patience."

"No," Kress said. "I am their master and their god, after all. Why should I wait on their impulses? They did not war often enough to suit me. I have corrected the situation."

"I see," said Wo. "I will discuss the matter with Shade."

"It is none of your concern, or his," Kress snapped.

"I must bid you good night, then," Wo said with resignation. But as she slipped into her coat to leave, she fixed him with a final, disapproving stare. "Look to your faces, Simon Kress," she warned him. "Look to your faces." And she departed.

Puzzled, he wandered back to the tank and stared at the castles. His faces were still there, as ever. Except—he snatched up his magnifying goggles and slipped them on. He studied the faces for long moments. Even then exactly what it was, was hard to make out. But it seemed to him that the expression on the faces had changed slightly, that his smile was somehow twisted so that it seemed a touch malicious. But it was a very subtle change—if it was a change at all. Kress finally put it down to his suggestibility, and he resolved not to invite Jala Wo to any more of his gatherings.

Over the next few months Kress and about a dozen of his favorites got together weekly for what he liked to call his "war games." Now that his initial fascination with the sandkings was past, Kress spent less time around his tank and more on his business affairs and his social life, but he still enjoyed having a few friends over for a war or two. He kept the combatants sharp on a constant edge of hunger. It had severe effects on the orange sandkings, which dwindled visibly until Kress began to wonder whether their maw was dead. But the others did well enough.

Sometimes at night when he could not sleep, Kress would take a bottle of wine into the living room, where the red gloom of his miniature desert provided the only light. He would drink and watch for hours, alone. There was usually a fight going on somewhere; when there was not, he could easily start one by dropping some small morsel of food into the tank.

Kress's companions began betting on the weekly battles, as Malada Blane had suggested. Kress won a goodly amount by betting on the whites, which had become the most powerful and most numerous colony in the tank and which had the grandest castle. One week he slid the corner of the tank top aside, and he dropped the food close to the white castle instead of on the central battleground, where he usually let food fall. So the others had to attack the whites in their stronghold to get any food at all. They tried. The whites were brilliant in defense. Kress won a hundred standards from Jad Rakkis.

Rakkis, in fact, lost heavily on the sandkings almost every week. He pretended to a vast knowledge of them and their ways, claiming that he had studied them after the first party, but he had no luck when it came to placing his bets. Kress suspected that Jad's claims were empty boasting. He had tried to study the sandkings a bit himself, in a moment of idle curiosity, tying in to the library to find out what world his pets originally came from. But the library had no listing for sandkings. He wanted to get in touch with Wo and ask her about it, but he had other concerns, and the matter kept slipping his mind.

Finally, after a month in which his losses totaled more than a thousand standards, Rakkis arrived at the war games. He was carrying a small plastic case under his arm. Inside was a spiderlike thing covered with fine golden hair.

"A sand spider," Rakkis announced. "From Cathaday. I got it this afternoon from l'Etherane the Petseller. Usually they remove the poison sacs, but this one is intact. Are you game, Simon? I want my money back. I'll bet a thousand standards, sand spider against sandkings."

Kress studied the spider in its plastic prison. His sandkings had grown—they were twice as large as Wo's, as she'd predicted—but they were still dwarfed by this thing. It was venomed, and they were not. Still, there were an awful lot of them. Besides, the endless sandking wars lately had begun to grow tiresome. The novelty of the match intrigued him.

"Done," Kress said. "Jad, you are a fool. The sandkings will just keep coming until this ugly creature of yours is dead."

"You are the fool, Simon," Rakkis replied, smiling. "The Cathadayan sand spider customarily feeds on burrowers that hide in nooks and crevices, and—well, watch—it will go straight into those castles and eat the maws.''

Kress scowled amid general laughter. He hadn't counted on that. ''Get on with it,'' he said irritably. Then he went to freshen his drink.

The spider was too large to be cycled conveniently through the food chamber. Two other guests helped Rakkis slide the tank top slightly to one side, and Malada Blane handed his case up to him. He shook the spider out. It landed lightly on a miniature dune in front of the red castle and stood confused for a moment, mouth working, legs twitching menacingly.

''Come on,'' Rakkis urged. They all gathered around the tank. Kress found his magnifiers and slipped them on. If he was going to lose a thousand standards, at least he wanted a good view of the action.

The sandkings had seen the invader. All over the red castle activity had ceased. The small scarlet mobiles were frozen, watching.

The spider began to move toward the dark promise of the gate. From the tower above, Simon Kress's countenance stared down impassively.

At once there was a flurry of activity. The nearest red mobiles formed themselves into two wedges and streamed over the sand toward the spider. More warriors erupted from inside the castle and assembled in a triple line to guard the approach to the underground chamber where the maw lived. Scouts came scuttling over the dunes, recalled to fight.

Battle was joined.

The attacking sandkings washed over the spider. Mandibles snapped shut on legs and abdomen, and clung. Reds raced up the golden legs to the invader's back. They bit and tore. One of them found an eye and ripped it loose with tiny yellow tendrils. Kress smiled and pointed.

But they were *small*, and they had no venom, and the spider did not stop. Its legs flicked sandkings off to either side. Its dripping jaws found others and left them broken and stiffening. Already a dozen of the reds lay dying. The sand spider came on and on. It strode straight through the triple line of guardians before the castle. The lines closed around it, covered it, waging desperate battle. A team of sandkings had bitten off one of the spider's legs. Defenders leaped from atop the towers to land on the twitching, heaving mass.

Lost beneath the sandkings, the spider somehow lurched down into the darkness and vanished.

Rakkis let out a long breath. He looked pale. ''Wonderful,'' someone else said. Malada Blane chuckled deep in her throat.

''Look,'' said Idi Noreddian, tugging Kress by the arm.

They had been so intent on the struggle in the corner that none of them had noticed the activity elsewhere in the tank. But now the castle was still, and the sands were empty save for dead red mobiles, and now they saw.

Three armies were drawn up before the red castle. They stood quite still, in perfect array, rank after rank of sandkings, orange and white and black—waiting to see what emerged from the depths.

Kress smiled. "A *cordon sanitaire*," he said. "And glance at the other castles, if you will, Jad."

Rakkis did, and he swore. Teams of mobiles were sealing up the gates with sand and stone. If the spider somehow survived this encounter, it would find no easy entrance at the other castles. "I should have brought four spiders," Rakkis said. "Still, I've won. My spider is down there right now, eating your damned maw."

Kress did not reply. He waited. There was motion in the shadows.

All at once red mobiles began pouring out of the gate. They took their positions on the castle and began repairing the damage that the spider had wrought. The other armies dissolved and began to retreat to their respective corners.

"Jad," Kress said, "I think you are a bit confused about who is eating whom."

The following week Rakkis brought four slim silver snakes. The sandkings dispatched them without much trouble.

Next he tried a large black bird. It ate more than thirty white mobiles and its thrashing and blundering virtually destroyed that castle, but ultimately its wings grew tired, and the sandkings attacked in force wherever it landed.

After that it was a case of insects, armored beetles not too unlike the sandkings themselves. But stupid, stupid. An allied force of oranges and blacks broke their formation, divided them, and butchered them.

Rakkis began giving Kress promissory notes.

It was around that time that Kress met Cath m'Lane again, one evening when he was dining in Asgard at his favorite restaurant. He stopped at her table briefly and told her about the war games, inviting her to join them. She flushed, then regained control of herself and grew icy. "Someone has to put a stop to you, Simon. I guess it's going to be me," she said.

Kress shrugged and enjoyed a lovely meal and thought no more about her threat.

Until a week later, when a small, stout woman arrived at his door and showed him a police wristband. "We've had complaints," she said. "Do you keep a tank full of dangerous insects, Kress?"

"Not insects," he said, furious. "Come, I'll show you."

When she had seen the sandkings, she shook her head. "This will never do. What do you know about these creatures anyway? Do you know what world they're from? Have they been cleared by the Ecological Board? Do you have a license for these things? We have a report that they're carnivores and possibly dangerous. We also have a report that they are semisentient. Where did you get these creatures anyway?"

"From Wo and Shade," Kress replied.

"Never heard of them," the woman said. "Probably smuggled them in, knowing our ecologists would never approve them. No, Kress, this won't do. I'm going to confiscate this tank and have it destroyed. And you're going to have to expect a few fines as well."

Kress offered her a hundred standards to forget all about him and his sandkings.

She *tsked.* "Now I'll have to add attempted bribery to the charges against you."

Not until he raised the figure to two thousand standards was she willing to be persuaded. "It's not going to be easy, you know," she said. "There are forms to be altered, records to be wiped. And getting a forged license from the ecologists will be time-consuming. Not to mention dealing with the complaint. What if she calls again?"

"Leave her to me," Kress said. "Leave her to me."

He thought about it for a while. That night he made some calls.

First he got l'Etherane the Petseller. "I want to buy a dog," he said. "A puppy."

The round-faced merchant gawked at him. "A puppy? That is not like you, Simon. Why don't you come in? I have a lovely choice."

"I want a very specific *kind* of puppy," Kress said. "Take notes. I'll describe to you what it must look like."

Afterwards he punched for Idi Noreddian. "Idi," he said, "I want you out here tonight with your holo equipment. I have a notion to record a sandking battle. A present for one of my friends."

The night after they made the recording, Kress stayed up late. He absorbed a controversial new drama in his sensorium, fixed himself a small snack, smoked a couple of joy sticks, and broke out a bottle of wine. Feeling very happy with himself, he wandered into the living room, glass in hand.

The lights were out. The red glow of the terrarium made the shadows look flushed and feverish. Kress walked over to survey his domain, curious as to how the blacks were doing in the repairs on their castle. The puppy had left it in ruins.

The restoration went well. But as Kress inspected the work through his magnifiers, he chanced to glance closely at the face on the sand-castle wall. It startled him.

He drew back, blinked, took a healthy gulp of wine, and looked again.

The face on the wall was still his. But it was all wrong, all *twisted*. His cheeks were bloated and piggish, his smile was a crooked leer. He looked impossibly malevolent.

Uneasy, he moved around the tank to inspect the other castles. They were each a bit different, but ultimately all the same.

The oranges had left out most of the fine detail, but the result still seemed monstrous, crude, a brutal mouth and mindless eyes.

The reds gave him a satanic, twitching sort of smile. His mouth did odd, unlovely things at its corners. The whites, his favorites, had carved a cruel idiot god.

Kress flung his wine across the room in rage. "You dare," he said under his breath. "Now you won't eat for a week, you damned . . ." His voice was shrill. "I'll teach you."

He had an idea. He strode out of the room, then returned a moment later with an antique iron throwing sword in his hand. It was a meter long, and the point was still sharp. Kress smiled, climbed up, and moved the tank cover aside just enough to give him working room, exposing one corner of the desert. He leaned down and jabbed the sword at the white castle below him. He waved it back and forth, smashing towers and ramparts and walls. Sand and stone collapsed, burying the scrambling mobiles. A flick of his wrist obliterated the features of the insolent, insulting caricature that the sandkings had made of his face. Then he poised the point of the sword above the dark mouth that opened down into the maw's chamber; he thrust with all his strength, meeting with resistance. He heard a soft, squishing sound. All the mobiles trembled and collapsed. Satisfied, Kress pulled back.

He watched for a moment, wondering whether he had killed the maw. The point of the throwing sword was wet and slimy. But finally the white sandkings began to move again—feebly, slowly—but they moved.

He was preparing to slide the cover back into place and move on to a second castle when he felt something crawling on his hand.

He screamed, dropping the sword, and brushed the sandking from his flesh. It fell to the carpet, and he ground it beneath his heel, crushing it thoroughly long after it was dead. It had crunched when he stepped on it. After that, trembling, he hurriedly sealed the tank up again. He rushed off to shower and inspected himself carefully. He boiled his clothing.

Later, after drinking several glasses of wine, he returned to the living room. He was a bit ashamed of the way he had been terrified by the sandking. But he was not about to open the tank again. From then on, the cover would stay sealed permanently. Still, he had to punish the others.

He decided to lubricate his mental processes with another glass of wine. As he finished it, an inspiration came to him. He went to the tank and made a few adjustments to the humidity controls.

By the time he fell asleep on the couch, his wine glass still in his hand, the sand castles were melting in the rain.

Kress woke to angry pounding on his door.

He sat up, groggy, his head throbbing. Wine hangovers were always the worst, he thought. He lurched to the entry chamber.

Cath m'Lane was outside. "You monster," she said, her face swollen and puffy and streaked with tears. "I cried all night, damn you. But no more, Simon, no more."

"Easy," he said, holding his head. "I've got a hangover."

She swore and shoved him aside and pushed her way into his house. The shambler came peering round a corner to see what the noise was. She spat at it and stalked into the living room, Kress trailing ineffectually after her. "Hold on," he said, "where do you . . . you can't . . ." He stopped, suddenly horror-struck. She was carrying a heavy sledgehammer in her left hand. "No," he said.

She went directly to the sandkings' tank. "You like the little charmers so much, Simon? Then you can live with them."

"Cath!" he shrieked.

Gripping the hammer with both hands, she swung as hard as she could against the side of the tank. The sound of the impact set Kress's head to screaming, and he made a low, blubbering sound of despair. But the plastic held.

She swung again. This time there was a *crack,* and a network of thin lines appeared in the wall of the tank.

Kress threw himself at her as she drew back her hammer to take a third swing. They went down flailing and rolled over. She lost her grip on the hammer and tried to throttle him, but Kress wrenched free and bit her on the arm, drawing blood. They both staggered to their feet, panting.

"You should see yourself, Simon," she said grimly. "Blood dripping from your mouth. You look like one of your pets. How do you like the taste?"

"Get out," he said. He saw the throwing sword where it had fallen the night before, and he snatched it up. "Get out," he repeated, waving the sword for emphasis. "Don't go near that tank again."

She laughed at him. "You wouldn't dare," she said. She bent to pick up her hammer.

Kress shrieked at her and lunged. Before he quite knew what was happening, the iron blade had gone clear through her abdomen. Cath m'Lane looked at him wonderingly and down at the sword. Kress fell back, whimpering. "I didn't mean . . . I only wanted . . ."

She was transfixed, bleeding, nearly dead, but somehow she did not fall. "You monster," she managed to say, though her mouth was full of blood. And she whirled, impossibly, the sword in her, and swung with her last strength at the tank. The tortured wall shattered, and Cath m'Lane was buried beneath an avalanche of plastic and sand and mud.

Kress made small hysterical noises and scrambled up onto the couch.

Sandkings were emerging from the muck on his living-room floor. They were crawling across Cath's body. A few of them ventured tentatively out across the carpet. More followed.

He watched as a column took shape, a living, writhing square of sandkings, bearing something—something slimy and featureless, a piece of raw meat as big as a man's head. They began to carry it away from the tank. It pulsed.

That was when Kress broke and ran.

Before he found the courage to return home, he ran to his skimmer and flew to the nearest city, some fifty kilometers away, almost sick with fear. But, once safely away, he found a small restaurant, downed several mugs of coffee and two anti-hangover tabs, ate a full breakfast, and gradually regained his composure.

It had been a dreadful morning, but dwelling on that would solve nothing. He ordered more coffee and considered his situation with icy rationality.

Cath m'Lane was dead at his hand. Could he report it and plead that it had been an accident? Unlikely. He had run her through, after all, and he had already told that policer to leave her to him. He would have to get rid of the evidence and hope that Cath had not told anyone her plans for the day. It was very unlikely she had. She could only have gotten his gift late last night. She said that she had cried all night, and she was alone when she arrived. Very well, he had one body and one skimmer to dispose of.

That left the sandkings. They might prove more of a difficulty. No doubt they had all escaped by now. The thought of them around his house, in his bed and his clothes, infesting his food—it made his flesh crawl. He shuddered and overcame his revulsion. It really shouldn't be too hard to kill them, he reminded himself. He didn't have to account for every mobile. Just the four maws, that was all. He could do that. They were large, as he'd seen. He would find them and kill them. He was their god; now he would be their destroyer.

He went shopping before he flew back to his home. He bought a set of skinthins that would cover him from head to foot, several bags of poison pellets for rockjock control, and a spray canister containing an illegally strong pesticide. He also bought a magnalock towing device.

When he landed late that afternoon, he went about things methodically. First he hooked Cath's skimmer to his own with the magnalock. Searching it, he had his first piece of luck. The crystal chip with Idi Noreddian's holo of the sandking fight was on the front seat. He had worried about that.

When the skimmers were ready, he slipped into his skinthins and went inside to get Cath's body.

It wasn't there.

He poked through the fast-drying sand carefully, and there was no doubt of it, the body was gone. Could she have dragged herself away? Unlikely, but Kress searched. A cursory inspection of his house turned up neither the body nor any sign of the sandkings. He did not have time for a more thorough investigation, not with the incriminating skimmer outside his front door. He resolved to try later.

Some seventy kilometers north of Kress's estate was a range of active volcanoes. He flew there, Cath's skimmer in tow. Above the glowering cone of the largest volcano he released the magnalock and watched the skimmer plummet down and vanish in the lava below.

It was dusk when he returned to his house. This gave him pause. Briefly he considered flying back to the city and spending the night there. He put the thought aside. There was work to do. He wasn't safe yet.

He scattered the poison pellets around the exterior of his house. No one would think this suspicious. He had always had a rockjock problem. When this task was completed, he primed the canister of pesticide and ventured back inside the house.

Kress went through the house, room by room, turning on lights everywhere he went until he was surrounded by a blaze of artificial illumination. He paused to clean up in the living room, shoveling sand and plastic fragments back into the broken tank. The sandkings were all gone, as he'd feared. The castles were shrunken and distorted, slagged by the watery bombardment Kress had visited upon them, and what little of them remained was crumbling as it dried.

He frowned and searched further, the canister of pest spray strapped across his shoulders.

Down in the wine cellar he could see Cath m'Lane's corpse.

It sprawled at the foot of a steep flight of stairs, the limbs twisted as if by a fall. White mobiles were swarming all over it, and as Kress watched, the body moved jerkily across the hard-packed dirt floor.

He laughed and twisted the illumination up to maximum. In the far corner a squat little earthen castle and a dark hole were visible between two wine racks. Kress could make out a rough outline of his face on the cellar wall.

The body shifted once again, moving a few centimeters toward the castle. Kress had a sudden vision of the white maw waiting hungrily. It might be able to get Cath's foot in its mouth, but no more. It was too absurd. He laughed again and started down into the cellar, finger poised on the trigger of the hose that snaked down his right arm. The sandkings—hundreds of them moving as one—deserted the body and assumed battle formation, a field of white between him and their maw.

Suddenly Kress had another inspiration. He smiled and lowered his firing hand. "Cath was always hard to swallow," he said, delighted at his wit. "Especially for one your size. Here, let me give you some help. What are gods for, after all?"

He retreated upstairs, returning shortly with a cleaver. The sand-kings, patient, waited and watched while Kress chopped Cath m'Lane into small, easily digestible pieces.

Kress slept in his skinthins that night, the pesticide close at hand, but he did not need it. The whites, sated, remained in the cellar, and he saw no sign of the others.

In the morning he finished the cleanup of the living room. When he was through, no trace of the struggle remained except for the broken tank.

He ate a light lunch and resumed his hunt for the missing sandkings. In full daylight it was not too difficult. The blacks had located in his rock garden, where they built a castle heavy with obsidian and quartz. The reds he found at the bottom of his long-disused swimming pool, which had partially filled with wind-blown sand over the years. He saw mobiles of both colors ranging about his grounds, many of them carrying poison pellets back to their maws. Kress felt like laughing. He decided his pesticide was unnecessary. No use risking a fight when he could just let the poison do its work. Both maws should be dead by evening.

That left only the burnt-orange sandkings unaccounted for. Kress circled his estate several times, in an ever-widening spiral, but he found no trace of them. When he began to sweat in his skinthins—it was a hot, dry day—he decided it was not important. If they were out here, they were probably eating the poison pellets, as the reds and blacks were.

He crunched several sandkings underfoot, with a certain degree of satisfaction, as he walked back to the house. Inside, he removed his skinthins, settled down to a delicious meal, and finally began to relax. Everything was under control. Two of the maws would soon be defunct, the third was safely located where he could dispose of it after it had served his purposes, and he had no doubt that he would find the fourth. As for Cath, every trace of her visit had been obliterated.

His reverie was interrupted when his viewscreen began to blink at him. It was Jad Rakkis, calling to brag about some cannibal worms he would bring to the war games tonight.

Kress had forgotten about that, but he recovered quickly. "Oh, Jad, my pardons. I neglected to tell you. I grew bored with all that and got rid of the sandkings. Ugly little things. Sorry, but there'll be no party tonight.''

Rakkis was indignant. ''But what will I do with my worms?''

''Put them in a basket of fruit and send them to a loved one,'' Kress said, signing off. Quickly he began calling the others. He did not need anyone arriving at his doorstep now, with the sandkings alive and infesting the estate.

As he was calling Idi Noreddian, Kress became aware of an annoying oversight. The screen began to clear, indicating that someone had answered at the other end. Kress flicked off.

Idi arrived on schedule an hour later. She was surprised to find the party had been canceled but perfectly happy to share an evening alone with Kress. He delighted her with his story of Cath's reaction to the holo they had made together. While telling it, he managed to ascertain that she had not mentioned the prank to anyone. He nodded, satisfied, and refilled their wine glasses. Only a trickle was left. ''I'll have to get a fresh bottle,'' he said. ''Come with me to my wine cellar, and help me pick out a good vintage. You've always had a better palate than I.''

She went along willingly enough but balked at the top of the stairs when Kress opened the door and gestured for her to precede him. ''Where are the lights?'' she asked. ''And that smell—what's that peculiar smell, Simon?''

When he shoved her, she looked briefly startled. She screamed as she tumbled down the stairs. Kress closed the door and began to nail it shut with the boards and air hammer he had left for that purpose. As he was finishing, he heard Idi groan. ''I'm hurt,'' she called. ''Simon, what is this?'' Suddenly she squealed, and shortly after that the screaming started.

It did not cease for hours. Kress went to his sensorium and dialed up a saucy comedy to blot it from his mind.

When he was sure she was dead, Kress flew her skimmer north to the volcanoes and discarded it. The magnalock was proving a good investment.

Odd scrabbling noises were coming from beyond the wine-cellar door the next morning when Kress went down to check things out. He listened for several uneasy moments, wondering whether Idi might possibly have survived and was scratching to get out. This seemed unlikely; it had to be the sandkings. Kress did not like the implications of this. He decided that he would keep the door sealed, at least for a while. He went outside with a shovel to bury the red and black maws in their own castles.

He found them very much alive.

The black castle was glittering with volcanic glass, and sandkings were all over it, repairing and improving. The highest tower was up to his waist, and on it was a hideous caricature of his face. When he approached the blacks halted in their labors and formed up into two threatening phalanxes. Kress glanced behind him and saw others closing off his escape. Startled, he dropped his shovel and sprinted out of the trap, crushing several mobiles beneath his boots.

The red castle was creeping up the walls of the swimming pool. The maw was safely settled in a pit, surrounded by sand and concrete and battlements. The reds crept all over the bottom of the pool. Kress watched them carry a rockjock and a large lizard into the castle. Horrified, he stepped back from the poolside and felt something crunch. Looking down, he saw three mobiles climbing up his leg. He brushed them off and stamped them to death, but others were approaching rapidly. They were larger than he remembered. Some were almost as big as his thumb.

He ran.

By the time he reached the safety of the house, his heart was racing and he was short of breath. He closed the door behind him and hurried to lock it. His house was supposed to be pestproof. He'd be safe in here.

A stiff drink steadied his nerve. *So poison doesn't faze them*, he thought. He should have known. Jala Wo had warned him that the maw could eat anything. He would have to use the pesticide. He took another drink for good measure, donned his skinthins, and strapped the canister to his back. He unlocked the door.

Outside, the sandkings were waiting.

Two armies confronted him, allied against the common threat. More than he could have guessed. The damned maws must be breeding like rockjocks. Mobiles were everywhere, a creeping sea of them.

Kress brought up the hose and flicked the trigger. A gray mist washed over the nearest rank of sandkings. He moved his hand from side to side.

Where the mist fell, the sandkings twitched violently and died in sudden spasms. Kress smiled. They were no match for him. He sprayed in a wide arc before him and stepped forward confidently over a litter of black and red bodies. The armies fell back. Kress advanced, intent on cutting through them to their maws.

All at once the retreat stopped. A thousand sandkings surged toward him.

Kress had been expecting the counterattack. He stood his ground, sweeping his misty sword before him in great looping strokes. They came at him and died. A few got through; he could not spray everywhere at once. He felt them climbing up his legs, then sensed their mandibles biting futilely at the reinforced plastic of his skinthins. He ignored them and kept spraying.

Then he began to feel soft impacts on his head and shoulders.

Kress trembled and spun and looked up above him. The front of his house was alive with sandkings. Blacks and reds, hundreds of them. They were launching themselves into the air, raining down on him. They fell all around him. One landed on his face-plate, its mandibles scraping at his eyes for a terrible second before he plucked it away.

He swung up his hose and sprayed the air, sprayed the house, sprayed until the airborne sandkings were all dead or dying. The mist settled back on him, making him cough. But he kept spraying. Only when the front of the house was clean did Kress turn his attention back to the ground.

They were all around him, on him, dozens of them scurrying over his body, hundreds of others hurrying to join them. He turned the mist on them. The hose went dead. Kress heard a loud *hiss*, and the deadly fog rose in a great cloud from between his shoulders, cloaking, choking him, making his eyes burn and blur. He felt for the hose, and his hand came away covered with dying sandkings. The hose was severed; they'd eaten it through. He was surrounded by a shroud of pesticide, blinded. He stumbled and screamed and began to run back to the house, pulling sandkings from his body as he went.

Inside, he sealed the door and collapsed on the carpet, rolling back and forth until he was sure he had crushed them all. The canister was empty by then, hissing feebly. Kress stripped off his skinthins and showered. The hot spray scalded him and left his skin reddened and sensitive, but it made his flesh stop crawling.

He dressed in his heaviest clothing, thick work pants and leathers, after shaking them out nervously. "Damn," he kept muttering, "damn." His throat was dry. After searching the entry hall thoroughly to make certain it was clean, he allowed himself to sit and pour a drink. "Damn," he repeated. His hand shook as he poured, slopping liquor on the carpet.

The alcohol settled him, but it did not wash away the fear. He had a second drink and went to the window furtively. Sandkings were moving across the thick plastic pane. He shuddered and retreated to his communications console. He had to get help, he thought wildly. He would punch through a call to the authorities, and policers would come out with flamethrowers, and . . .

Kress stopped in mid-call and groaned. He couldn't call in the police. He would have to tell them about the whites in his cellar, and they'd find the bodies there. Perhaps the maw might have finished Cath m'Lane by now, but certainly not Idi Noreddian. He hadn't even cut her up. Besides, there would be bones. No, the police could be called in only as a last resort.

He sat at the console, frowning. His communications equipment filled a whole wall. From here he could reach anyone on Baldur. He had plenty of money and his cunning; he had always prided himself on his cunning. He would handle this somehow.

Briefly he considered calling Wo, but he soon dismissed the idea. Wo knew too much and she would ask questions, and he did not trust her. No, he needed someone who would do as he asked *without* questions.

His frown slowly turned into a smile. Kress had contacts. He put through a call to a number he had not used in a long time.

A woman's face took shape on his viewscreen—white-haired, blank of expression, with a long, hooked nose. Her voice was brisk and efficient. "Simon," she said. "How is business?"

"Business is fine, Lissandra," Kress replied. "I have a job for you."

"A removal? My price has gone up since last time, Simon. It has been ten years, after all."

"You will be well paid," Kress said. "You know I'm generous. I want you for a bit of pest control."

She smiled a thin smile. "No need to use euphemisms, Simon. The call is shielded."

"No, I'm serious. I have a pest problem. Dangerous pests. Take care of them for me. No questions. Understood?"

"Understood."

"Good. You'll need . . . oh, three to four operatives. Wear heat-resistant skinthins, and equip them with flamethrowers or lasers, something on that order. Come out to my place. You'll see the problem. Bugs, lots and lots of them. In my rock garden and the old swimming pool you'll find castles. Destroy them, kill everything inside them. Then knock on the door, and I'll show you what else needs to be done. Can you get out here quickly?"

Her face remained impassive. "We'll leave within the hour."

Lissandra was true to her word. She arrived in a lean, black skimmer with three operatives. Kress watched them from the safety of a second-story window. They were all faceless in dark plastic skinthins. Two of them wore portable flamethrowers; a third carried lasercannon and explosives. Lissandra carried nothing; Kress recognized her by the way she gave orders.

Their skimmer passed low overhead first, checking out the situation. The sandkings went mad. Scarlet and ebony mobiles ran everywhere, frenetic. Kress could see the castle in the rock garden from his vantage point. It stood tall as a man. Its ramparts were crawling with black defenders, and a steady stream of mobiles flowed down into its depths.

Lissandra's skimmer came down next to Kress's, and the operatives vaulted out and unlimbered their weapons. They looked inhuman, deadly.

The black army drew up between them and the castle. The reds— Kress suddenly realized that he could not see the reds. He blinked. Where had they gone?

Lissandra pointed and shouted, and her two flamethrowers spread out and opened up on the black sandkings. Their weapons coughed dully and began to roar, long tongues of blue-and-scarlet fire licking out before them. Sandkings crisped and shriveled and died. The operatives began to play the fire back and forth in an efficient, interlocking pattern. They advanced with careful, measured steps.

The black army burned and disintegrated, the mobiles fleeing in a thousand different directions, some back toward the castle, others toward the enemy. None reached the operatives with flamethrowers. Lissandra's people were very professional.

Then one of them stumbled.

Or seemed to stumble. Kress looked again and saw that the ground had given way beneath the man. Tunnels, he thought with a tremor of fear, tunnels, pits, traps. The flamer was sunk in sand up to his waist, and suddenly the ground around him seemed to erupt, and he was covered with scarlet sandkings. He dropped the flamethrower and began to claw wildly at his own body. His screams were horrible to hear.

His companion hesitated, then swung and fired. A blast of flame swallowed human and sandkings both. The screaming stopped abruptly. Satisfied, the second flamer turned back to the castle, took another step forward, and recoiled as his foot broke through the ground and vanished up to the ankle. He tried to pull it back and retreat, and the sand all around him gave way. He lost his balance and stumbled, flailing, and the sandkings were everywhere, a boiling mass of them, covering him as he writhed and rolled. His flamethrower was useless and forgotten.

Kress pounded wildly on the window, shouting for attention. "The castle! Get the castle!"

Lissandra, standing back by her skimmer, heard and gestured. Her third operative sighted with the lasercannon and fired. The beam throbbed across the grounds and sliced off the top of the castle. He brought the cannon down sharply, hacking at the sand and stone parapets. Towers fell. Kress's face disintegrated. The laser bit into the ground, searching round and about. The castle crumbled. Now it was only a heap of sand. But the black mobiles continued to move. The maw was buried too deeply. The beams hadn't touched it.

Lissandra gave another order. Her operative discarded the laser, primed an explosive, and darted forward. He leaped over the smoking corpse of the first flamer, landed on solid ground within Kress's rock garden, and heaved. The explosive ball landed square atop the ruins of the black castle. White-hot light seared Kress's eyes, and there was a tremendous gout of sand and rock and mobiles. For a moment dust obscured everything. It was raining sandkings and pieces of sandkings.

Kress saw that the black mobiles were dead and unmoving.

"The pool!" he shouted down through the window. "Get the castle in the pool!"

Lissandra understood quickly; the ground was littered with motionless blacks, but the reds were pulling back hurriedly and re-forming. Her operative stood uncertain, then reached down and pulled out another explosive ball. He took one step forward, but Lissandra called him, and he sprinted back in her direction.

It was all so simple then. He reached the skimmer, and Lissandra took him aloft. Kress rushed to another window in another room to watch. They came swooping in just over the pool, and the operative pitched his bombs down at the red castle from the safety of the skimmer. After the fourth run, the castle was unrecognizable, and the sandkings stopped moving.

Lissandra was thorough. She had him bomb each castle several additional times. Then he used the lasercannon, crisscrossing methodically until he was certain that nothing living could remain intact beneath those small patches of ground.

Finally they came knocking at his door. Kress was grinning maniacally when he let them in. "Lovely," he said, "lovely."

Lissandra pulled off the mask of her skinthins. "This will cost you, Simon. Two operatives gone, not to mention the danger to my own life."

"Of course," Kress blurted. "You'll be well paid, Lissandra. Whatever you ask, just so you finish the job."

"What remains to be done?"

"You have to clean out my wine cellar," Kress said. "There's another castle down there. And you'll have to do it without explosives. I don't want my house coming down around me."

Lissandra motioned to her operative. "Go outside and get Rajk's flamethrower. It should be intact."

He returned armed, ready, silent. Kress led them to the wine cellar.

The heavy door was still nailed shut, as he had left it. But it bulged outward slightly, as if warped by some tremendous pressure. That made Kress uneasy, as did the silence that reigned about them. He stood well away from the door while Lissandra's operative removed his nails and planks. "Is that safe in here?" he found himself muttering, pointing at the flamethrower. "I don't want a fire, either, you know."

"I have the laser," Lissandra said. "We'll use that for the kill. The flamethrower probably won't be needed. But I want it here just in case. There are worse things than fire, Simon."

He nodded.

The last plank came free of the cellar door. There was still no sound from below. Lissandra snapped an order, and her underling fell back, took up a position behind her, and leveled the flamethrower squarely at the door. She slipped her mask back on, hefted the laser, stepped forward, and pulled the door open.

No motion. No sound. It was dark down there.

"Is there a light?" Lissandra asked.

"Just inside the door," Kress said. "On the right-hand side. Mind the stairs. They're quite steep."

She stepped into the doorway, shifted the laser to her left hand, and reached up with her right, fumbling inside for the light panel. Nothing happened. "I feel it," Lissandra said, "but it doesn't seem to . . ."

Then she was screaming, and she stumbled backward. A great white sandking had clamped itself around her wrist. Blood welled through her skinthins where its mandibles had sunk in. It was fully as large as her hand.

Lissandra did a horrible little jig across the room and began to smash her hand against the nearest wall. Again and again and again. It landed with a heavy, meaty thud. Finally the sandking fell away. She whimpered and fell to her knees.

"I think my fingers are broken," she said softly. The blood was still flowing freely. She had dropped the laser near the cellar door.

"I'm not going down there," her operative announced in clear, firm tones.

Lissandra looked up at him. "No," she said. "Stand in the door and flame it all. Cinder it. Do you understand?"

He nodded.

Kress moaned. "My *house*," he said. His stomach churned. The white sandking had been so *large*. How many more were down there? "Don't," he continued. "Leave it alone. I've changed my mind."

Lissandra misunderstood. She held out her hand. It was covered with blood and greenish-black ichor. "Your little friend bit clean through my glove, and you saw what it took to get it off. I don't care about your house, Simon. Whatever is down there is going to die."

Kress hardly heard her. He thought he could see movement in the shadows beyond the cellar door. He imagined a white army bursting out, each soldier as big as the sandking that had attacked Lissandra. He saw himself being lifted by a hundred tiny arms and being dragged down into the darkness, where the maw waited hungrily. He was afraid. "Don't," he said.

They ignored him.

Kress darted forward, and his shoulder slammed into the back of Lissandra's operative just as the man was bracing to fire. The operative grunted, lost his balance, and pitched forward into the black. Kress listened to him fall down the stairs. Afterwards there were other noises— scuttlings and snaps and soft, squishing sounds.

Kress swung around to face Lissandra. He was drenched in cold sweat, but a sickly kind of excitement possessed him. It was almost sexual.

Lissandra's calm, cold eyes regarded him through her mask. "What are you doing?" she demanded as Kress picked up the laser she had dropped. "*Simon!*"

"Making a peace," he said, giggling. "They won't hurt god, no, not so long as god is good and generous. I was cruel. Starved them. I have to make up for it now, you see."

"You're insane," Lissandra said. It was the last thing she said. Kress burned a hole in her chest big enough to put his arm through. He dragged the body across the floor and rolled it down the cellar stairs. The noises were louder—chitinous clackings and scrapings and echoes that were thick and liquid. Kress nailed up the door once again.

As he fled, he was filled with a deep sense of contentment that coated his fear like a layer of syrup. He suspected it was not his own.

He planned to leave his home, to fly to the city and take a room for a night, or perhaps for a year. Instead he started drinking. He was not quite sure why. He drank steadily for hours and retched it all up violently on his living-room carpet. At some point he fell asleep. When he woke, it was pitch-dark in the house.

He cowered against the couch. He could hear *noises*. Things were moving in the walls. They were all around him. His hearing was extra- ordinarily acute. Every little creak was the footstep of a sandking. He closed his eyes and waited, expecting to feel their terrible touch, afraid to move lest he brush against one.

Kress sobbed and then was very still.

Time passed, but nothing happened.

He opened his eyes again. He trembled. Slowly the shadows began to soften and dissolve. Moonlight was filtering through the high win- dows. His eyes adjusted.

The living room was empty. Nothing there, nothing, nothing. Only his drunken fears.

Kress steeled himself and rose and went to a light.

Nothing there. The room was deserted.

He listened. Nothing. No sound. Nothing in the walls.

It had all been his imagination, his fear.

The memories of Lissandra and the thing in the cellar returned to him unbidden. Shame and anger washed over him. Why had he done that? He could have helped her burn it out, kill it. *Why* . . . he knew why. The maw had done it to him, had put fear in him. Wo had said it was psionic, even when it was small. And now it was large, so large. It had feasted on Cath and Idi, and now it had two more bodies down there. It would keep growing. And it had learned to like the taste of human flesh, he thought.

He began to shake, but he took control of himself again and stopped. It wouldn't hurt him, he was god, the whites had always been his favorites.

He remembered how he had stabbed it with his throwing sword. That was before Cath came. Damn her, anyway.

He couldn't stay here. The maw would grow hungry again. Large as it was, it wouldn't take long. Its appetite would be terrible. What would it do then? He had to get away, back to the safety of the city while the maw was still contained in his wine cellar. It was only plaster and hard-packed earth down there, and the mobiles could dig and tunnel. When they got free . . . Kress didn't want to think about it.

He went to his bedroom and packed. He took three bags. Just a single change of clothing, that was all he needed; the rest of the space he filled with his valuables, with jewelry and art and other things he could not bear to lose. He did not expect to return to this place ever again.

His shambler followed him down the stairs, staring at him from its baleful, glowing eyes. It was gaunt. Kress realized that it had been ages since he had fed it. Normally it could take care of itself, but no doubt the pickings had grown lean of late. When it tried to clutch at his leg, he snarled at it and kicked it away, and it scurried off, obviously hurt and offended.

Carrying his bags awkwardly, Kress slipped outside and shut the door behind him.

For a moment he stood pressed against the house, his heart thudding in his chest. Only a few meters between him and his skimmer. He was afraid to take those few steps. The moonlight was bright, and the grounds in front of his house were a scene of carnage. The bodies of Lissandra's two flamers lay where they had fallen, one twisted and burned, and the other swollen beneath a mass of dead sandkings. And the mobiles, the black and red mobiles, they were all around him. It took an effort to remember that they were dead. It was almost as if they were simply waiting, as they had waited so often before.

Nonsense, Kress told himself. More drunken fears. He had seen the castles blown apart. They were dead, and the white maw was trapped in his cellar. He took several deep and deliberate breaths and stepped forward onto the sandkings. They crunched. He ground them into the sand savagely. They did not move.

Kress smiled and walked slowly across the battleground, listening to the sounds, the sounds of safety.

Crunch, crackle, crunch.

He lowered his bags to the ground and opened the door to his skimmer.

Something moved from shadow into light. A pale shape on the seat of his skimmer. It was as long as his forearm. Its mandibles clacked together softly, and it looked up at him from six small eyes set all around its body.

Kress wet his pants and backed away slowly.

There was more motion from inside the skimmer. He had left the door open. The sandking emerged and came toward him, cautiously. Others followed. They had been hiding beneath his seats, burrowed into the upholstery. But now they emerged. They formed a ragged ring around the skimmer.

Kress licked his lips, turned, and moved quickly to Lissandra's skimmer.

He stopped before he was halfway there. Things were moving inside that one, too. Great maggoty things half-seen by the light of the moon.

Kress whimpered and retreated back toward the house. Near the front door, he looked up.

He counted a dozen long, white shapes creeping back and forth across the walls of the building. Four of them were clustered close together near the top of the unused belfry, where the carrion hawk had once roosted. They were carving something. A face. A very recognizable face.

Kress shrieked and ran back inside. He headed for his liquor cabinet.

A sufficient quantity of drink brought him the easy oblivion he sought. But he woke. Despite everything, he woke. He had a terrific headache, and he stank, and he was hungry. Oh, so very hungry! He had never been so hungry.

Kress knew it was not his *own* stomach hurting.

A white sandking watched him from atop the dresser in his bedroom, its antennae moving faintly. It was as big as the one in the skimmer the night before. He tried not to shrink away. "I'll . . . I'll feed you," he said to it. "I'll feed you." His mouth was horribly dry, sandpaper-dry. He licked his lips and fled from the room.

The house was full of sandkings; he had to be careful where he put his feet. They all seemed busy on errands of their own. They were making modifications in his house, burrowing into or out of his walls, carving things. Twice he saw his own likeness staring out at him from unexpected places. The faces were warped, twisted, livid with fear.

He went outside to get the bodies that had been rotting in the yard, hoping to appease the white maw's hunger. They were gone, both of them. Kress remembered how easily the mobiles could carry things many times their own weight.

It was terrible to think that the maw was *still* hungry after all that.

When Kress reentered the house, a column of sandkings was wending its way down the stairs. Each carried a piece of his shambler. The head seemed to look at him reproachfully as it went by.

Kress emptied his freezers, his cabinets, everything, piling all the food in the house in the center of his kitchen floor. A dozen whites waited to take it away. They avoided the frozen food, leaving it to thaw in a great puddle, but carried off everything else.

When all the food was gone, Kress felt his own hunger pangs abate just a bit, though he had not eaten a thing. But he knew the respite would be short-lived. Soon the maw would be hungry again. He had to feed it.

Kress knew what to do. He went to his communicator. "Malada," he began casually when the first of his friends answered, "I'm having a small party tonight. I realize this is terribly short notice, but I hope you can make it. I really do."

He called Jad Rakkis next, and then the others. By the time he had finished, five of them had accepted his invitation. Kress hoped that would be enough.

Kress met his guests outside—the mobiles had cleaned up remarkably quickly, and the grounds looked almost as they had before the battle—and walked them to his front door. He let them enter first. He did not follow.

When four of them had gone through, Kress finally worked up his courage. He closed the door behind his latest guest, ignoring the startled exclamations that soon turned into shrill gibbering, and sprinted for the skimmer the man had arrived in. He slid in safely, thumbed the starplate, and swore. It was programmed to lift only in response to its owner's thumbprint, of course.

Rakkis was the next to arrive. Kress ran to his skimmer as it set down and seized Rakkis by the arm as he was climbing out. "Get back in, quickly," he said, pushing. "Take me to the city. Hurry, Jad. *Get out of here!*"

But Rakkis only stared at him and would not move. "Why, what's wrong, Simon? I don't understand. What about your party?"

And then it was too late, because the loose sand all around them was stirring, and the red eyes were staring at them, and the mandibles were clacking. Rakkis made a choking sound and moved to get back in his skimmer, but a pair of mandibles snapped shut about his ankle, and suddenly he was on his knees. The sand seemed to boil with subterranean activity. Rakkis thrashed and cried terribly as they tore him apart. Kress could hardly bear to watch.

After that, he did not try to escape again. When it was all over, he cleaned out what remained in his liquor cabinet and got extremely drunk. It would be the last time he would enjoy that luxury, he knew. The only alcohol remaining in the house was stored down in the wine cellar.

Kress did not touch a bite of food the entire day, but he fell asleep feeling bloated, sated at last, the awful hunger vanquished. His last thoughts before the nightmares took him were about whom he could ask out tomorrow.

Morning was hot and dry. Kress opened his eyes to see the white sandking on his dresser again. He shut his eyes again quickly, hoping the dream would leave him. It did not, and he could not go back to sleep, and soon he found himself staring at the thing.

He stared for almost five minutes before the strangeness of it dawned on him; the sandking was not moving.

The mobiles could be preternaturally still, to be sure. He had seen them wait and watch a thousand times. But always there was some motion about them: The mandibles clacked, the legs twitched, the long, fine antennae stirred and swayed.

But the sandking on his dresser was completely still.

Kress rose, holding his breath, not daring to hope. Could it be dead? Could something have killed it? He walked across the room.

The eyes were glassy and black. The creature seemed swollen, somehow, as if it were soft and rotting inside, filling up with gas that pushed outward at the plates of white armor.

Kress reached out a trembling hand and touched it.

It was warm, hot even, and growing hotter. But it did not move.

He pulled his hand back, and as he did, a segment of the sandking's white exoskeleton fell away from it. The flesh beneath was the same color, but softer-looking, swollen and feverish. And it almost seemed to throb.

Kress backed away and ran to the door.

Three more white mobiles lay in his hall. They were all like the one in his bedroom.

He ran down the stairs, jumping over sandkings. None of them moved. The house was full of them, all dead, dying, comatose, whatever. Kress did not care what was wrong with them. Just so they could not move.

He found four of them inside his skimmer. He picked them up, one by one, and threw them as far as he could. Damned monsters. He slid back in, on the ruined half-eaten seats, and thumbed the starplate.

Nothing happened.

Kress tried again and again. Nothing. It wasn't fair. This was *his* skimmer. It ought to start. Why wouldn't it lift? He didn't understand.

Finally he got out and checked, expecting the worst. He found it. The sandkings had torn apart his gravity grid. He was trapped. He was still trapped.

Grimly Kress marched back into the house. He went to his gallery and found the antique sword he had used on Cath m'Lane. He set to work. The sandkings did not stir even as he chopped them to pieces. But they splattered when he made the first cut, the bodies almost bursting. Inside was awful; strange half-formed organs, a viscous reddish ooze that looked almost like human blood, and the yellow ichor.

Kress destroyed twenty of them before he realized the futility of what he was doing. The mobiles were nothing, really. Besides, there were so *many* of them. He could work for a day and a night and still not kill all of them.

He had to go down into the wine cellar and use the sword on the maw.

Resolute, he started toward the cellar. He got within sight of the door, then stopped.

It was not a door anymore. The walls had been eaten away, so that the hole was twice the size it had been, and round. A pit, that was all. There was no sign that there had ever been a door nailed shut over that black abyss.

A ghastly, choking, fetid odor seemed to come from below.

And the walls were wet and bloody and covered with patches of white fungus.

And worst, it was *breathing*.

Kress stood across the room and felt the warm wind wash over him as it exhaled, and he tried not to choke, and when the wind reversed direction, he fled.

Back in the living room he destroyed three more mobiles and collapsed. What was *happening*? He didn't understand.

Then he remembered the only person who might understand. Kress went to his communicator again, stepped on a sandking in his haste, and prayed fervently that the device still worked.

When Jala Wo answered, he broke down and told her everything.

She let him talk without interruption, no expression save for a slight frown on her gaunt, pale face. When Kress had finished, she said only, "I ought to leave you there."

Kress began to blubber. "You can't. Help me, I'll pay—"

"I ought to," Wo repeated, "but I won't."

"Thank you," Kress said. "Oh, thank—"

"Quiet," said Wo. "Listen to me. This is your own doing. Keep your sandkings well, and they are courtly ritual warriors. You turned yours into something else, with starvation and torture. You were their god. You made them what they are. That maw in your cellar is sick, still suffering from the wound you gave it. It is probably insane. Its behavior is . . . unusual.

"You have to get out of there quickly. The mobiles are not dead, Kress. They are dormant. I told you the exoskeleton falls off when they grow larger. Normally, in fact, it falls off much earlier. I have never heard of sandkings growing as large as yours while still in the insectoid stage. It is another result of crippling the white maw, I would say. That does not matter.

"What matters is the metamorphosis your sandkings are now undergoing. As the maw grows, you see, it gets progressively more intelligent. Its psionic powers strengthen, and its mind becomes more sophisticated, more ambitious. The armored mobiles are useful enough when the maw is tiny and only semisentient, but now it needs better servants, bodies with more capabilities. Do you understand? The mobiles are all going to give birth to a new breed of sandking. I can't say exactly what it will look like. Each maw designs its own, to fit its perceived needs and desires. But it will be biped, with four arms and opposable thumbs. It will be able to construct and operate advanced machinery. The individual sandkings will not be sentient. But the maw will be very sentient indeed."

Kress was gaping at Wo's image on the viewscreen. "Your workers," he said, with an effort. "The ones who came out here . . . who installed the tank . . ."

Wo managed a faint smile. "Shade," she said.

"Shade is a sandking," Kress repeated numbly. "And you sold me a tank of . . . of . . . infants, ah . . ."

"Do not be absurd," Wo said. "A first-stage sandking is more like a sperm than like an infant. The wars temper and control them in nature. Only one in a hundred reaches the second stage. Only one in a thousand achieves the third and final plateau and becomes like Shade. Adult sandkings are not sentimental about the small maws. There are too many of them, and their mobiles are pests." She sighed.

"And all this talk wastes time. That white sandking is going to waken to full sentience soon. It is not going to need you any longer, and it hates you, and it will be very hungry. The transformation is taxing. The maw must eat enormous amounts both before and after. So you have to get out of there. Do you understand?"

"I *can't*," Kress said. "My skimmer is destroyed, and I can't get any of the others to start. I don't know how to reprogram them. Can you come out for me?"

"Yes," said Wo. "Shade and I will leave at once, but it is more than two hundred kilometers from Asgard to you, and there is equipment that we will need to deal with the deranged sandking you've created. You cannot wait there. You have two feet. Walk. Go due east, as near as you can determine, as quickly as you can. The land out there is pretty desolate. We can find you easily with an aerial search, and you'll be safely away from the sandkings. Do you understand?''

"Yes," Kress said. "Yes, oh, yes."

They signed off, and he walked quickly toward the door. He was halfway there when he heard the noise, a sound halfway between a pop and a crack.

One of the sandkings had split open. Four tiny hands covered with pinkish-yellow blood came up out of the gap and began to push the dead skin aside.

Kress began to run.

He had not counted on the heat.

The hills were dry and rocky. Kress ran from the house as quickly as he could, ran until his ribs ached and his breath was coming in gasps. Then he walked, but as soon as he had recovered, he began to run again. For almost an hour he ran and walked, ran and walked, beneath the fierce, hot sun. He sweated freely and wished that he had thought to bring some water, and he watched the sky in hopes of seeing Wo and Shade.

He was not made for this. It was too hot and too dry, and he was in no condition. But he kept himself going with the memory of the way the maw had breathed and the thought of the wriggling little things that by now were surely crawling all over his house. He hoped Wo and Shade would know how to deal with them.

He had his own plans for Wo and Shade. It was all their fault, Kress had decided, and they would suffer for it. Lissandra was dead, but he knew others in her profession. He would have his revenge. This he promised himself a hundred times as he struggled and sweated his way eastward.

At least he hoped it was east. He was not that good at directions, and he wasn't certain which way he had run in his initial panic, but since then he had made an effort to bear due east, as Wo had suggested.

When he had been running for several hours, with no sign of rescue, Kress began to grow certain that he had miscalculated his direction.

When several more hours passed, he began to grow afraid. What if Wo and Shade could not find him? He would die out here. He hadn't eaten in two days, he was weak and frightened, his throat was raw for want of water. He couldn't keep going. The sun was sinking now, and he'd be completely lost in the dark. What was wrong? Had the sandkings eaten Wo and Shade? The fear was on him again, filling him, and with it a great thirst and a terrible hunger. But Kress kept going. He stumbled now when he tried to run, and twice he fell. The second time he scraped his hand on a rock, and it came away bloody. He sucked at it as he walked, and he worried about infection.

The sun was on the horizon behind him. The ground grew a little cooler, for which Kress was grateful. He decided to walk until last light and settle down for the night. Surely he was far enough from the sandkings to be safe, and Wo and Shade would find him come morning.

When he topped the next rise, he saw the outline of a house in front of him.

It wasn't as big as his own house, but it was big enough. It was habitation, safety. Kress shouted and began to run toward it. Food and drink, he had to have nourishment, he could taste the meal already. He was aching with hunger. He ran down the hill toward the house, waving his arms and shouting to the inhabitants. The light was almost gone now, but he could still make out a half-dozen children playing in the twilight. "Hey there," he shouted. "Help, help."

They came running toward him.

Kress stopped suddenly. "No," he said, "oh, no. Oh, no." He backpedaled, slipped on the sand, got up, and tried to run again. They caught him easily. They were ghastly little things with bulging eyes and dusky orange skin. He struggled, but it was useless. Small as they were, each of them had four arms, and Kress had only two.

They carried him toward the house. It was a sad, shabby house, built of crumbling sand, but the door was quite large, and dark, and it breathed. That was terrible, but it was not the thing that set Simon Kress to screaming. He screamed because of the others, the little orange children who came crawling out of the castle, and watched impassively as he passed.

All of them had his face.

Born in Oklahoma City, Oklahoma, Hugo and Nebula winner Joe Halde-
man took a B.S. degree in physics and astronomy from the University of
Maryland, and did postgraduate work in mathematics and computer
science. His plans for a career in science were cut short by the U.S.
Army, which sent him to Vietnam in 1968 as a combat engineer. Seriously
wounded in action, Haldeman returned home in 1969, and began to
write—and the consequent loss to the scientific world has been a substan-
tial gain for SF. Haldeman sold his first story to Galaxy *in 1969, and by*
1976 had already garnered Nebula and Hugo awards for his famous
novel The Forever War *(Ballantine). His next novel,* Mindbridge *(Avon),*
sold for a record six-figure advance, and he took another Hugo Award in
1977 for his story "Tricentennial." His other books include a main-
stream novel War Year *(Pocket Books), an SF novel* All My Sins
Remembered *(Avon), a short-story collection,* Infinite Dreams *(Avon),*
and, as editor, the anthologies Study War No More *(Avon) and* Cosmic
Laughter *(Holt). Soon forthcoming is a new novel,* Worlds, *and a*
collaborative novel, Starschool, *written with his brother, SF writer Jack*
C. Haldeman II. His story "Armaja Das" was in our Sixth Annual
Collection. *He lives in Ormand Beach, Florida, with his wife Gay.*

In the exciting and imaginative story that follows, Haldeman depicts
a crisis in the career of a hard-boiled twenty-first-century private detec-
tive, who has to deal with problems that Sam Spade or Philip Marlowe
never even dreamed *of. . . .*

JOE HALDEMAN
Bloodsisters

So I used to carry two different business cards: J. Michael Loomis, Data
Concentration, and Jack Loomis, Private Investigator. They mean the
same thing, nine cases out of ten. You have to size up a potential
customer, decide whether he'd feel better hiring a shamus or a clerk.

Some people still have these romantic notions about private detectives and get into a happy sweat at the thought of using one. But it *is* the
21st century and, endless Bogart reruns notwithstanding, most of my
work consisted in sitting at my office console and using it to subvert the
privacy laws of various states and countries—finding out embarrassing
things about people, so other people could divorce them or fire them or
get a piece of the slickery.

Not to say I didn't go out on the street sometimes; not to say I didn't have a gun and a ticket for it. There are forces of evil out there, friends, though most of them would probably rather be thought of as businessmen who use the law rather than fear it. Same as me. I was always happy, though, to stay on this side of murder, treason, kidnaping—any lobo offense. This brain may not be much, but it's all I have.

I should have used it when the woman walked into my office. She had a funny way of saying hello:

"Are you licensed to carry a gun?"

Various retorts came to mind, most of them having to do with her expulsion, but, after a period of silence, I said yes and asked who had referred her to me. Asked politely, too, to make up for staring. She was a little more beautiful than anyone I'd ever seen before.

"My lawyer," she said. "Don't ask who he is."

With that, I was pretty sure that this was some sort of elaborate joke. Story detectives always have beautiful mysterious customers. My female customers tend to be dowdy and too talkative, and much more interested in alimony than in romance.

"What's your name, then? Or am I not supposed to ask that, either?"

She hesitated. "Ghentlee Arden."

I turned the console on and typed in her name, then a seven-digit code. "Your legal firm is Lee, Chu, and Rosenstein. And your real name is Maribelle Four Ghentlee, fourth clone of Maribelle Ghentlee."

"Arden is my professional name. I dance." She had a nice blush.

I typed in another string of digits. Sometimes that sort of thing would lose a customer. "Says here you're a registered hooker."

"Callgirl," she said frostily. "Class-one courtesan. I was getting to that."

I'm a liberal-minded man; I don't have anything against hookers *or* clones. But I like my customers to be frank with me. Again, I should have shown her the door—then followed her through it.

Instead: "So. You have a problem?"

"Some men are bothering me, one man in particular. I need some protection."

That gave me pause. "Your union has a Pinkerton contract for that sort of thing."

"*My* union." Her face trembled a little. "They don't let clones in the union. I'm an associate, for classification. No protection, no medical, no *anything*."

"Sorry, I didn't know that. Pretty old-fashioned." I could see the reasoning, though. Dump 1000 Maribelle Ghentlees on the market and a merely ravishing girl wouldn't have a chance.

"Sit down." She was on the verge of tears. "Let me explain to you what I can't do.

"I can't hurt anyone physically. I can't trace this cod down and wave a gun in his face, tell him to back off."

"I know," she sobbed. I took a box of tissues out of my drawer, passed it over.

"Listen, there are laws about harassment. If he's really bothering you, the cops'll be glad to freeze him."

"I can't go to the police." She blew her nose. "I'm not a citizen."

I turned off the console. "Let me see if I can fill in some blanks without using the machine. You're an unauthorized clone."

She nodded.

"With bought papers."

"Of course I have papers. I wouldn't be in your *machine* if I didn't."

Well, she wasn't dumb, either. "This cod. He isn't just a disgruntled customer."

"No." She didn't elaborate.

"One more guess," I said, "and then you do the talking for a while. He knows you're not legal."

"He should. He's the one who pulled me."

"Your own daddy. Any other surprises?"

She looked at the floor. "Mafia."

"Not the legal one, I assume."

"Both."

The desk drawer was still open; the sight of my own gun gave me a bad chill. "There are two reasonable courses open to me. I could handcuff you to the doorknob and call the police or I could knock you over the head and call the Mafia. That would probably be safer."

She reached into her purse; my hand was halfway to the gun when she took out a credit flash, thumbed it and passed it over the desk. She easily had five times as much money as I make in a good year, and I'm in a comfortable 70 percent bracket.

"You must have one hell of a case of bedsores."

"Don't be stupid," she said, suddenly hard. "You can't make that kind of money on your back. If you take me on as a client, I'll explain."

I erased the flash and gave it back to her. "Ms. Ghentlee. You've already told me a great deal more than I want to know. I don't want the police to put me in jail. I don't want the courts to scramble my brains with a spoon. I don't want the Mafia to take boltcutters to my appendages."

"I could make it worth your while."

"I've got all the money I can use. I'm only in this profession because I'm a snoopy bastard." It suddenly occurred to me that that was more or less true.

"That wasn't completely what I meant."

"I assumed that. And you tempt me, as much as any woman's beauty has ever tempted me."

She turned on the waterworks again. "Christ. Go ahead and tell your story. But I don't think you can convince me to do anything for you."

"My real clone mother wasn't named Maribelle Ghentlee."

"I could have guessed that."

"She was Maxine Kraus." She paused. "Maxine . . . Kraus."

"Is that supposed to mean something to me?"

"Maybe not. What about *Werner* Kraus?"

"Yeah." Swiss industrialist, probably the richest man in Europe. "Some relation?"

"She's his daughter and only heir."

I whistled. "Why would she want to be cloned, then?"

"She didn't know she was being cloned. She thought she was having a Pap test." She smiled a little. "Ironic posture."

"And they pulled you from the scraping."

She nodded. "The Mafia bought her physician. Then killed him."

"You mean the real Mafia?" I said.

"That depends on what you call real. Mafia, Incorporated, comes into it, too, in a more or less legitimate way. I was supposedly one of six Maribelle Ghentlee clones that they had purchased to set up as courtesans in New Orleans, to provoke a test case. They claimed that the sisterhood's prohibition against clone prostitutes constituted unfair restraint of trade."

"Never heard of the case. I guess they lost."

"Of course. They wouldn't have done it in the South if they'd wanted to win."

"Wait a minute. Jumping ahead. Obviously, they plan ultimately to use you as a substitute for the real Maxine Kraus."

"When the old man dies, which will be soon."

"Then why would they parade you around in public?"

"Just to give me an interim identity. They chose Ghentlee as a clone mother because she was the closest one available to Maxine Kraus's physical appearance. I had good make-up; none of the real Ghentlee clones suspected I wasn't one of them."

"Still . . . what happens if you run into someone who knows what the real Kraus looks like? With your face and figure, she must be all over the gossip sheets in Europe."

"You're sweet." Her smile could make me do almost anything. Short of taking on the Mafia. "She's a total recluse, though, for fear of kidnapers. She probably hasn't seen twenty people in her entire life.

"And she isn't beautiful, though she has the raw materials for it. Her mother died when she was still a baby—killed by kidnapers."

"I remember that."

"So she's never had a woman around to model herself after. No one ever taught her how to do her hair properly or use make-up. A man buys all her clothes. She doesn't have anyone to be beautiful *for*."

"You feel sorry for her."

"More than that." She looked at me with an expression that somehow held both defiance and hopelessness. "Can you understand? She's my mother. I was force-grown, so we're the same apparent age, but she's still my only parent. I love her. I won't be part of a plan to kill her."

"You'd rather die?" I said softly. She was going to.

"Yes. But that wouldn't accomplish anything, not if the Mafia did it. They'd take a few cells and make another clone. Or a dozen, or a hundred, until one came along with a personality to go along with matricide."

"Once they know you feel this way—"

"They *do* know. I'm running."

That galvanized me. "They know who your lawyer is?"

"My lawyer?" She gasped when I took the gun out of the drawer. People who see guns only on the cube are usually surprised at how solid and heavy they actually look.

"Could they trace you here? is what I mean." I crossed the room and slid open the door. No one in the corridor. I twisted a knob and 12 heavy magnetic bolts slammed home.

"I don't think so. The lawyers gave me a list of names and I just picked one I liked."

I wondered whether it was Jack or J. Michael. I pushed a button on the wall and steel shutters rolled down over the view of Central Park. "Did you take a cab here?"

"No, subway. And I went up to a hundred and twenty-fifth and back."

"Smart." She was staring at the gun. "It's a forty-eight magnum recoilless. Biggest handgun a civilian can buy."

"You need one so big?"

"Yes. I used to carry a twenty-five Beretta, small enough to conceal in a bathing suit. I used to have a partner, too." It was a long story and I didn't like to tell it.

"Look," I said. "I have a deal with the Mafia. They don't do divorce work and I don't drop bodies into the East River. Understand?" I put the gun back into the drawer and slammed it shut.

"I don't blame you for being afraid—"

"Afraid? Ms. Four Ghentlee, I'm not afraid. I'm *terrified*! How old do you think I am?"

"Call me Belle. You're thirty-five, maybe forty. Why?"

"You're kind—and I'm rich. Rich enough to buy youth: I've been in this *business* almost forty years. I take lots of vitamins and try not to fuck with the Mafia.''

She smiled and then was suddenly somber. Like a baby. "Try to understand me. You've lived sixty years?''

I nodded. "Next year.''

"Well, I've been alive barely sixty *days*. After four years in a tank, growing and learning.

"Learning isn't *being*, though. Everything is new to me. When I walk down a street, the sights and sounds and smells . . . it's, it's like a great flower opening to the sun. Just to sit alone in the dark—'' Her voice broke.

"You can't even *know* how much I want to live—and that's not condescending: it's a statement of fact. Yet I want you to kill me.''

I could only shake my head.

"If you can't hide me, you have to kill me.'' She was crying now and wiped the tears savagely from her cheeks. "Kill me and make sure every cell in my body is destroyed.''

She started walking around the desk. Along the way, she did something with a clasp and her dress slithered to the floor. The sudden naked beauty was like an electric shock. "If you save me, you can have me. Friend, lover, wife . . . slave. Forever.'' She held a posture of supplication for a moment, then eased toward me. Watching the muscles of her body work made my mouth go dry. She reached down and started unbuttoning my shirt.

I cleared my throat. "I didn't know clones had navels.''

"Only special ones. I have other special qualities.''

Idiot, something reminded me, every woman you've ever loved has sucked you dry and left you for dead. I clasped her hips with my big hands and drew her warmth to me. Close up, the navel wasn't very convincing; nobody's perfect.

I'd done dry-cleaning jobs before, but never so cautiously or thoroughly. That she was a clone made the business a little more delicate than usual, since clones' lives are more rigidly supervised by the Government than ours are. But the fact that her identity was false to begin with made it easier; I could second-guess the people who had originally dry-cleaned her.

I hated to meddle with her beauty, and that beauty made plastic surgery out of the question. Any legitimate doctor would be suspicious, and going to an underworld doctor would be suicidal. So we dyed her hair black and bobbed it. She stopped wearing make-up and bought some truly froppy clothes. She kept a length of tape stuck across her buttocks to give her a virgin-schoolgirl kind of walk. For everyone but me.

The Mafia had given her a small fortune—birdseed to them—both to ensure her loyalty and to accustom her to having money, for impersonating Kraus. We used about half of it for the dry-cleaning.

A month or so later, there was a terrible accident on a city bus. Most of the bodies were burned beyond recognition: I did some routine bribery and two of them were identified as the clone Maribelle Four Ghentlee and John Michael Loomis, private eye. When we learned the supposed clone's body had disappeared from the morgue, we packed up our money—long since converted into currency—and a couple of toothbrushes and pulled out.

I had a funny twinge when I closed the door on that console. There couldn't be more than a half-dozen people in the world who were my equals at using that instrument to fish information out of the system. But I had to either give it up or send Belle off on her own.

We flew to the West Indies and looked around. Decided to settle on the island of St. Thomas. I'd been sailing all my life, so we bought a 50-foot boat and set up a charter service for tourists. Some days we took parties out to skindive or fish. Other days we anchored in a quiet cove and made love like happy animals.

After about a year, we read in the little St. Thomas paper that Werner Kraus had died. It mentioned Maxine but didn't print a picture of her. Neither did the San Juan paper. We watched all the news programs for a couple of days (had to check into a hotel to get access to a video cube) and collected magazines for a month. No pictures, to our relief, and the news stories remarked that *Fräulein* Kraus went to great pains to stay out of the public eye.

Sooner or later, we figured some paparazzi would find her and there would be pictures. But by then, it shouldn't make any difference. Belle had let her hair grow out to its natural chestnut, but we kept it cropped boyishly short. The sun and wind had darkened her skin and roughed it, and a year of fighting the big boat's rigging had put visible muscle under her sleekness.

The marina office was about two broom closets wide. It was a beautiful spring morning and I'd come in to put my name on the list of boats available for charter. I was reading the weather print-out when Belle sidled through the door and squeezed in next to me at the counter. I patted her on the fanny. "With you in a second, honey."

A vise grabbed my shoulder and spun me around.

He was over two meters tall and so wide at the shoulders that he literally couldn't get through the door without turning sideways. Long white hair and pale-blue eyes. White sports coat with a familiar cut: tailored to de-emphasize the bulge of a shoulder holster.

"You don't do that, friend," he said with a German accent.

I looked at the woman, who was regarding me with aristocratic amusement. I felt the blood drain from my face and damned near said her name out loud.

She frowned. "*Helmuth,*" she said to the guard, "*Sie sind ihm erschrocken.* I'm sorry," she said to me, "but my friend has quite a temper." She had a perfect North Atlantic accent and her voice sent a shiver of recognition down my back.

"I am sorry," he said heavily. Sorry he hadn't had a chance to throw me into the water, he was.

"I must look like someone you know," she said. "Someone you know rather well."

"My wife. The similarity is . . . quite remarkable."

"Really? I should like to meet her." She turned to the woman behind the counter. "We'd like to charter a sailing boat for the day."

The clerk pointed at me. "He has a nice fifty-foot one."

"That's fine! Will your wife be aboard?"

"Yes . . . yes, she helps me. But you'll have to pay the full rate," I said rapidly. "The boat normally takes six passengers."

"No matter. Besides, we have two others."

"And you'll have to help with the rigging."

"I should hope so. We love to sail." That was pretty obvious. We had been wrong about the wind and sun, thinking that Maxine would have led a sheltered life; she was almost as weathered as Belle. Her hair was probably long, but she had it rolled up in a bun and tied back with a handkerchief.

We exchanged false names: Jack Jackson and Lisa von Hollerin. The bodyguard's name was Helmuth Zwei Kastor. A clone; there was at least one other chunk of overmuscled *Bratwurst* around. Lisa paid the clerk and called her friends at the marina hotel, telling them to meet her at the Abora, slip 39.

I didn't have any chance to warn Belle. She came up from the galley as we were swinging aboard. She stared open-mouthed and staggered, almost fainting. I took her by the arm and made introductions, everybody staring.

After a few moments of strange silence, Helmuth Two whispered, "*Du bist ein Klone.*"

"She can't be a clone, silly man," Lisa said. "When did you ever see a clone with a navel?" Belle was wearing shorts and a halter. "But we could be twin sisters. That *is* remarkable."

Helmuth Two shook his head solemnly. Belle had told me that a clone can always recognize a fellow clone, by the eyes. Never be fooled by a man-made navel.

The other two came aboard. Helmuth One was, of course, a Xerox copy of Helmuth Two. Lisa introduced Maria Salamanca as her lover: a small olive-skinned Basque woman, no stunning beauty, but having an attractive air of friendly mystery about her.

Before we cast off, Lisa came to me and apologized. "We are a passing strange group of people. You deserve something extra for putting up with us." She pressed a gold Krugerrand into my palm—worth at least triple the charter fare—and I tried to act suitably impressed. We had over 1000 of them in the keel, for ballast.

The Ahora didn't have an engine: getting it in and out of the crowded marina was something of an accomplishment. Belle and Lisa handled the sails expertly, while I manned the wheel. They kept looking at each other, then touching. When we were in the harbor, they sat together at the prow, holding hands. Once we were in open water, they went below together. Maria went into a sulk, but the two clones jollied her out of it.

I couldn't be jealous of Lisa. An angel can't sin. But I did wonder what you would call what they were doing. Was it a weird kind of incest? Transcendental masturbation? I only hoped Belle would keep her mouth shut, at least figuratively.

After about an hour, Lisa came up and sat beside me at the wheel. Her hair was long and full, and flowed like dark liquid in the wind, and she was naked. I tentatively rested my hand on her thigh. She had been crying.

"She told me. She had to tell me." Lisa shook her head in wonder. "Maxine One Kraus. She had to stay below for a while. Said she couldn't trust her legs." She squeezed my hand and moved it back to the wheel.

"Later, maybe. And don't worry; your secret is safe with us." She went forward and put an arm around Maria, speaking rapid German to her and the two Helmuths. One of the guards laughed and they took off their incongruous jackets, then carefully wrapped up their weapons and holsters. The sight of a .48 magnum recoilless didn't arouse any nostalgia in me. Maria slipped out of her clothes and stretched happily. The guards did the same. They didn't have navels but were otherwise adequately punctuated.

Belle came up then, clothed and flushed, and sat quietly next to me. She stroked my biceps and I ruffled her hair. Then I heard Lisa's throaty laugh and suddenly turned cold.

"Hold on a second," I whispered. "We haven't been using our heads."

"Speak for yourself." She giggled.

"Oh, be serious. This stinks of coincidence. That she should turn up here, that she should wander into the office just as—"

"Don't worry about it."

"Listen. She's no more Maxine Kraus than you are. They've found us. She's another clone, one that's going to—"

"She's Maxine. If she were a clone, I could tell immediately."

"Spare me the mystical claptrap and take the wheel. I'm going below." In the otherwise empty aftercompartment, I'd stored an interesting assortment of weapons and ammunition.

She grabbed my arm and pulled me back down to the seat. "You spare *me* the private-eye claptrap and listen—you're right, it's no coincidence. Remember that old foreigner who came by last week?"

"No."

"You were up on the stern, folding sail. He was just at the slip for a second, to ask directions. He seemed flustered—"

"I remember. Frenchman."

"I thought so, too. He was Swiss, though."

"And that was no coincidence, either."

"No, it wasn't. He's on the board of directors of one of the banks we used to liquefy our credit. When the annual audit came up, they'd managed to put together all our separate transactions—"

"Bullshit. That's impossible."

She shook her head and laughed. "You're good, but they're good, too. They were curious about what we were trying to hide, using their money, and traced us here. Found we'd started a business with only one percent of our capital.

"Nothing wrong with that, but they were curious. This director was headed for a Caribbean vacation, anyhow; he said he'd come by and poke around."

It sounded too fucking complicated for a Mafia hit. They know it's the cute ones who get caught. If they wanted us, they'd just follow us out to the middle of nowhere and blow us away.

"He'd been a lifelong friend of Werner Kraus. That's why he was so rattled. One look at me and he had to rush to the phone."

"And you want me to believe," I said, "that the wealthiest woman in the world would come down herself, to see what sort of innocent game we were playing. With only two bodyguards."

"Five bodyguards and the Swiss Foreign Legion; so what? Look at them. If they're armed, they've got little tiny weapons stashed away where the sun don't shine. I could—"

"That proves my point."

"In a pig's ass. It doesn't mesh. She's spent all her life locked away from her own shadow—"

"That's just it. She's tired of it. She turned twenty-five last month and came into full control of the fortune. Now she wants to take control of her own life."

"If that's true, it's damned stupid. What would you do, in her position? You'd send the giants down alone. Not just walk into enemy territory with your flanks exposed."

She had to smile at that. "I probably would." She looked thoughtful. "Maxine and I are the same woman, in some ways, but you and the Mafia taught me caution. Maxine has been in a cage all her life and just wants out. Wants to see what the world looks like when it's not locked in a cube show. Wants to sail someplace besides her own lake."

I almost had to believe it. We'd been in open water for over an hour before the Helmuths wrapped up their guns and started tanning their privates. We would've long been shark chum if that's what they'd wanted. Getting sloppy in your old age, Loomis.

"It was still a crazy chance to take. Damned crazy."

"So she's a little crazy. Romantic, too, in case you haven't noticed."

"Really? When I peeked in, you were playing checkers. Jumping each other."

"Bastard." She knew the one place I was ticklish. Trying to get away, I jerked the wheel and nearly tipped us all into the drink.

We anchored in a small cove where I knew there was a good reef. Helmuth One stayed aboard to guard while the rest of us went diving.

The fish and coral were as beautiful as ever, but I could only watch Maxine and Belle. They swam slowly hand in hand, kicking with unconscious synchrony, totally absorbed. Although the breathers kept their hair wrapped up identically, it was easy to tell them apart, since Maxine had an allover tan. Still, it was an eerie kind of ballet like a mirror that didn't quite work. Maria and Helmuth Two were also hypnotized by the sight.

I went aboard early, to start lunch. I'd just finished slicing ham when I heard the drone of a boat, rather far away. Large siphon jet, by the rushing sound of it.

The guard shouted, "*Zwei—komn' herauf*!"

Hoisted myself up out of the galley. The boat was about two kilometers away and coming roughly in our direction, fast.

"Trouble coming?" I asked him.

"Cannot tell yet, sir. I suggest you remain below." He had a gun in each hand, behind his back.

Below, good idea. I slid the hatch off the aftercompartment and tipped over the cases of beer that hid the weaponry. Fished out two heavy plastic bags, left the others in place for the time being. It was all up-to-date American Coast Guard issue and had cost more than the boat.

I'd rehearsed this a thousand times in my mind but hadn't planned on the bags' being slippery with oil and condensation, impossible to grip and tear. I stood up to get a knife from the galley, and it was almost the last thing I ever did.

I looked back at the loud noise and saw a line of holes zipping toward me from the bow, letting in blue light and lead. I dropped and heard bullets hissing over my head, tried not to flinch at the sting of splinters driving into my arm and face. Heard the regular cough-cough-cough of Helmuth One's return fire, while at the stern there was a strangled cry of pain and then a splash; they must have gotten the older guard while he was coming up the ladder.

For a second, I thought I was bleeding, but it was only urine; that wasn't in the rehearsals, either. Neither was the sudden clatter of the bilge pump; they'd hit us below the water line.

I controlled the trembling well enough to cut open the bag that held the small-caliber spitter, and it took only three times to lock the cassette of ammunition into the receiver. Jerked back the arming lever and hurried up to the galley hatch.

The spitter was made for sinking boats, quickly. It fired tiny flechettes, small as old-fashioned stereo needles, 50 rounds per second. Each carried a small explosive charge and moved faster than sound. In ten seconds, they could make a boat look as if a man had been working over it all afternoon with a chain saw.

I resisted the urge to squeeze off a blast and duck back under cover (not that the hull gave much protection against whatever they were using). We had clamped traversing mounts for the gun onto three sides of the galley hatch, to hold it steady. The spitter's most effective if you can hold the point of aim right on the water line.

They were concentrating their fire on the bow—lucky for me, unlucky for Helmuth—most of it going high. He must have been shooting from a prone position, difficult target. I slid the spitter onto its mount and cranked the scope up to maximum power.

When I looked through its scope, a lifetime of target-shooting reflexes took hold: deep breath, let half out, do the Zen thing. Their boat surged toward the center of the scope's field, and I waited. It was a Whaler Unsinkable. One man crouched at the bow, firing what looked like a 20mm recoilless, clamped onto the rail above an apron of steel plate. There were several splashes of silver on the metal shield; Helmuth had been doing some fancy shooting.

The Whaler slewed in a sharp starboard turn, evidently to give the gunner a better angle on our bow. Good boatmanship, good tactics but bad luck. Their prow touched the junction of my cross hairs right at the water line and I didn't even have to track. I just pressed the trigger and watched a cloud of black smoke and steam whip from prow to stern. Not even an Unsinkable can stay upright with its keel chewed off. It nosed

down suddenly—crushing the gunner behind a 50-knot wall of water—
and then flipped up into the air, scattering people. It landed upright with a
great splash and turned turtle. Didn't sink, though.

I snapped a fresh cassette into place and tried to remember where the
hydrogen tank was on that model. Second blast found it and the boat
dutifully exploded. Vaporized. The force of the blast, even at our distance, was enough to ram the scope's eyepiece back into my eye, and it
set the Abora to rocking. None of them could have lived through it, but I
checked with the scope. No one swimming.

Helmuth One peered down at me. "What is that?"

I patted it. "Coast Guard weapon, a spitter."

"May I try it?"

"Sure." I traded places with him, glad to be up in the breeze. My
boat was a mess. The mainmast had been shattered by a direct hit,
waist-high. The starboard rail was chewed to splinters, forward, and near
misses had gouged up my nice teak foredeck. The bilge pump coughed
out irregular spews of water; evidently, we weren't in danger of sinking.

"Are you all right?" Belle called from the water.

"Yes . . . looks all clear. Come on—" I was interrupted by the
spitter, a scream like a large animal dying slowly.

I unshipped a pair of binoculars to check his marksmanship. It was
excellent. He was shooting at the floating bodies. What a spitter did to
one was terrible to see.

"Jesus Christ, Helmuth. What do you do for fun when you don't
have dead people to play with?"

"Some of them may yet live," he said neutrally.

At least one did. Wearing a life jacket, she had been floating face
down but suddenly began treading water. She was holding an automatic
pistol in both hands. She looked exactly like Belle and Maxine.

I couldn't say anything; couldn't take my eyes off her. She fired two
rounds and I felt them slap into the hull beneath me. I heard Helmuth
curse and suddenly her shoulders dissolved in a spray of meat and bone
and her head fell into the water.

My knees buckled and I sat down suddenly. "You see?" Helmuth
shouted. "You see?"

"I saw." In fact, I would never stop seeing it.

Helmuth Two, it turned out, had been hit in the side of the neck, but
it was a big neck and he survived. Maxine called a helicopter, which
came out piloted by Helmuth Three.

After an hour or so, Helmuth Four joined us in a large speedboat
loaded down with gasoline, thermite and shark chum. He also had a little
electrical gadget that made sharks feel hungry whether they actually were
or not.

By that time, we had transferred the gold and a few more important things from my boat onto the helicopter. We chummed the area thoroughly and, as the water began to boil with sharks, towed both hulks out to deep water, where they burned brightly and sank.

The Helmuths spent the next day sprinkling the island with money and threats, while Maxine got to know Belle and me better, locked behind the heavily guarded door of the honeymoon suite of the quaint old Sheraton that overlooked the marina. She made us a job offer—a life offer, really—and we accepted without hesitation. That was six years ago.

Sometimes I do miss our old life—the sea, the freedom, the friendly island, the lazy idyls with Belle. Sometimes I even miss New York's hustle and excitement, and the fierce independence of my life there. I'm still a mean son of a bitch, but I never get to prove it.

We do travel sometimes, but with extreme caution. The clone that Helmuth ripped apart in the placid cove might have been Belle's own daughter, since the Mafia had plenty of opportunities to collect cells from her body. It's immaterial. If they could make one, they could make an army of them.

Like our private army of Helmuths and Lamberts and Delias. I'm chief of security, among other things, and the work is interesting, most of it at a console as good as the one I had in Manhattan. No violence since that one afternoon six years ago, not yet. I did have to learn German, though, which is a kind of violence, at least to a brain as old as mine.

We haven't made any secret of the fact that Belle is Maxine's clone. The official story is that *Fräulein* Kraus had a clone made of herself, for "companionship." This started a fad among the wealthy, being the first new sexual diversion since the invention of the vibrator.

Belle and Maxine take pains to dress alike and speak alike, and have even unconsciously assimilated each other's mannerisms. Most of the nonclone employees, and the occasional guests, can't tell them apart. Even I sometimes confuse them, at a distance.

Close up, which happens happily often, there's no problem. Belle has a way of looking at me that Maxine could never duplicate. And Maxine is literally a trifle prettier: You can't beat a real navel.

*At first look, a hospital and a concentration camp would seem to have
little in common, but not so—survival in either death camp or death ward
draws on similar secret reserves of mind and heart and spirit, as you will
learn in this tense, brilliant, and finely executed story about a man who is
haunted by someone else's past.*

*Jack Dann is one of the finest of the "new" SF writers, and also one
of the most respected editor-anthologists of the seventies. He began
writing in 1970, and first established his reputation with the critically
acclaimed novella "Junction," which was a Nebula finalist in 1973; he
has been a Nebula finalist twice more since then. His books include a
novel,* Starhiker *(Harper & Row), and a recently-released collection of
his short fiction,* Timetipping *(Doubleday). As an anthologist, he edited
one of the most famous anthologies of the decade,* Wandering Stars
*(Pocket Books), a collection of fantasy and SF on Jewish themes; his
other anthologies include* Immortal *(Harper & Row),* Future Power
(Random House), coedited with Gardner Dozois, and Faster Than Light
*(Harper & Row), coedited with George Zebrowski. Upcoming are an
anthology called* Aliens!, *coedited with Gardner Dozois, from Pocket
Books, and* Wandering Stars II, *from Doubleday. Also upcoming are
three novels:* The Man Who Melted, Distances, *and* Junction, *a full-
length expansion of the novella of the same name, from Dell. Dann lives
in Johnson City, New York.*

JACK DANN
Camps

As Stephen lies in bed, he can think only of pain.

He imagines it as sharp and blue. After receiving an injection of
Demerol, he enters pain's cold regions as an explorer, an objective
visitor. It is a country of ice and glass, monochromatic plains and valleys
filled with wash-blue shards of ice, crystal pyramids and pinnacles,
squares, oblongs, and all manner of polyhedron—block upon block of
painted blue pain.

Although it is midafternoon, Stephen pretends it is dark. His eyes
are tightly closed, but the daylight pouring into the room from two large
windows intrudes as a dull red field extending infinitely behind his
eyelids.

"Josie," he asks through cotton mouth, "aren't I due for another shot?'' Josie is crisp and fresh and large in her starched white uniform. Her peaked nurse's cap is pinned to her mouse-brown hair.

"I've just given you an injection, it will take effect soon." Josie strokes his hand, and he dreams of ice.

"Bring me some ice," he whispers.

"If I bring you a bowl of ice, you'll only spill it again."

"Bring me some ice . . ." By touching the ice cubes, by turning them in his hand like a gambler favoring his dice, he can transport himself into the beautiful blue country. Later, the ice will melt, and he will spill the bowl. The shock of cold and pain will awaken him.

Stephen believes that he is dying, and he has resolved to die properly. Each visit to the cold country brings him closer to death; and death, he has learned, is only a slow walk through icefields. He has come to appreciate the complete lack of warmth and the beautifully etched face of his magical country.

But he is connected to the bright flat world of the hospital by plastic tubes—one breathes cold oxygen into his left nostril; another passes into his right nostril and down his throat to his stomach; one feeds him intravenously, another draws his urine.

"Here's your ice," Josie says. "But mind you, don't spill it." She places the small bowl on his tray table and wheels the table close to him. She has a musky odor of perspiration and perfume; Stephen is reminded of old women and college girls.

"Sleep now, sweet boy."

Without opening his eyes, Stephen reaches out and places his hand on the ice.

"Come now, Stephen, wake up. Dr. Volk is here to see you."

Stephen feels the cool touch of Josie's hand, and he opens his eyes to see the doctor standing beside him. The doctor has a gaunt, long face and thinning brown hair; he is dressed in a wrinkled green suit.

"Now we'll check the dressing, Stephen," he says as he tears away a gauze bandage on Stephen's abdomen.

Stephen feels the pain, but he is removed from it. His only wish is to return to the blue dreamlands. He watches the doctor peel off the neat crosshatchings of gauze. A terrible stink fills the room.

Josie stands well away.

"Now we'll check your drains." The doctor pulls a long drainage tube out of Stephen's abdomen, irrigates and disinfects the wound, inserts a new drain, and repeats the process by pulling out another tube just below the rib cage.

Stephen imagines that he is swimming out of the room. He tries to cross the hazy border into cooler regions, but it is difficult to concentrate.

He has only a half-hour at most before the Demerol will wear off. Already, the pain is coming closer, and he will not be due for another injection until the night nurse comes on duty. But the night nurse will not give him an injection without an argument. She will tell him to fight the pain.

But he cannot fight without a shot.

"Tomorrow we'll take that oxygen tube out of your nose," the doctor says, but his voice seems far away, and Stephen wonders what he is talking about.

He reaches for the bowl of ice, but cannot find it.

"Josie, you've taken my ice."

"I took the ice away when the doctor came. Why don't you try to watch a bit of television with me; Soupy Sales is on."

"Just bring me some ice," Stephen says. "I want to rest a bit." He can feel the sharp edges of pain breaking through the gauzy wraps of Demerol.

"I love you, Josie," he says sleepily as she places a fresh bowl of ice on his tray.

As Stephen wanders through his ice-blue dreamworld, he sees a rectangle of blinding white light. It looks like a doorway into an adjoining world of brightness. He has glimpsed it before on previous Demerol highs. A coal-dark doorway stands beside the bright one.

He walks toward the portals, passes through white-blue cornfields.

Time is growing short. The drug cannot stretch it much longer. Stephen knows that he has to choose either the bright doorway or the dark, one or the other. He does not even consider turning around, for he has dreamed that the ice and glass and cold blue gemstones have melted behind him.

It makes no difference to Stephen which doorway he chooses. On impulse he steps into blazing, searing whiteness.

Suddenly he is in a cramped world of people and sound.

The boxcar's doors were flung open. Stephen was being pushed out of the cramped boxcar that stank of sweat, feces, and urine. Several people had died in the car, and added their stink of death to the already fetid air.

"Carla, stay close to me," shouted a man beside Stephen. He had been separated from his wife by a young woman who pushed between them, as she tried to return to the dark safety of the boxcar.

SS men in black, dirty uniforms were everywhere. They kicked and pummeled everyone within reach. Alsatian guard dogs snapped and barked. Stephen was bitten by one of the snarling dogs. A woman beside him was being kicked by soldiers. And they were all being methodically herded past a high barbed-wire fence. Beside the fence was a wall.

Stephen looked around for an escape route, but he was surrounded by other prisoners, who were pressing against him. Soldiers were shooting indiscriminately into the crowd, shooting women and children alike. The man who had shouted to his wife was shot.

"Sholom, help me, help me," screamed a scrawny young woman whose skin was as yellow and pimpled as chicken flesh.

And Stephen understood that *he* was Sholom. He was a Jew in this burning, stinking world, and this woman, somehow, meant something to him. He felt the yellow star sewn on the breast of his filthy jacket. He grimaced uncontrollably. The strangest thoughts were passing through his mind, remembrances of another childhood: morning prayers with his father and rich uncle, large breakfasts on Saturdays, the sounds of his mother and father quietly making love in the next room, *Yortzeit* candles burning in the living room, his brother reciting the "four questions" at the Passover table.

He touched the star again and remembered the Nazi's facetious euphemism for it: *Pour le Semite*.

He wanted to strike out, to kill the Nazis, to fight and die. But he found himself marching with the others, as if he had no will of his own. He felt that he was cut in half. He had two selves now; one watched the other. One self wanted to fight. The other was numbed; it cared only for itself. It was determined to survive.

Stephen looked around for the woman who had called out to him. She was nowhere to be seen.

Behind him were railroad tracks, electrified wire, and the conical tower and main gate of the camp. Ahead was a pitted road littered with corpses and their belongings. Rifles were being fired and a heavy, sickly sweet odor was everywhere. Stephen gagged, others vomited. It was the overwhelming stench of death, of rotting and burning flesh. Black clouds hung above the camp, and flames spurted from the tall chimneys of ugly buildings, as if from infernal machines.

Stephen walked onward; he was numb, unable to fight or even talk. Everything that happened around him was impossible, the stuff of dreams.

The prisoners were ordered to halt, and the soldiers began to separate those who would be burned from those who would be worked to death. Old men and women and young children were pulled out of the crowd. Some were beaten and killed immediately while the others looked on in disbelief. Stephen looked on, as if it was of no concern to him. Everything was unreal, dreamlike. He did not belong here.

The new prisoners looked like *Musselmänner*, the walking dead. Those who became ill, or were beaten or starved before they could "wake up" to the reality of the camps, became *Musselmänner*. *Musselmänner* could not think, or feel. They shuffled around, already dead in spirit, until a guard or disease or cold or starvation killed them.

"Keep marching," shouted a guard, as Stephen stopped before an emaciated old man crawling on the ground. "You'll look like him soon enough."

Suddenly, as if waking from one dream and finding himself in another, Stephen remembered that the chicken-skinned girl was his wife. He remembered their life together, their children and crowded flat. He remembered the birthmark on her leg, her scent, her hungry love-making. He had once fought another boy over her.

His glands opened up with fear and shame; he had ignored her screams for help.

He stopped and turned, faced the other group. "Fruma," he shouted, then started to run.

A guard struck him in the chest with the butt of his rifle, and Stephen fell into darkness.

He spills the icewater again and awakens with a scream.

"It's my fault," Josie says, as she peels back the sheets. "I should have taken the bowl away from you. But you fight me."

Stephen lives with the pain again. He imagines that a tiny fire is burning in his abdomen, slowly consuming him. He stares at the television high on the wall and watches Soupy Sales.

As Josie changes the plastic sac containing his intravenous saline solution, an orderly pushes a cart into the room and asks Stephen if he wants a print for his wall.

"Would you like me to choose something for you?" Josie asks.

Stephen shakes his head and asks the orderly to show him all the prints. Most of them are familiar still-lifes and pastorals, but one catches his attention. It is a painting of a wheat field. Although the sky looks ominously dark, the wheat is brightly rendered in great broad strokes. A path cuts through the field and crows fly overhead.

"That one," Stephen says. "Put that one up."

After the orderly hangs the print and leaves, Josie asks Stephen why he chose that particular painting.

"I like Van Gogh," he says dreamily, as he tries to detect a rhythm in the surges of abdominal pain. But he is not nauseated, just gaseous.

"Any particular reason why you like Van Gogh?" asks Josie. "He's my favorite artist, too."

"I didn't say he was my favorite," Stephen says, and Josie pouts, an expression which does not fit her prematurely lined face. Stephen closes his eyes, glimpses the cold country, and says, "I like the painting because it's so bright that it's almost frightening. And the road going through the field"—he opens his eyes—"doesn't go anywhere. It just ends in the field. And the crows are flying around like vultures."

"Most people see it as just a pretty picture," Josie says.

"What's it called?"

"*Wheatfield with Blackbirds.*"

"Sensible. My stomach hurts, Josie. Help me turn over on my side." Josie helps him onto his left side, plumps up his pillows, and inserts a short tube into his rectum to relieve the gas. "I also like the painting with the large stars that all look out of focus," Stephen says. "What's it called?"

"*Starry Night.*"

"That's scary, too," Stephen says. Josie takes his blood pressure, makes a notation on his chart, then sits down beside him and holds his hand. "I remember something," he says. "Something just—" He jumps as he remembers, and pain shoots through his distended stomach. Josie shushes him, checks the intravenous needle, and asks him what he remembers.

But the memory of the dream recedes as the pain grows sharper. "I hurt all the fucking time, Josie," he says, changing position. Josie removes the rectal tube before he is on his back.

"Don't use such language. I don't like to hear it. I know you have a lot of pain," she says, her voice softening.

"Time for a shot."

"No, honey, not for some time. You'll just have to bear with it."

Stephen remembers his dream again. He is afraid of it. His breath is short and his heart feels as if it is beating in his throat, but he recounts the entire dream to Josie.

He does not notice that her face has lost its color.

"It's only a dream, Stephen. Probably something you studied in history."

"But it was so real, not like a dream at all."

"That's enough!" Josie says.

"I'm sorry I upset you. Don't be angry."

"I'm *not* angry."

"I'm sorry," he says, fighting the pain, squeezing Josie's hand tightly. "Didn't you tell me that you were in the Second World War?"

Josie is composed once again. "Yes, I did, but I'm surprised you remembered. You were very sick. I was a nurse overseas, spent most of the war in England. But I was one of the first service women to go into any of the concentration camps."

Stephen drifts with the pain; he appears to be asleep.

"You must have studied very hard," Josie whispers to him. Her hand is shaking just a bit.

It is twelve o'clock and his room is death-quiet. The sharp shadows seem to be the hardest objects in the room. The fluorescents burn steadily in the hall outside.

Stephen looks out into the hallway, but he can see only the far white wall. He waits for his night nurse to appear: it is time for his injection. A young nurse passes by his doorway. Stephen imagines that she is a cardboard ship sailing through the corridors.

He presses the buzzer, which is attached by a clip to his pillow. The night nurse will take her time, he tells himself. He remembers arguing with her. Angrily, he presses the buzzer again.

Across the hall, a man begins to scream, and there is a shuffle of nurses into his room. The screaming turns into begging and whining. Although Stephen has never seen the man in the opposite room, he has come to hate him. Like Stephen, he has something wrong with his stomach, but he cannot suffer well. He can only beg and cry, try to make deals with the nurses, doctors, God, and angels. Stephen cannot muster any pity for this man.

The night nurse finally comes into the room, says, "You have to try to get along without this," and gives him an injection of Demerol.

"Why does the man across the hall scream so?" Stephen asks, but the nurse is already edging out of the room.

"Because he's in pain."

"So am I," Stephen says in a loud voice. "But I can keep it to myself."

"Then stop buzzing me constantly for an injection. That man across the hall has had half of his stomach removed. He's got something to scream about."

So have I, Stephen thinks; but the nurse disappears before he can tell her. He tries to imagine what the man across the hall looks like. He thinks of him as being bald and small, an ancient baby. Stephen tries to feel sorry for the man, but his incessant whining disgusts him.

The drug takes effect; the screams recede as he hurtles through the dark corridors of a dream. The cold country is dark, for Stephen cannot persuade his night nurse to bring him some ice. Once again, he sees two entrances. As the world melts behind him, he steps into the coal-black doorway.

In the darkness he hears an alarm, a bone-jarring clangor.

He could smell the combined stink of men pressed closely together. They were all lying upon two badly constructed wooden shelves. The floor was dirt; the smell of urine never left the barrack.

"Wake up," said a man Stephen knew as Viktor. "If the guard finds you in bed, you'll be beaten again."

Stephen moaned, still wrapped in dreams. "Wake up, wake up," he mumbled to himself. He would have a few more minutes before the guard arrived with the dogs. At the very thought of dogs, Stephen felt revulsion. He had once been bitten in the face by a large dog.

He opened his eyes, yet he was still half-asleep, exhausted. You are in a death camp, he said to himself. You must wake up. You must fight by waking up. Or you will die in your sleep. Shaking uncontrollably, he said, "Do you want to end up in the oven; perhaps you will be lucky today and live."

As he lowered his legs to the floor, he felt the sores open on the soles of his feet. He wondered who would die today and shrugged. It was his third week in the camp. Impossibly, against all odds, he had survived. Most of those he had known in the train had either died or become *Musselmänner*. If it was not for Viktor, he, too, would have become a *Musselmänner*. He had a breakdown and wanted to die. He babbled in English. But Viktor talked him out of death, shared his portion of food with him, and taught him the new rules of life.

"Like everyone else who survives, I count myself first, second, and third—then I try to do what I can for someone else," Viktor had said.

"I will survive," Stephen repeated to himself, as the guards opened the door, stepped into the room, and began to shout. Their dogs growled and snapped but heeled beside them. The guards looked sleepy; one did not wear a cap, and his red hair was tousled.

Perhaps he spent the night with one of the whores, Stephen thought. Perhaps today would not be so bad . . .

And so begins the morning ritual: Josie enters Stephen's room at quarter to eight, fusses with the chart attached to the footboard of his bed, pads about aimlessly, and finally goes to the bathroom. She returns, her stiff uniform making swishing sounds. Stephen can feel her standing over the bed and staring at him. But he does not open his eyes. He waits a beat.

She turns away, then drops the bedpan. Yesterday it was the metal ashtray; day before that, she bumped into the bedstand.

"Good morning, darling, it's a beautiful day," she says, then walks across the room to the windows. She parts the faded orange drapes and opens the blinds.

"How do you feel today?"

"Okay, I guess."

Josie takes his pulse and asks, "Did Mr. Gregory stop in to say hello last night?"

"Yes," Stephen says. "He's teaching me how to play gin rummy. What's wrong with him?"

"He's very sick."

"I can see that; has he got cancer?"

"I don't know," says Josie, as she tidies up his night table.

"You're lying again," Stephen says, but she ignores him. After a time, he says, "His girlfriend was in to see me last night. I bet his wife will be in today."

"Shut your mouth about that," Josie says. "Let's get you out of that bed so I can change the sheets."

Stephen sits in the chair all morning. He is getting well but is still very weak. Just before lunchtime, the orderly wheels his cart into the room and asks Stephen if he would like to replace the print hanging on the wall.

"I've seen them all," Stephen says. "I'll keep the one I have." Stephen does not grow tired of the Van Gogh painting; sometimes, the crows seem to have changed position.

"Maybe you'll like this one," the orderly says as he pulls out a cardboard print of Van Gogh's *Starry Night*. It is a study of a village nestled in the hills, dressed in shadows. But everything seems to be boiling and writhing as in a fever dream. A cypress tree in the foreground looks like a black flame, and the vertiginous sky is filled with great blurry stars. It is a drunkard's dream. The orderly smiles.

"So you did have it," Stephen says.

"No. I traded some other pictures for it. They had a copy in the West Wing."

Stephen watches him hang it, thanks him, and waits for him to leave. Then he gets up and examines the painting carefully. He touches the raised facsimile brushstrokes and turns toward Josie, feeling an odd sensation in his groin. He looks at her, as if seeing her for the first time. She has an overly full mouth which curves downward at the corners when she smiles. She is not a pretty woman—too fat, he thinks.

"Dance with me," he says, as he waves his arms and takes a step forward, conscious of the pain in his stomach.

"You're too sick to be dancing just yet," but she laughs at him and bends her knees in a mock plié.

She has small breasts for such a large woman, Stephen thinks. Feeling suddenly dizzy, he takes a step toward the bed. He feels himself slip to the floor, feels Josie's hair brushing against his face, dreams that he's all wet from her tongue, feels her arms around him, squeezing, then feels the weight of her body pressing down on him, crushing him . . .

He wakes up in bed, catheterized. He has an intravenous needle in his left wrist, and it is difficult to swallow, for he has a tube down his throat.

He groans, tries to move.

"Quiet, Stephen," Josie says, stroking his hand.

"What happened?" he mumbles. He can only remember being dizzy.

"You've had a slight setback, so just rest. The doctor had to collapse your lung; you must lie very still."

"Josie, I love you," he whispers, but he is too far away to be heard. He wonders how many hours or days have passed. He looks toward the window. It is dark, and there is no one in the room.

He presses the buzzer attached to his pillow and remembers a dream . . .

"You must fight," Viktor said.

It was dark, all the other men were asleep, and the barrack was filled with snoring and snorting. Stephen wished they could all die, choke on their own breath. It would be an act of mercy.

"Why fight?" Stephen asked, and he pointed toward the greasy window, beyond which were the ovens that smoked day and night. He made a fluttering gesture with his hand—smoke rising.

"You must fight, you must live, living is everything. It is the only thing that makes sense here."

"We're all going to die, anyway," Stephen whispered. "Just like your sister . . . and my wife."

"No, Sholom, we're going to live. The others may die, but we're going to live. You must believe that."

Stephen understood that Viktor was desperately trying to convince himself to live. He felt sorry for Viktor; there could be no sensible rationale for living in a place like this.

Stephen grinned, tasted blood from the corner of his mouth, and said, "So we'll live through the night, maybe."

And maybe tomorrow, he thought. He would play the game of survival a little longer.

He wondered if Viktor would be alive tomorrow. He smiled and thought: if Viktor dies, then I will have to take his place and convince others to live. For an instant, he hoped Viktor would die so that he could take his place.

The alarm sounded. It was three o'clock in the morning, time to begin the day.

This morning Stephen was on his feet before the guards could unlock the door.

"Wake up," Josie says, gently tapping his arm. "Come on, wake up."

Stephen hears her voice as an echo. He imagines that he has been flung into a long tunnel; he hears air whistling in his ears but cannot see anything.

"Whassimatter?" he asks. His mouth feels as if it is stuffed with cotton; his lips are dry and cracked. He is suddenly angry at Josie and the plastic tubes that hold him in his bed as if he were a latter-day Gulliver. He wants to pull out the tubes, smash the bags filled with saline, tear away his bandages.

"You were speaking German," Josie says. "Did you know that?"

"Can I have some ice?"

"No," Josie says impatiently. "You spilled again, you're all wet."

" . . . for my mouth, dry . . ."

"Do you remember speaking German, honey? I have to know."

"Don't remember, bring ice, I'll try to think about it."

As Josie leaves to get him some ice, he tries to remember his dream.

"Here, now, just suck on the ice." She gives him a little hill of crushed ice on the end of a spoon.

"Why did you wake me up, Josie?" The layers of dream are beginning to slough off. As the Demerol works out of his system, he has to concentrate on fighting the burning ache in his stomach.

"You were speaking German. Where did you learn to speak like that?"

Stephen tries to remember what he said. He cannot speak any German, only a bit of classroom French. He looks down at his legs (he has thrown off the sheet) and notices, for the first time, that his legs are as thin as his arms. "My God, Josie, how could I have lost so much weight?"

"You lost about forty pounds, but don't worry, you'll gain it all back. You're on the road to recovery now. Please, try to remember your dream."

"I can't, Josie! I just can't seem to get a hold of it."

"Try."

"Why is it so important to you?"

"You weren't speaking college German, darling. You were speaking slang. You spoke in a patois that I haven't heard since the forties."

Stephen feels a chill slowly creep up his spine. "What did I say?"

Josie waits a beat, then says, "You talked about dying."

"Josie?"

"Yes," she says, pulling at her fingernail.

"When is the pain going to stop?"

"It will be over soon." She gives him another spoonful of ice. "You kept repeating the name Viktor in your sleep. Can you remember anything about that?"

Viktor, Viktor, deep-set blue eyes, balding head and broken nose, called himself a Galitzianer. Saved my life. "I remember," Stephen says. "His name is Viktor Shmone. He is in all my dreams now."

Josie exhales sharply.

"Does that mean anything to you?" Stephen asks anxiously.

"I once knew a man from one of the camps." She speaks very slowly and precisely. "His name was Viktor Shmone. I took care of him. He was one of the few people left alive in the camp after the Germans fled." She reaches for her purse, which she keeps on Stephen's night table, and fumbles an old, torn photograph out of a plastic slipcase.

As Stephen examines the photograph, he begins to sob. A thinner and much younger Josie is standing beside Viktor and two other emaciated-looking men. "Then I'm not dreaming," he says, "and I'm going to die. That's what it means." He begins to shake, just as he did in his dream, and, without thinking, he makes the gesture of rising smoke to Josie. He begins to laugh.

"Stop that," Josie says, raising her hand to slap him. Then she embraces him and says, "Don't cry, darling, it's only a dream. Somehow, you're dreaming the past."

"Why?" Stephen asks, still shaking.

"Maybe you're dreaming because of me, because we're so close. In some ways, I think you know me better than anyone else, better than any man, no doubt. You might be dreaming for a reason: maybe I can help you."

"I'm afraid, Josie."

She comforts him and says, "Now tell me everything you can remember about the dreams."

He is exhausted. As he recounts his dreams to her, he sees the bright doorway again. He feels himself being sucked into it. "Josie," he says, "I must stay awake, don't want to sleep, dream . . ."

Josie's face is pulled tight as a mask; she is crying.

Stephen reaches out to her, slips into the bright doorway, into another dream.

It was a cold cloudless morning. Hundreds of prisoners were working in the quarries; each work gang came from a different barrack. Most of the gangs were made up of *Musselmänner*, the faceless majority of the camp. They moved like automatons, lifting and carrying the great stones to the numbered carts, which would have to be pushed down the tracks.

Stephen was drenched with sweat. He had a fever and was afraid that he had contracted typhus. An epidemic had broken out in the camp last week. Every morning several doctors arrived with the guards. Those who were too sick to stand up were taken away to be gassed or experimented upon in the hospital.

Although Stephen could barely stand, he forced himself to keep moving. He tried to focus all his attention on what he was doing. He made a ritual of bending over, choosing a stone of a certain size, lifting it, carrying it to the nearest cart, and then taking the same number of steps back to his dig.

A *Musselmänn* fell to the ground, but Stephen made no effort to help him. When he could help someone in a little way, he would, but he would not stick his neck out for a *Musselmänn*. Yet something niggled at Stephen. He remembered a photograph in which Viktor and this *Musselmänn* were standing with a man and a woman he did not recognize. But Stephen could not remember where he had ever seen such a photograph.

"Hey, you," shouted a guard. "Take the one on the ground to the cart."

Stephen nodded to the guard and began to drag the *Musselmänn* away.

"Who's the new patient down the hall?" Stephen asks as he eats a bit of cereal from the breakfast tray Josie has placed before him. He is feeling much better now; his fever is down, and the tubes, catheter, and intravenous needle have been removed. He can even walk around a bit.

"How did you find out about that?" Josie asks.

"You were talking to Mr. Gregory's nurse. Do you think I'm dead already? I can still hear."

Josie laughs and takes a sip of Stephen's tea. "You're far from dead! In fact, today is a red-letter day; you're going to take your first shower. What do you think about that?"

"I'm not well enough yet," he says, worried that he will have to leave the hospital before he is ready.

"Well, Dr. Volk thinks differently, and his word is law."

"Tell me about the new patient."

"They brought in a man last night who drank two quarts of motor oil; he's on the dialysis machine."

"Will he make it?"

"No, I don't think so; there's too much poison in his system."

We should all die, Stephen thinks. It would be an act of mercy. He glimpses the camp.

"Stephen!"

He jumps, then awakens.

"You've had a good night's sleep; you don't need to nap. Let's get you into that shower and have it done with." Josie pushes the tray table away from the bed. "Come on, I have your bathrobe right here."

Stephen puts on his bathrobe, and they walk down the hall to the showers. There are three empty shower stalls, a bench, and a whirlpool bath. As Stephen takes off his bathrobe, Josie adjusts the water pressure and temperature in the corner stall.

"What's the matter?" Stephen asks, after stepping into the shower. Josie stands in front of the shower stall and holds his towel, but she will not look at him. "Come on," he says, "you've seen me naked before."

"That was different."

"How?" He touches a hard, ugly scab that has formed over one of the wounds on his abdomen.

"When you were sick, I washed you in bed, as if you were a baby. Now it's different." She looks down at the wet tile floor, as if she is lost in thought.

"Well, I think it's silly," he says. "Come on, it's hard to talk to someone who's looking the other way. I could break my neck in here and you'd be staring down at the fucking floor."

"I've asked you not to use that word," she says in a very low voice.

"Do my eyes still look yellowish?"

She looks directly at his face and says, "No, they look fine."

Stephen suddenly feels faint, then nauseated; he has been standing too long. As he leans against the cold shower wall, he remembers his last dream. He is back in the quarry. He can smell the perspiration of the men around him, feel the sun baking him, draining his strength. It is so bright . . .

He finds himself sitting on the bench and staring at the light on the opposite wall. I've got typhus, he thinks, then realizes that he is in the hospital. Josie is beside him.

"I'm sorry," he says.

"I shouldn't have let you stand so long; it was my fault."

"I remembered another dream." He begins to shake; and Josie puts her arms around him.

"It's all right now, tell Josie about your dream."

She's an old, fat woman, Stephen thinks. As he describes the dream, his shaking subsides.

"Do you know the man's name?" Josie asks. "The one the guard ordered you to drag away."

"No," Stephen says. "He was a *Musselmänn*, yet I thought there was something familiar about him. In my dream I remembered the photograph you showed me. He was in it."

"What will happen to him?"

"The guards will give him to the doctors for experimentation. If they don't want him, he'll be gassed."

"You must not let that happen," Josie says, holding him tightly.

"Why?" asks Stephen, afraid that he will fall into the dreams again.

"If he was one of the men you saw in the photograph, you must not let him die. Your dreams must fit the past."

"I'm afraid."

"It will be all right, baby," Josie says, clinging to him. She is shaking and breathing heavily.

Stephen feels himself getting an erection. He calms her, presses his face against hers, and touches her breasts. She tells him to stop, but does not push him away.

"I love you," he says as he slips his hand under her starched skirt. He feels awkward and foolish and warm.

"This is wrong," she whispers.

As Stephen kisses her and feels her thick tongue in his mouth, he begins to dream . . .

Stephen stopped to rest for a few seconds. The *Musselmänn* was dead weight. I cannot go on, Stephen thought; but he bent down, grabbed the *Musselmänn* by his coat, and dragged him toward the cart. He glimpsed the cart, which was filled with the sick and dead and exhausted; it looked no different than a cartload of corpses marked for a mass grave.

A long, gray cloud covered the sun, then passed, drawing shadows across gutted hills.

On impulse, Stephen dragged the *Musselmänn* into a gully behind several chalky rocks. Why am I doing this? he asked himself. If I'm caught, I'll be ash in the ovens, too. He remembered what Viktor had told him: "You must think of yourself all the time, or you'll be no help to anyone else."

The *Musselmänn* groaned, then raised his arm. His face was gray with dust and his eyes were glazed.

"You must lie still," Stephen whispered. "Do not make a sound. I've hidden you from the guards, but if they hear you, we'll all be punished. One sound from you and you're dead. You must fight to live, you're in a death camp, you must fight so you can tell of this later."

"I have no family, they're all—"

Stephen clapped his hand over the man's mouth and whispered, "Fight, don't talk. Wake up, you cannot survive the death by sleeping."

The man nodded, and Stephen climbed out of the gully. He helped two men carry a large stone to a nearby cart.

"What are you doing?" shouted a guard.

"I left my place to help these men with this stone; now I'll go back where I was."

"What the hell are you trying to do?" Viktor asked.

Stephen felt as if he was burning up with fever. He wiped the sweat from his eyes, but everything was still blurry.

"You're sick, too. You'll be lucky if you last the day."

"I'll last," Stephen said, "but I want you to help me get him back to the camp."

"I won't risk it, not for a *Musselmänn*. He's already dead, leave him."

"Like you left me?"

Before the guards could take notice, they began to work. Although Viktor was older than Stephen, he was stronger. He worked hard every day and never caught the diseases that daily reduced the barrack's numbers. Stephen had a touch of death, as Viktor called it, and was often sick.

They worked until dusk, when the sun's oblique rays caught the dust from the quarries and turned it into veils and scrims. Even the guards sensed that this was a quiet time, for they would congregate together and talk in hushed voices.

"Come, now, help me," Stephen whispered to Viktor. "I've been doing that all day," Viktor said. "I'll have enough trouble getting you back to the camp, much less carry this *Musselmänn*."

"We can't leave him."

"Why are you so preoccupied with this *Musselmänn*? Even if we can get him back to the camp, his chances are nothing. I know, I've seen enough, I know who has a chance to survive."

"You're wrong this time," Stephen said. He was dizzy and it was difficult to stand. The odds are I won't last the night, and Viktor knows it, he told himself. "I had a dream that if this man dies, I'll die, too. I just feel it."

"Here we learn to trust our dreams," Viktor said. "They make as much sense as this . . ." He made the gesture of rising smoke and gazed toward the ovens, which were spewing fire and black ash.

The western portion of the sky was yellow, but over the ovens it was red and purple and dark blue. Although it horrified Stephen to consider it, there was a macabre beauty here. If he survived, he would never forget these sense impressions, which were stronger than anything he had ever experienced before. Being so close to death, he was, perhaps for the first time, really living. In the camp, one did not even consider suicide. One grasped for every moment, sucked at life like an infant, lived as if there was no future.

The guards shouted at the prisoners to form a column; it was time to march back to the barracks.

While the others milled about, Stephen and Viktor lifted the *Musselmänn* out of the gully. Everyone nearby tried to distract the guards. When the march began, Stephen and Viktor held the *Musselmänn* between them, for he could barely stand.

"Come on, dead one, carry your weight," Viktor said. "Are you so dead that you cannot hear me? Are you as dead as the rest of your family?" The *Musselmänn* groaned and dragged his legs. Viktor kicked him. "You'll walk or we'll leave you here for the guards to find."

"Let him be," Stephen said.

"Are you dead or do you have a name?" Viktor continued.

"Berek," croaked the *Musselmänn*. "I am not dead."

"Then we have a fine bunk for you," Viktor said. "You can smell the stink of the sick for another night before the guards make a selection." Viktor made the gesture of smoke rising.

Stephen stared at the barracks ahead. They seemed to waver as the heat rose from the ground. He counted every step. He would drop soon, he could not go on, could not carry the *Musselmänn.*

He began to mumble in English.

"So you're speaking American again," Viktor said.

Stephen shook himself awake, placed one foot before the other.

"Dreaming of an American lover?"

"I don't know English and I have no American lover."

"Then who is this Josie you keep talking about in your sleep . . .?"

"Why were you screaming?" Josie asks, as she washes his face with a cold washcloth.

"I don't remember screaming," Stephen says. He discovers a fever blister on his lip. Expecting to find an intravenous needle in his wrist, he raises his arm.

"You don't need an I.V.," Josie says. "You just have a bit of a fever. Dr. Volk has prescribed some new medication for it."

"What time is it?" Stephen stares at the whorls in the ceiling.

"Almost three P.M. I'll be going off soon."

"Then I've slept most of the day away," Stephen says, feeling something crawling inside him. He worries that his dreams still have a hold on him. "Am I having another relapse?"

"You'll do fine," Josie says.

"I should be fine now. I don't want to dream anymore."

"Did you dream again, do you remember anything?"

"I dreamed that I saved the *Musselmänn,*" Stephen says.

"What was his name?" asks Josie.

"Berek, I think. Is that the man you knew?"

Josie nods and Stephen smiles at her. "Maybe that's the end of the dreams," he says, but she does not respond. He asks to see the photograph again.

"Not just now," Josie says.

"But I have to see it. I want to see if I can recognize myself . . ."

Stephen dreamed he was dead, but it was only the fever. Viktor sat beside him on the floor and watched the others. The sick were moaning and crying; they slept on the cramped platform, as if proximity to one another could ensure a few more hours of life. Wan moonlight seemed to fill the barrack.

Stephen awakened, feverish. "I'm burning up," he whispered to Viktor.

"Well," Viktor said, "you've got your *Musselmänn.* If he lives, you live. That's what you said, isn't it?"

"I don't remember. I just knew that I couldn't let him die."

"You'd better go back to sleep, you'll need your strength. Or we may have to carry *you*, tomorrow."

Stephen tried to sleep, but the fever was making lights and spots before his eyes. When he finally fell asleep, he dreamed of a dark country filled with gemstones and great quarries of ice and glass.

"What?" Stephen asked, as he sat up suddenly, awakened from damp-black dreams. He looked around and saw that everyone was watching Berek, who was sitting under the window at the far end of the room.

Berek was singing the *Kol Nidre* very softly. It was the Yom Kippur prayer, which was sung on the most holy of days. He repeated the prayer three times, and then once again in a louder voice. The others responded, intoned the prayer as a recitative. Viktor was crying quietly, and Stephen imagined that the holy spirit animated Berek. Surely, he told himself, that face and those pale unseeing eyes were those of a dead man. He remembered the story of the golem, shuddered, found himself singing and pulsing with fever.

When the prayer was over, Berek fell back into his fever trance. The others became silent, then slept. But there was something new in the barrack with them tonight, a palpable exultation. Stephen looked around at the sleepers and thought: We're surviving, more dead than alive, but surviving . . .

"You were right about that *Musselmänn*," Viktor whispered. "It's good that we saved him."

"Perhaps we should sit with him," Stephen said. "He's alone." But Viktor was already asleep; and Stephen was suddenly afraid that if he sat beside Berek, he would be consumed by his holy fire.

As Stephen fell through sleep and dreams, his face burned with fever.

Again he wakes up screaming.

"Josie," he says, "I can remember the dream, but there's something else, something I can't see, something terrible . . ."

"Not to worry," Josie says, "it's the fever." But she looks worried, and Stephen is sure that she knows something he does not.

"Tell me what happened to Viktor and Berek," Stephen says. He presses his hands together to stop them from shaking.

"They lived, just as you are going to live and have a good life." Stephen calms down and tells her his dream.

"So you see," she says, "you're even dreaming about surviving." "I'm burning up."

"Dr. Volk says you're doing very well." Josie sits beside him, and he watches the fever patterns shift behind his closed eyelids.

"Tell me what happens next, Josie."

"You're going to get well."

"There's something else . . ."

"Shush, now, there's nothing else." She pauses, then says, "Mr. Gregory is supposed to visit you tonight. He's getting around a bit; he's been back and forth all day in his wheelchair. He tells me that you two have made some sort of a deal about dividing up all the nurses."

Stephen smiles, opens his eyes, and says, "It was Gregory's idea. Tell me what's wrong with him."

"All right, he has cancer, but he doesn't know it, and you must keep it a secret. They cut the nerve in his leg because the pain was so bad. He's quite comfortable now, but, remember, you can't repeat what I've told you."

"Is he going to live?" Stephen asks. "He's told me about all the new projects he's planning. So I guess he's expecting to get out of here."

"He's not going to live very long, and the doctor didn't want to break his spirit."

"I think he should be told."

"That's not your decision to make, nor mine."

"Am I going to die, Josie?"

"No!" she says, touching his arm to reassure him.

"How do I know that's the truth?"

"Because I say so, and I couldn't look you straight in the eye and tell you if it wasn't true. I should have known it would be a mistake to tell you about Mr. Gregory."

"You did right," Stephen says. "I won't mention it again. Now that I know, I feel better." He feels drowsy again.

"Do you think you're up to seeing him tonight?"

Stephen nods, although he is bone tired. As he falls asleep, the fever patterns begin to dissolve, leaving a bright field. With a start, he opens his eyes: he has touched the edge of another dream.

"What happened to the man across the hall, the one who was always screaming?"

"He's left the ward," Josie says. "Mr. Gregory had better hurry, if he wants to play cards with you before dinner. They're going to bring the trays up soon."

"You mean he died, don't you?"

"Yes, if you must know, he died. But *you're* going to live."

There is a crashing noise in the hallway. Someone shouts, and Josie runs to the door.

Stephen tries to stay awake, but he is being pulled back into the cold country.

"Mr. Gregory fell trying to get into his wheelchair by himself,"

Josie says. "He should have waited for his nurse, but she was out of the room and he wanted to visit you."

But Stephen does not hear a word she says.

There were rumors that the camp was going to be liberated. It was late, but no one was asleep. The shadows in the barrack seemed larger tonight.

"It's better for us if the Allies don't come," Viktor said to Stephen.

"Why do you say that?"

"Haven't you noticed that the ovens are going day and night? The Nazis are in a hurry."

"I'm going to try to sleep," Stephen said.

"Look around you, even the *Musselmänner* are agitated." Viktor said. "Animals become nervous before the slaughter. I've worked with animals. People are not so different."

"Shut up and let me sleep," Stephen said, and he dreamed that he could hear the crackling of distant gunfire.

"Attention," shouted the guards as they stepped into the barrack. There were more guards than usual, and each one had two Alsatian dogs. "Come on, form a line. Hurry."

"They're going to kill us," Viktor said, "then they'll evacuate the camp and save themselves."

The guards marched the prisoners toward the north section of the camp. Although it was still dark, it was hot and humid, without a trace of the usual morning chill. The ovens belched fire and turned the sky aglow. Everyone was quiet, for there was nothing to be done. The guards were nervous and would cut down anyone who uttered a sound, as an example for the rest.

The booming of big guns could be heard in the distance. If I'm going to die, Stephen thought, I might as well go now and take a Nazi with me. Suddenly, all of his buried fear, aggression, and revulsion surfaced; his face became hot and his heart felt as if it was pumping in his throat. But Stephen argued with himself. There was always a chance. He had once heard of some women who were waiting in line for the ovens; for no apparent reason the guards sent them back to their barracks. Anything could happen. There was always a chance. But to attack a guard would mean certain death.

The guns became louder. Stephen could not be sure, but he thought the noise was coming from the west. The thought passed through his mind that everyone would be better off dead. That would stop all the guns and screaming voices, the clenched fists and wildly beating hearts. The Nazis should kill everyone, and then themselves, as a favor to humanity.

The guards stopped the prisoners in an open field surrounded on three sides by forestland. Sunrise was moments away; purple-black clouds drifted across the sky, touched by gray in the east. It promised to be a hot, gritty day.

Half-step Walter, a Judenrat sympathizer who worked for the guards, handed out shovel heads to everyone.

"He's worse than the Nazis," Viktor said to Stephen.

"The Judenrat thinks he will live," said Berek, "but he will die like a Jew with the rest of us."

"Now, when it's too late, the *Musselmänn* regains consciousness," Viktor said.

"Hurry," shouted the guards, "or you'll die now. As long as you dig, you'll live."

Stephen hunkered down on his knees and began to dig with the shovel head.

"Do you think we might escape?" Berek whined.

"Shut up and dig," Stephen said. "There is no escape, just stay alive as long as you can. Stop whining, are you becoming a *Musselmänn* again?" Stephen noticed that other prisoners were gathering up twigs and branches. So the Nazis plan to cover us up, he thought.

"That's enough," shouted a guard. "Put your shovels down in front of you and stand in a line."

The prisoners stood shoulder to shoulder along the edge of the mass grave. Stephen stood between Viktor and Berek. Someone screamed and ran and was shot immediately.

I don't want to see trees or guards or my friends, Stephen thought as he stared into the sun. I only want to see the sun, let it burn out my eyes, fill up my head with light. He was shaking uncontrollably, quaking with fear.

Guns were booming in the background.

Maybe the guards won't kill us, Stephen thought, even as he heard the crackcrack of their rifles. Men were screaming and begging for life. Stephen turned his head only to see someone's face blown away.

Screaming, tasting vomit in his mouth, Stephen fell backward, pulling Viktor and Berek into the grave with him.

Darkness. Stephen thought. His eyes were open, yet it was dark. I must be dead, this must be death . . .

He could barely move. Corpses can't move, he thought. Something brushed against his face; he stuck out his tongue, felt something spongy. It tasted bitter. Lifting first one arm and then the other, Stephen moved some branches away. Above, he could see a few dim stars; the clouds were lit like lanterns by a quarter moon.

He touched the body beside him; it moved. That must be Viktor, he thought. "Viktor, are you alive, say something if you're alive." Stephen whispered, as if in fear of disturbing the dead.

Viktor groaned and said, "Yes, I'm alive, and so is Berek,"

"And the others?"

"All dead. Can't you smell the stink? You, at least, were unconscious all day."

"They can't *all* be dead," Stephen said, then he began to cry.

"Shut up," Viktor said, touching Stephen's face to comfort him. "We're alive, that's something. They could have fired a volley into the pit."

"I thought I was dead," Berek said. He was a shadow among shadows.

"Why are we still here?" Stephen asked.

"We stayed in here because it is safe," Viktor said.

"But they're all dead," Stephen whispered, amazed that there could be speech and reason inside a grave.

"Do you think it's safe to leave now?" Berek asked Viktor.

"Perhaps. I think the killing has stopped. By now the Americans or English or whoever they are have taken over the camp. I heard gunfire and screaming. I think it's best to wait a while longer."

"Here?" asked Stephen. "Among the dead?"

"It's best to be safe."

It was the afternoon when they climbed out of the grave. The air was thick with flies. Stephen could see bodies sprawled in awkward positions beneath the covering of twigs and branches. "How can I live when all the others are dead?" he asked himself aloud.

"You live, that's all," answered Viktor.

They kept close to the forest and worked their way back toward the camp.

"Look there," Viktor said, motioning Stephen and Berek to take cover. Stephen could see trucks moving toward the camp compound.

"Americans," whispered Berek.

"No need to whisper now," Stephen said. "We're safe."

"Guards could be hiding anywhere," Viktor said. "I haven't slept in the grave to be shot now."

They walked into the camp through a large break in the barbed-wire fence, which had been hit by an artillery shell. When they reached the compound, they found nurses, doctors, and army personnel bustling about.

"You speak English," Viktor said to Stephen, as they walked past several quonsets. "Maybe you can speak for us."

"I told you, I can't speak English."

"But I've heard you!"

"Wait," shouted an American army nurse. "You fellows are going the wrong way." She was stocky and spoke perfect German. "You must check in at the hospital; it's back that way."

"No," said Berek, shaking his head. "I won't go in there."

"There's no need to be afraid now," she said. "You're free. Come along, I'll take you to the hospital."

Something familiar about her, Stephen thought. He felt dizzy and everything turned gray.

"Josie," he murmured, as he fell to the ground.

"What is it?" Josie asks. "Everything is all right, Josie is here."

"Josie," Stephen mumbles.

"You're all right."

"How can I live when they're all dead?" he asks.

"It was a dream," she says as she wipes the sweat from his forehead. "You see, your fever has broken, you're getting well."

"Did you know about the graves?"

"It's all over now, forget the dream."

"Did you know?"

"Yes," Josie says. "Viktor told me how he survived the grave, but that was so long ago, before you were even born. Dr. Volk tells me you'll be going home soon."

"I don't want to leave, I want to stay with you."

"Stop that talk, you've got a whole life ahead of you. Soon, you'll forget all about this, and you'll forget me, too."

"Josie," Stephen asks, "let me see that old photograph again. Just one last time."

"Remember, this is the last time," she says as she hands him the faded photograph.

He recognizes Viktor and Berek, but the young man standing between them is not Stephen. "That's not me," he says, certain that he will never return to the camp.

Yet the shots still echo in his mind.

Nebula winner Edward Bryant was born in White Plains, New York, but now lives in Denver, Colorado, where he manages the famous Milford Writer's Conference. One of the most popular and prolific writers of the seventies, Bryant's stories have appeared everywhere from Orbit *to* National Lampoon *to* Penthouse, *and his books include* Phoenix Without Ashes *(Fawcett Gold Medal), a novelization of a television script by Harlan Ellison, two short-story collections,* Among the Dead *(Collier) and* Cinnabar *(Bantam), and, as editor, the anthology* 2076: The American Tricentennial *(Pyramid). His memorable novelette "Particle Theory" was in our* Seventh Annual Collection, *and his story "Stone" won him a Nebula in 1979.*

Here he takes on a theme usually reserved for cheap-jack horror movies, and treats it—and the people thrown together because of it—with subtlety, compassion, and grace.

EDWARD BRYANT
giANTS

Paul Chavez looked from the card on the silver plate to O'Hanlon's face and back to the card. "I couldn't find the tray," she said. "Put the thing away maybe twelve years ago and didn't have time to look. Never expected to need it." Her smile folded like parchment and Chavez thought he heard her lips crackle.

He reached out and took the card. Neat black-on-white printing asserted that one Laynie Bridgewell was a bona fide correspondent for the UBC News Billings bureau. He turned the card over. Sloppy cursive scripts deciphered as: "*Imperitive I talk to you about New Mexico Project.*" "Children of electronic journalism," Chavez said amusedly. He set the card back on the plate. "I suppose I ought to see her in the drawing room—if I were going to see her, which I'm not."

"She's a rather insistent young woman," said O'Hanlon.

Chavez sat stiffly down on the couch. He plaited his fingers and rested the palms on the crown of his head. "It's surely time for my nap. Do be polite."

"Of course, Dr. Chavez," said O'Hanlon, sweeping silently out of the room, gracefully turning as she exited to close the doors of the library.

Pain simmered in the joints of his long bones. Chavez shook two capsules from his omnipresent pill case and poured a glass of water from the carafe on the walnut desk. Dr. Hansen had said it would only get worse. Chavez lay on his side on the couch and felt weary—seventy-two years weary. He supposed he should have walked down the hall to his bedroom, but there was no need. He slept better here in the library. The hardwood panels and the subdued Mondrian originals soothed him. Endless ranks of books stood vigil. He loved to watch the wind-blown patterns of the pine boughs beyond the French windows that opened onto the balcony. He loved to study the colors as sunlight spilled through the leaded DNA double-helix pane Annie had given him three decades before.

Chavez felt the capsules working faster than he had expected. He thought he heard the tap of something hard against glass. But then he was asleep.

In its basics, the dream never changed.

They were there in the desert somewhere between Albuquerque and Alamogordo, all of them: Ben Peterson, the tough cop; the FBI man Robert Graham; Chavez himself; and Patricia Chavez, his beautiful, brainy daughter.

The wind, gusting all afternoon, had picked up; it whistled steadily, atonally, obscuring conversation. Sand sprayed abrasively against their faces. Even the gaunt stands of spiny cholla bowed with the wind.

Patricia had struck off on her own tangent. She struggled up the base of a twenty-foot dune. She began to slip back almost as far as each step advanced her.

They all heard it above the wind—the shrill, ululating chitter.

"What the hell is that?" Graham yelled.

Chavez shook his head. He began to run toward Patricia. The sand, the wind, securing the brim of his hat with one hand; all conspired to make his gait clumsy.

The immense antennae rose first above the crest of the dune. For a second, Chavez thought they surely must be branches of windblown cholla. Then the head itself heaved into view, faceted eyes coruscating with changing hues of red and blue. Mandibles larger than a farmer's scythes clicked and clashed. The ant paused, apparently surveying the creatures downslope.

"Look at the size of it," said Chavez, more to himself than to the others.

He heard Peterson's shout. "It's as big as a horse!" He glanced back and saw the policeman running for the car.

Graham's reflexes were almost as prompt. He had pulled his .38 Special from the shoulder holster and swung his arm, motioning Patricia to safety, yelling, "Back, get back!" Patricia began to run from the dune all too slowly, feet slipping on the sand, legs constricted by the ankle-length khaki skirt. Graham fired again and again, the gun popping dully in the wind.

The ant hesitated only a few seconds longer. The wind sleeked the tufted hair on its purplish green thorax. Then it launched itself down the slope, all six articulated legs churning with awful precision.

Chavez stood momentarily frozen. He heard a coughing stutter from beside his shoulder. Ben Peterson had retrieved a Thompson submachine gun from the auto. Gouts of sand erupted around the advancing ant. The creature never hesitated.

Patricia lost her race in a dozen steps. She screamed once as the crushing mandibles closed around her waist. She looked despairingly at her father. Blood ran from both corners of her mouth.

There was an instant eerie tableau. The Tommy gun fell silent as Peterson let the muzzle fall in disbelief. The hammer of Graham's pistol clicked on a spent cylinder. Chavez cried out.

Uncannily, brutally graceful, the ant wheeled and, still carrying Patricia's body, climbed the slope. It crested the dune and vanished. Its chittering cry remained a moment more before raveling in the wind.

Sand flayed his face as Chavez called out his daughter's name over and over. Someone took his shoulder and shook him, telling him to stop it, to wake up. It wasn't Peterson or Graham.

It was his daughter.

She was his might-have-been daughter.

Concerned expression on her sharp-featured face, she was shaking him by the shoulder. Her eyes were dark brown and enormous. Her hair, straight and cut short, was a lighter brown.

She backed away from him and sat in his worn, leather-covered chair. He saw she was tall and very thin. For a moment he oscillated between dream-orientation and wakefulness. "Patricia?" Chavez said.

She did not answer.

Chavez let his legs slide off the couch and shakily sat up. "Who in the world are you?"

"My name's Laynie Bridgewell," said the young woman.

Chavez's mind focused. "Ah, the reporter."

"Correspondent."

"A semantic distinction. No essential difference." One level of his mind noted with amusement that he was articulating well through the confusion. He still didn't know what the hell was going on. He yawned deeply, stretched until a dart of pain cut the movement short, said, "Did you talk Ms. O'Hanlon into letting you up here?"

"Are you kidding?" Bridgewell smiled. "She must be a great watchdog."

"She's known me a long while. How *did* you get up here?"

Bridgewell looked mildly uncomfortable. "I, uh, climbed up."

"Climbed?"

"Up one of the pines. I shinnied up a tree to the balcony. The French doors were unlocked. I saw you inside sleeping, so I came in and waited."

"A criminal offense," said Chavez.

"They were unlocked," she said defensively.

"I meant sitting and watching me sleep. Terrible invasion of privacy. A person could get awfully upset, not knowing if another human being, a strange one at that, is secretly watching him snore or drool or whatever."

"You slept very quietly," said Bridgewell. "Very still. Until the nightmare."

"Ah," said Chavez. "It was that apparent?"

She nodded. "You seemed really upset. I thought maybe I ought to wake you."

Chavez said, "Did I say anything?"

She paused and thought. "Only two words I could make out. A name—Patricia. And you kept saying 'them.' "

"That figures." He smiled. He felt orientation settling around him like familiar wallpaper in a bedroom, or old friends clustering at a departmental cocktail party. "You're from the UBC bureau in Billings?"

"I drove down this morning."

"Work for them long?"

"Almost a year."

"First job?"

She nodded. "First real job."

"You're what—twenty-one?" said Chavez.

"Twenty-two."

"Native?"

"Of Montana?" She shook her head. "Kansas."

"University of Southern California?"

Another shake. "Missouri."

"Ah," he said. "Good school." Chavez paused. "You're here on assignment?"

A third shake. "My own time."

"Ah," said Chavez again. "Ambitious. And you want to talk to me about the New Mexico Project?"

Face professionally sober, voice eager, she said, "Very much. I didn't have any idea you lived so close until I read the alumni bulletin from the University of Wyoming."

"I wondered how you found me out." Chavez sighed. "Betrayed by my alma mater . . ." He looked at her sharply. "I don't grant interviews, even if I occasionally conduct them." He stood and smiled. "Will you be wanting to use the stairs, or would you rather shinny back down the tree?"

"Who is Patricia?" said Bridgewell.

"My daughter," Chavez started to say. "Someone from my past," he said.

"I lost people to the bugs," said Bridgewell quietly. "My parents were in Biloxi at the wrong time. Bees never touched them. The insecticide offensive got them both."

The pain in Chavez's joints became ice needles. He stood—and stared.

Even more quietly, Bridgewell said, "You don't have a daughter. Never had. I did my homework." Her dark eyes seemed even larger. "I don't know everything about the New Mexico Project—that's why I'm here. But I can stitch the rumors together." She paused. "I even had the bureau rent an old print of the movie. I watched it four times yesterday."

Chavez felt the disorientation return, felt exhausted, felt—damn it!—old. He fumbled the container of pain pills out of his trouser pocket, then returned it unopened. "Hungry?" he said.

"You better believe it. I had to leave before breakfast."

"I think we'll get some lunch," said Chavez. "Let's go downtown. Try not to startle Ms. O'Hanlon as we leave."

O'Hanlon had encountered them in the downstairs hall, but reacted only with a poker face. "Would you and the young lady like some lunch, Dr. Chavez?"

"Not today," said Chavez, "but thank you. Ms. Bridgewell and I are going to eat in town."

O'Hanlon regarded him. "Have you got your medicine?"

Chavez patted his trouser leg and nodded.

"And you'll be back before dark?"

"Yes," he said. "Yes. And if I'm not, I'll phone. You're not my mother. I'm older than you."

"Don't be cranky," she said. "Have a pleasant time."

Bridgewell and Chavez paused in front of the old stone house. "Why don't we take my car?" said Bridgewell. "I'll run you back after lunch." She glanced at him. "You're not upset about being driven around by a kid, are you?" He smiled and shook his head. "Okay."

They walked a hundred meters to where her car was pulled off the blacktop and hidden in a stand of spruce. It was a Volkswagen beetle of a vintage Chavez estimated to be a little older than its driver.

As if reading his thoughts, Bridgewell said, "Runs like a watch—the old kind, with hands. Got a hundred and ten thousand on her third engine. I call her Scarlett." The car's color was a dim red like dried clay.

"Do you really miss watches with hands?" said Chavez, opening the passenger-side door.

"I don't know—I guess I hadn't really thought about it. I know I don't miss slide rules."

"*I* miss hands on timepieces." Chavez noticed there were no seatbelts. "A long time ago, I stockpiled all the Timexes I'd need for my lifetime."

"Does it really make any difference?"

"I suppose not." Chavez considered that as Bridgewell drove onto the highway and turned downhill.

"You love the past a lot, don't you?"

"I'm nostalgic," said Chavez.

"I think it goes a lot deeper than that."

Silence enveloped both driver and rider. Chavez suspected what she meant by that last observation. He wondered how much he *did* talk in his sleep, and how sharply she had noted the double-helix pattern.

Bridgewell handled the VW like a racing Porsche. Chavez held onto the bar screwed onto the glove-box door with both hands. Balding radial tires shrieked as she shot the last curve and they began to descend the slope into Casper. To the east, across the city, they could see a ponderous dirigible-freighter settling gracefully toward a complex of blocks and domes.

"Why," she said, "are they putting a pilot fusion plant squarely in the middle of the biggest coal deposits in the country?"

Chavez shrugged. "When man entered the atomic age he opened a door into a new world. What he may eventually find in that new world no one can predict."

"Huh?" Bridgewell said. Then: "Oh, the movie. Doesn't it ever worry you—having that obsession?"

"No," said Chavez. Bridgewell slowed slightly as the road became city street angling past blocks of crumbling budget housing. "Turn left on Rosa. Head downtown."

"Where are we eating? I'm hungry enough to eat coal byproducts."

"Close. We're going to the oil can."

"Huh?" Bridgewell said again.

"The Petroleum Tower. Over there." Chavez pointed at a forty-story cylindrical pile. It was windowed completely with bronze reflective panes. "The rooftop restaurant's rather good."

They left Scarlett in an underground lot and took the high-speed exterior elevator to the top of the Petroleum Tower. Bridgewell closed her eyes as the ground level rushed away from them. At the fortieth floor she opened her eyes to stare at the glassed-in restaurant, the lush hanging plants, the noontime crowd. "Who *are* these people? They all look so, uh, professional."

"They are that," said Chavez, leading the way to the maître d'.

"Oil people. Uranium people. Coal people. Slurry people. Shale people. Coal gasification—"

"I've got the point," Bridgewell said. "I feel a little under-dressed."

"They know me."

And so, apparently, they did. The maître d' issued orders and Bridgewell and Chavez were instantly ushered to a table beside a floor-to-ceiling window.

"Is this a part of being maybe the world's greatest molecular biologist?"

Chavez shook his head. "More a condition of originally being a local boy. Even with the energy companies, this is still a small town at heart." He fell silent and looked out the window. The horizon was much closer than he remembered from his childhood. A skiff of brown haze lay over the city. There was little open land to be seen.

They ordered drinks.

They made small talk.

They ordered food.

"This is very pleasant," said Bridgewell, "but I'm still a cor-respondent. I think you're sitting on the biggest story of the decade."

"That extraterrestrial ambassadors are shortly to land near Albu-querque? That they have picked America as a waystation to repair their ship?"

Bridgewell looked bemused. "I'm realizing I don't know when you're kidding."

"Am I now?"

"Yes."

"So why do you persist in questioning me?"

She hesitated. "Because I suspect you want to tell someone. It might as well be me."

He thought about that a while. The waiter brought the garnish tray and Chavez chewed on a stick of carrot. "Why don't you tell me the pieces you've picked up."

"And then?"

"We'll see," he said. "I can't promise anything."

Bridgewell said, "You're a lot like my father. I never knew when he was kidding either."

"Your turn," said Chavez.

The soup arrived. Bridgewell sipped a spoonful of French onion and set the utensil down. "The New Mexico Project. It doesn't seem to have anything to do with New Mexico. You wouldn't believe the time I've spent on the phone. All my vacation I ran around that state in Scarlett."

Chavez smiled a long time, finally said, "Think metaphorically. The Manhattan Project was conducted under Stagg Field in Chicago."

"I don't think the New Mexico Project has anything to do with nuclear energy," she said. "But I have heard a lot of mumbling about DNA chimeras."

"So far as I know, no genetic engineer is using recombinant DNA to hybridize creatures with all the more loathsome aspects of snakes, goats, and lions. The state of the art improves, but we're not that good yet."

"But I shouldn't rule out DNA engineering?" she said.

"Keep going."

"Portuguese is the official language of Brazil."

Chavez nodded.

"UBC's stringer in Recife has it that, for quite a while now, nothing's been coming out of the Brazilian nuclear power complex at Xique-Xique. I mean there's *news*, but it's all through official release. Nobody's going in or out."

Chavez said, "You would expect a station that new and large to be a concern of national security. Shaking down's a long and complex process."

"Maybe." She picked the ripe olives out of the newly arrived salad and carefully placed them in a line on the plate. "I've got a cousin in movie distribution. Just real scutwork so far, but she knows what's going on in the industry. She told me that the U.S. Department of Agriculture ordered a print from Warner Brothers dubbed in Portuguese and had it shipped to Brasilia. The print was that movie you're apparently so concerned with—*Them!* The one about the ants mutating from radioactivity in the New Mexico desert. The one about giant ants on the rampage."

"Only a paranoid could love this chain of logic," said Chavez.

Her face looked very serious. "If it takes a paranoid to come up with this story and verify it," she said, "then that's what I am. Maybe nobody else is willing to make the jumps. I am. I know nobody else has the facts. I'm going to get them."

To Chavez, it seemed that the table had widened. He looked across the linen wasteland at her. "The formidable Formicidae family . . ." he said. "So have you got a conclusion to state?" He felt the touch of tiny legs on his leg. He felt feathery antennae tickle the hairs on his thigh. He jerked back from the table and his water goblet overturned, the waterstain spreading smoothly toward the woman.

"What's wrong?" said Bridgewell. He heard concern in her voice. He slapped at his leg, stopped the motion, drew a deep breath.

"Nothing." Chavez hitched his chair closer to the table again. A waiter hovered at his shoulder, mopping the water with a towel and refilling the goblet. "Your conclusion." His voice strengthened. "I asked about your theory."

"I know this sounds crazy," said Bridgewell. "I've read about how the Argentine fire ants got to Mobile, Alabama. And I damned well know about the bees—I told you that."

Chavez felt the touch again, this time on his ankle. He tried unobtrusively to scratch and felt nothing. Just the touch. Just the tickling, chitinous touch.

"Okay," Bridgewell continued. "All I can conclude is that somebody in South America's created some giant, mutant ants, and now they're marching north. Like the fire ants. Like the bees."

"Excuse me a moment," said Chavez, standing.

"Your face is white," said Bridgewell. "Can I help you?"

"No." Chavez turned and, forcing himself not to run, walked to the restroom. In a stall, he lowered his trousers. As he had suspected, there was no creature on his leg. He sat on the toilet and scratched his skinny legs until the skin reddened and he felt the pain. "Damn it," he said to himself. "Stop." He took a pill from the case and downed it with water from the row of faucets. Then he stared at himself in the mirror and returned to the table.

"You okay?" Bridgewell had not touched her food.

He nodded. "I'm prey to any number of ailments; goes with the territory. I'm sorry to disturb your lunch."

"I'm apparently disturbing yours more."

"I offered." He picked up knife and fork and began cutting a slice of cold roast beef. "I offered—so follow this through. Please."

Her voice softened. "I have the feeling this all ties together somehow with your wife."

Chavez chewed the beef, swallowed without tasting it. "Did you look at the window?" Bridgewell looked blank. "The stained glass in the library."

Her expression became mobile. "The spiral design? The double helix? I loved it. The colors are incredible."

"It's exquisite; and it's my past." He took a long breath. "Annie gave it to me for my forty-first birthday. As well, it was our first anniversary. Additionally it was on the occasion of the award. It meant more to me than the trip to Stockholm." He looked at her sharply. "You said you did your homework. How much *do* you know?"

"I know that you married late," said Bridgewell, "for your times."

"Forty."

"I know that your wife died of a freak accident two years later. I didn't follow up."

"You should have," said Chavez. "Annie and I had gone on a picnic in the Florida panhandle. We were driving from Memphis to Tampa. I was cleaning some catfish. Annie wandered off, cataloguing insects and plants. She was an amateur taxonomist. For whatever reason—God only knows—I don't—she disturbed a mound of fire ants. They swarmed over her. I heard her screaming. I ran to her and dragged her away and brushed off the ants. Neither of us had known about her protein allergy—she'd just been lucky enough never to have been bitten or stung.'' He hesitated and shook his head. ''I got her to Pensacola. Annie died in anaphylactic shock. The passages swelled, closed off. She suffocated in the car.''

Bridgewell looked stricken. She started to say, ''I'm sorry, Dr. Chavez. I had no—''

He held up his hand gently. ''Annie was eight months pregnant. In the hospital they tried to save our daughter. It didn't work.'' He shook his head again, as if clearing it. ''You and Annie look a bit alike—coltish, I think is the word. I expect Patricia would have looked the same.''

The table narrowed. Bridgewell put her hand across the distance and touched his fingers. ''You never remarried.''

''I disengaged myself from most sectors of life.'' His voice was dispassionate.

''Why didn't you re-engage?''

He realized he had turned his hand over, was allowing his fingers to curl gently around hers. The sensation was warmth. ''I spent the first half of my life singlemindedly pursuing certain goals. It took an enormous investment of myself to open my life to Annie.'' As he had earlier in the morning when he'd first met Bridgewell, he felt profoundly weary. ''I suppose I decided to take the easier course; to hold onto the past and call it good.''

She squeezed his hand. ''I won't ask if it's been worth it.''

''What about you?'' he said. ''You seem to be in ferocious pursuit of your goals. Do you have a rest of your life hidden off to the side?''

Bridgewell hesitated. ''No. Not yet. I've kept my life directed, very concentrated, since—since everyone died. But someday . . .'' Her voice trailed off. ''I still have time.''

''Time,'' Chavez said, recognizing the sardonicism. ''Don't count on it.''

Her voice very serious, she said, ''Whatever happens, I won't let the past dictate to me.''

He felt her fingers tighten. ''Never lecture someone three times your age,'' he said. ''It's tough to be convincing.'' He laughed and banished the tension.

''This *is* supposed to be an interview,'' she said, but didn't take her hand away.

''Did you ever have an ant farm as a child?'' Chavez said. She shook her head. ''Then we're going to go see one this afternoon.'' He glanced at the food still in front of her. ''Done?'' She nodded. ''Then let's go out to the university field station.''

They stood close together in the elevator. Bridgewell kept her back to the panoramic view. Chavez said, "I've given you no unequivocal statements about the New Mexico Project."

"I know."

"And if I should tell you now that there are indeed monstrous ant mutations—creatures large as horses—tramping toward us from the Mata Grosso?"

This time she grinned and shook her head silently.

"You think me mad, don't you?"

"I still don't know when you're kidding," she said.

"There are no giant ants," said Chavez. "Yet." And he refused to elaborate.

The field station of the Wyoming State University at Casper was thirty kilometers south, toward the industrial complex at Douglas River Bend. Two kilometers off the freeway, Scarlett clattered and protested across the pot-holed access road, but delivered them safely. They crossed the final rise and descended toward the white dome and the cluster of out-buildings.

"That's huge," said Bridgewell. "Freestanding?"

"Supported by internal pressure," said Chavez. "We needed something that could be erected quickly. It was necessary that we have a thoroughly controllable internal environment. It'll be hell to protect from the snow and wind come winter, but we shouldn't need it by then."

There were two security checkpoints with uniformed guards. Armed men and women dubiously inspected the battered VW and its passengers, but waved them through when Chavez produced his identification.

"This is incredible," said Bridgewell.

"It wasn't my idea," said Chavez. "Rules."

She parked Scarlett beside a slab-sided building that adjoined the dome. Chavez guided her inside, past another checkpoint in the lobby, past obsequious underlings in lab garb who said, "Good afternoon, Dr. Chavez," and into a sterile-appearing room lined with electronic gear.

Chavez gestured at the rows of monitor screens. "We can't go into the dome today, but the entire installation is under surveillance through remotely controlled cameras." He began flipping switches. A dozen screens jumped to life in living color.

"It's all jungle," Bridgewell said.

"Rain forest." The cameras panned past vividly green trees, creepers, seemingly impenetrable undergrowth. "It's a reasonable duplication of the Brazilian interior. Now, listen." He touched other switches.

At first the speakers seemed to be crackling with electronic noise. "What am I hearing?" she finally said.

"What does it sound like?"

She listened longer. "Eating?" She shivered. "It's like a thousand mouths eating."

"Many more," Chavez said. "But you have the idea. Now watch."

The camera eye of the set directly in front of her dollied in toward a wall of greenery wound round a tree. Chavez saw the leaves ripple, undulating smoothly as though they were the surface of an uneasy sea. He glanced at Bridgewell; she saw it too. "Is there wind in the dome?"

"No," he said.

The view moved in for a closeup. "Jesus!" said Bridgewell.

Ants. Ants covered the tree, the undergrowth, the festooned vines.

"You may have trouble with the scale," Chavez said. "They're about as big as your thumb."

The ants swarmed in efficient concert, mandibles snipping like garden shears, stripping everything green, everything alive. Chavez stared at them and felt only a little hate. Most of the emotion had long since been burned from him.

"Behold *Eciton*," said Chavez. "Driver ants, army ants, the *maripunta*, whatever label you'd like to assign."

"I've read about them," said Bridgewell. "I've seen documentaries and movies at one time or another. I never thought they'd be this frightening when they were next door."

"There is fauna in the environment too. Would you like to see a more elaborate meal?"

"I'll pass."

Chavez watched the leaves ripple and vanish, bit by bit. Then he felt the tentative touch, the scurrying of segmented legs along his limbs. He reached out and tripped a single switch; all the pictures flickered and vanished. The two of them sat staring at the opaque gray monitors.

"Those are the giant ants?" she finally said.

"I told you the truth." He shook his head. "Not yet."

"No kidding now," she said.

"The following is a deliberate breach of national security," he said, "so they tell me." He raised his hands. "So what?" Chavez motioned toward the screens. "The *maripunta* apparently are mutating into a radically different form. It's not an obvious physical change, not like in *Them!* It's not by deliberate human agency, as with the bees. It may be through accidental human action—the Brazilian double-X nuclear station is suspected. We just don't know. What we do understand is that certain internal regulators in the *maripunta* have gone crazy."

"And they're getting bigger?" She looked bewildered.

He shook his head violently. "Do you know the square-cube law? No? It's a simple rule of nature. If an insect's dimensions are doubled, its strength and the area of its breathing passages are increased by a factor of four. But the mass is multiplied by eight. After a certain point, and that point isn't very high, the insect can't move or breathe. It collapses under its own mass."

"No giant ants?" she said.

"Not yet. Not exactly. The defective mechanism in the *maripunta* is one which controls the feeding and foraging phases. Ordinarily the ants—all the millions of them in a group—spend about two weeks in a nomadic phase. Then they alternate three weeks in place in a statary phase. That's how it used to be. Now only the nomadic phase remains."

"So they're moving," said Bridgewell. "North?" She sat with hands on knees. Her fingers moved as though with independent life.

"The *maripunta* are ravenous, breeding insanely, and headed our way. The fear is that, like the bees, the ants won't proceed linearly. Maybe they'll leapfrog aboard a charter aircraft. Maybe on a Honduran freighter. It's inevitable."

Bridgewell clasped her hands; forced them to remain still in her lap.

Chavez continued, "Thanks to slipshod internal Brazilian practices over the last few decades, the *maripunta* are resistant to every insecticide we've tried."

"They're unstoppable?" Bridgewell said.

"That's about it," said Chavez.

"And that's why the public's been kept in the dark?"

"Only partially. The other part is that we've found an answer." Chavez toyed with the monitor switches but stopped short of activating them. "The government agencies involved with this project fear that the public will misunderstand our solution to the problem. Next year's an election year." Chavez smiled ruefully. "There's a precedence to politics."

Bridgewell glanced from the controls to his face. "You're part of the solution. How?"

Chavez decisively flipped a switch and they again saw the ant-ravaged tree. The limbs were perceptibly barer. He left the sound down. "You know my background. You were correct in suspecting the New Mexico Project had something to do with recombinant DNA and genetic engineering. You're a good journalist. You were essentially right all down the line." He looked away from her toward the screen. "I and my people here are creating giant ants."

Bridgewell's mouth dropped open slightly. "I—but, you—"

"Let me continue. The purpose of the New Mexico Project has been to tinker with the genetic makeup of the *maripunta*—to create a virus-borne mutagen that will single out the queens. We've got that agent now."

All correspondent again, Bridgewell said, "What will it do?"

"At first we were attempting to readjust the ants' biological clocks and alter the nomadic phase. Didn't work; too sophisticated for what we can accomplish. So we settled for something more basic, more physical. We've altered the ants to make them huge.''

"Like in *Them!*''

"Except that *Them!* was a metaphor. It stated a physical impossibility. Remember the square-cube law?'' She nodded. "Sometime in the near future, bombers will be dropping payloads all across Brazil, Venezuela, the Guianas . . . anywhere we suspect the ants are. The weapon is dispersal bombs, aerosol canisters containing the viral mutagen to trigger uncontrolled growth in each new generation of ants.''

"The square-cube law . . .'' said Bridgewell softly.

"Exactly. We've created monsters—and gravity will kill them.''

"It'll work?''

"It should.'' Then Chavez said very quietly, "I hope I live long enough to see the repercussions.''

Bridgewell said equally quietly, "I *will* file this story.''

"I know that.''

"Will it get you trouble?''

"Probably nothing I can't handle.'' Chavez shrugged. "Look around you at this multi-million dollar installation. There were many more convenient places to erect it. I demanded it be built here.'' His smile was only a flicker. "When you're a giant in your field—and needed—the people in power tend to indulge you.''

"Thank you, Dr. Chavez,'' she said.

"Dr. Chavez? After all this, it's still not Paul?''

"Thanks, Paul.''

They drove north, back toward Casper, and watched the western photochemical sunset. The sun sank through the clouds in a splendor of reds. They talked very little. Chavez found the silence comfortable.

Why didn't you re-engage?

The question no longer disturbed him. He hadn't truly addressed it. Yet it was no longer swept under the carpet. That made all the difference.

I'll get to it, he thought. Chavez stared into the windshield sun-glare and saw his life bound up in a leaded pane like an ambered insect.

Bridgewell kept glancing at him silently as she drove up the long mountain road to Chavez's house. She passed the stand of pine where she had hidden Scarlett earlier in the day and braked to a stop in front of the stone house. They each sat still for the moment.

"You'll want to be filing your story,'' said Chavez.

She nodded.

"Now that you know the way up my tree, perhaps you'll return to visit in a more conventional way?''

Bridgewell smiled. She leaned across the seat and kissed him on the lips. It was, Chavez thought, a more than filial kiss. "Now *I'm* not kidding," she said.

Chavez got out of the Volkswagen and stood on the flagstone walk while Bridgewell backed Scarlett into the drive and turned around. As she started down the mountain, she turned and waved. Chavez waved. He stood there and watched until the car vanished around the first turn.

He walked back to the house and found O'Hanlon waiting, arms folded against the twilight chill, on the stone step. Chavez hesitated beside her and they both looked down the drive and beyond. Casper's lights began to blossom into a growing constellation.

"Does she remind you considerably of what Patricia might have been like?" said O'Hanlon.

Chavez nodded, and then said quickly, "Don't go for easy Freud. There's more to it than that—or there may be."

A slight smile tugged at O'Hanlon's lips. "Did I say anything?"

"Well, no." Chavez stared down at the city. He said, with an attempt at great dignity, "We simply found, in a short time, that we liked each other very much."

"I thought that might be it." O'Hanlon smiled a genuine smile. "Shall we go inside? Much longer out here and we'll be ice. I'll fix some chocolate."

He reached for the door. "With brandy?"

"All right."

"And you'll join me?"

"You know I ordinarily abstain, Dr. Chavez, but—" Her smile impossibly continued. "It is rather a special day, isn't it?" She preceded him through the warm doorway.

Chavez followed with a final look at the city. Below the mountain, Casper's constellation winked and bloomed into the zodiac.

Twelve hours later, the copyrighted story by Laynie Bridgewell made the national news and the wire services.

Eighteen hours later, her story was denied by at least five governmental agencies of two sovereign nations.

Twelve days later, Paul Chavez died quietly in his sleep, napping in the library.

Twenty-two days later, squadrons of jet bombers dropped cargoes of hissing aerosol bombs over a third of the South American continent. The world was saved. For a while, anyway. The grotesquely enlarged bodies of *Eciton burchelli* would shortly litter the laterite tropical soil.

Twenty-seven days later, at night, an intruder climbed up to the balcony of Paul Chavez's house on Casper Mountain and smashed the stained glass picture in the French doors leading into the library. No item was stolen. Only the window was destroyed.

Space colonies—"L5 colonies" as they are sometimes called—have recently become a popular theme in SF, popular enough, in fact, to prompt the editor of Analog *to remark that he now receives more SF stories that take place on space colonies than stories that take place on other planets. Self-contained "cities in space," life on an L5 colony is usually thought of as precisely planned, controlled, socially-engineered, with even the smallest details worked out minutely in advance. But as Dean Ing reminds us here, every world—even small artificial ones—has an underworld, and behind the scenes and out of sight things might be very different indeed, different enough even to disrupt the best laid plans of mice and men and social engineers. . . .*

Dean Ing has managed to become very popular in a very short span of time. His story "The Devil You Don't Know" was on last year's Nebula ballot, and his first novel Soft Targets *(Ace) was published this year as a large-format, illustrated trade paperback. Another novel,* Anasazi, *is forthcoming from Ace. Ing lives in Eugene, Oregon.*

DEAN ING

Down and Out on Ellfive Prime

Responding to Almquist's control, the little utility tug wafted from the North dock port and made its gentle pirouette. Ellfive Prime Colony seemed to fall away. Two hundred thousand kilometers distant, blue-white Earth swam into view, cradle of mankind, cage for too many. Almquist turned his long body in its cushions and managed an obligatory smile over frown lines. "If that won't make you homesick, Mr. Weston, nothing will."

The fat man grunted, looking not at the planet he had deserted but at something much nearer. From the widening of Weston's eyes, you could tell it was something big, closing fast. Torin Almquist knew what it was; he eased the tug out, watching his radar, to give Weston the full benefit of it.

When the tip of the great solar mirror swept past, Weston blanched and cried out. For an instant, the view port was filled with cables and the mirror pivot mechanism. Then once again there was nothing but Earth and sharp pinpricks of starlight. Weston turned toward the engineering manager, wattles at his jawline trembling. "Stupid bastard," he grated. "If that'll be your standard joke on new arrivals, you must cause a lot of coronaries."

Abashed, disappointed: "A mirror comes by every fourteen seconds, Mr. Weston. I thought you'd enjoy it. You asked to see the casting facility, and this is where you can see it best. Besides, if you were retired as a heart case, I'd know it." *And the hell with you,* he added silently. Almquist retreated into an impersonal spiel he knew by heart, moving the tug back to gain a panorama of the colony with its yellow legend, L-5', proud and unnecessary on the hull. He moved the controls gently, the blond hairs on his forearm masking the play of tendons within.

The colony hung below them, a vast shining melon the length of the new Hudson River Bridge and nearly a kilometer thick. Another of its three mirror strips, anchored near the opposite South end cap of Ellfive Prime and spread like curved petals toward the sun, hurtled silently past the view port. Almquist kept talking. " . . . Prime was the second industrial colony in space, dedicated in 2007. These days it's a natural choice for a retirement community. A fixed population of twenty-five hundred—plus a few down-and-out bums hiding here and there. Nowhere near as big a place as Orbital General's new industrial colony out near the asteroid belt."

Almquist droned on, backing the tug farther away. Beyond the South end cap, a tiny mote sparkled in the void, and Weston squinted, watching it. "The first Ellfive was a General Dynamics–Lever Brothers project in close orbit, but it got snuffed by the Chinese in 2012, during the war."

"I was only a cub then," Weston said, relaxing a bit. "This colony took some damage too, didn't it?"

Almquist glanced at Weston, who looked older despite his bland flesh. Well, living Earthside with seven billion people tended to age you. "The month I was born," Almquist nodded, "a nuke was intercepted just off the centerline of Ellfive Prime. Thermal shock knocked a tremendous dimple in the hull, from inside, of course, it looked like a dome poking up through the soil south of center."

Weston clapped pudgy hands, a gesture tagging him as neo-Afrikaner. "That'll be the hill, then. The one with the pines and spruce, near Hilton Prime?"

A nod. "Stress analysts swore they could leave the dimple if they patched the hull around it. Cheapest solution—and for once, a pretty one. When they finished bringing new lunar topsoil and distributing it inside, they saw there was enough dirt on the slope for spruce and ponderosa pine roots. To balance thousands of tons of new processed soil, they built a blister out on the opposite side of the hull and moved some heavy hardware into it."

The fat man's gaze grew condescending as he saw the great metal blister roll into view like a tumor on the hull. "Looks slap-dash," he said.

"Not really; they learned from DynLever's mistakes. The first Ellfive colony was a cylinder, heavier than an ellipsoid like ours." Almquist pointed through the view port. "DynLever designed for a low ambient pressure without much nitrogen in the cylinder and raised hell with water transpiration and absorption in a lot of trees they tried to grow around their living quarters. I'm no botanist, but I know Ellfive Prime has an Earthside ecology—the same air you'd breathe in Peru, only cleaner. We don't coddle our grass and trees, and we grow all our crops right in the North end cap below us."

Something new and infinitely pleasing shifted Weston's features. "You used to have an external crop module to feed fifty thousand people, back when this colony was big in manufacturing—"

"Sold it," Almquist put in. "Detached the big rig and towed it out to a belt colony when I was new here. We didn't really need it anymore—"

Weston returned the interruption pointedly: "You didn't let me finish. I put that deal over. OrbGen made a grand sum on it—which is why the wife and I can retire up here. One hand washes the other, eh?"

Almquist said something noncommittal. He had quit wondering why he disliked so many newcomers. He *knew* why. It was a sling-cast irony that he, Ellfive Prime's top technical man, did not have enough rank in OrbGen to be slated for colony retirement. Torin Almquist might last as Civil Projects Manager for another ten years, if he kept a spotless record. Then he would be Earthsided in the crowds and smog and would eat fish cakes for the rest of his life. Unlike his ex-wife, who had left him to teach in a belt colony so that she would never have to return to Earth. And who could blame her? *Shit.*

"I beg your pardon?"

"Sorry; I was thinking. You wanted to see the high-g casting facility? It's that sphere strapped on to the mirror that's swinging toward us. It's moving over two hundred meters per second, a lot faster than the colony floor, being a kilometer and a half out from the spin axis. So at the mirror tip, instead of pulling around one standard g they're pulling over three g's. Nobody spends more than an hour there. We balance the sphere with storage masses on the other mirror tips."

Restive, only half-interested: "Why? It doesn't look very heavy."

"It isn't," Almquist conceded, "but Ellfive Prime has to be balanced just so if she's going to spin on center. That's why they filled that blister with heavy stored equipment opposite the hill—though a few tons here and there don't matter."

Weston wasn't listening. "I keep seeing something like barn doors flipping around, past the other end, ah, end cap." He pointed. Another brief sparkle. "There," he said.

Almquist's arm tipped the control stick, and the tug slid farther from the colony's axis of rotation. "Stacking mirror cells for shipment," he explained. "We still have slag left over from a nitrogen-rich asteroid they towed here in the old days. Fused into plates, the slag makes good protection against solar flares. With a mirror face, it can do double duty. We're bundling up a pallet load, and a few cargo men are out there in P-suits—pressure suits. They—"

Weston would never know, and have cared less, what Almquist had started to say. The colony manager clapped the fingers of his free hand against the wireless speaker in his left ear. His face stiffened with zealot intensity. Fingers flickering to the console as the tug rolled and accelerated, Almquist began to speak into his throat mike—something about a Code Three. Weston knew something was being kept from him. He didn't like it and said so. Then he said so again.

". . . happened before," Almquist was saying to someone, "but this time you keep him centered, Radar Prime. I'll haul him in myself. Just talk him out of a panic; you know the drill. Please be quiet, Mr. Weston," he added in a too-polite aside.

"Don't patronize me," Weston spat. "Are we in trouble?"

"I'm swinging around the hull; give me a vector," Almquist continued, and Weston felt his body sag under acceleration. "Are you in voice contact?" Pause. "Doesn't he acknowledge? He's on a work-crew-scrambler circuit, but you can patch me in. Do it."

"You're treating me like a child."

"If you don't shut up, Weston, I *will*. Oh, hell, it's easier to humor you." He flicked a toggle, and the cabin speaker responded.

". . . be okay. I have my explosive riveter," said an unfamiliar voice, adult male, thinned and tightened by tension. "Starting to retro-fire now."

Almquist counted aloud at the muffled sharp bursts. "Not too fast, Versky," he cautioned. "You overheat a rivet gun, and the whole load could detonate."

"Jeez, I'm cartwheeling," Versky cut in. "Hang tight, guys." More bursts, now a staccato hammer. Versky's monologue gave no sign that he had heard Almquist, had all the signs of impending panic.

"Versky, listen to me. Take your goddamn finger off the trigger. We have you on radar. Relax. This is Torin Almquist, Versky. I say again—"

But he didn't. Far beyond, streaking out of the ecliptic, a brief nova flashed against the stars. The voice was cut off instantly. Weston saw Almquist's eyes blink hard, and in that moment the manager's face seemed aged by compassion and hopelessness. Then, very quietly: "Radar Prime, what do you have on scope?"

"Nothing but confetti, Mr. Almquist. Going everywhere at once."

"Should I pursue?"

"Your option, sir."

"And your responsibility."

"Yes, sir. No, don't pursue. Sorry."

"Not your fault. I want reports from you and Versky's cargo-team leader with all possible speed." Almquist flicked toggles with delicate savagery, turned his little vessel around, arrowed back to the dock port. Glancing at Weston, he said, "A skilled cargo man named Yves Versky. Experienced man; should've known better. He floated into a mirror support while horsing those slag cells around and got grazed by it. Batted him hell to breakfast." Then, whispering viciously to himself, "God-*damn* those big rivet guns. They can't be used like control jets. Versky knew that."

Then, for the first time, Weston realized what he had seen. A man in a pressure suit had just been blown to small pieces before his eyes. It would make a lovely anecdote over sherry, Weston decided.

Even if Almquist had swung past the external hull blister he would have failed to see, through a darkened view port, the two shabby types looking out. Nobody had official business in the blister. The younger man grimaced nervously, heavy cords bunching at his neck. He was half a head taller than his companion. "What d'you think, Zen?"

The other man yielded a lopsided smile. "Sounds good." He unplugged a pocket communicator from the wall and stuffed it into his threadbare coverall, then leaned forward at the view port. His chunky, muscular torso and short legs ill-matched the extraordinary arms that reached halfway to his knees, giving him the look of a tall dwarf. "I think they bought it, Yves."

"What if they didn't?"

Zen swung around, now grinning outright, and regarded Yves Versky through a swatch of brown hair that was seldom cut. "Hey, do like boss Almquist told you. Relax! They *gotta* buy it."

"I don't follow you."

"Then you'd better learn to. Look, if they recover any pieces, they'll find human flesh. How can they know it was a poor rummy's body thawed after six months in deep freeze? And if they *did* decide it's a scam, they'd have to explain how we planted him in your P-suit. And cut him loose from the blister, when only a few people are supposed to have access here; *and* preset the audio tape and the explosive, *and* coaxed a decent performance out of a lunk like you, *and*," he spread his apelike arms wide, his face comically ugly in glee, "nobody can afford to admit there's a scam counterculture on Ellfive Prime. All the way up to Torin Almquist there'd be just too much egg on too many faces. It ain't gonna happen, Versky."

The hulking cargo man found himself infected by the grin, but: "I wonder how long it'll be before *I* see another egg."

Zen snorted, "First time you lug a carton of edible garbage out of

Hilton Prime, me lad, Jean Neruda's half-blind when you put on the right coverall, he won't know he has an extra in his recycling crew, and after two days you won't mind pickin' chicken out of the slop. Just sit tight in your basement hidey-hole when you're off duty for a while. Stay away from crews that might recognize you until your beard grows. And keep your head shaved like I told you.''

Versky heaved a long sigh, sweeping a hand over his newly bald scalp. ''You'll drop in on me? I need a lot of tips on the scam life. And—and I don't know how to repay you.''

''A million ways. I'll think of a few, young fella. And sure, you'll see me—whenever I like.''

Versky chuckled at the term *young fella*. He knew Zen might be in his forties, but he seemed younger. Versky followed his mentor to the air lock into the colony hull. ''Well, just don't forget your friend in the garbage business,'' he urged, fearful of his unknown future.

Zen paused in the conduit that snaked beneath the soil of Ellfive Prime. ''Friendship,'' he half-joked, ''varies directly with mutual benefit and inversely with guilt. Put another way,'' he said, lapsing into scam language as he trotted toward the South end cap, ''a friend who's willing to be understood is a joy. One that demands understanding is a pain in the ass.''

''You think too much,'' Versky laughed. They moved softly now, approaching an entry to the hotel basement.

Zen glanced through the spy hole, paused before punching the wall in the requisite place. ''Just like you work too much.'' He flashed his patented gargoyle grin. ''Trust me. Give your heart a rest.''

Versky, much too tall for his borrowed clothing, inflated his barrel chest in challenge. ''Do I *look* like a heart murmur?''

A shrug. ''You did to OrbGen's doctors, rot their souls—which is why you were due to be Earthsided next week. Don't lay that on *me*, ol' scam; I'm the one who's reprieved you to a low-g colony, if you'll just stay in low-g areas near the end caps.'' He opened the door.

Versky saw the hand signal and whispered, ''I got it: Wait thirty seconds.'' He chuckled again. ''Sometimes I think you should be running this colony.''

Zen slipped through, left the door nearly closed, waited until Versky had moved near the slit. ''In some ways,'' he stage-whispered back, ''I do.'' Wink. Then he scuttled away.

At mid-morning the next day, Almquist arranged the accident report and its supporting documents into a neat sequence across his video console. Slouching behind his desk with folded arms, he regarded the display for a moment before lifting his eyes. ''What've I forgot, Emory?''

Emory Reina cocked his head sparrowlike at the display. Almquist gnawed a cuticle, watching the soulful Reina's eyes dart back and forth in sober scrutiny. "It's all there," was Reina's verdict. "The only safety infraction was Versky's, I think."

"You mean the tether he should've worn?"

A nod; Reina started to speak but thought better of it, the furrows dark on his olive face.

"Spit it out, dammit," Almquist goaded. Reina usually thought a lot more than he talked, a trait Almquist valued in his assistant manager.

"I am wondering," the little Brazillian said, "if it was really accidental." Their eyes locked again, held for a long moment. "Ellfive Prime has been orbiting for fifty years. Discounting early casualties throughout the war, the colony has had twenty-seven fatal mishaps among OrbGen employees. Fourteen of them occurred during the last few days of the victim's tour on the colony."

"That's hard data?"

Another nod.

"You're trying to say they're suicides."

"I am trying not to think so." A devout Catholic, Reina spoke hesitantly.

Maybe he's afraid God is listening. I wish I thought He would. "Can't say I'd blame some of them," Almquist said aloud, remembering. "But not Yves Versky. Too young, too much to live for."

"You must account for my pessimism," Reina replied.

"It's what we pay you for," Almquist said, trying in vain to make it airy. "Maybe the insurance people could convince OrbGen to sweeten the Earthside trip for returning people. It might be cheaper in the long run."

Emory Reina's face said that was bloody likely. "After I send a repair crew to fix the drizzle from that rain pipe, I could draft a suggestion from you to the insurance group," was all he said.

"Do that," Almquist turned his attention to the desk console. As Reina padded out of the low Center building into its courtyard, the manager committed the accident report to memory storage, then paused. His fingers twitched nervously over his computer-terminal keyboard. Oh, yes, he'd forgotten something, all right. Conveniently.

In moments, Almquist had queried Prime memory for an accident report ten years past. It was an old story in more ways than one. Philip Elroy Hazen: technical editor, born 14 September 2014, arrived on L-5' for first tour to write modification work orders 8 May 2039. Earthsided on 10 May 2041; a standard two-year tour for those who were skilled enough to qualify. A colony tour did not imply any other bonus: The tour *was* the bonus. It worked out very well for the owning conglomerates that controlled literally everything on their colonies. Almquist's mouth twitched: *well, maybe not literally . . .*

Hazen had wangled a second tour to the colony on 23 February 2045, implying that he'd been plenty good at his work. Fatal injury accident report filed 20 February 2047.

Uh-*huh*; uh-*huh!* Yes, by God, there was a familiar ring to it: a malf in Hazen's radio while he was suited up, doing one last check on a modification to the casting facility. Flung off the tip of the mirror and—*Jesus, what a freakish way to go*—straight into a mountain of white-hot slag that radiated like a dying sun near a temporary processing module outside the colony hull. No recovery attempted; why sift ashes?

Phil Hazen; Zen, they'd called him. The guy they used to say needed rollerskates on his hands; but that was envy talking. Almquist had known Zen slightly, and the guy was an absolute terror at sky-bike racing along the zero-g axis of the colony. Built his own tri-wing craft, even gave it a Maltese cross, scarlet polymer wingskin, and a funny name. The *Red Baron* had looked like a joke, just what Zen had counted on. He'd won a year's pay before other sky bikers realized it wasn't a streak of luck.

Hazen had always made his luck. With his sky bike—it was with young seasoned spruce and the foam polymer, fine engineering and better craftsmanship, all disguised to lure the suckers. And all without an engineering degree. Zen had just picked up expertise, never seeming to work at it.

And when his luck ran out, it was—Almquist checked the display— only days before he was slated for Earthside. Uh-*huh!*

Torin Almquist knew about the shadowy wraiths who somehow dropped from sight on the colony, to be caught later or to die for lack of medical attention or, in a few cases, to find some scam—some special advantage—to keep them hidden on Ellfive Prime. He'd been sure Zen was a survivor, no matter what the accident report said. What was the phrase? *A scam, not a bum*; being on the scam wasn't quite the same. A scam wasn't down and out of resources; he was down and out of sight. Maybe the crafty Zen had engineered another fatality that wasn't fatal.

Almquist hadn't caught anyone matching the description of Zen. Almost, but not quite. He thought about young Yves Versky, whose medical report hadn't been all that bad, then considered Versky's life expectancy on the colony versus his chances Earthside. Versky had been a sharp hardworker too. Almquist leaned back in his chair again and stared at his display. He had no way of knowing that Reina's rainpipe crew was too late to ward off disaster.

A rain pipe had been leaking long before Grounds Maintenance realized they had a problem. Rain was a simple matter on Ellfive Prime: You built a web of pipes with spray nozzles that ran the length of the colony. From ground level the pipes were nearly invisible, thin lines connected by crosspieces in a great cylindrical net surrounding the colony's zero-g axis. Gravity loading near the axis was so slight that the rain pipes could be anchored lightly.

Yet now and then, a sky biker would pedal foolishly from the zero-g region or would fail to compensate for the gentle rolling movement generated by the air itself. That was when the rain pipes saved somebody's bacon and on rare occasions suffered a kink. At such times, Almquist was tempted to press for the outlawing of sky bikes until the rabid sports association could raise money for a safety net to protect people and pipes alike. But the cost would have been far too great: It would have amounted to a flat prohibition of sky bikes.

The problem had started a month earlier with a mild collision between a sky bike and a crosspiece. The biker got back intact, but the impact popped a kink on the underside of the attached rain pipe. The kink could not be seen from the colony's axis. It might possibly have been spotted from floor level with a good, powerful telescope.

Inspection crews used safety tethers, which loaded the rain pipe just enough to close the crack while the inspector passed. Then the drizzle resumed for as long as the rain continued. Thereafter, the thrice-weekly afternoon rain from that pipe had been lessened in a line running from Ellfive Prime's Hilton Hotel, past the prized hill, over the colony's one shallow lake, to work-staff apartments that stretched from the lake to the North end cap, where crops were grown. Rain was lessened, that is, everywhere but over the pine-covered hill directly below the kink. Total rainfall was unchanged; but the hill got three times its normal moisture, which gradually soaked down through a forty-year accumulation of ponderosa needles and humus, into the soil below.

In this fashion the hill absorbed one hundred thousand kilograms too much water in a month. A little water percolated back to the creek and the lake it fed. Some of it was still soaking down through the humus overburden. And much of it—far too much—was held by the underlying slope soil, which was gradually turning to ooze. The extra mass had already caused a barely detectable shift in the colony's spin axis. Almquist had his best troubleshooter, Lee Shumway, quietly checking the hull for a structural problem near the hull blister.

Suzanne Nagel was a lissome widow whose second passion was for her sky bike. She had been idling along in zero-g, her chain-driven propeller a soft whirr behind her, when something obscured her view of the hill far below. She kept staring at it until she was well beyond the leak, then realized the obstruction was a spray of water. Suzy sprint-pedaled the rest of the way to the end cap, and five minutes later the rains were canceled by Emory Reina.

Thanks to Suzy Nagel's stamina, the slope did not collapse that day. But working from inspection records, Reina tragically assumed that the leak had been present for perhaps three days instead of a month. The hill needed something—a local vibration, for example—to begin the mud slide that could abruptly displace up to two hundred thousand tons of mass downslope. Which would inevitably bring on the nightmare more feared than meteorites by every colony manager: spinquake. Small meteorites could only damage a colony, but computer simulations had proved that if the spin axis shifted suddenly a spinquake could crack a colony like an egg.

The repair crew was already in place high above when Reina brought his electrabout three-wheeler to a halt near a path that led up to the pines. His belt-comm set allowed direct contact with the crew and instant access to all channels, including his private scrambler to Torin Almquist.

"I can see the kink on your video," Reina told the crew leader, studying his belt-slung video. "Sleeve it and run a pressure check. We can be thankful that a leak that large was not over Hilton Prime," he added, laughing. The retired OrbGen executives who luxuriated in the hotel would have screamed raw murder, of course. And the leak would have been noticed weeks before.

Scanning the dwarf apple trees at the foot of the slope, Reina's gaze moved to the winding footpath. In the forenoon quietude, he could hear distant swimmers cavorting in the slightly reduced gravity of the Hilton pool near the South end cap. But somewhere above him on the hill, a large animal thrashed clumsily through the pine. It wasn't one of the half-tame deer; only maladroit humans made that much commotion on Ellfive Prime. Straining to locate the hiker, Reina saw the leaning trees. He blinked. No trick of eyesight, they were really leaning. Then he saw the long shallow mud slide, no more than a portent of its potential, that covered part of the footpath. For perhaps five seconds, his mind grasping the implication of what he saw, Reina stood perfectly still. His mouth hung open.

In deadly calm, coding the alarm on his scrambler circuit: "Torin, Emory Reina. I have a Code Three on the hill. And," he swallowed hard, "potential Code One. I say again, Code One: mud slides on the main-path side of the hill. Over." Then Reina began to shout toward the pines.

Code Three was bad enough: a life in danger. Code Two was more serious still, implying an equipment malfunction that could affect many lives. Code One was reserved for colony-wide disaster. Reina's voice shook. He had never called a Code One before.

During the half-minute it took for Almquist to race from a conference to his office, Reina's shouts flushed not one but two men from the hillside. The first, a heavy individual in golf knickers, identified himself testily as Voerster Weston. He stressed that he was not accustomed to peremptory demands from an overall-clad worker. The second man emerged far to Reina's right but kept hidden in a stand of mountain laurel, listening, surmising, sweating.

Reina's was the voice of sweet reason. "If you want to live, Mr. Weston, please lie down where you are. Slowly. The trees below you are leaning outward, and they were not that way yesterday."

"Damnation, I know that much," Weston howled; "that's what I was looking at. Do you know how wet it is up here? I will not lie down on this muck!"

The man in the laurels made a snap decision, cursed, and stood up. "If you don't, two-belly, I'll shoot you here and now," came the voice of Philip Elroy Hazen. Zen had one hand thrust menacingly into a coverall pocket. He was liberally smeared with mud, and his aspect was not pleasant.

"O demonio, another one," Reina muttered. The fat man saw himself flanked, believed Zen's implied lie about a weapon, and carefully levered himself down to the blanket of pine needles. At this moment Torin Almquist answered the Mayday.

There was no way to tell how much soil might slide, but through staccato interchanges Emory Reina described the scene better than his video could show it. Almquist was grim. "We're already monitoring an increase in the off-center spin, Emory; not a severe shift, but it could get to be. Affirmative on that potential Code One. I'm sending a full emergency crew to the blister, now that we know where to start."

Reina thought for a moment, glumly pleased that neither man on the slope had moved. "I believe we can save these two by lowering a safety sling from my crew. They are directly overhead. Concur?"

An instant's pause. "Smart, Emory. And you get your butt out of there. Leave the electrabout, man, just go!"

"With respect, I cannot. Someone must direct the sling deployment from here."

"It's your bacon. I'll send another crew to you."

"Volunteers only," Reina begged, watching the slope. For the moment it seemed firm. Yet a bulge near cosmetically placed slag boulders suggested a second mass displacement. Reina then explained their predicament to the men on the slope, to ensure their compliance.

"It's worse than that," Zen called down. "There was a dugout over there," he pointed to the base of a boulder, "where a woman was living. She's buried, I'm afraid."

Reina shook his head sadly, using his comm set to his work crew. Over four hundred meters above, men were lashing tether lines from crosspieces to distribute the weight of a sling. Spare tethers could be linked by carabiners to make a lifeline reaching to the colony floor. The exercise was familiar to the crew, but only as a drill until now. And they would be hoisting, not lowering.

Diametrically opposite from the hill, troubleshooters converged on the blister where the colony's long-unused reactor and coolant tanks were stored. Their job was simple—in principle.

The reactor subsystems had been designed as portable elements, furnished with lifting and towing lugs. The whole reactor system weighed nearly ten thousand tons, including coolant tanks. Since the blister originally had been built around the stored reactor elements to balance the hill mass, Almquist needed only to split the blister open to space, then lower the reactor elements on quartz cables. As the mass moved out of the blister and away from the hull, it would increase in apparent weight, balancing the downward flow of mud across the hull. Almquist was lucky in one detail: The reactor was not in line with the great solar-mirror strips. Elements could be lowered a long way while repairs were carried out to redistribute the soil.

Almquist marshaled forces from his office. He heard the colony-wide alarm whoop its signal, watched monitors as the colony staff and two thousand other residents hurried toward safety in end-cap domes. His own P-suit, ungainly and dust-covered, hung in his apartment ten paces away. There was no time to fetch it while he was at his post. *Never again*, he promised himself. He divided his attention among monitors showing the evacuation, the blister team, and the immediate problem above Emory Reina.

Reina was optimistic as the sling snaked down. "South a bit," he urged into his comm set, then raised his voice, "Mr. Weston, a sling is above you, a little north. Climb in and buckle the harness. They will reel you in."

Weston looked around him, the whites of his eyes visible from fifty meters away. He had heard the alarm and remembered only that it meant mortal danger. He saw the sling turning gently on its thin cable as it neared him.

"Now, steady as she goes," Reina said, then, "Stop." The sling collapsed on the turf near the fat man. Reina, fearful that the mud-covered stranger might lose heart, called to assure him that the sling would return.

"I'll take my chances here," Zen called back. The sling could mean capture. The fat man did not understand that any better than Reina did.

Voerster Weston paused halfway into his harness, staring up. Suddenly he was scrambling away from it, tripping in the sling, mindless with the fear of rising into a synthetic sky. Screaming, he fled down the slope. And brought part of it with him.

Reina saw apple trees churning toward him in time to leap atop his electrabout and kept his wits enough to grab branches as the first great wave slid from the slope. He saw Weston disappear in two separate upheavals, swallowed under the mud slide he had provoked. Mauled by hardwood, mired to his knees, Reina spat blood and turf. He hauled one leg free, then the other, pulling at tree limbs. The second man, he saw, had slithered against a thick pine and was now trying to climb it.

Still calm, voice indistinct through his broken jaw, Reina redirected the sling crew. The sling harness bounced upslope near the second man. "Take the sling," Reina bawled.

Now Reina's whole world shuddered. It was a slow, perceptible motion, each displacement of mud worsening the off-center rotation and slight acceleration changes that could bring more mud that could bring worse . . . Reina forced his mind back to the immediate problem. He could not see himself at its focus.

Almquist felt the tremors, saw what had to be done. "Emory, I'm sending your relief crew back. Shumway's in the blister. They don't have time to cut the blister now; they'll have to blow it open. You have about three minutes to get to firm ground. Then you run like hell to South end cap."

"As soon as this man is in the sling," Reina mumbled. Zen had already made his decision, seeing the glistening ooze that had buried the fat man.

"Now! Right fucking *now*," Almquist pleaded. "I can't delay it a millisecond. When Shumway blows the blister open it'll be a sudden shake, Emory. You know what that means?"

Reina did. The sharp tremor would probably bring the entire middle of the slope thundering down. Even if the reactor could be lowered in minutes, it would take only seconds for the muck to engulf him. Reina began to pick his way backward across fallen apple trees, wondering why his left arm had an extra bend above the wrist. He kept a running fire of instructions to the rain-pipe crew as Zen untangled the sling harness. Reina struggled toward safety in pain, patience, reluctance. And far too slowly.

"He is buckled in," Reina announced. His last words were, "Haul away." He saw the mud-spattered Zen begin to rise, swinging in a broad arc, and they exchanged "OK" hand signals before Reina gave full attention to his own escape. He had just reached the edge of firm ground when Lee Shumway, moving with incredible speed in a full P-suit, ducked through a blister airlock and triggered the charges.

The colony floor bucked once, throwing Reina off stride. He fell on his fractured ulna, rolled, opened his mouth—perhaps to moan, perhaps to pray. His breath was bottled by mud as he was flung beneath a viscous gray tide that rolled numberless tons of debris over him.

The immense structure groaned, but held. Zen swayed sickeningly as Ellfive Prime shook around him. He saw Reina die, watched helplessly as a retiree home across the valley sagged and collapsed. Below him, a covey of Quetzal birds burst from the treetops like jeweled scissors in flight. As he was drawn higher he could see more trees slide.

The damage worsened; too many people had been too slow. The colony was rattling everything that would rattle. Now it was all rattling louder. Somewhere, a shrill whistle keened as precious air and more precious water vapor rushed toward a hole in the sunlight windows.

When the shouts above him became louder than the carnage below, Zen began to hope. Strong arms reached for his and moments later he was attached to another tether. "I can make it from here," he said, calling his thanks back as he hauled himself toward the end-cap braces.

A crew man with a video comm set thrust it toward Zen as he neared a ladder. "It's for you," he said, noncommittal.

For an instant, an eon, Zen's body froze, though he continued to waft nearer. Then he shrugged and took the comm set as though it were ticking. He saw a remembered face in the video. Wrapping an arm around the ladder, he nodded to the face. "Don Bellows here," he said innocently.

Pause, then a snarl: "You wouldn't believe my mixed emotions when I recognized you on the monitor. Well, *Mister* Bellows, Adolf Hitler here." Almquist went on. "Or you'll think so damned quick unless you're in my office as fast as your knuckles will carry you."

The crew man was looking away, but he was tense. He knew. Zen cleared his throat for a whine. "I'm scared—"

"You've been dead for ten years, Hazen. How can you be scared? Frazer there will escort you; his instructions are to brain you if he has to. I have sweeping powers right now. Don't con me and don't argue; I need you right here, right now."

By the time Zen reached the terraces with their felled, jumbled crops, the slow shakes had subsided. They seemed to diminish to nothing as he trotted, the rangy Frazer in step behind, to an abandoned electrabout. Damage was everywhere, yet the silence was oppressive. A few electrical fires were kindling in apartments as they moved toward the Colony Center building. Some fires would be out, others out of control, in minutes. The crew man gestured Zen through the courtyard and past two doors. Torin Almquist stood looming over his console display, ignoring huge shards of glass that littered his carpet.

Almquist adjusted a video monitor. "Thanks, Frazer; would you wait in the next room?" The crew man let his face complain of his idleness but complied silently. Without glancing from the monitors, Almquist transfixed the grimy Zen. "If I say the word, you're a dead man. If I say a different word, you go Earthside in manacles. You're still here only because I wanted you here all the time, just in case I ever needed you. Well, I need you now. If you hadn't been dropped into my lap we'd have found you on a Priority One. Never doubt that.

"If I say a third word, you get a special assistant's slot—I can swing that—for as long as I'm here. All I'm waiting for is one word from *you*. If it's a lie, you're dead meat. Will you help Ellfive Prime? Yes or no?"

Zen considered his chances. Not past that long-legged Frazer. They could follow him on monitors for some distance anyhow unless he had a head start. "Given the right conditions," Zen hazarded.

Almquist's head snapped up. "My best friend just died for you, against my better judgment. *Yes or no.*"

"Yes. I owe you nothin', but I owe him somethin'."

Back to the monitors, speaking to Zen; "Lee Shumway's crew has recovered our mass balance, and they can do it again if necessary. I doubt there'll be more mud slides, though; five minutes of spinquakes should've done it all."

Zen moved to watch over the tall man's bare arms. Two crews could be seen from a utility tug monitor, rushing to repair window leaks where water vapor had crystallized in space as glittering fog. The colony's external heat radiator was in massive fragments, and the mirrors were jammed in place. It was going to get hot in Ellfive Prime. "How soon will we get help from other colonies?"

Almquist hesitated. Then, "We won't, unless we fail to cope. OrbGen is afraid some other corporate pirate will claim salvage rights. And when you're on my staff, everything I tell you is privileged data."

"You think the danger is over?"

"Over?" Almquist barked a laugh that threatened to climb out of control. He ticked items off on his fingers. "We're losing water vapor; we have to mask mirrors and repair the radiator, or we fry; half our crops are ruined and food stores may not last; and most residents are hopeless clods who have no idea how to fend for themselves. *Now* d'you see why I diverted searches when I could've taken you twice before?"

Zen's mouth was a cynical curve.

Almquist: "Once when you dragged a kid from the lake filters I could've had you at the emergency room." Zen's eyebrows lifted in surprised agreement. "And once when a waiter realized you were scamming food from the Hilton service elevator."

"That was somebody else, you weren't even close. But okay, you've been a real sweetheart. Why?"

"Because you've learned to live outside the system! Food, shelter, medical help, God knows what else; you have another system that hardly affects mine, and now we're going to teach your tricks to the survivors. This colony is going to make it. You were my experimental group, Zen. You just didn't know it.'' He rubbed his chin reflectively. ''By the way, how many guys are on the scam? Couple of dozen?'' An optimist, Torin Almquist picked what he considered a high figure.

A chuckle. ''Couple of hundred, you mean.'' Zen saw slackjawed disbelief and went on: ''They're not all guys. A few growing families. There's Wandering Mary, Maria Polyakova; our only registered nurse, but I found her dugout full of mud this morning. I hope she was sleepin' out.''

''Can you enlist their help? If they don't help, this colony can still die. The computer says it will, as things stand now. It'll be close, but we won't make it. How'd you like to take your chances with a salvage crew?''

''Not a chance. But I can't help just standing her swappin' wind with you.''

''Right.'' Eyes bored into Zen's, assessing him. The thieves' argot, the be-damned-to-you gaze, suggested a man who was more than Hazen *had* been. ''I'll give you a temporary pass. See you here tomorrow morning; for now, look the whole colony over, and bring a list of problems and solutions as you see 'em.''

Zen turned to leave, then looked back. ''You're really gonna let me just walk right out.'' A statement of wonder, and of fact.

''Not without this,'' Almquist said, scribbling on a plastic chit. He thrust it toward Zen. ''Show it to Frazer.''

Inspecting the cursive scrawl: ''Doesn't look like much.''

''*Mas que nada*,'' Almquist smiled, then looked quickly away as his face fell. *Better than nothing,* his private joke with Emory Reina. He glanced at the retreating Zen and rubbed his forehead. Grief did funny things to people's heads. To deny a death you won't accept, you invest his character in another man. Not very smart when the other man might betray you for the sheer fun of it. Torin Almquist massaged his temples and called Lee Shumway. They still had casualties to rescue.

Zen fought a sense of unreality as he moved openly in broad daylight. Everyone was lost in his own concerns. Zen hauled one scam from his plastic bubble under the lake surface, half dead in stagnant air after mud from the creek swamped his air exchanger. An entire family of scams, living as servants in the illegal basement they had excavated for a resident, had been crushed when the foundation collapsed.

But he nearly wept to find Wandering Mary safe in a secret conduit, tending to a dozen wounded scams. He took notes as she told him where her curative herbs were planted and how to use them. The old girl flatly refused to leave her charges, her black eyes flashing through wisps of gray hair, and Zen promised to send food.

The luck of Sammy the Touch was holding strong. The crop compost heap that covered his half-acre foam shell seemed to insulate it from ground shock as well. Sammy patted his little round tummy, always a cheerful sign, as he ushered Zen into the bar where, on a good night, thirty scams might be gathered. If Zen was the widest-ranging scam on Ellfive Prime, Sammy the Touch was the most secure.

Zen accepted a glass of potato vodka—Sammy was seldom *that* easy a touch—and allowed a parody of the truth to be drawn from him. He'd offered his services to an assistant engineer, he said, in exchange for unspecified future privileges. Sammy either bought the story or took a lease on it. He responded after some haggling with the promise of a hundred kilos of "medicinal" alcohol and half his supply of bottled methane. Both were produced from compost precisely under the noses of the crop crew, and both were supplied on credit. Sammy also agreed to provision the hidden infirmary of Wandering Mary. Zen hugged the embarrassed Sammy and exited through one of the conduits, promising to pick up the supplies later.

Everywhere he went, Zen realized, the scams were coping better than legal residents. He helped a startlingly handsome middle-aged blonde douse the remains of her smoldering wardrobe. Her apartment complex had knelt into its courtyard and caught fire.

"I'm going to freeze tonight," Suzy Nagel murmured philosophically.

He eyed her skimpy costume and doubted it. Besides, the temperature was slowly climbing, and there wouldn't *be* any night until the solar mirrors could be pivoted again. There were other ways to move the colony to a less reflective position, but he knew Almquist would try the direct solutions first.

Farmer Brown—no one knew his original name—wore his usual stolen agronomy-crew coverall as he hawked his pack load of vegetables among residents in the low-rent area. He had not assessed all the damage to his own crops, tucked and espaliered into corners over five square kilometers of the colony. Worried as he was, he had time to hear a convincing story. "Maybe I'm crazy to compete against myself," he told Zen, "but you got a point. If a salvage outfit takes over, it's kaymag." KMAG: Kiss my ass good-bye. "I'll sell you seeds, even breeding pairs of hamsters, but don't ask me to face the honchos in person. You remember about the vigilantes, ol' scam."

Zen nodded. He gave no thought to the time until a long shadow striped a third of the colony floor. One of the mirrors had been coaxed into pivoting. Christ, he was tired—but why not? It would have been dark long before, on an ordinary day. He sought his sleeping quarters in Jean

Neruda's apartment, hoping Neruda wouldn't insist on using Zen's eyesight to fill out receipts. Their arrangement was a comfortable quid pro quo, but please, thought Zen, not tonight!

He found a more immediate problem than receipts. Yves Versky slumped, trembling, in the shambles of Neruda's place, holding a standard emergency oxygen mask over the old man's face. The adjoining office had lost one wall in the spinquake, moments after the recycling crew ran for end-cap domes.

"I had to hole up here," Versky gasped, exhausted. "Didn't know where else to go. Neruda wouldn't leave either. Then the old fool smelled smoke and dumped his goldfish bowl on a live power line. Must've blown half the circuits in his body." Like a spring-wound toy, Versky's movements and voice diminished. "Took me two hours of mouth-to-mouth before he was breathing steady, Zen. Boy, have I got a headache."

Versky fell asleep holding the mask in place. Zen could infer the rest. Neruda, unwilling to leave familiar rooms in his advancing blindness. Versky, unwilling to abandon a life, even that of a half-electrocuted, crotchety old man. Yet Neruda was right to stay put: Earthside awaited the OrbGen employee whose eyes failed.

Zen lowered the inert Versky to the floor, patted the big man's shoulder. More than unremitting care, he had shown stamina and first-aid expertise. Old Neruda awoke once, half-manic, half-just disoriented. Zen nursed him through it with surface awareness. On another level he was cataloguing items for Almquist, for survivors, for Ellfive Prime.

And on the critical level a voice in him jeered, *bullshit: For yourself.* Not because Almquist or Reina had done him any favors, but because Torin Almquist was right. The colony manager could find him eventually; maybe it was better to rejoin the system now, on good terms. Besides, as the only man who could move between the official system and the scam counterculture, he could really wheel and deal. It might cause some hard feelings in the conduits, but . . . Zen sighed, and slept. Poorly.

It was two days before Zen made every contact he needed, two more when Almquist announced that Ellfive Prime would probably make it. The ambient temperature had stabilized. Air and water losses had ceased. They did not have enough stored food to provide three thousand daily calories per person beyond twenty days, but crash courses in multicropping were suddenly popular, and some immature crops could be eaten.

"It'd help if you could coax a few scams into instructing," Almquist urged as he slowed to match Zen's choppy pace. They turned from the damaged crop terraces toward the Center.

"Unnn-likely," Zen intoned. "We still talk about wartime, when vigilantes tried to clean us out. They ushered a couple of nice people out of airlocks, naked, which we think was a little brusque. Leave it alone; it's working.''

A nod. ''Seems to be. But I have doubts about the maturing rates of your seeds. Why didn't my people know about those hybrid daikon radishes and tomatoes?''

''You were after long-term yield,'' Zen shrugged. ''This hot weather will ripen the stuff faster, too. We've been hiding a dozen short-term crops under your nose, including dandelions better than spinach. Like hamster haunch is better'n rabbit, and a lot quicker to grow.''

Almquist could believe the eighteen-day gestation period, but was astonished at the size of the breeding stock. ''You realize your one-kilo hamsters could be more pet than protein?''

''Not in our economy,'' Zen snorted. ''It's hard to be sentimental when you're down and out. Or stylish either.'' He indicated his frayed coverall. ''By the time the rag man gets this, it won't yield three meters of dental floss.''

Almquist grinned for the first time in many days. What his new assistant had forgotten in polite speech, he made up in the optimism of a young punk. He corrected himself: an *old* punk. ''You know what hurts? You're nearly my age and look ten years younger. How?''

It wasn't a specific exercise, Zen explained. It was attitude. ''You're careworn,'' he sniffed. ''Beat your brains out for idling plutocrats fifty weeks a year and then wonder why you age faster than I do.'' Wondering headshake.

They turned toward the Center courtyard. Amused, Almquist said, ''You're a plutocrat?''

''Ain't racin' my motors. Look at all the Indians who used to live past a hundred. A Blackfoot busted his ass like I do, maybe ten or twenty weeks a year. They weren't dumb, just scruffy.''

Almquist forgot his retort; his deck console was flashing for attention. Zen wandered out of the office, returning with two cups of scam ''coffee.'' Almquist sipped it between calls, wondering if it was really brewed from ground dandelion root, considering how this impudent troll was changing his life, could change it further.

Finally he sat back. ''You hear OrbGen's assessment,'' he sighed. ''I'm a God-damned hero, for now. Don't ask me about next year, if they insist on making poor Emory a sacrificial goat to feed ravening stockholders, I can't help it.''

Impassive: ''Sure you could. You just let 'em co-opt you.'' Zen sighed, then released a sad troglodyte's smile. ''Like you co-opted me.''

''I can unco-opt. Nothing's permanent.''

''You said it, bubba.''

Almquist took a long breath, then cantilevered a forefinger in warning. "Watch your tonuge, Hazen. When I pay your salary, you pay some respect." He saw the sullen look in Zen's eyes and bored in. "Or would you rather go on the scam again and get Earthsided the first chance I get? I haven't *begun* to co-opt you yet," he glowered. "I have to meet with the Colony Council in five minutes—to explain a lot of things, including you. When I get back, I want a map of those conduits the scams built, to the best of your knowledge."

A flood of ice washed through Zen's veins. Staring over the cup of coffee that shook in his hands: "You *know* I can't do that."

Almquist paused in the doorway, his expression smug. "You know the alternative. Think about it," he said, and turned and walked out.

When Torin Almquist returned, his wastebasket was overturned on his desk. A ripe odor wrinkled his nose for him even before he saw what lay atop the wastebasket like an offering on a pedestal: a lavish gift of human excrement. His letter opener, an antique, protruded from the turd. It skewered a plastic chit, Zen's pass. On the chit, in draftsman's neat printing, full caps: I THOUGHT ABOUT IT.

Well, you sure couldn't mistake his answer, Almquist reflected as he dumped the offal into his toilet. Trust Zen to make the right decision.

Which way had he gone? Almquist could only guess at the underground warrens built during the past fifty years, but chose not to guess. He also knew better than to mention Zen to the Colony Council. The manager felt a twinge of guilt at the choice, truly no choice at all, that he had forced on Zen—but there was no other way.

If Zen knew the whole truth, he might get careless, and a low profile was vital for the scams. The setup benefited all of Ellfive Prime. Who could say when the colony might once more need the counterculture and its primitive ways?

And that meant Zen had to disappear again, genuinely down and out of reach. If Almquist himself didn't know exactly where the scams hid, he couldn't tell OrbGen even under drugs. And he didn't intend to tell. Sooner or later OrbGen would schedule Torin Almquist for permanent Earthside rotation, and when that day came he might need help in his own disappearance. *That* would be the time to ferret out a secret conduit, to contact Zen. The scams could use an engineering manager who knew the official system inside out.

Almquist grinned to himself and brewed a cup of dandelion coffee. Best to get used to the stuff now, he reasoned; it would be a staple after he retired, down and out on Ellfive Prime.

Here's another story that deals, obliquely at least, with the concept of space colonies, but rather more cynically than did Dean Ing's piece. Space colonies have been touted as achievable Utopias, and as Utopias is how they have been primarily portrayed in SF—some even see space colonies as the only hope of mankind, the heir and successor to terrestrial civilization. But a close reading of history will show that today's Utopia is often tomorrow's Dystopia, that even the brightest hopes tarnish, and that the child can often turn upon and savage its parents. . . .

Nebula winner Gregory Benford is one of the most acclaimed writers of his generation. His novel In the Ocean of the Night *(Dell) was widely hailed as one of the very best novels to appear during the seventies, and his collaborative novella "If the Stars Are Gods," written with Gordon Eklund, won him a Nebula award in 1974. His other books include* The Stars in Shroud *(Berkley),* Jupiter Project *(Nelson), and, in collaboration with Gordon Eklund,* If the Stars Are Gods *(Berkley) a novelization of their award-winning story. Upcoming projects include a novel* Timescape, *due from Pocket Books, another novel in collaboration with Gordon Eklund,* Find the Changeling, *due from Dell, and a novel in collaboration with William Rotsler,* Shiva Descending, *due from Ace. His story "In Alien Flesh" was in our* Eighth Annual Collection. *Benford lives in Irvine, California, where he works in the physics department of the University of California.*

GREGORY BENFORD
Redeemer

He had trouble finding it. The blue-white exhaust plume was a long trail of ionized hydrogen scratching a line across the black. It had been a lot harder to locate out here than Central said it would be.

Nagara came up on the *Redeemer* from behind, their blind side. They wouldn't have any sensors pointed aft. No point in it when you're on a one-way trip, not expecting visitors and haven't seen anybody for seventy-three years.

He boosted in with the fusion plant, cutting off the translight to avoid overshoot. The translight rig was delicate and still experimental, and it had already pushed him over seven light-years out from Earth. And anyway, when he got back to Earth there would be an accounting, and he would have to pay off from his profit anything he spent for overexpenditure of the translight hardware.

The ramscoop vessel ahead was running hot. It was a long cylinder, fluted fore and aft. The blue-white fire came boiling out of the aft throat, pushing *Redeemer* along at a little below a tenth of light velocity. Nagara's board buzzed. He cut in the null-mag system. The ship's skin visible outside fluxed into its superconducting state, gleaming like chrome. The readout winked and Nagara could see on the sim board his ship slipping like a silver fish through the webbing of magnetic field lines that protected *Redeemer*.

The field was mostly magnetic dipole. He cut through it and glided in parallel to the hot exhaust streamer. The stuff was spitting out a lot of UV and he had to change filters to see what he was doing. He came up along the aft section of the ship and matched velocities. The magnetic throat up ahead sucked in the interstellar hydrogen for the fusion motors. He stayed away from it. There was enough radiation up there to fry you for good.

Redeemer's midsection was rotating but the big clumsy-looking lock aft was stationary. Fine. No trouble clamping on.

The couplers seized *clang* and he used a waldo to manually open the lock. He would have to be fast now, fast and careful.

He pressed a code into the keyin plate on his chest to check it. It worked. The slick aura enveloped him, cutting out the ship's hum. Nagara nodded to himself.

He went quickly through the *Redeemer*'s lock. The pumps were still laboring when he spun the manual override to open the big inner hatch. He pulled himself through in the zero-g with one powerful motion, through the hatch and into a cramped suitup room. He cut in his magnetos and settled to the grid deck.

As Nagara crossed the deck a young man came in from a side hatchway. Nagara stopped and thumped off his protective shield. The man didn't see Nagara at first because he was looking the other way as he came through the hatchway, moving with easy agility. He was studying the subsystem monitoring panels on the far bulkhead. The status phosphors were red but they winked green as Nagara took three steps forward and grabbed the man's shoulder and spun him around. Nagara was grounded and the man was not. Nagara hit him once in the stomach and then shoved him against a bulkhead. The man gasped for breath. Nagara stepped back and put his hand into his coverall pocket and when it came out there was a dart pistol in it. The man's eyes didn't register anything at first and when they did he just stared at the pistol, getting his breath back, staring as though he couldn't believe either Nagara or the pistol was there.

"What's your name?" Nagara demanded in a clipped, efficient voice.

"What? I—"

"Your name. Quick."

"I . . . Zak."

"All right, Zak, now listen to me. I'm inside now and I'm not staying long. I don't care what you've been told. You do just what I say and nobody will blame you for it."

" . . . Nobody . . .?" Zak was still trying to unscramble his thoughts and he looked at the pistol again as though that would explain things.

"Zak, how many of you are manning this ship?"

"Manning? You mean crewing?" Confronted with a clear question, he forgot his confusion and frowned. "Three. We're doing our five-year stint. The Revealer and Jacob and me."

"Fine. Now, where's Jacob?"

"Asleep. This isn't his shift."

"Good." Nagara jerked a thumb over his shoulder. "Personnel quarters that way?"

"Uh, yes."

"Did an alarm go off through the whole ship, Zak?"

"No, just on the bridge."

"So it didn't wake up Jacob?"

"I . . . I suppose not."

"Fine, good. Now, where's the Revealer?"

So far it was working well. The best way to handle people who might give you trouble right away was to keep them busy telling you things before they had time to decide what they should be doing. And Zak plainly was used to taking orders.

"She's in the forest."

"Good. I have to see her. You lead the way, Zak."

Zak automatically half turned to kick down the hatchway he'd come in through and then the questions came out. "What—who *are* you? How—"

"I'm just visiting. We've got faster ways of moving now, Zak. I caught up with you."

"A faster ramscoop? But we—"

"Let's go, Zak." Nagara waved the dart gun and Zak looked at it a moment and then, still visibly struggling with his confusion, he kicked off and glided down the drift tube.

The forest was one half of a one hundred meter long cylinder, located near the middle of the ship and rotating to give one g. The forest was dense with pines and oak and tall bushes. A fine mist hung over the tree tops, obscuring the other half of the cylinder, a gardening zone that hung over their heads. Nagara hadn't been in a small cylinder like this for decades. He was used to seeing a distant green carpet overhead, so far away you couldn't make out individual trees, and shrouded by the cottonball clouds that accumulated at the zero-g along the cylinder axis. This whole place felt cramped to him.

Zak led him along footpaths and into a bamboo-walled clearing. The Revealer was sitting in lotus position in the middle of it. She was wearing a Flatlander robe and cowl just like Zak. He recognized it from a historical fax readout.

She was a plain-faced woman, wrinkled and wiry, her hands thick and calloused, the fingers stubby, the nails clipped off square. She didn't go rigid with surprise when Nagara came into view and that bothered him a little. She didn't look at the dart pistol more than once, to see what it was, and that surprised him, too.

"What's your name?" Nagara said as he walked into the bamboo-encased silence.

"I am the Revealer." A steady voice.

"No, I meant your name."

"That is my name."

"I mean—"

"I am the Revealer for this stage of our exodus."

Nagara watched as Zak stopped halfway between them and then stood uncertainly, looking back and forth.

"All right. When they freeze you back down, what'll they call you then?"

She smiled at this. "Michele Astanza."

Nagara didn't show anything in his face. He waved the pistol at her and said, "Get up."

"I prefer to sit."

"And I prefer you stand."

"Oh."

He watched both of them carefully. "Zak, I'm going to have to ask you to do a favor for me."

Zak glanced at the Revealer and she moved her head a few millimeters in a nod. He said, "Sure."

"This way." Nagara gestured with the pistol to the woman. "You lead."

The woman nodded to herself as if this confirmed something and got up and started down a footpath to the right, her steps so soft on the leafy path that Nagara could not hear them over the tinkling of a stream on the overhead side of the cylinder. Nagara followed her. The trees trapped the sound in here and made him jumpy.

He knew he was taking a calculated risk by not getting Jacob, too. But the odds against Jacob waking up in time were good and the whole point of doing it this way was to get in and out fast, exploit surprise. And he wasn't sure he could handle the three of them together. That was just it—he was doing this alone so he could collect the whole fee, and for that you had to take some extra risk. That was the way this thing worked. The forest gave onto some corn fields and then some wheat, all with UV phosphors netted above. The three of them skirted around the nets and through a hatchway in the big aft wall. Whenever Zak started to say anything Nagara cut him off with a wave of the pistol. Then Nagara saw that with some time to think Zak was adding some things up and the lines around his mouth were tightening, so Nagara asked him some questions about the ship's design. That worked. Zak rattled on about quintuple-redundant failsafe subsystems he'd been repairing until they were at the entrance to the freezing compartment.

It was bigger than Nagara had thought. He had done all the research he could, going through old faxes of *Redeemer*'s prelim designs, but plainly the Flatlanders had changed things in some later design phase.

One whole axial section of *Redeemer* was given over to the freeze-down vaults. It was at zero-g because otherwise the slow compression of tissues in the corpses would do permanent damage. They floated in their translucent compartments, like strange fish in endless rows of pale, blue-white aquariums.

The vaults were stored in a huge array, each layer a cylinder slightly larger than the one it enclosed, all aligned along the ship's axis. Each cylinder was two compartments thick, a corpse in every one, and the long cylinders extended into the distance until the chilly fog steaming off them blurred the perspective and the eye could not judge the size of the things. Despite himself Nagara was impressed. There were thousands upon thousands of Flatlanders in here, all dead and waiting for the promised land ahead, circling Tau Ceti. And with seventy-five more years of data to judge by, Nagara knew something this Revealer couldn't reveal: the failure rate when they thawed them out would be thirty percent.

They had come out on the center face of the bulwark separating the vault section from the farming part. Nagara stopped them and studied the front face of the vault array, which spread away from them radially like an immense spider web. He reviewed the old plans in his head. The axis of the whole thing was a tube a meter wide, the same translucent organiform. Liquid nitrogen flowed in the hollow walls of the array and the phosphor light was pale and watery.

"That's the DNA storage," Nagara said, pointing at the axial tube.

"What?" Zak said. "Yes, it is."

"Take them out."

"What?"

"They're in failsafe self-refrigerated canisters, aren't they?"

"Yes."

"That's fine." Nagara turned to the Revealer. "You've got the working combinations, don't you?"

She had been silent for some time. She looked at him steadily and said, "I do."

"Let's have them."

"Why should I give them?"

"I think you know what's going on."

"Not really."

He knew she was playing some game but he couldn't see why. "You're carrying DNA material for over ten thousand people. Old genotypes, undamaged. It wasn't so rare when you collected it seventy-five years ago but it is now. I want it."

"It is for our colony."

"You've got enough corpses here."

"We need genetic diversity."

"The System needs it more than you. There's been a war. A lot of radiation damage."

"Who won?"

"Us. The outskirters."

"That means nothing to me."

"We're the environments in orbit around the sun, not sucking up to Earth. We knew what was going on. We're mostly in Bernal spheres. We got the jump on—"

"You've wrecked each other genetically, haven't you? That was always the trouble with your damned cities. No place to dig a hole and hide."

Nagara shrugged. He was watching Zak. From the man's face Nagara could tell he was getting to be more insulted than angry—outraged at somebody walking in and stealing their future. And from the way his leg muscles were tensing against a foothold Nagara guessed Zak was also getting more insulted than scared, which was trouble for sure. It was a lot better if you dealt with a man who cared more about the long odds against a dart gun at this range, than about some principle. Nagara knew he couldn't count on Zak ignoring all the Flatlander nonsense the Revealer and others had pumped into him.

They hung there in zero-g, nobody moving in the wan light, the only sound a gurgling of liquid nitrogen. The Revealer was saying something and there was another thing bothering Nagara, some sound, but he ignored it.

"How did the planetary enclaves hold out?" the woman was asking. "I had many friends—"

"They're gone."

Something came into the woman's face. "You've lost man's *birthright?*"

"They sided with the—"

"Abandoned the planets altogether? Made them unfit to *live* on? All for your awful *cities*—" and she made a funny jerky motion with her right hand.

That was it. When she started moving that way Nagara saw it had to be a signal and he jumped to the left. He didn't take time to place his boots right and so he picked up some spin but the important thing was to get away from that spot fast. He heard a *chuung* off to the right and a dart smacking into the bulkhead and when he turned his head to the right and up behind him a burly man with black hair and the same Flatlander robes and a dart gun was coming at him on a glide.

Nagara had started twisting his shoulder when he leaped and now the differential angular momentum was bringing his shooting arm around. Jacob was already aiming again. Nagara took the extra second to make his shot and allow for the relative motions. His dart gun puffed and Nagara saw it take Jacob in the chest, just right. The man's face went white and he reached down to pull the dart out but by that time the nerve inhibitor had reached the heart and abruptly Jacob stopped plucking at the dart and his fingers went slack and the body drifted on in the chilly air, smacking into a vault door and coming to rest.

Nagara wrenched around to cover the other two. Zak was coming at him. Nagara leaped away, braked. He turned and Zak had come to rest against the translucent organiform, waiting.

"That's a lesson," Nagara said evenly. "Here's another."

He touched the key in on his chest and his force screen flickered on around him, making him look metallic. He turned it off in time to hear the hollow boom that came rolling through the ship like a giant's shout.

"That's a sample. A shaped charge. My ship set it off two hundred meters from Redeemer. The next one's keyed to go on impact with your skin. You'll lose pressure too fast to do anything about it. My force field comes on when the charge goes, so it won't hurt me."

"We've never seen such a field," the woman said unsteadily.

"Outskirter invention. That's why we won."

He didn't bother watching Zak. He looked at the woman as she clasped her thick worker's hands together and began to realize what choices were left. When she was done with that she murmured, "Zak, take out the canisters."

The woman sagged against a strut. Her robes clung to her and made her look gaunt and old.

"You're not giving us a chance, are you?" she said.

"You've got a lot of corpses here. You'll have a big colony out at Tau Ceti." Nagara was watching Zak maneuver the canisters onto a mobile carrier. The young man was going to be all right now, he could tell that. There was the look of weary defeat about him.

"We need the genotypes for insurance. In a strange ecology there will be genetic drift."

"The System has worse problems right now."

"With Earth dead you people in the artificial worlds are *finished*," she said savagely, a spark returning. "That's why we left. We could see it coming."

Nagara wondered if they'd have left at all if they'd known a faster than light drive would come along. But no, it wouldn't have made any difference. The translight transition cost too much and only worked for small ships. He narrowed his eyes and made a smile without humor.

"I know quite well why you left. A bunch of scum-lovers. Purists. Said Earth was just as bad as the cylinder cities, all artificial, all controlled. Yeah, I know. You flatties sold off everything you had and built *this*—" His voice became bitter. "Ransacked a fortune—*my* fortune."

For once she looked genuinely curious, uncalculating. "Yours?"

He flicked a glance at her and then back at Zak. "Yeah. I would've inherited some of your billions you made out of those smelting patents."

"You—"

"I'm one of your great-grandsons."

Her face changed. "No."

"It's true. Stuffing the money into this clunker made all your descendants have to bust ass for a living. And it's not so easy these days."

"I . . . didn't . . ."

He waved her into silence. "I knew you were one of the mainstays, one of the rich Flatlanders. The family talked about it a lot. We're not doing so well now. Not as well as you did, not by a thousandth. I thought that would mean you'd get to sleep right through, wake up at Tau Ceti. Instead"—he laughed—"they've got you standing watch."

"Someone has to be the Revealer of the word, grandson."

"Great-grandson. Revealer? If you'd 'revealed' a little common sense to that kid over there, he would've been alert and I wouldn't be in here."

She frowned and watched Zak, who was awkwardly shifting the squat modular canisters stenciled GENETIC BANK. MAX SECURITY. "We are not military types."

Nagara grinned. "Right. I was looking through the family records and I thought up this job. I figured you for an easy setup. A max of three or four on duty, considering the size of the life-support systems and redundancies. So I got the venture capital together for time in a translight and here I am."

"We're not your kind. Why can't you give us a chance, grandson?"

"I'm a businessman."

She had a dry, rasping laugh. "A few centuries ago everybody thought space colonies would be the final answer. Get off the stinking old Earth and everything's solved. Athens in the sky. But look at you—a paid assassin. A 'businessman.' You're no grandson of *mine*.''

"Old ideas." He watched Zak.

"Don't you see it? The colony environments aren't a social advance. You need discipline to keep life-support systems from springing a leak or poisoning you. Communication and travel have to be regulated for simple safety. So you don't get democracies, you get strong men. And then they turned on *us*—on Earth.''

"You were out of date," he said casually, not paying much attention.

"Do you ever read any history?"

"No." He knew this was part of her spiel—he'd seen it on a fax from a century ago—but he let her go on to keep her occupied. Talkers never acted when they could talk.

"They turned Earth into a handy preserve. The Berbers and Normans had it the same way a thousand years ago. They were seafarers. They depopulated Europe's coastline by raids, taking what or who they wanted. You did the same to us, from orbit, using solar lasers. But to—"

"Enough," Nagara said. He checked the long bore of the axial tube. It was empty. Zak had the stuff secured on the carrier. There wasn't any point in staying here any longer than necessary.

"Let's go," he said.

"One more thing," the woman said.

"What?"

"We went peacefully, I want you to remember that. We have no defenses."

"Yeah," Nagara said impatiently.

"But we have huge energies at our disposal. The scoop fields funnel an enormous flux of relativistic particles. We could've temporarily altered the magnetic multipolar fields and burned your sort to death."

"But you didn't."

"No, we didn't. But remember that."

Nagara shrugged. Zak was floating by the carrier ready to take orders, looking tired. The kid had been easy to take, too easy for him to take any pride in doing it. Nagara liked an even match. He didn't even mind losing if it was to somebody he could respect. Zak wasn't in that league, though.

"Let's go," he said.

The loading took time but he covered Zak on every step and there were no problems. When he cast off from *Redeemer* he looked around by reflex for a planet to sight on, relaxing now, and it struck him that he was more alone than he had ever been, the stars scattered like oily jewels on velvet were the nearest destination he could have. That woman in *Re-deemer* had lived with this for years. He looked at the endless long night out here, felt it as a shadow that passed through his mind, and then he punched in instructions and *Redeemer* dropped away, its blue-white arc a fuzzy blade that cut the darkness, and he slipped with a hollow clapping sound into translight.

He was three hours from his dropout point when one of the canisters strapped down behind the pilot's couch gave a warning buzz from thermal overload. It popped open.

Nagara twisted around and fumbled with the latches. He could pull the top two access drawers a little way out and when he did he saw that inside there was a store of medical supplies. Boxes and tubes and fluid cubes. Cheap stuff. No DNA manifolds.

Nagara sat and stared at the complete blankness outside. *We could've temporarily altered the magnetic multipolar fields and burned your sort to death*, she had said. *Remember that.*

If he went back she would be ready. They could rig some kind of aft sensor and focus the ramscoop fields on him when he came tunneling in through them. Fry him good.

They must have planned it all from the first. Something about it, something about the way she'd looked, told him it had been the old woman's idea.

The risky part of it had been the business with Jacob. That didn't make sense. But maybe she'd known Jacob would try something and since she couldn't do anything about it she used it. Used it to relax him, make him think the touchy part of the job was done so that he didn't think to check inside the stenciled canisters.

He looked at the medical supplies. Seventy-three years ago the woman had known they couldn't protect themselves from what they didn't know, ships that hadn't been invented yet. So on her five-year watch she had arranged a dodge that would work even if some System ship caught up to them. Now the Flatlanders knew what to defend against.

He sat and looked out at the blankness and thought about that.

When he popped out into System space the A47 sphere was hanging up to the left at precisely the relative coordinates and distance he'd left it.

A47 was big and inside there were three men waiting to divide up and classify and market the genotypes and when he told them what was in the canisters it would all be over, his money gone and theirs and no hope of his getting a stake again. And maybe worse than that. Maybe a lot worse.

He squinted at A47 as he came in for rendezvous. It looked different. Some of the third quadrant damage from the war wasn't repaired yet. The skin that had gleamed once was smudged now and twisted gray girders stuck out of the ports. It looked pretty beat up. It was the best high-tech fortress they had and A47 had made the whole difference in the war. It broke the African shield by itself. But now it didn't look like so much. All the dots of light orbiting in the distance were pretty nearly the same or worse and now they were all that was left in the system.

Nagara turned his ship about to vector on the landing bay, listening to the rumble as the engines cut in. The console phosphors rippled blue, green, yellow as Central reffed him.

This next part was going to be pretty bad. Damned bad. And out there his great-grandmother was on the way still, somebody he could respect now, and for the first time he thought the Flatlanders probably were going to make it. In the darkness of the cabin something about the thought made him smile.

How many times have you said to yourself, "If only I'd known better—if only I could go back and tell myself not to do that!" Well, suppose you could do precisely that: when would you choose to visit yourself . . . and what would you say? This is the intriguing premise of the following story by James P. Girard, and under his adroit hand it becomes a moving and deeply compassionate tale of communication across gulfs of time . . . and of a strange but very real sacrifice.

James P. Girard is one of the most promising of the new writers who have come on the scene at the end of the seventies, and has appeared in F&SF, Penthouse, *and* New Dimensions. *His story "September Song" appeared in our* Eighth Annual Collection. *Girard lives in Newton, Kansas.*

JAMES P. GIRARD
In Trophonius's Cave

The wire slipped off again, stinging the back of Max Kufus's hand, and he jerked backward with a grunt and then said, "Shit!" and sat back heavily on the shed's dirt floor, catching himself on one hand. He wiped the other across his forehead, then reached out absent-mindedly for the bottle standing on the busted chair against the wall, and took a swallow.

His hand was slippery with sweat, where he'd wiped his forehead, and he took care not to drop the bottle. He'd left one of the heavy wooden doors open, for light as well as air, but it was still dark and close in the shed. When he'd begun, a little after noon, there'd been a wind, and clouds had been racing overhead, but it was still now, and he knew that the clouds had bunched up overhead, even without seeing them.

He stared at the bicycle wheel a minute, thinking of saying the hell with it, then reminded himself of how he'd feel tomorrow, when he'd be completely sober, if he let himself give up. It had been bad enough when he'd busted it, what with Dougie going around all day trying to pretend it didn't really matter to him, though he'd finally managed to put the guilt out of his mind—something he'd had a lot of practice at over the years. He sighed and put it away again, letting himself remember instead the moments he'd already spent enjoying Dougie's reaction when he found the spokes repaired, his own rare moment of self-congratulation. Over the years he'd come to know which disappointments hurt the most; this would be one, if he let it. He rocked forward onto his feet again, nearly

119

losing his balance, and come to rest in a squat, fumbling at the bent spoke.

The other one had been fairly easy because the little metal socket had still been in the rim and there'd been enough wire to work with. So he'd been able to thread it and then nip the end enough to keep the wire from pulling back out. It looked like it ought to be soldered or something; it probably wasn't the way they'd do it at a bike shop. But it looked like the wheel would ride straight enough for the time being, especially if he could fix the other busted spoke. Maybe by the time it came loose again, he'd be able to figure out something better, or he'd have enough money to get it done right or to get a new wheel or even a new bike for the kid. He smiled and took another swallow of whiskey; that was on old joke.

The problem with the remaining spoke was that the socket had pulled out along with the spoke and gotten lost, leaving only the hole in the rim—too much hole and not enough wire, so that no matter how he contrived to twist the end, it slipped out again. What he really needed was something to replace the socket with.

He laid the wheel down on its axle and rose stiffly to his feet, then picked his way gingerly through old paint buckets and odd lengths of wood, laid edgewise, getting close enough to the shelf holding the nail and screw jars to reach over and lift out the one he wanted, holding two fingers inside the dusty rim. He carried it to the chair and poured out an assortment of oddball bits of metal beside the whiskey bottle.

He frowned and pushed the stuff around with one finger, hunched over to peer at it in the half-light, but nothing suggested itself. There were some little L-shaped braces he'd once used to make a bookshelf for Georgette, a few rusty springs, some old brackets from the window-shades that had once hung in the kitchen, where the window now was unadorned, and a lot of other odd metal things whose uses were long lost to memory. He sighed and scooped the stuff back into the jar, along with dust from the chair, then left the jar sitting where it was and turned back to the bicycle wheel, beginning to feel defeated.

He had always been good at figuring things out, at thinking of ways to do things that most people wouldn't have thought of. One year in school, they'd put him in a special class with all the gifted kids. But he hadn't been like them; he hadn't cared enough about it, and so he hadn't made good grades. Anyway, he'd known, as everyone else had, that he was only going to wind up working at the processing plant, like his old man. Being able to figure out different ways of doing things didn't count for much there.

If he could have figured out how to kick booze, that would have been worth something to him at one time, but it had had him stumped, just like this damned bicycle wheel. He shrugged and took another drink.

Suppose his bigself showed up right now and told him to go on the wagon, even gave him some good reason for doing so? It was a fantasy he'd enjoyed for a while after the bigselves started coming around, as if it might somehow be a way out, although it was mostly little kids who got visited. Anyway, it hadn't taken him long to reason it out: If his bigself came back with that kind of advice, it would mean he hadn't kicked the habit, up ahead in the future, and was trying to go back and change things. And why should he take the advice from himself, 30 years older, that he wouldn't take from himself now? The thing to do would be to go back to when he was 17, when he'd started drinking, and give himself a good kick in the ass—except that there hadn't been any visits until two years ago, that anybody knew about. So it probably wasn't possible.

He stared at the far corner of the shed, not seeing it, thinking that a kick in the ass probably wouldn't be necessary; All he'd have to do would be to show himself where he was going to end up. You know what they call me? he'd say. Old Max, the alky, that's you, 30 years ahead. He remembered vividly the first time he'd heard it, down at the gas station when he was filling the car, from somebody talking in a normal tone of voice, not bothering to whisper, as if it wouldn't matter to him.

He shook his head sharply and grabbed the wheel, putting that too out of his mind. He spread his feet a bit, to brace himself, and got a better grip on the pliers. It looked like this job was going to boil down to brute force more than anything else—and strength had never been something he was long on.

Dougie Kufus walked home as slowly as he could, feeling the gray sky like a weight on the top of his head, pushing him into the earth. He didn't want to go home, but there was nowhere else he wanted to go either—especially not back to the schoolground, where the other kids were. And he couldn't just stand still; it'd get dark and some grown-up would come around and make him go home anyway. So he walked slowly, as if each step were the last.

Already he was thinking how it was going to be tomorrow in school—and not just tomorrow, but the whole rest of the seventh grade. He'd never in a million years figured on Jeff getting a visit from his bigself. They'd talked about it sometimes, imagining, but he'd always thought of it as one of those things that just happened to the kids on the other side of town, like stereoviewers and kiddicomputers and other expensive things. But now it was as if Jeff was one of those other kids, as if he'd changed somehow. What if all the other kids got visited, all over town, and he was the only one left? Suddenly he felt sure that was how it was going to be, that that was the way it was supposed to be for someone like him, Old Max's kid, the drunk's kid. Really, when he thought about it, Jeff had always been different from him: he had a mother, for one thing, and his father didn't drink much, even though he didn't work much either, and he was kind of mean; at least, he didn't get drunk all over town, so that the police had to bring him home sometimes, like Pop.

He kicked a rock hard, wanting it to smash against something, but it just skipped out into the street and bounced a couple of times and stopped. Maybe Jeff had just been fooling him all the time, pretending to be his friend; maybe everybody had been doing that, pretending he was just like them when really everybody knew that he was the only one different. He stopped for a moment, feeling desolate, on the verge of believing it, then shrugged and started walking again, thinking: Maybe it's better to be that way. But it didn't make him feel any better.

When he got home the door was standing open even though it looked like it was going to rain, and he half expected to find Pop passed out on the couch or in the bedroom, but he wasn't anywhere around. Dougie went into the kitchen, feeling vaguely hungry, but all he could find was a package of the chipped beef Pop made gravy with sometimes. He tore it open and ate the thin slices one at a time, taking little bites to make it last longer, then went into the living room and flicked on the TV, throwing himself down on the armchair, sitting sideways against the sag so he'd be more or less upright.

The news was on, which he was supposed to watch for social studies, but he couldn't keep his mind on it. He wondered what Jeff's bigself had said. He hadn't asked because it was usually a secret and it wasn't polite to ask, though he'd wanted to. Jeff had told him that it happened while he was alone, while his mom and dad were out partying the night before. Everyone said that's how it always was—that the bigselves always showed up when you were by yourself because they couldn't stay very long, for some reason, and they didn't want to be interrupted. Jeff said his bigself had said he'd remembered that night because it was his parents' anniversary and they'd decided he was old enough to stay home by himself without a sitter. Jeff had said that was funny because they'd let him stay by himself a couple of times before, but he guessed his bigself must have forgotten about that.

It had never really occurred to Dougie before that the bigselves would have to remember when to show up, but it made sense, so they didn't have to waste time finding their littleselves or having to talk to a bunch of other people. He tried to think of when he'd go back and visit himself if he was a bigself now. It could be just about any night, he guessed, since he never knew whether Pop was going to be around or not. He frowned. If he had to figure out a time to visit himself, even just last week, he couldn't do it for sure. He was by himself a lot, but he wasn't sure exactly which days it had been. He tried to think back further, to some memorable time when he'd been all alone, but he couldn't remember the exact date of any particular time.

He leaned forward in the chair. That meant his bigself couldn't have visited him, up to now, because, if he couldn't remember a time for a visit, even last week, how was his bigself going to remember a time, 30 years from now?

He got up and walked distractedly into the kitchen, not with any purpose, just walking and thinking. Suppose he made a time for his bigself to visit—a time and a place he'd be sure to remember even if he had to scratch it on his skin. He stopped, his eyes growing suddenly wide. Whenever he did, it might be the time his bigself came, if he was ever going to come, and he could do it right now, tonight.

He put one thumb in his mouth and chewed at the nail, making a fist. It couldn't be here; Pop might show up anytime. He stared at the graying kitchen window, not seeing it, running down possibilities in his mind, then suddenly thought of the place where he and Jeff had made a hideout once, over on the far side of town, out past the houses along the river. But it was a long way away—a long way to ride a bike, let alone walk. He winced, remembering what had happened to the bike, and then realized for the first time that he was staring out the kitchen window at the shed, where the bike was, and he noticed that the big door was open and there was a light on inside.

He stood still for a moment, his lips pursed, wondering what to do about it. If he just slipped out the front door, he could be gone before Pop even knew he'd come home; on the other hand, Pop might be able to get the old car started. He probably wouldn't be willing to take Dougie where he really wanted to go, but he could tell Pop he had to go downtown for something, and that would get him halfway; he could figure it out from there.

He nodded to himself abruptly and headed out the back door and across the yard to the shed.

Pop was slumped against one wall, asleep, a pair of pliers in his hand and an empty whisky bottle lying beside him. Dougie's bike was sitting upside down, balanced on the seat and handlebars, and the back wheel was off, lying at an angle in front of Pop. The tire and the deflated tube were hanging on the end of a shelf just above the busted chair.

Dougie stepped on into the shed, keeping quiet for the moment, and examined the wheel. One of the busted spokes looked like it had been fixed, but one was still disconnected. He licked his lips, then grabbed the wheel and slid it into the prongs of the bike frame, giving it a slight spin. It still wobbled from side to side but not nearly as badly as before, the one spoke seemed to make a lot of difference. It looked like it would turn, at least, without rubbing against the frame. He glanced around at the scattered parts. He'd never put a bike tire on from scratch, but he'd seen it done. He reached down and eased the pliers out of Pop's hand.

It was nearly dark outside by the time he finished, and it was growing windy again. Getting the tire onto the rim had had him baffled for a while until he'd figured out how to use a screwdriver to hold it down in one place while he forced it in the rest of the way around with the plier handle. Then he'd had to work on the axle nuts a long time to get the wheel centered enough not to rub. And when that was done, he'd realized that the disconnected spoke, which he'd tried to bend back out of the way, was going to come loose eventually and catch on the frame. So he'd gripped it with the pliers, down near the hub, and twisted it back and forth until it broke off. That left nothing but airing the tire, and he'd have to walk it down to the gas station to do that.

As he was wheeling it out, he glanced back at Pop and thought for a second that he ought to wake him up and make him go in the house and get in bed, but he didn't want to have to explain what he was up to or make up something. So he went on, closing the door behind him, in case it started raining.

Something loud woke Max up, and he struggled briefly, not recognizing the hot, dark place he awoke in, thinking it might be a jail cell. But then lightning struck again outside; thunder rattled the shed's roof, showing him where he was and reminding him of what he had been doing.

But the bike was gone, and the wheel with it—even the tire and tube. He licked his lips and looked around for the whisky bottle, found it lying empty beside the chair. The inside of his mouth was dry, and he needed something for it, but the rest of him was wet; sweat made his body itch all over.

He rose clumsily to all fours, then to his feet, and looked at his watch but couldn't read it in the dark. He pushed through the heavy door, surprised to find a cool wind blowing outside, and twisted his wrist to catch the little light there was. It was only 7:20, though it looked dark enough to be 9 or 10 because of the clouds packed overhead. The scraggly backyard was dry and dust-patched. So it hadn't rained yet. He stretched his neck and scratched it, feeling the sweat drying quickly in the wind.

He supposed Dougie had come and found the bike half-fixed and had gone ahead and put it together and then gone for a ride. That made Max feel good, not only because he'd apparently fixed the bike enough to make it ridable but also because Dougie had been able to put it together by himself. Evidence that Dougie could take care of himself always made Max feel a little less guilty about things.

In the kitchen he checked the icebox for something to eat or drink but found neither. He thought about going after a bottle, but he wasn't sure the car would start, and it looked like it was going to rain like hell anytime. Anyway, he didn't have to have it, no matter what people thought.

He went into the living room, where the TV was on, and threw himself down on the sofa without bothering to turn on any lights. There was a nice breeze coming in the window at the far end of the room, and he really felt, as he did now and then, that he could get along without booze without too much effort. It he didn't go after a bottle the rest of the evening, then pretty soon it would be too late, and he'd have to wait until morning, and then it would be broad daylight, and he might be able to make himself go the whole day without a drink, and what he could do for one day he could do for one more, and so on, and he might never take another drink. He propped his hands behind his head, feeling generally optimistic about himself, although he knew that this was only a game he played with himself from time to time. He still had a few hours before the liquor stores closed, and he might fall asleep and spend the whole night without another drink and that would be a plus, of sorts—though there was no real chance that he'd be able to make it through the day tomorrow or that he'd even think about doing so, once it was morning. But it was nice to halfway believe in the possibility for a while, when it didn't seem threatening, and he was feeling good anyway about Dougie's bike.

Thinking of that, he twisted his neck slightly and looked toward the front door, where he expected to see Dougie momentarily. He was pretty sure the kid had sense enough to come in out of the rain, unlike his old man.

He frowned, realizing for the first time that Dougie hadn't bothered to wake him up and make him go to bed, as he usually did. He shrugged. The kid had probably been excited about his bike and in a hurry to take a ride before it got too dark. It wasn't like him to leave the TV on, either, come to think of it.

Max looked at the TV again, thinking for a moment it was a scene from a movie he'd seen somewhere, but then realizing it was one of the new shows, he wondered momentarily whether it might be one of the R-rated ones they were showing now but then remembered they were only showing them after 9 P.M. The window lightened briefly and thunder banged outside, and he frowned again, hoping Dougie would get back soon.

The tire still wobbled enough to make him concentrate on keeping his balance, but after a couple of blocks he had the hang of it, and he began to feel good. There was a little bit of breeze coming up behind him now, drying the sweat he'd worked up in the shed and walking the bike to the gas station, and he was happy to be riding again, going as fast as he dared down the broad street running between bars and used-car lots toward the nice side of town, where streetlamps were just beginning to glow faintly ahead of him, reminding him of why he was taking the ride. As he thought of it, his stomach gave a quick jerk from excitement. He wondered if his bigself might even be waiting for him when he got there, and he rose a little on the pedals, sending the bike shooting on ahead a little faster.

It wasn't until he'd had to turn off the big road into the darker neighborhood streets leading toward the river that he began to feel less confident. What if his bigself didn't show up? Would it mean he wasn't coming? Or would it just mean that he'd have to remember the time and place until he was the bigself, so he could go back? He sat back on the seat, noticing that his legs were growing tired, and let the bike coast a little, just pedaling every now and then when he had to swing out to pass a parked car. There was no traffic here, and the houses blocked the wind that had been blowing down the big boulevard. So there was no sound except his breathing and the crunch of his tires over occasional pebbles, and now and then an unseen dog in some backyard complaining of his passage.

If he did come back and visit himself when he got to be a bigself, then wouldn't he remember being visited when he was a littleself? He remembered now that they'd talked about that in science class one day—it had something to do with what they called a paradox—but he couldn't remember now what the teacher had said about it, and he wished he could. Because if the only bigselves who went back were the ones who remembered being visited, then that's how they'd remember the time and place—it wouldn't take any special remembering, like he was planning on.

But if it was just the bigselves who remembered being visited . . . why should they bother to go back? In that case, it wouldn't change anything. But if they didn't go back, how could they remember being visited? So it had to be the ones who didn't remember being visited, who wanted to change things by going back. But did that mean that all the kids who were being visited now wouldn't bother to go back when they got to be bigselves? Because, really, if things were changed, then by the time they got to be bigselves, they'd be different bigselves from the ones who visited them in the first place . . .

He shook his head, feeling slightly nauseous. It just kept going around and around in his mind, like one of those dreams that kept repeating and waking you up all night long, so that it seemed like you never got any sleep.

The important thing, he thought, forcing himself to grab onto the thought, was that things had to change—that's what it was all about; that's why the bigselves started coming in the first place, to make things change. So, if his bigself showed up tonight, that would be great. But if he didn't, it would just mean that Dougie would have to plan on coming back himself eventually and that he'd have this time and place to do it.

He leaned forward again, pedaling steadily, anxious now to get beyond the neat, dark houses that made him feel small and alone. He had been this way in daylight, and he knew kids who lived in this part of town, but nothing looked familiar in the dark. He saw faces at the bright windows now and then and realized that none of them could see him passing by outside, and it made him feel as if he were somehow beyond their reach, for good or ill, as if he were a ghost.

By the time he reached the gravel stretch leading to the riverbank, he was tired and winded and confused and even a little scared; it was darker out beyond the houses, and there was a strong wind behind him now, seeming to stand between him and the town, as if he couldn't turn back, and the insect sounds made it seem like a long way from anywhere.

The wobbly tire made it too hard to fight the bike through the gravel. So he got off and pushed it, breathing hard, and it took him a while to find the path in the darkness. When he did, it seemed as if the bank were steeper than he remembered, so that it was scary going down toward the narrow level path just above the dark water, and then the place where the big concrete pipe ran out of the earth—their old hideout—looked like a black pit, so that he stood for a moment working up his courage, remembering for the first time tales of snakes and wild animals.

When he did finally enter, leaving his bike on the path, he was surprised to find himself walking in a narrow stream of water. It had never really occurred to him before to wonder what the pipe was for; he had sort of vaguely supposed it was to keep the river from overflowing by taking in water when it rose that high. Now it occurred to him that there might be some danger in hanging around in it, although he planned to stick close to the end, and he figured he could get out quick enough if he had to.

Once he got a few feet inside, it didn't seem so dark anymore, thanks to the gray light filtering in from the opening. It was hot, though, and none of the wind seemed to get in. He began to itch and jerk after a few minutes, but he couldn't tell if it was from nighttime insects or sweat. After some experimentation he found a way to half sit and half lie with his knees arched over the stream, his back against one slope of the pipe.

Once he had gotten used to the heat and the darkness, the silence began to bother him, so that he kept still and listened hard for outside noises. But then he began to think he heard faint sounds from further inside the pipe, and that worried him a lot until he decided it must just be the echoes of his own small sounds, and he even sang a couple of songs, in a low voice, to prove it to himself but stopped that when the echo began to seem kind of scary.

Finally, he decided to concentrate on listening for the sound of footsteps from outside, but he listened for a long time and nothing happened—although now and then there was a flash of light which might have been distant lightning or passing headlights on the road above—and he grew bored and even began to feel a little silly about the whole thing.

He thought of Pop and felt guilty for having left him on the floor of the shed, and he thought maybe he'd better be starting back soon because, anyway, he was beginning to feel kind of sleepy and the pipe was uncomfortable. But it was going to be an awful long ride back, and he thought he'd better rest awhile before he started. So he laid his head back against the arching concrete and closed his eyes for a moment.

He was cold and wet, and when he woke up he thought at first he might have peed on himself in his sleep, but then he felt the wind from the window and saw the strip of water running clear from the window to the couch, and he shivered and sat up, feeling dizzy. There was a kind of flapping light from somewhere, making it hard to focus on things, and it took him a moment to realize it came from the TV, where a test pattern was rolling over and over.

He got up and turned it off, feeling stiff and sore, then went and closed the window. He was on his way down the hall to his bedroom when he remembered about Dougie, and so he looked in the kid's room just to make sure, but he couldn't tell whether there was anyone in the bed or not, and so he turned on the hall light, which showed him clearly that the bed was empty.

Confused, he went on to his own bedroom, half expecting to find him there, but it was empty too. He sat down on the edge of his bed and began untying one shoe, as if he might just go ahead and go to sleep, but then he realized that he couldn't do that; the kid might be in some kind of trouble.

That thought woke him up. Where could Dougie be, in the middle of the night? He turned on the bedroom light and checked his watch, then shook his head, perplexed. It was after 1 A.M., and it looked like it must have been raining like hell outside. He stood up uncertainly and began to wander through the rest of the little house, thinking Dougie might be there somewhere, after all, but he wasn't in the kitchen or the bathroom, and that was it.

Max stood in the middle of the dark kitchen and licked his lips, wishing to hell he had a bottle. What could have happened? Maybe the spoke busted again, and the kid was out in the middle of nowhere, walking his bike home. Or maybe he'd just had to hole up somewhere for a long time because of the rain. He nodded, trying to decide that that must be it. But the time worried him. It was awful goddamn late; he couldn't quite convince himself that Dougie wouldn't have tried to make it home before now, rain or no rain.

He was beginning to feel a little scared, and he decided he'd better do what he could, which was get in the car and take a swing around the area. He patted his pants pocket, out of habit, to make sure the keys were there and then went out the back door to where the car was parked beside the shed.

He'd left the window open, as usual, and the whole front seat was soaked. So he went back in the house and hunted up an old ragged army blanket to put over it. But then when he tried to start the car, it didn't even turn over. There was just a kind of clicking sound, and then even that died away.

He sat for a moment in the dark front seat, feeling helpless. As if on cue, it started raining again, big drops coming nearly straight down that struck the window ledge and splattered his face, making him blink. He put his face in his hands and then lifted his eyes slowly to look over his fingertips at the dark windshield, where water ran in wavy lines. He felt certain now that something very bad had happened to Dougie while he had slept on the sofa, oblivious to a storm that splashed water clear across the living room. Maybe there'd been a flood or a tornado; how would he have known?

He fought his way out of the car, filled with the old ache of anger at himself, as if it were a pain that was with him always, but that he only noticed when he was most vulnerable. He went back into the kitchen, not bothering to close the door behind him, and then to the front hall, where he searched in vain for his raincoat, finally settling instead for an old brown leather jacket. He started out the front door, then turned back to the closet and rummaged again for a moment, coming up at last with a wadded white sailor's cap which he jammed onto his head, letting the brim sag all around. Thus equipped, he plunged out the door and into the rain, heading toward the gas station at the corner and the big boulevard that led downtown.

"Dougie? Hey, Dougie, wake up."

He was lost for a moment, forgetting where he had been, but then it came back to him and he sat up straight, straining to see in the darkness. He looked first at the gray circle of the pipe's end, but then realized the voice had come from the other direction. Looking that way, open-mouthed, he could barely make out the form of someone sitting a few feet further into the pipe's interior.

"Don't be scared, Dougie. I come here on purpose, to tell you something."

He nodded, unable for the moment to say anything. He noticed that it was colder and that his legs were wet, and he thought the water must have risen while he slept.

"You gotta get out of here, Dougie. It ain't safe. Don't you know this is a drainage pipe? All that rainwater's gonna be rushin' down here before you know it."

The voice sounded older than he'd expected. He twisted his head a little to one side, but there was no way he could make out the face.

"Are you my bigself?" he blurted suddenly, surprising himself.

There was a silence, and then the voice said "Uhh . . . yeah. Yeah, that's right. I figured you knew that already. That's why you came here, isn't it? Course it is. Since I'm you, I knew that already, you see?"

Dougie caught a faint, familiar smell and frowned.

"Are you drinking whisky?" he asked.

There was another brief silence.

"Uhh . . . well, I did have a drink before I come down here, Dougie. Lots of folks have a drink now and then and it don't mean nothin'. I mean, don't let it worry you none, that you're gonna have a drink every now and then, like anyone else, when you get to be big."

Dougie nodded, feeling some of his initial elation fade.

"You're not rich, are you?" he asked.

His bigself chuckled.

"No, not exactly. No, I don't think you could say I was rich." His voice changed suddenly, the way Pop's did sometimes when he tried to make himself be serious. "But, now, that don't mean I ain't happy, does it? You don't have to be rich to be happy with your life, Dougie. I mean . . ." But then he seemed to run down, as if he couldn't think of anything more to say about it.

"You're just like Pop," Dougie said, and it was an accusation.

This time the silence went on a little longer. When the bigself spoke again, his voice had softened, become matter-of-fact.

"Yeah, you're right, Dougie. I guess that's what I really come to tell you, besides getting out of this pipe. I'm an alky, just like your old man . . . just like our old man . . . and that means you're an alky, too, up ahead. But, see, things can change. That's why us bigselves come back, ain't it? Here's the thing, Dougie: You got this sickness in you, just like your old man, that makes you an alcoholic if you let it. It's genetic . . . inherited . . . they found that out for sure up ahead. And the only way you can ever lick it is just never to start, never to take that first drink. 'Cause once you do, it's got you. You see what I mean? That's what I come to tell, and it's up to you to take it or leave it. I don't know what you can make out of your life—I don't say you're gonna get rich if you don't drink—but I do know you can keep from ending up like me, for sure. That's entirely up to you."

Dougie nodded, feeling a little ashamed, and beginning to feel intensely grateful to his bigself, who had somehow managed to come back and tell him this.

"How . . . ?" he started to ask, but the bigself cut him off.

"Listen, Dougie, I wasn't kiddin' about that rainwater. You gotta clear out of here, for sure, the sooner the better."

Dougie half stood, getting control of his stiff legs on the slanting pipe and trying to keep his feet out of the water. He started to turn away, toward the outside, but then looked back.

"What about you?" he asked.

It looked as though the bigself shrugged.

"Don't sweat it. They're gonna jerk me back anytime now. I'm gonna be just fine." There was a sharp clinking sound, and Dougie realized that the bigself had picked up a bottle. He turned again toward the opening.

"Say, Dougie," the bigself said. "One more thing, I just happened to remember. You don't know it, but your old man's out lookin' for you tonight. He got worried when he woke up and you weren't around anywhere. And the thing is, if you don't go find him and get him home, he's gonna get sick and be in the hospital a long time. Let's see . . . if you head straight back out to the highway and then toward home, you oughta run into him."

"I will," Dougie said. "I'll find him. Thanks a lot."

The figure of the bigself gave him a little wave, and Dougie turned and headed out, nearly stumbling over his bike on the path outside. He wrestled it up the slope and then along the gravel stretch to where the pavement began, then jumped on and pedaled hard into the cold wind, feeling an occasional heavy raindrop against his face and arms.

Max Kufus took another big swallow, which made his eyes water, and then giggled, lying back against the curve of the pipe. When he put his ear against the concrete, he thought he could hear the roar of a lot of water coming up fast.

That had been a good one, all right, that business about the drinking, and he'd just thought it up on the spur of the moment. If he'd scared the kid enough to keep him off the sauce for good, that would be a big bonus. Things were working out even better than he'd planned.

He took another swallow and then coughed for a time. It had been a long time since he'd had anything to drink, and he hated to guzzle his body back, it had to look like he'd just fallen off the wagon and gotten himself drowned by accident.

That way, with luck, they wouldn't bother to go back and check on him, and they'd never find out he hadn't visited his own younger self, and they'd never know that Dougie was alive this time around, and so no government agent would be sent back to "rectify" things.

Shit, he'd even saved himself a round of pneumonia, it looked like, and a hell of a lot of hospital bills. It looked like a bargain all the way around, from where he sat. He held the bottle out toward the darkness, toasting it, and then took as big a swallow as he could stand.

The vampire is an archetype that has haunted the human mind for thousands of years—and to judge from the numbers of books, movies, plays, television shows, picture books, and so forth that are still being produced about vampires every year, the archetype of the undead is still as alive in the night fears of twentieth-century city-dwellers as ever it was to the huddled isolated villagers of the Dark Ages. Over the centuries, though, the archetype of the vampire has acquired an encumbrance of legend that does tend to distance it a bit from skeptical moderns: its aversion to garlic and crucifixes, its inability to cast a reflection or cross running water, its vulnerability to sunlight and wooden stakes, its ability to change itself into a bat or stealthy fog . . . all a bit silly, to people no longer steeped in medieval mystique. But what if the vampire were real, *a corporate being instead of a garlic-loathing ambulatory corpse? We tend to forget—until stories like the hair-raising one that follows remind us—what the vampire would be if it really existed: a* predator, *or, in the author's words, "a sort of intellectual saber-toothed tiger making his way as secretly as he can in our modern world," and hunting his prey . . . us.*

Suzy McKee Charnas is the author of the critically acclaimed novel Walk to the End of the World *(Berkley), and its recent sequel* Motherlines *(Berkley). A new novel,* The Vampire Tapestry, *of which "The Ancient Mind at Work" is a part, is upcoming from Pocket Books. Born in Manhattan, Charnas, after a sojourn in Nigeria, now resides in Albuquerque, New Mexico, with her husband and family.*

SUZY McKEE CHARNAS
The Ancient Mind at Work

On a Tuesday morning Katje discovered that Dr. Weyland was a vampire, like the one in the movie she'd seen last week.

Jackson's friend on the night cleaning crew had left his umbrella hooked over the bike rack outside the lab building. Since Katje liked to take a stroll in the dawn quiet before starting work, she went over to see if the umbrella was still there. As she started back empty-handed through the heavy mist, she heard the door of the lab building boom behind her, and she looked back.

Two men had come out. One of them, clearly hurt or ill, sank down on his knees and reached out a hand to steady himself on the damp and glistening surface of the parking lot. The other, a tall man with gray hair, turned his head to look full at the kneeling figure—and continued walking without hesitation. He didn't even take his hands out of his raincoat pockets until he stooped to unlock his shimmering, dark Mercedes. He got inside and drove off.

Katje started back toward the lot. But the young man pushed himself upright, looked around in a bewildered manner, and making his way unsteadily to his own car also drove away.

So, there was the vampire, sated and cruel, and there was his victim, wilted, pale and confused—although the movie vampire had swirled about in a black cloak, not a trench coat, and had gone after bosomy young females. Walking over the lawn to the club, Katje smiled at her own fancy.

What she had really seen, she knew, was the star of the Cayslin Center for the Study of Man, Dr. Weyland, leaving the lab with one of his sleep-subjects after a debilitating all-night session. Dr. Weyland must have thought the young man was stooping to retrieve dropped car keys.

The Cayslin Club was an old mansion donated years before to the college. It served now as the faculty club. Its grandeur had been severely challenged by the lab building and attendant parking lot constructed on half of the once spacious lawn, but the club was still imposing within.

This morning when she stepped inside, Katje found a woman in a T-shirt, shorts, and red shoes running from the dining area through the hall and down the length of the living room, making a turn of quick little steps at the fireplace, and running back again. It was Miss Donelly's latest guest lecturer, who was surely old enough to have more dignity. Nothing could hurt the synthetic carpeting that had replaced the fine old rugs, but really, what a way for a grown woman to behave!

She glared. The runner waved cheerfully.

Jackson was in the green room, plugging leaks; it had begun to rain now. The green room was a glassed-in terrace, tile-floored and furnished with chairs of lacy wrought iron.

"Did you find it, Mrs. de Groot?" Jackson asked.

"No, I'm sorry." Katje never called him by his name because she didn't know whether he was Jackson Somebody or Somebody Jackson, and she had learned to be careful about everything to do with blacks in this country.

"Thanks for looking, anyway," Jackson said.

In the kitchen she stood by the sinks, staring out at the dreary day. She had never grown used to these chill, watery winters, though after so many years she couldn't quite recall the exact quality of the African sunlight in which she had grown up. It was no great wonder that Henrik had died here. The gray climate had finally quenched even his ardent nature six years ago.

Her savings from her own salary as housekeeper at the Cayslin Club would eventually finance her return home. She needed enough to buy not a farm but a house with a garden patch somewhere high and cool. She frowned, trying to picture the ideal site, but nothing clear came into her mind. She had been away so long.

While Katje was scrubbing out the sinks, Miss Donelly burst in, shrugging off her dripping coat. "Of all the high-handed, Goddamn—oh, hello, Mrs. de Groot; sorry for the language. Look, we won't be having the women's faculty lunch here tomorrow after all. Dr. Weyland is giving a special money pitch to a couple of fat-cat alumni, and he wants a nice, quiet setting—our lunch corner here at the club, as it turns out. Dean Wacker's already said yes, so that's that." She cocked her head to one side. "What in the world is that thumping noise?"

"Someone running," Katje said, thinking abstractedly of the alumni lunching with the vampire. Would he eat? The one in the movie hadn't.

Miss Donelly's face got red patches over the sharp cheekbones. "My God, is that my lecturer doing her jogging in here because of the weather? I'm so sorry, Mrs. de Groot—I did mean to find her someplace to run, but even in free periods the gyms are full of great hulking boys playing basketball—"

She smiled. "You know, Mrs. de Groot, I've been meaning to ask you to be my next guest lecturer. Would you come talk to my students?"

"Me? What about?"

"Oh, about colonial Africa, what it was like growing up there. These kids' experience is so narrow and protected. I look for every chance to expand their thinking."

Katje wrung out the rag. "My grandfather and Uncle Jan whipped the native boys to work like cattle and kicked them hard enough to break bones for not showing respect. Otherwise we would have been overrun and driven out. I used to go hunting. I shot rhino, elephant, leopard, and I was proud of doing it and doing it well. Your students don't want to know about such things. They have nothing to fear but tax collectors and nothing to do with nature except giving money for whales and seals."

"But that's what I mean," Miss Donelly said. "Different viewpoints."

"There are plenty of books about Africa."

"Okay, forget I asked." Miss Donelly gnawed at her thumbnail, frowning. "I guess I could get the women together over at Corrigan tomorrow instead of here if I spend an hour on the phone. We'll miss your cooking, Mrs. de Groot."

Katje said, "Will Dr. Weyland expect me to cook for his guests?"

"Not Weyland," Miss Donelly said drily. "It's nothing but the best for him, which means the most expensive. They'll probably have a banquet brought in from Borchard's."

She went to collect her guest.

Katje put on coffee and phoned Buildings and Grounds. Yes, Dr. Weyland and two companions were on at the club for tomorrow; no, Mrs. de Groot wouldn't have to do anything but tidy up afterward; yes, it was short notice, and please write it in on the club calendar; and yes, Jackson had been told to check the eaves over the east bedrooms before he left.

"Wandering raincoat," Miss Donelly said, darting in to snatch it up from the chair where she'd left it. "Just watch out for Weyland, Mrs. de Groot."

"What, an old woman of fifty, more gray than blond, with lines and bones in the face? I am not some slinky graduate student trying not only for an A but for the professor also."

"I don't mean romance," Miss Donelly grinned, "though God knows half the faculty—of both sexes—are in love with the man." Honestly, Katje thought, the things people talked about these days! "To no avail, alas, since he's a real loner. But he will try to get you into his expensive sleep lab and make your dreams part of the world-shaking, history-changing research that he stole off poor old Joel Milnes."

Milnes, Katje thought when she was alone again; Professor Milnes, who had gone away to some sunny place to die of cancer. Then Dr. Weyland had come from a small southern school and taken over Milnes's dream project, saving it from being junked—or stealing it, in Miss Donelley's version. A person who looked at a thing in too many ways was bound to get confused.

Jackson came in and poured coffee for himself. He leaned back in his chair and flipped the schedules where they hung on the wall by the phone. He was as slender as a Kikuyu youth—she could see his ribs arch under his shirt. He ate a lot of starch and junk food, but he was too nervous to fatten on it. By rights he belonged in a red blanket, skin gleaming with oil, hair plaited. This life pulled him out of his nature.

"Try and don't put nobody in that number-six bedroom till I get to it the end of the week," he said. "The rain drips in behind the casement. I laid out towels to soak up the water. I see you got Weyland in here tomorrow. My buddy Maurice on the cleaning crew says that guy got the best lab in the place."

"What is Dr. Weyland's research?" Katje asked.

" 'Dream mapping,' they call it. Maurice says there's nothing interesting in his lab—just equipment, you know, recording machines and computers and like that. I'd like to see all that hardware sometime. Only you won't catch me laying out my dreams on tape!

"Well, I got to push along. There's some dripping faucets over at Joffey I got to look at. Hans Brinker, that's me. Thanks for the coffee."

Katje began pulling out the fridge racks for cleaning, listening to him whistle as he gathered up his tools in the green room.

The people from Borchard's left her very little to do. She was stacking the rinsed dishes in the washer when a man said from the doorway, "I am very obliged to you, Mrs. de Groot."

Dr. Weyland stood poised there, slightly stoop-shouldered, head thrust inquisitively forward as he examined the kitchen. She was surprised that he knew her name, for he did not frequent the club. She had seen his tall figure only once or twice in the dining room.

"There was just a bit remaining to do, Dr. Weyland," she said.

"Still, this is your territory," he said, advancing. "I'm sure you were helpful to the Borchard's people. I've never been back here. Are those freezers or refrigerators?"

She showed him around the kitchen and the pantries. He seemed impressed. He was, she realized, unexpectedly personable: lean and grizzled, but with the hint of vulnerability common among rangy men. You couldn't look at him without imagining the gawky scarecrow he must have been as a boy. His striking features—craggy nose and brow, strong mouth, lank jaw—no doubt outsize and homely then, were now impressively united by the long creases of experience on his cheeks and forehead.

"No more scullions cranking the spit," he remarked over the rotisserie. "You come originally from East Africa, Mrs. de Groot? Things must have been very different there."

"Yes. I left a long time ago."

"Surely not so very long," he said, and his eyes flicked over her from head to foot.

Relaxing in the warmth of his interest she said, "Are you from elsewhere also?"

A mistake; he frosted up at once. "Why do you ask?"

"Excuse me. I thought I heard just the trace of an accent."

"My family were Europeans. We spoke German at home. May I sit down?" His big hands, capable- and strong-looking, graced the back of a chair. He smiled briefly. "Would you mind sharing your coffee with an institutional fortune hunter? That is my job—persuading rich men and the guardians of foundations to spend a little of their money in support of work that offers no immediate result. I don't enjoy dealing with these shortsighted men."

"Everyone says you do it well." Katje filled a cup for him.

"It takes up my time," he said. "It wearies me." His large and brilliant eyes, in sockets darkened with fatigue, had a withdrawn, somber aspect. How old was he? Katje wondered.

Suddenly he gazed at her and said, "Didn't I see you over by the lab the other morning? There was mist on my windshield; I couldn't be sure."

She told him about Jackson's friend's umbrella, thinking now he'll explain, this is what he came to say. But he added nothing, and she found herself hesitant to ask about the student in the parking lot. "Is there anything else I can do for you, Dr. Weyland?"

"I don't mean to keep you from your work. One thing. Would you come over and do a session for me in the sleep lab?"

She shook her head.

"All the information goes on tapes under coded I.D. numbers, Mrs. de Groot. Your privacy would be strictly guarded."

"I would prefer not to."

"Excuse me then. It was a pleasure to talk with you," he said, rising. "If you find a reason to change your mind, my extension is one sixty-three."

She was close to tears, but Uncle Jan made her strip down the gun again—her first gun, her own gun—and then the lion coughed, and she saw with the wide gaze of fear his golden form crouched, tail lashing, in the thornbush. As her pony shied she threw up her gun and fired, and the dust boiled up from the thrashings of the wounded cat.

Then Scotty's patient voice said, "Do it again," and she was tearing down the rifle once more by lamplight at the worn wooden table while her mother sewed with angry stabs of the needle and spoke words Katje didn't bother hearing because she knew the gist by heart. "If only Jan had children of his own! Sons, preferably, to take out hunting with Scotty. Because he has no sons, he takes Katje out shooting instead so he can show how tough Boer youngsters are, even a girl. For whites to kill for sport, as Jan and Scotty do, is to go backward into the barbaric past of Africa. Now the farm is producing; there is no need to kill for hides to get cash for coffee, salt, and tobacco. And to train a *girl* to go stalking and killing animals like scarcely more than an animal herself!"

"Again," said Scotty, and the lion coughed, making the pony shiver under her; Katje woke.

She was sitting in front of the TV, blinking at the sharp, knowing face of the talk-show host. The sound had gone off again, and she had dozed.

She didn't often dream, hardly ever of Africa. Why now? Because, she thought, Dr. Weyland had roused her memory. She thought he looked a bit like Scotty, the neighboring farmer whom Uncle Jan had begun by calling a damned *rooinek* and ended treating like a brother.

She got up and hit the TV to make it speak again and sat down to watch with an apple in her hand. Lately she ate too much, out of boredom. Would she grow stout like her mother? It was Dr. Weyland who had brought this worry to the surface of her mind, no proper concern of a middle-aged widow. It was Dr. Weyland who had stirred up that long-ago girlhood spent prowling for game in the bright, dissolving landscape of tan grass.

"Under the bed, do you think?" Miss Donelly dropped on her knees to look. The guest lecturer had left her hairbrush behind. Katje forbore to point out that this was the sort of thing to be expected of someone who put on track clothes and ran inside the house.

A student flung open the bedroom door and leaned in: "Is it too late to hand in my paper, Miss Donelly?"

"For God's sake, Mickey," Miss Donelly burst out, "where did you get that?"

Across the chest of the girl's T-shirt where her coat gaped open were emblazoned the words SLEEP WITH WEYLAND. HE'S A DREAM. She grinned. "Some hustler is selling them right outside the co-op. Better hurry if you want one—Security's already been sent for." She giggled, put a sheaf of dog-eared papers down on the chair by the door, added "Thanks, Miss Donelly," and clattered away down the stairs.

Miss Donelly sat back on her heels and laughed. "Well, I never, as my grandma used to say. That man is turning this school into a circus!"

"These young people have no respect for anything," Katje said. "What will Dr. Weyland say, seeing his name used like that? He should have her expelled."

"Him? He'll barely notice. But Wacker will throw fits." Miss Donelly got up, dusting her hands. She ran a finger over the blistered paint on the windowsill. "Pity they can't use some of the loot Weyland brings in to really fix this old place up. But I guess we can't complain. Without Weyland this would be just another expensive little backwater school for the not so bright children of the upper middle class. And it isn't all roses even for him; this T-shirt thing will bring on a fresh bout of backbiting among his colleagues, you watch. This kind of incident brings out the jungle beast in even the mildest academics."

Katje snorted. She didn't think much of academic infighting.

"I know we must seem pretty tame to you," Miss Donelly said wryly, "but there are some real ambushes and even killings here, in terms of careers. It's not the cushy life it sometimes seems, and not so secure either.

"Even you may be in a little trouble, Mrs. de Groot, though I hope not. Only a few weeks ago there was a complaint from a faculty member that you upset his guests by something you said—"

"I said they couldn't set up a dart board in here," Katje responded crisply.

"There are others who don't like your politics—"

"I never speak about politics," Katje said, offended. That was the first thing Henrik had demanded of her here. She had acquiesced like a good wife; not that she was ashamed of her political beliefs. She had loved and married Henrik not because but in spite of his radical politics.

"From your silence they assume you're some kind of reactionary racist," Miss Donelly said. "And because you're a Boer and don't carry on your husband's crusade. Then there are the ones who say you're just too old and stuffy for the job, meaning you scare them a little, and they'd rather have a giggly cocktail waitress or a downtrodden mouse of a working student. But you've got plenty of partisans too and even Wacker knows you give this place tone and dignity. They ought to double your salary. You're solid and dependable, even if you are a little, well, old-fashioned. And you lived a real life in the world, whatever your values, which is more than most of our faculty has ever done." She stopped, blushing, and moved toward the door. "Well, when that hair-brush turns up just put it aside for me, will you? Thank you, Mrs. de Groot."

Katje said, "Thank you, too." That girl was as softheaded as everyone around here, but she had a good heart.

Many of the staff had already left for vacation during intersession, now that new scheduling had freed everyone from doing special intensive courses between semesters. The last cocktail hour at the club was thinly attended. Katje moved among the drinkers, gathering loaded ashtrays, used glasses, rumpled napkins. A few people greeted her as she passed.

There were two major topics of conversation: the bio student who had been raped last night as she left the library, and the Weyland T-shirt, or, rather, Weyland himself.

They said he was a disgrace, encouraging commercial exploitation of his name. He was probably getting a cut of the profits; no he wasn't, didn't need to, he was a superstar with plenty of income, no dependents, and no tastes except for study and work. And that beautiful Mercedes-Benz of his, don't forget. No doubt that was where he was this evening— not off on a holiday or drinking cheap club booze but tearing around the countryside in his beloved car.

Better a ride in the country than burying himself in the library and feeding his insatiable appetite for books. But what can a workaholic do if he's also an insomniac? The two conditions reinforce each other. It was unhealthy for him to push so hard. Just look at him, so haggard and preoccupied, so lean and lonely-looking. The man deserved a prize for his shy-bachelor-hopelessly-hooked-on-the-pursuit-of-knowledge act.

How many students were in the sleep project now? More than were in his classes. They called his course in ethnography "The Ancient Mind at Work," but the girls found his formality charming, and his absent-mindedness, too—did you hear how he wore two vests one on top of the other to class and never knew it? He wasn't formal; he was rigid and too old-fashioned in his thinking to make a first-rate contribution to anthropology. So he'd simply appropriated poor Milnes's beautiful adaptation of the Richman-Steinmolle recording system to the documentation of dreams, throwing in some "cross-cultural" terminology to bring the project into his own field. And there was doubt that Weyland fully understood the computer end of the process. No wonder he couldn't keep an assistant for long.

Here was Petersen leaving him because of some brouhaha over a computer run. Charming, yes, but Weyland could also be a sarcastic bastard. He was apt to be testy, yes; the great are often quarrelsome, nothing new in that. Remember how he almost came to blows with young Denton over that scratch Denton put on the Mercedes' fender? When Denton lost his temper and threw a punch, Weyland jumped into the car and tried to run him down. Well, that's how Denton told it, but was it likely, considering that Weyland was big enough to flatten Denton with a slap? Denton should have been given a medal for trying to get Weyland off the street. Have you seen him drive? Roars along just barely in control of that great big machine—

Weyland himself wasn't there. Of course not. Weyland was a disdainful, snobbish son-of-a-bitch; Weyland was a shy, socially maladroit scholar absorbed in his great work; Weyland had a secret sorrow too painful to share; Weyland was a charlatan; Weyland was a genius working himself to death to keep alive the Cayslin Center for the Study of Man.

Dean Wacker brooded by the huge, empty fireplace and said several times in a carrying voice that he had talked with Weyland and that the students involved in the T-shirt scandal would face firm disciplinary action.

Miss Donelly came in late with a woman from Economics. They talked heatedly in the window bay, and the two other women in the room drifted over to join them. Katje followed.

" . . . from off-campus, but that's what they always say," one of them snapped. Miss Donelly caught Katje's eye, smiled a strained smile, and plunged back into the discussion. They were talking about the rape. Katje wasn't interested. A woman who used her sense and carried herself with self-respect didn't get raped, but saying so to these intellectual women wasted breath. They didn't understand real life. Katje headed back toward the kitchen.

Buildings and Grounds had sent Nettie Ledyard over from the student cafeteria to help out. She was rinsing glasses and squinting at them through the smoke of her cigarette. She wore a T-shirt bearing a bulbous fish shape across the front and the words SAVE OUR WHALES. These "environmental messages" vexed Katje; only naive, citified people could think of wild animals as pets. The shirt undoubtedly belonged to one of Nettie's long-haired, bleeding-heart boyfriends. Nettie herself smoked too much to pretend to an environmental conscience. She was no hypocrite, at least. But she should come properly dressed to do a job at the club, just in case a professor came wandering back here for more ice or whatever.

"I'll be helping you with the club inventory again during intersession," Nettie said. "Good thing too. You'll be spending a lot of time over here until school starts again, and the campus is really emptying out. Now there's this sex maniac cruising around—though what I could do but run like hell and scream my head off I can't tell you.

"Listen, what's this about Jackson sending you on errands for him?" she added irritably. She flicked ash off her bosom, which was high like a shelf, pushed up by her too tight brassiere. "His pal Maurice can pick up his own umbrella; he's no cripple. Having you wandering around out there alone at some godforsaken hour—"

"Neither of us knew about the rapist," Katje said, wiping out the last of the ashtrays.

"Just don't let Jackson take advantage of you, that's all."

Katje grunted. She had been raised not to let herself be taken advantage of by blacks. At home they had all practiced that art.

Later, helping to dig out a fur hat from under the pile of coats in the foyer, Katje heard someone saying, " . . . other people's work, glomming on and taking all the credit; a real bloodsucker."

Into her mind came the image of Dr. Weyland's tall figure moving without a break in stride past the stricken student.

Jackson came down from the roof with watering eyes. A damp wind was rising.

"That leak is fixed for a while," he said, hunching to blow on his chapped hands. "But the big shots at Buildings and Grounds got to do something better before the next snow piles up and soaks through again."

Katje polished the silver plate with a gray flannel. "What do you know about vampires?" she said.

"How bad you want to know?"

He had no right to joke with her like that, he whose ancestors had been heathen savages. "What do you know about vampires?" she repeated firmly.

"Not a thing." He grinned. "But you just keep on going to the movies with Nettie, and you'll find out all about that kind of stuff. She got to have the dumbest taste in movies there ever was. Horrible stuff!"

Katje looked down from the landing at Nettie, who had just let herself in to the club. Nettie's hair was all in tight little rings like pigs' tails. She called, "Guess what I went and did."

"Your hair," Katje said. "You got it done curly."

Nettie hung her coat crookedly on the rack and peered into the foyer mirror. "I've been wanting to try a permanent for months, but I couldn't find the money. So the other night I went over to the sleep lab." She came upstairs.

"What was it like?" Katje said, looking more closely at Nettie's face: Was she paler than usual? Yes, Katje thought with sudden apprehension.

"It's nothing much. You just lie down on this couch, and they plug you in to their machines, and you sleep. Next morning you unplug and go collect your pay. That's all there is to it."

"You slept well?"

"I felt pretty dragged out yesterday. Dr. Weyland gave me a list of stuff I'm supposed to eat to fix that, and he got me the day off too. Wait a minute. I need a smoke before we go into the linens."

They stood together on the upper landing. From down in the living room rose the murmur of quiet conversation.

Nettie said, "I'd go back for another sleep session in a minute if they'd have me. Good money for no work; not like this." She blew a stream of smoke contemptuously toward the closet door.

Katje said, "Someone has to do what we do."

"Yeah, but why us?" Nettie lowered her voice. "We ought to get old Grauer and Rhine in there with the bedding and the inventory lists, and us two go sit in their big leather chairs and drink coffee like ladies."

Katje had already done that as Henrik's wife. What she wanted now was to sit on the *stoep* after a day's hunting, sipping drinks and trading stories of the kill in the pungent dusk, away from the smoky, noisy hole of a kitchen: a life that Henrik had rebelled against as parasitical, narrow, and dull. His grandfather, like Katje's, had trekked right out of the Transvaal when it became too staid for him and had started over, and what was wrong with that kind of courage and strength? Henrik had carried on the tradition. He had the guts to fight Uncle Jan and everybody else over the future of the land, the government, the natives—that courage had drawn her to him, and had lost her that fine old life and landed her here, now.

Nettie, still hanging back from the linen closet, grudgingly ground out her cigarette on the sole of her shoe. "Coming to the meeting Friday?"

"No. I told you, they're all Reds in those unions. I do all right for myself." Besides, Dr. Weyland was giving a lecture that same Friday night. Katje opened the closet.

"Okay; if you think it's fine to make what we make doing this stuff. Me, I'm glad there's something like a gig in the sleep lab now and then so I can make a little extra and live like a person once in a while. You ought to go over there, you know? There's hardly anything doing during intersession with almost everybody gone. They could take you right away. You get extra pay and time off, and besides, Dr. Weyland's kind of cute, in a gloomy, old sort of way. He leaned over me to plug something into the wall, and I said, 'Go ahead, you can bite my neck any time.' ''

Katje gave her a startled glance, but Nettie, not noticing, moved past her into the closet and pulled out the step stool. Katje said in a neutral voice, ''What did he say to that?''

''Nothing, but he smiled.'' Nettie climbed onto the step stool. ''We'll start up top, all right? I bet all the guys who work nights at the labs get those kind of jokes all the time. Later he said he was hoping you'd come by, and I said he just likes his blood in different flavors.''

Taking a deep breath of the sweet sunshine smell of the clean linens, Katje said, ''He asked you to ask me to come?''

''He said to remind you.''

The first pile of blankets was handed down from the top shelf. Katje said, ''He really accepts anyone into this project?''

''Unless you're sick, or if you've got a funny metabolism or whatever. They do a blood test on you, like at the doctor's.''

That was when Katje noticed the little round Band-Aid on the inside of Nettie's elbow, right over the vein.

Miss Donelly was sharing a jug of cheap wine with three other faculty women in the front lounge. Katje made sure the coffee machine was filled for them and then slipped outside.

She still walked alone on campus when she chose. She wasn't afraid of the rapist, who hadn't been heard from in several days. A pleasurable tension drove her toward the lighted windows of the labs. This was like moving through the sharp air of the bushveldt at dusk.

The lab blinds, tilted down, let out only threads of light. She could see nothing. She hovered a moment, then turned back, hurrying now. The mood was broken, and she felt silly; Daniel from Security would be furious to find her alone out here, and what would she tell him? That she felt herself to be on the track of something wild and it made her feel young?

Miss Donelly and the others were still talking. Katje was glad to hear their wry voices and gusts of laughter, equally glad not to have to sit with them. At first she had been hurt by the social exclusions that had followed her hiring on at the club; now she was grateful.

She had more on her mind than school gossip, and she needed to think. Her own impulsive act excited and appalled her: sallying forth at dusk at some risk (her mind swerved neatly around the other, the imaginary danger), and for what? To sniff the breeze and search the ground for tracks?

The thought of Dr. Weyland haunted her: Dr. Weyland as the restless visitor to the club kitchen; Dr. Weyland as the enigma of faculty gossip; Dr. Weyland as she had first thought of him the other morning in the lab-building parking lot.

She was walking to the bus stop when Jackson drove up and offered her a lift. She was glad to accept. The lonesomeness of the campus was accentuated by darkness and the empty circles of light around the lamp posts.

Jackson pulled aside a jumble of equipment on the front seat—radio parts, speakers, and wires—to make room for her. Two books were on the floor by her feet. He said, "The voodoo book is left over from my brother Paul. He went through a thing, you know, trying to trace back our family, down in Louisiana. The other one was just lying around."

The other one was *Dracula*. Katje felt the gummy spot where the price sticker had been peeled off. Jackson must have bought it for her at the discount bookstore downtown. She didn't know how to thank him easily, so she said nothing.

"It's a long walk out to the bus stop," Jackson said, scowling as he drove out of the stone gates of the college drive. "They should've let you stay on in faculty housing after your husband died."

"They needed the space for another teacher," Katje said. She missed the cottage on the east side of campus, but her present rooming-house lodgings away from school offered more privacy.

He shook his head. "Well, I think it's a shame, you being a foreign visitor and all."

Katje laughed. "After twenty-five years in this country, a visitor?"

He laughed too. "Yeah. Well, you sure have moved around in our society more than most while you been here; from lady of leisure to, well, maid work." She saw the flash of his grin. "Just like my old auntie that used to do for white women up the hill. Don't you mind?"

She minded when she thought working at the club would never end. Sometimes the Africa she remembered seemed too vague a place to go back to now, and the only future she could see was keeling over at the end while vacuuming the club, like a farmer worn to death at his plow . . .

None of this was Jackson's business. "Did your auntie mind her work?" she snapped.

Jackson pulled up opposite the bus stop. "She said you just do what it comes to you to do and thank God for it."

"I say the same."

He sighed. "You're a lot like her, you know? Someday I got a bunch of questions to ask you about how it was when you lived in Africa. I mean, was it like they show in the movies, you know, *King Solomon's Mines* and like that?"

Katje had never seen that movie, but she knew that nothing on film could be like her Africa. "No," she said. "You should go to Africa sometime and see for yourself."

"I'm working on it. There's your bus coming. Wait a minute, listen—no more walking alone out here after dark. There's not enough people around now. You got to arrange to be picked up. Didn't you hear? That guy jumped another girl last night. She got away, but still. Daniel says he found one of the back doors to the club unlocked. You be careful, will you? I don't want to have to come busting in there to save you from some deranged, six-foot pre-med on the rampage, know what I mean? Skinny dude like me could get real ruined that way."

"Oh, I will take care of myself," Katje said, touched and annoyed and amused all at once by his solicitude.

"Sure. Only I wish you were about fifteen years younger and studying karate, you know?"

As she climbed out of the car with the books on her arm he added, "You do any shooting in Africa? Hunting and stuff?"

"Yes, quite a lot."

"Okay, take this." He pulled metal out of his pocket and put it in her hand. It was a gun. "Just in case. You know how to use it, right?"

She closed her fingers on the compact weight of it. "But where did you get this? Do you have papers for it? The laws here are very strict—"

He tugged the door shut and said through the open window, "I live in a rough neighborhood, and I got friends. Hurry up, you'll miss your bus."

Dracula was a silly book. She had to force herself to read on in spite of the phony Dutchman Ven Helsing, an insult to anyone of Dutch descent. The voodoo book was impenetrable, and she soon gave it up in disgust.

The handgun was another matter. She sat at the formica-topped table in her kitchenette and turned the shiny little automatic in the light, thinking. How had Jackson come by such a thing, or for that matter, how did he afford his fancy sports car and all that equipment he carried in it from time to time—where did it all come from and where did it go? He was up to something, probably lots of things—what they called "hustling" nowadays. A good thing he had given her the gun. It could only get him into trouble to carry it around with him. She knew how to handle weapons, and surely with a rapist at large the authorities would be understanding about her lack of a license for it.

The gun needed cleaning. She worked on it as best she could without the right tools. It was a cheap .25-caliber gun. Back home your gun was a fine rifle, made to drop a charging rhino in his tracks, not a stubby little nickel toy like this for scaring off muggers and rapists.

Yet she wasn't sorry to have it. Her own hunting gun that she had brought from Africa years ago was in storage with the extra things from the cottage. She realized now that she had missed its presence lately—since the beginning of the secret stalking of Dr. Weyland.

She went to sleep with the gun on the night table next to her bed.

She woke listening for the roar so she would know in what direction to look tomorrow for the lion's spoor. There was a hot, rank odor of African dust in the air, and she sat up in bed thinking, he's been here.

It was a dream. But it had been so clear! She went to look out the front window without turning on the light, and it was the ordinary street below that seemed unreal. Her heart drummed in her chest. Not that he would come after her here on Dewer Street, but he had sent Nettie to the club, and now he had sent this dream into her sleep. Creatures stalking one another over time grew a bond from mind to mind. But that was in another life.

Was she losing her sanity? She read for a little in the Afrikaans Bible she had brought with her from home but so seldom opened in recent years. What gave comfort in the end was to put Jackson's automatic into her purse to carry with her. A gun was supposedly of no use against a vampire—you needed a wooden stake, she remembered reading, or you had to cut off his head to kill him—but the weight of the weapon in her handbag reassured her.

The lecture hall was full in spite of the scarcity of students on campus this time of year. These special talks were open to the town as well.

Dr. Weyland read his lecture in a stiff, abrupt manner. He stood cramped slightly over the lectern, which was low for his height, and rapped out his sentences, rarely raising his eyes from his notes. In his tweeds and heavy-rimmed glasses he was the picture of the scholarly recluse drawn out of the study into the limelight. His lecture was brief; he fulfilled with unmistakable impatience the duty set every member of the faculty to give one public address per year on an aspect of his work.

The audience didn't mind. They had come prepared to be spellbound by the great Dr. Weyland speaking on the demonology of dreams. At the end there were questions, most of them obviously designed to show the questioner's cleverness rather than to elicit information. The discussions after these lectures were usually the real show. Katje, lulled by the abstract talk, came fully to attention when a young woman asked, "Professor, have you considered whether the legends of such supernatural creatures as werewolves, vampires, and dragons are not distortions out of nightmares, as many think; that maybe the legends reflect the existence of real, though rare, prodigies of evolution?"

Dr. Weyland hesitated, coughed, sipped water. "The forces of evolution are capable of prodigies, certainly," he said. "You have chosen an excellent word. But we must understand that we are not speaking—in the case of the vampire, for example—of a blood-sipping phantom who cringes from a clove of garlic. How could nature design such a being?

"The corporeal vampire, if it existed, would be by definition the greatest of all predators, living as he would off the top of the food chain. Man is the most dangerous animal, the devourer or destroyer of all others, and the vampire would choose to avoid the risks of attacking humans by tapping the blood of lower animals if he could; so we must assume that our vampire cannot. Perhaps animal blood can tide him over a lean patch, as seawater can sustain a castaway for a few miserable days but can't permanently replace fresh water to drink. Humanity would remain the vampire's livestock, albeit fractious and dangerous to deal with, and where they live, so must he.

"In the sparsely settled early world he would be bound to a town or village to assure his food supply. He would learn to live on little— perhaps a half-liter of blood per day—since he could hardly leave a trail of drained corpses and hope to go unnoticed. Periodically, he would withdraw for his own safety and to give the villagers time to recover from his depredations. A sleep several generations long would provide him with an untouched, ignorant population in the same location. He would have to be able to slow his metabolism, to induce in himself naturally a state of suspended animation; mobility in time would become his alternative to mobility in space."

Katje listened intently, thinking yes, he is the sort of animal that lies in wait for the prey to come his way. His daring in speaking this way stirred her; she could see he was beginning to enjoy the game, growing more at ease at the podium as he warmed to his subject.

"The vampire's slowed body functions during these long rest periods might help extend his lifetime; so might living for long periods, waking or sleeping, on the edge of starvation. We know that minimal feeding produces striking longevity in some other species. Long life would be a highly desirable alternative to reproduction, since a vampire would flourish best with the least competition. The great predator would not wish to sire his own rivals. It could not be true that his bite would turn his victims into vampires like himself—"

"Or we'd be up to our necks in fangs," whispered someone in the audience rather loudly.

"Fangs are too noticeable and not efficient for blood sucking," observed Dr. Weyland. "Large, sharp canine teeth are designed to tear meat. Polish versions of the vampire legend would be closer to the mark: They tell of some sort of puncturing device, perhaps a needle in the tongue like a sting that would secrete an anticlotting substance. That way the vampire could seal his lips around the wound and draw the blood freely without having to rip great, spouting, wasteful holes in his unfortunate prey." Dr. Weyland smiled.

The younger members of the audience produced appropriate retching noises.

Would a vampire sleep in a coffin? someone asked.

"Certainly not," Dr. Weyland retorted. "Would you, given a choice? The corporeal vampire would require physical access to the world, which is something that burial customs generally prevent. He might retire to a cave or take his rest in a tree like Merlin, or Ariel in the cloven pine, provided he could find either tree or cave safe from wilderness freaks and developers' bulldozers.

"Finding a secure resting place is one obvious problem for our vampire in modern times," he continued. "There are others. Upon each waking he must quickly adapt to his new surroundings, a task that, we may imagine, has grown progressively more difficult with the rapid acceleration of cultural change since the Industrial Revolution. In the past century and a half he has no doubt had to limit his sleeps to shorter and shorter periods for fear of completely losing touch. This curtailment of his rest might be expected to wear him down and render him increasingly irritable."

He paused to adjust his glasses, now as visibly relaxed as Katje had seen him in her kitchen at the club. Someone called out, "Could a corporeal vampire get a toothache?"

"Assuredly," replied Dr. Weyland. "He is, after all, a stage of humanity, real though hard to come by. He would no doubt also need a haircut now and then and could only put his pants on, as humorists have said since the widespread adoption of trousers, one leg at a time.

"Since we posit a natural rather than a supernatural being, he grows older, but slowly. Meanwhile, each updating of himself is more challenging and demands more from him—more imagination, more energy, more cunning. While he must adapt sufficiently to disguise his anomalous existence, he must not succumb to current ideologies of Right or Left— that is, to the cant of individual license or to the cant of the infallibility of the masses—lest either allegiance interfere with the exercise of his predatory survival skill."

Meaning, Katje thought grimly, he can't afford scruples about drinking our blood.

Emrys Williams raised a giggle by commenting that a lazy vampire could always take home a pretty young instructor to show him the new developments in interpersonal relations.

Dr. Weyland fixed him with a cold glance. "You are mixing up dinner with sex," he remarked, "and not, I gather, for the first time."

They roared. Williams—the "tame Wild Welshman of the Lit.

Department'' to his less admiring colleagues—turned a gratified pink.

One of Dr. Weyland's associates in Anthropology pointed out at boring length that the vampire, born in an earlier age, would become dangerously conspicuous for his diminutive height as the human race grew taller.

"Not necessarily," commented Dr. Weyland. "Remember that we speak of a highly specialized physical form. It may be that during his waking periods his metabolism is so sensitive that he responds to the stimuli in the environment by growing in his body as well as in his mind. Perhaps while he's awake his entire being exists at an intense inner level of activity and change. The stress of these great rushes to catch up all at once with physical, mental, and cultural evolution must be enormous. No wonder he needs his long sleeps."

He glanced at the clock on the wall. "As you can see, by the application of a little logic and imagination we come up with a creature bearing superficial resemblances to the vampire of legend, but at base one quite different from your standard strolling corpse with an aversion to crosses. Next question?"

They weren't willing to end this flight of fancy. Someone asked how he accounted for the superstitions about crosses and garlic and so on.

Dr. Weyland sipped water from the glass at hand while contemplating the audience. He said finally, "Primitive men first encountering the vampire would be unaware that they themselves were products of evolution. They would have no way of knowing that he was a still higher product of the same process. They would make up stories to account for him and to try to control him. In early times the vampire himself might even believe in some of these legends—the silver bullet, the oaken stake. .

"But waking at length in a more rational age, he would abandon these notions just as everyone else did. A clever vampire might even make use of the folklore. For instance, it is generally supposed that Bram Stoker was inspired to write *Dracula* by his meeting with a Rumanian professor of Oriental languages from Pest University; I refer you to a recent biography of Stoker by Daniel Farson. Why was this Professor Arminius Vambery in London at just the right time, a guest at a certain eating club along with Stoker on a certain night? How did Vambery come to have a wealth of tantalizing detail about the vampire superstition at his fingertips? Ladies and gentlemen, take note: There is a research paper in it somewhere."

He didn't wait for their laughter to die away but continued, "Any intelligent vampire sensitive to the questing spirit of those times would have developed a passionate interest in his own origin and evolution. Now, who was Arminius Vambery, and why his ceaseless exploration of that same subject?

"Eventually our vampire prudently retires. Imagine his delight upon waking half a century later to find vampire legends a common currency of the popular culture and *Dracula* a classic.''

''Wouldn't he be lonely?'' sighed a girl standing in the side aisle, her posture eloquent of the desire to comfort that loneliness.

''The young lady will forgive me,'' Dr. Weyland responded, ''if I observe that this is a question born of a sheltered life. Predators in nature do not indulge in the sort of romantic moonings that humans impute to them. As for our vampire, even if he had the inclination he wouldn't have the time. On each waking he has more to learn. Perhaps someday the world will return to a reasonable rate of change, permitting him some leisure in which to feel lonely or whatever suits him.''

A nervous girl ventured the opinion that a perpetually self-educating vampire would always have to find himself a place in a center of learning in order to have access to the information he would need.

''Naturally,'' agreed Dr. Weyland dryly. ''Perhaps a university, where strenuous study and other eccentricities of the living intellect would be accepted behavior in a grown man. Possibly even a modest institution like Cayslin College would serve.''

Under the chuckling following this came a question too faint for Katje to hear. Dr. Weyland, having bent to listen, straightened up and announced sardonically, ''The lady desires me to comment upon the vampire's 'Satanic pride.' Madam, here you enter the area of the literary imagination and its devices, where I dare not tread under the eyes of my colleagues from the English Department. Perhaps they will pardon me if I merely point out that a tiger who falls asleep in a jungle and on waking finds a thriving city overgrowing his lair has no energy to spare for displays of Satanic pride.''

That's nerve, Katje thought; Dr. Weyland expounding on a vampire's pride—what an exercise in arrogance!

Williams, intent on having the last word as always, spoke up once more: ''The vampire as time traveler—you ought to be writing science fiction, Weyland,'' which provoked a growing patter of applause. It was evident that the evening was ending.

Katje went out with the crowd, but withdrew to stand outside under the portico of the Union Building. She saw Dr. Weyland's car across the street, gleaming in the lamplight: his access to physical mobility and a modern mechanical necessity that he had mastered. No wonder he loved it.

With the outwash of departing audience came Miss Donelly. She asked if Katje needed a lift: ''There's my car, the rusty, trusty Volks.'' Katje explained that a group of women from the staff cafeteria went bowling together each Friday night and had promised to come by and pick her up.

"I'll wait with you just in case," Miss Donelly said. "You know, Wild Man Williams is a twerp, but he was right: Weyland's vampire would be a time traveler. He could only go forward, of course, never back, and only by long, unpredictable leaps—this time, say, into our age of what we like to think of as technological marvels; maybe next time into an age of interstellar travel. Who knows, he might get to taste Martian blood, if there are Martians, and if they have blood.

"Frankly, I wouldn't have thought Weyland could come up with anything so imaginitive as that—the vampire as a sort of living saber-toothed tiger prowling the pavements, a truly endangered species. That's next term's T-shirt: SAVE THE VAMPIRE."

Miss Donelly might banter, but she would never believe. It was all a joke to her, a clever mental game invented by Dr. Weyland for his audience. No point consulting her.

Miss Donelly added ruefully, 'You've got to hand it to the man. He's got a tremendous stage presence, and he sure knows how to turn on the charm when he feels like it. Nothing too smooth, mind you, just enough unbending, enough slightly caustic graciousness, to set suscepti-ble hearts a-beating. You could almost forget what a ruthless, self-centered bastard he can be. Did you notice that most of the comments came from women? Is that your lift?"

It was. While the women in the station wagon shuffled themselves around to make room, Katje stood with her hand on the door and watched Dr. Weyland emerge from the building with admiring students at either hand. He loomed above them, his hair silver under the lamplight. For over-civilized people to experience the approach of such a predator as sexually attractive was not strange. She remembered Scotty saying once that the great cats were all beautiful, and maybe beauty helped them to capture their prey.

He turned his head, and she thought for a moment that he was looking at her as she got into the station wagon.

What could she do that wouldn't arouse total disbelief and a suspi-cion that she herself was crazy? She couldn't think amid the tired, satisfied ramblings of her bowling friends, and she declined to stay up socializing with them. They didn't press her. She was not one of their regular group.

Sitting alone at home, Katje had a cup of hot milk to calm herself for sleep. To her perplexity, her mind kept wandering from thoughts of Dr. Weyland to memories of drinking cocoa at night with Henrik and the African students he used to bring to dinner. They had been native boys to her, dressed up in suits and talking politics like white men, flashing photographs of black babies playing with toy trucks and walkie-talkie sets. Sometimes they had gone to see documentary films of an Africa full of cities and traffic and black professionals exhorting, explaining, running things, as these students expected to do in their turn when they went home.

She thought about home now. She recalled clearly all those indicators of irrevocable change in Africa, and she saw suddenly that the old life there had gone. She would return to an Africa largely as foreign to her as America had been at first. Reluctantly, she admitted one of her feelings when listening to Dr. Weyland's talk had been an unwilling empathy with him: if he was a one-way time traveler, so was she.

As the vampire could not return to simpler times, so Katje saw herself cut off from the life of raw vigor, the rivers of game, the smoky village air, all viewed from the lofty heights of white privilege. One did not have to sleep half a century to lose one's world these days; one had only to grow older.

Next morning she found Dr. Weyland leaning, hands in pockets, against one of the columns flanking the entrance to the club. She stopped some yards from him, her purse hanging heavily on her arm. The hour was early, the campus deserted-looking. Stand still, she thought; show no fear.

He looked at her. "I saw you after the lecture last night, and earlier in the week, outside the lab one evening. You must know better than to wander alone at night, the campus empty, no one around—anything might happen. If you are curious, Mrs. de Groot, come do a session for me. All your questions will be answered. Come over tonight. I could stop by here for you in my car on the way back to the lab after dinner. There is no problem with scheduling, and I would welcome your company. I sit alone over there these nights hoping some impoverished youngster, unable to afford a trip home at intersession, will be moved by an uncontrollable itch for travel to come to my lab and earn his fare."

She felt fear knocking heavily in her body. She shook her head, no.

"My work would interest you, I think," he went on, watching her. "You are an alert, fine-looking woman; they waste your qualities here. Couldn't the college find you something better than to be a housekeeper for them after your husband died? You might consider coming over regularly to help me with some clerical chores until I get a new assistant. I pay well."

Astonished out of her fear at the offer of work in the vampire's lair, she found her voice: "I am a country woman, Dr. Weyland, a daughter of farmers. I have no proper education. Never read books at home, except the Bible. My husband didn't want me to work. I have spent my time in this country learning English and cooking and how to shop for the right things. I have no skills, no knowledge but the little that I remember of the crops and weather and customs of another country—and even that is probably out of date. I would be no use in work like yours."

Hunched in his coat with the collar up-turned, looking at her slightly askance, his tousled hair gleaming with the damp, he had the aspect of an old hawk, intent but aloof. He broke the pose, yawned behind his large-knuckled hand, and straightened up.

"As you like. Here comes your friend Nellie."

"Nettie," Katje corrected, suddenly outraged: he's drunk Nettie's blood; the least he could do was remember her name properly. But he was vanishing over the lawn toward the lab.

Nettie came panting up. "Who was that? Did he try to attack you?"

"It was Dr. Weyland," Katje said. She hoped Nettie didn't notice her trembling, which Katje tried to conceal.

Nettie laughed. "What is this, a secret romance?"

Miss Donelly came into the kitchen toward the end of the luncheon for the departing Emeritus. She plumped herself down between Nettie and Katje, who were taking a break and preparing dessert, respectively. Katje spooned whipped cream carefully into each glass dish of fruit.

Miss Donelly said, "In case I get too smashed to say this later, thanks. On the budget I gave you, you did just great. The Department will put on something official with Beef Wellington and trimmings, over at Borchard's, but it was really important for some of us lowly types to give Sylvia our own alcoholic farewell feast, which we couldn't have done without your help."

Nettie nodded and stubbed out her cigarette.

"Our pleasure," Katje said, preoccupied. Dr. Weyland had come for her, would come back again; he was hers to deal with, but how? She no longer thought of sharing her fear, not with Nettie with her money worries or with Miss Donelly, whose eyes were just now faintly swimmy-looking with drink. Weyland the vampire was not for a committee to deal with. Only fools left it to committees to handle life and death.

"The latest word," Miss Donelly added bitterly, "is that the Department plans to fill Sylvia's place with some guy from Oregon, which means the salary goes up half as much again or more inside of six months."

"Them's the breaks," Nettie said, not very pleasantly. She caught Katje's eye with a look that said, Look who makes all the money and look who does all the complaining.

"Them is," Miss Donelly agreed glumly. "As for me, the word is no tenure, so I'll be moving on in the fall. Me and my big mouth. Wacker nearly fainted at my prescription for stopping the rapes: You trap the guy, disembowel him, and hang his balls over the front gate. Our good dean doesn't know me well enough to realize it's all front. On my own I'd be too petrified to try anything but talking the bastard out of it. You know: 'Now you just let me get my dress back on, and I'll make us each a cup of coffee, and you tell me all about why you hate women.' '' She stood up, groaning.

"Did you hear what happened to that girl last night, the latest victim? He cut her throat. Ripped her pants off but didn't even bother raping her; that's how desperate for sex he is.''

Katje said, "Jackson told us about the killing this morning.''

"Jackson? Oh, the maintenance man. Look out, it could even be him. Any of them, damn them,'' she muttered savagely as she turned away, "living off us, kicking our bodies out of the way when they're through—''

She stumbled out of the kitchen.

Nettie snorted. "She's always been one of those libbers. No wonder Wacker's getting rid of her. Some men act like hogs, but you can't let yourself be turned into a man-hater. A man's the only chance a girl has of getting up in the world, you know?'' She pulled on a pair of acid-yellow gloves and headed for the sink. "If I want out of these rubber gloves I have to marry a guy who can afford to pay a maid.''

Katje sat looking at the fruit dishes with their plump cream caps. It was just as the Bible said. She felt it happen: The scales fell from her eyes. She saw clearly and thought, I am a fool.

Bad pay is real, rape is real, killing is real. The real world worries about real dangers, not childish fancies of a night prowler who drinks blood. Dr. Weyland took the trouble to be concerned, to offer extra work, while I was thinking idiot things about him. Where does it come from, this nonsense of mine? My life is dull since Henrik died; so I make up drama in my head, and that way I get to think about Dr. Weyland, a distinguished and learned gentleman, being interested in me.

She resolved to go to the lab building later and leave a note for Dr. Weyland, an apology for her reluctance, an offer to stop by soon and make an appointment at the sleep lab.

Nettie looked at the clock and said over her shoulder, "Time to take the ladies their dessert.''

At last the women had dispersed, leaving the usual fog of smoke behind. Katje and Nettie had finished the cleaning up. Katje said, "I'm going for some air.''

Nettie, wreathed by smoke of her own making, drowsed in one of the big living-room chairs. She shook her head. "Not me. I'm pooped.'' She sat up. "Unless you want me along. It's still light out, so you're safe from the Cayslin Ripper.''

"Don't disturb yourself,'' Katje said.

Away on the far edge of the lawn three students danced under the sailing shape of a Frisbee. Katje looked up at the sun, a silver disc behind a thin place in the clouds; more rain coming, probably. The campus still wore a deserted look. Katje wasn't worried; there was no vampire, and the gun in her purse would suffice for anything else.

The sleep lab was locked. She tucked her note of apology between the lab door and the jamb and left.

As she started back across the lawn someone stepped behind her, and long fingers closed on her arm: It was Dr. Weyland. Firmly and without a word he bent her course back toward the lab.

"What are you doing?" she said, astonished.

"I almost drove off without seeing you. Come sit in my car, I want to talk to you." She held back, alarmed, and he gave her a sharp little shake. "Making a fuss is pointless. No one is here to notice. No one would believe."

There was only his car in the parking lot; even the Frisbee players had gone. Dr. Weyland opened the door of his Mercedes and pushed Katje into the front passenger seat with a deft, powerful thrust of his arm. He got in on the driver's side, snapped down the automatic door locks, and sat back. He looked up at the gray sky, then at his watch.

Katje said, "You wanted to say something to me?"

He didn't answer.

She said, "What are we waiting for?"

"For the day man to leave and lock up the lab. I don't like to be interrupted."

This is what it's like, Katje thought, feeling lethargic detachment stealing through her, paralyzing her. No hypnotic power out of a novelist's imagination held her, but the spell cast on the prey of the hunting cat, the shock of being seized in the deadly jaws, though not a drop of blood was yet spilled. "Interrupted," she whispered.

"Yes," he said, turning toward her. She saw the naked craving in his gaze. "Interrupted at whatever it pleases me to do with you. You are on my turf now, Mrs. de Groot, where you have persisted in coming time after time. I can't wait any longer for you to make up your mind. You are healthy—I looked up your records—and I am hungry. You may live to walk away after, I don't know yet—who would listen to a mad old woman? I can tell you this much: Your chances are better if you don't speak."

The car smelled of cold metal, leather, and tweed. At length a man came out of the lab building and bent to unlock the chain from the only bicycle in the bike rack. By the way Dr. Weyland shifted in his seat, Katje saw that this was the departure he had been awaiting.

"Look at that idiot," he muttered. "Is he going to take all night?" She saw him turn restlessly toward the lab windows. That would be the place, after a bloodless blow to stun her—he wouldn't want any mess in his Mercedes.

In her lassitude she was sure that he had attacked that girl, drunk her blood, and then killed her. He was using the rapist's activities as cover. When subjects did not come to him at the sleep lab, hunger drove him out to hunt. Perhaps he was glad then to put aside his civilized disguise.

She thought, *But I am myself a hunter!*

Cold anger coursed through her. Her thoughts flew: She needed time, a moment out of his reach to plan her survival. She had to get out of the car—any subterfuge would do.

She gulped and turned toward him, croaking, "I'm going to be sick."

He swore furiously. The locks clicked; he reached roughly past her and shoved open the door on her side: "Out!"

She stumbled out into the drizzling, chilly air and backed several hasty paces, hugging her purse to her body like a shield, looking quickly around. The man on the bike had gone. The upper story of the Cayslin Club across the lawn showed a light—Nettie would be missing her now. Maybe Jackson would be just arriving to pick them up. But no help could come in time.

Dr. Weyland had gotten out of the car. He stood with his arms folded on the roof of the Mercedes, looking across at her with a mixture of annoyance and contempt. "Mrs. de Groot, do you think you can outrun me?"

He started around the front of his car toward her.

Scotty's voice sounded quietly in her ear: "Yours," he said, as the leopard tensed to charge. Weyland too was an animal, not an immortal monster out of legend—just a wild beast, however smart and strong and hungry. He had said so himself.

She jerked out the automatic, readying it to fire as she brought it swiftly up to eye level in both hands while her mind told her calmly that a head shot would be best but that a hit was surer if she aimed for the torso.

She shot him twice, two slugs in quick succession, one in the chest and one in the abdomen. He did not fall but bent to clutch at his torn body, and he screamed and screamed so that she was too shaken to steady her hands for the head shot afterward. She cried out also, involuntarily: His screams were dreadful. It was long since she had killed anything.

Footsteps rushed behind her, arms flung round her, pinning her hands to her sides so that the gun pointed at the ground and she couldn't fire at Weyland again. Jackson's voice gasped in her ear, "Jesus Creeping Christ!"

His car stood where he had braked it, unheard by Katje. Nettie jumped out and rushed toward Katje, crying, "My God, he's shot, she shot him!"

Breaking off his screaming, Weyland tottered away from them around his car and fetched up, leaning on the front. His face, a hollow-cheeked, starving mask, gaped at them.

"It's him?" Jackson said incredulously. "*He* tried to rape you?"

Katje shook her head. "He's a vampire."

"Vampire, hell!" Jackson exploded in a breathless laugh. "He's a Goddamn dead rapist, that's what he is! Jesus!"

Weyland panted, "Stop staring, cattle!"

He wedged himself heavily into the driver's seat of his car. They could see him slumped there, his forehead against the curve of the steering wheel. Blood spotted the Mercedes where he had leaned.

"Mrs. de Groot, give me the gun," Jackson said.

Katje clenched her fingers around the grip. "No."

She could tell by the way Jackson's arms tightened that he was afraid to let go of her and grab for the gun. He said, "Nettie, take my car and go get Daniel!"

Nettie moaned, "My God, look! What's he doing?"

Weyland had lifted his red-smeared hands to his face, and he was licking the blood from his fingers. Katje could see his throat working as he strained to swallow his food, his life.

A siren sounded. Nettie cried in wild relief, "That's Daniel's car coming!"

Weyland raised his head. His gray face was rigid with determination. He snarled, "I won't be put on show! The door—one of you shut the door!" he started the engine.

His glaring face commanded them. Nettie darted forward, slammed the door, and recoiled, wiping her hand on her sweater.

Eyes blind to them now, Weyland drove the Mercedes waveringly past them, out of the parking lot toward the gateway road. Rain swept down in heavy gusts. Katje heard the siren again and woke to her failure: She had not made a clean kill. The vampire was getting away.

She lunged toward Jackson's car. He held her back, shouting, "Nothing doing, come on, you done *enough!*"

The Mercedes crawled haltingly down the middle of the road, turned at the stone gates, and was gone.

Jackson said, "*Now* will you give me that gun?"

Katje snapped on the safety and dropped the automatic on the wet paving at their feet.

Nettie was pointing toward the club. "There's people coming. They must have heard the shooting and called Daniel. Listen, Jackson, we're in trouble. Nobody's going to believe that Dr. Weyland is the rapist—or the other thing either." Her glance flickered nervously over Katje. "Whatever we say, they'll think we're crazy."

"Oh, shit," said Jackson tiredly, letting Katje go at last. He stopped to retrieve the gun. Katje saw the apprehension in his face as he weighed Nettie's assessment of their situation; a wild story from some cleaning people about the eminent professor—

"We've got to say something," Nettie went on desperately. "All that blood—" She fell silent, staring.

There was no blood. The rain had washed the tarmac clean.

Jackson faced Katje and said urgently, "Listen, Mrs. de Groot, we don't know a thing about any shooting, you hear?" He slipped the gun into an inside pocket of his jacket. "You came over to make an appointment at the sleep lab, only Dr. Weyland wasn't around. You waited for him, and Nettie got worried when you didn't come back, so she called me, and we drove over here looking for you. We all heard shooting, but nobody saw anything. There was nothing to see. Like now."

Katje was furious with him and herself. She should have chanced the head shot; she shouldn't have let Jackson hold her back.

She could see Daniel's car now, wheeling into the parking lot.

Jackson said quietly, "I got accepted to computer school in Rochester for next semester. You can bet they don't do vampires down there, Mrs. de Groot; and they don't do black guys who can get hold of guns, either. Me and Nettie got to live here; we don't get to go away to Africa."

She grew calmer; he was right. The connection had been between herself and the vampire all along, and what had happened here was her own affair. It had nothing to do with these young people.

"All right, Jackson," she said. "There was nothing to see."

"Not a thing," he said in his old, easy manner, and he turned toward Daniel's car.

He would do all right; maybe someday he would come visit her in Africa, in a smart suit and carrying an attaché case, on business. Surely they had computers there now too.

Daniel stepped out of his car into the rain, one hand on the butt of his pistol. Katje saw the disappointment sour his florid face as Nettie put a hand on his arm and began to talk quietly.

Katje picked up her purse from where she had dropped it—how light it felt now, without the gun in it. She fished out her plastic rain hood, though her hair was already wet. Tying the hood on, she thought about her old Winchester 270, her lion gun. About taking it from storage, putting it in working order, tucking it well back into the broom closet at the club. In case Weyland didn't die, in case he couldn't sleep with two bullets in him and came limping back on to familiar ground, to look for her. He would come next week, when the students returned, or never. She didn't think he would come, but she would be ready just in case.

And then, as she had planned, she would go home to Africa. Her mind flashed; a new life, whatever life she could make for herself there these days. If Weyland could fit himself to new futures, so could she.

But if he did sleep, and woke again fifty years from now? Each generation must look out for itself. She had done her part, although perhaps not well enough to boast about. Still, what a tale it would make some evening over the smoke of a campfire on the veldt, beginning with the tall form of Dr. Weyland seen striding across the parking lot past a kneeling student in the heavy mist of morning . . .

Katje walked toward Daniel's car to tell the story that Buildings and Grounds would understand.

The modern concept of the child as someone to be cherished over the span of a long, leisurely growth and protected from the world's rough edges is a comparatively recent one—go back only to the end of the nineteenth century and such sentimental notions vanish, and you will find children of eight and nine working grueling eighteen-hour shifts in the mines and factories and mills, children barely old enough to walk harnessed to loads like sledge-dogs and made to haul them until they drop. These were poor people's children, admittedly. But go back only a few hundred years before that, and you will find even the children of the rich and mighty treated more casually and with rather less care than that usually lavished on a household pet today; there was no sense wasting much time on them until it could be seen that they had a chance to survive into their teens. . . .

Here Michael Bishop—one of the best of the new SF writers, author of Catacomb Years *(Berkley),* Transfigurations *(Berkley/Putnam),* Stolen Faces *(Dell), and* Eyes of Fire *(Pocket Books)—shows us how easily in a disintegrating world, such a state of affairs might come about again. . . .*

MICHAEL BISHOP
Vernalfest Morning

Priesman calls the place us kids live Little Camp Fuji. Fuji is short for refugee, and Priesman is—was—a lieutenant with the guerrillas on the rampart side of City. Since most of our mothers and daddies were sympathizers, one of Priesman's jobs is seeing after the kids in our camp. Already he's shown us how to keep the Fujiniles from Deeland, Viperhole, Poohburgh, and the other nearby kiddie camps out of our gardens and barracks, and twice in the last month he's been through Fuji with a side of wild greyhound.

I like Priesman. I like the way he takes care of us, and I like the way he looks. He always wears dappled fatigues, creased combat boots, an automatic carbine slung over his shoulder, and a pair of bristly 'rilla burns that sweep down from his ears and out across his cheeks like wings. My father (I have a photograph of him with his last bullet wound showing on his left temple) had 'rilla burns just like Priesman's.

A little over a week ago, four days before Vernalfest, Priesman came into Little Camp Fuji's central barracks, number 3, and dropped a bloody side of greyhound on the floor. I was sitting on Little Mick's winter thermals playing a game of bodycount with Lajosipha Joiner, our twelve-year-old self-appointed witchwoman. Lajosipha had made the bodycount markers out of spent machine-gun shells and several old rampart-side safe-passage tokens. A bunch of kids got up to look at the meat Priesman had just dropped, but the lieutenant turned my way.

"You're the oldest one here, aren't you, Neddie?"

"I'm fifteen."

Hands on hips, Priesman twisted at the waist to stare all the other kids right in the eye. "Anyone older than Neddie?" When no one fessed to being older, the lieutenant swaggered toward me, hooked a finger inside my shirt, and led me out onto the porch. While his big hands were squeezing my shoulders together, all I could see was the broken button just below the X of his cartridge belts.

"Fifteen, huh? If you weren't so damn puny, Neddie, you'd've probably been promoted out of Fuji by now."

I didn't say anything; I didn't look into Priesman's face. He already knew that in the last six months his own unit had run me back to camp half a dozen times. Finally, Priesman's beetle-browed colonel, Simpson, had said, "Don't come back before you're asked, little boy, or I'll have your scrotum for a dice bag . . ."

"Listen, Neddie," Priesman was saying, "do you know who Maud Turska is? Ever heard her name?"

"She's in your unit. She's the Poohburgher proctor."

"That's right. Well, Simpson thinks she's passing holdfast locations and potential bomb targets to the airport-siders. He thinks she's using some of her kids as runners."

I looked up, wrinkling my forehead.

"Listen, now. We can't give you any metal, Neddie—no hard ammo, you understand—but on Vernalfest morning we want you to hit 'em. Hit Poohburgh, I mean. Do it right, and you'll have your promotion out of Fuji, I can tell you that."

When I went back inside to tell the others, most of the kids had rumbled down the rear steps to spit Priesman's gift and build a fire under it. Lajosipha was still there, though, hunched over the shells and tokens, and when I told her about racking through Poohburgh she jumped up and paced all over the barracks like a stork on stilts. Her legs were so long I sometimes used to think her head sat right on top of them.

"It didn't matter, them not giving us any metal. Other ways will do; beautiful ways. We need cardboard, Neddie. We need cardboard. And lumber. And rags. And eight or ten old automobile tires. I think Lieutenant Priesman's asked the right folks to get this done, Neddie, I really do."

The next day, three days before Vernalfest, I led Little Mick, Awkward Alice Gomez, and a couple of other Fujiniles from barracks number 4 through the rampart-side ruins to the old trucking warehouses under the expressway. Little Mick had a wagon, a noisy one with wheels that we'd wrapped with torn bedding, and it bumped along, going clink-clank-clatter, and slowing us up.

Over the drooping expressway bridges, drifting up from City's burnt-out heart, oily plumes of smoke wriggled on the sky, and I could imagine Lajosipha trying to conjure with them, voodooing the airport-siders but blessing us rampart 'rillas with magical gobbledygook. She wasn't worth a poot on a scavenger hunt, though, and I was glad we hadn't brought her.

As it was, Little Mick nearly did us in while we were flattening pasteboard crates near the warehouse incinerator and laying them out in our wagon. He got punchy with success, I guess, and started jigging around the parking lot each time we flattened and stacked a box. Just as a huge, gray-green copter with rocket launchers under its carriage was tilting over the expressway toward the ack-ack emplacements on the mountain, Alice tripped Little Mick and hauled him up against the dumpster. That probably saved our bums. Priesman says the airport-siders like to go frog-gigging.

But we got back to Little Camp Fuji okay, and the next day while two other dog-parties were out for paint and lumber, Brian Rabbek took the wagon and a couple of thirteen-year-olds over toward the Pits. They were going to dig inner tubes and tires out of the sand. They ended up being gone 'til way past dark. Lajosipha, in fact, started muttering about death and weaving her arms around in front of her face like two black geese trying to knot a double hitch with their necks. The littler kids got spooked, and I told her to go do her witchwomaning in a closet some-where. She ignored me and kept it up. Brian and the others eventually got back okay, though, and that pretty well undid the spookiness of her mumbling and jerking about. Damn good thing.

The day before Vernalfest broke clean and clear. Awkward Alice, just as if she was old enough to know, said that the smoke hanging over the airport across town and among the trees on the mountainside looked laundered. It *was* white, white and fluffy.

That was the day everyone in Little Camp Fuji really worked. We sat crosslegged out in the yard between barracks and worked at cutting the tires and inner tubes into long pieces. We made breastplates, helmets, and shields out of cardboard. We painted designs on the shields and cuirasses we'd finished. The plans for all this get-up and for the coats-of-arms and mottoes we painted on it were all Lajosipha Joiner's; she told us what everything was supposed to be called, showed us how to use strips of rubber as flexings on our shin- and armguards, and insisted that every flimsy lance have a banner tied to it somewhere along its length. A few of us made broad swords out of scrap lumber, and Little Mick found a number of odd-sized tins which he cobbled together on a board for a set of marching drums. Lajosipha supervised everything. Her hands were streaked with three different colors of paint right up to her elbows. We were really busy.

Priesman came by in the afternoon. He was sweaty and crotchety, he had gray circles under his eyes. "What the hell is this, Neddie? You think you're going on a goddamn *crusade?*"

"No metal, you said. We've made our own stuff."

"Listen, the first Children's Crusade was a fiasco. If I know anything at all about first-strike advantage, Neddie, this one isn't going to go a bit better. They'll hear you coming. They'll *see* you coming. It'll all turn out a botch, and Simpson'll have my neck."

"He'll have your scrotum for a dice bag," I corrected Priesman.

"That'll all right," Lajosipha said, answering the Lieutenant instead of me. "We don't sneak." She was wearing a cardboard breastplate with a drippy red eagle outlined a little off-center against it. A white hand print lay on her left cheek like Indian war paint.

Priesman turned to me. "Neddie—"

"It'll be okay," I assured him. "We don't have to sneak to hit 'em right. We really don't."

Not looking at anybody, the Lieutenant said, "Shit!" Then he unslung his carbine, fired three quick, pinging shots at the weather vane on the number 4 barracks, and stalked to the entrance of Little Camp Fuji. Here he turned around and spoke only to me: "*Our* scrotums, Neddie. Yours and mine. Simpson wants Turska taken down and out, but her daddy was a field commander with the original rampart force, fifteen years ago, and it's got to be done obliquely." He let his eyes rove disgustedly over our medieval get-ups. "Obliquely doesn't mean back-asswardly, Neddie. I swear, you just don't seem to understand."

He wiped his forehead with his sleeve, sent a blob of spittle into the dust, and disappeared up the hillside between an ashy-black automobile and a row of trashed phone booths.

On Vernalfest morning Lajosipha was the first one off the floor. And the first one to get down on it again in order to pray. Keening, moaning low, coughing from the spring cold, she woke the rest of us up. The barracks were dark, and when some of the kids in number 3 started slamming doors to the dormitories next to us, it was hard not to think of gun shots.

With Little Mick's thermals under me for a mattress I lay staring at the ribbed ceiling and remembering how until I was four I had lived in the lobby of the International Hotel. Then the airport-siders had collapsed the building with mortars, and it was almost two years—I got real good at looting and grubbing, even as a little kid—before the first kiddie camps were "bilaterally organized." Priesman says there's a six-year-old treaty outlawing military activity in or around the camps, but Fuji's been strafed before and so have Viperhole and Mouse Town. Maybe the kids on airport side have caught it, too, I don't know. But if you just look up, you can see the colander holes above the rafters . . .

"Come on, Neddie," Brian Rabbek said. "If we don't get started, it'll be light soon."

Everyone dressed. Everyone pulled on their cuirasses, casques, and greaves, old Lajosipha right there to say which was which and to help lace you in if you couldn't do it yourself. Outside, as the aspens on the mountain ridge began to twinkle, we grabbed our lances and formed up in two columns. Little Mick started bongoing his peppermint and tobacco tins, but someone knocked him on his ass, and the stillness got thick and nerve-tweaking again. Pretty soon, we were all shuffling out of Little Camp Fuji like the pallbearers at a propaganda funeral. It was eerie, marching in front of them before first light.

I wasn't really in front, though. Lajosipha Joiner marched ahead of me, wearing a long white dress that had once been her mother's and not an ounce of cardboard armoring. Her goose-neck arms weaved back and forth as she walked, as if she was spelling the sun to come up. I didn't mind her going ahead of even me, because I kept waiting for a 'rilla unit—ours or theirs—to spring out of the rubble into our path and mow everybody down with words or rifle fire. In the cool, spooky morning rifle fire didn't seem much worse than words. Also, it was okay by me if Lajosipha wanted to lead us to Poohburgh, because it sits about two miles off the perimeter expressway in an area of rocks called Sand Spire and I felt like she knew where we were going maybe even better than I did. She had a sense for that kind of thing. So all I had to do that morning was wonder why, except for the flapping of our banners, it was so still and quiet.

"Truce today," Brian Rabbek whispered. "Vernalfest truce. We're breaking it, Neddie."

I guess we were, going against a rampart-side camp on the first Sunday after the spring's first full moon—but what mattered to me was doing what Priesman had asked and getting promoted into an adult unit bivouacked on the mountain face overlooking City. I was too old for Little Camp Fuji. Only a couple of the kids had ever really seemed like family to me, which was how Priesman said I ought to think of *all* of them. Anyhow, I've heard Simpson say truces are made to be broken, that's what they're for . . .

"Play, Little Mick," Lajosipha commanded loudly as we straggled into Sand Spire toward the quonsets of Poohburgh. "Give us a tat-and-a-too to march to."

So Little Mick, with permission this time, began bongoing his tins, and all us Fujiniles flapped and fluttered along, holding our lances high and squinting against the pale light seeping across the eastern plains and through the ruins of City to the rock garden surrounding Poohburgh.

A sentry heard or saw us coming. He raised a piping, echoing shout to rouse his barracksmates. They got up in a hurry, too. They got up a lot faster than we had, in fact, so that whatever "first-strike advantage" Preisman had wished for us was lost by our fluttering and drumming. That didn't seem to matter, though. Our get-ups—our visors, our shields, our other cardboard whatnots—put even the older Poohburghers in a panic, and Lajosipha led us right up their main avenue before any of them thought of picking up a rock and flinging it at our funny-looking heads.

By this time our lances had come down and we were spreading out across the camp like iodine seeping through a bucket of water, scuffling along beside each other with our broad swords and lances pricking at whoever not from Fuji got in our way. I don't remember a whole lot of what happened, except that it didn't seem cool after we'd tramped into the Sand Spire area. I remember that a lot of the younger kids on the other side came out of their quonsets without many clothes on, and a couple of little boys were stiff from the dawn shock. When we chased them up against a porch railing or a boulder of sandstone, their bellies gave way as easily as a wet sponge would. What I remember mostly, I guess, is scuffling and screaming and myself feeling sick because everything seemed to take so long. It all just went on and on, and in the midst of it all I remember Lajosipha Joiner weaving spells with her arms and charming us invincible.

Finally, someone thought of picking up a rock. The first one thrown struck Lajosipha in the eye, and she crumpled down into her tattered white dress like a wilting flower. Then more rocks came, and while I was trying to pull Lajosipha out of camp I could hear the rocks bouncing off shields and breastplates with sickening *thwumps*. On one side of me I saw Brian Rabbek retrieving stones from the ground and chunking them back at the kids who had thrown them. Awkward Alice Gomez was doing the same thing on the other side. Pulling Lajosipha along, I noticed that the dust was clotted and sticky, but didn't really think about anything but getting her home. Throwing rocks and jabbing with our lances, we retreated. We backed out of the Poohburgh kiddie camp, tore our armor off, and tossed aside our weapons, and, after regrouping on the far side of the Sand Spire overpass, helped each other get home to Fuji.

Lajosipha was dead. We buried her in her mother's dress in the trough of dirt where we used to spit and roast the greyhounds Priesman brought us. Little Mick and a couple of kids from the number 2 barracks never came back at all. Not counting one kid's mild concussion and some really-nothing scrapes and bruises, though, these were the only casualties we suffered. Brian Rabbek says we were gone only an hour and twenty minutes, and most of that time was used getting down to Sand Spire for the attack and then returning home. Three days later, in spite of how bad my memory is concerning what we did down there, I feel like we spent the whole day in Poohburgh. The rest of Vernalfest is just a shadow thrown by the morning, even poor Lajosipha's burial. We just dug her down and covered her up. I don't think a single one of us thought about carrying her in a prop-procession through the main streets here on rampart side, and that's too bad.

That's why I say that the rest of Vernalfest was just a shadow thrown by the morning.

It wasn't until yesterday that Priesman got by to see us again. I had myself so worked up waiting for him that two or three times I nearly went out looking for his unit's bivouac, just to ask him how us Fujiniles had done. When he finally came strolling in, though, Priesman was wearing *two* carbines and a smile that made his 'rilla burns stand out.

"Turska broke, tough old Maud herself. Her daughter by an airport-sider was in Poohburgh Vernalfest morning, and that just wiped her out. She fessed the whole schmeer under sedation, and Simpson's higher than a migrating goose." Priesman tossed a rifle at me. "Here's your carbine, Theodore. Let's get the hell out of Little Camp Fuji."

"I've been promoted?"

"Sure." He bent his fatigue collar down so that I could see the new insignia on it. "And so have I, Theodore, so have I."

Here's another excellent story by George R. R. Martin, a powerful and exotic study of the future of religion, and a very special kind of heresy. . . .

GEORGE R. R. MARTIN
The Way of Cross and Dragon

"Heresy," he told me. The brackish waters of his pool sloshed gently.

"Another one?" I said wearily. "There are so many these days."

My Lord Commander was displeased by that comment. He shifted position heavily, sending ripples up and down the pool. One broke over the side, and a sheet of water slid across the tiles of the receiving chamber. My boots were soaked yet again. I accepted that philosophically. I had worn my worst boots, well aware that wet feet are among the inescapable consequences of paying call on Torgathon Nine-Klariis Tûn, elder of the ka-Thane people, and also Archbishop of Vess, Most Holy Father of the Four Vows, Grand Inquisitor of the Order Militant of the Knights of Jesus Christ, and councillor to His Holiness, Pope Daryn XXI of New Rome.

"Be there as many heresies as stars in the sky, each single one is no less dangerous, Father," the Archbishop said solemnly. "As Knights of Christ, it is our ordained task to fight them one and all. And I must add that this new heresy is particularly foul."

"Yes, my Lord Commander," I replied. "I did not intend to make light of it. You have my apologies. The mission to Finnegan was most taxing. I had hoped to ask you for a leave of absence from my duties. I need a rest, a time for thought and restoration."

"Rest?" The Archbishop moved again in his pool, only a slight shift of his immense bulk, but it was enough to send a fresh sheet of water across the floor. His black, pupilless eyes blinked at me. "No, Father, I am afraid that is out of the question. Your skills and your experience are vital for this new mission." His bass tones seemed to soften somewhat then. "I have not had time to go over your reports on Finnegan," he said. "How did your work go?"

"Badly," I told him, "though ultimately I think we will prevail. The Church is strong on Finnegan. When our attempts at reconciliation were rebuffed, I put some standards into the right hands, and we were able to shut down the heretics' newspaper and broadcast faciles. Our friends also saw to it that their legal action came to nothing."

"That is not *badly*," the Archbishop said. "You won a considerable victory for the Lord."

"There were riots, my Lord Commander," I said. "More than a hundred of the heretics were killed, and a dozen of our own people. I fear there will be more violence before the matter is finished. Our priests are attacked if they so much as enter the city where the heresy has taken root. Their leaders risk their lives if they leave that city. I had hoped to avoid such hatreds, such bloodshed."

"Commendable, but not realistic," said Archbishop Torgathon. He blinked at me again, and I remembered that among people of his race that was a sign of impatience. "The blood of martyrs must sometimes be spilled, and the blood of heretics as well. What matters it if a being surrenders his life, so long as his soul is saved?"

"Indeed," I agreed. Despite his impatience, Torgathon would lecture for another hour if given a chance. That prospect dismayed me. The receiving chamber was not designed for human comfort, and I did not wish to remain any longer than necessary. The walls were damp and moldy, the air hot and humid and thick with the rancid-butter smell characteristic of the ka-Thane. My collar was chafing my neck raw, I was sweating beneath my cassock, my feet were thoroughly soaked, and my stomach was beginning to churn. I pushed ahead to the business at hand. "You say this new heresy is unusually foul, my Lord Commander?"

"It is," he said.

"Where has it started?"

"On Arion, a world some three weeks distance from Vess. A human world entirely. I cannot understand why you humans are so easily corrupted. Once a ka-Thane has found the faith, he would scarcely abandon it."

"That is well known," I said politely. I did not mention that the number of ka-Thane to find the faith was vanishingly small. They were a slow, ponderous people, and most of their vast millions showed no interest in learning any ways other than their own, or following any creed but their own ancient religion. Torgathon Nine-Klariis Tûn was an anomaly. He had been among the first converts almost two centuries ago, when Pope Vidas L had ruled that non-humans might serve as clergy. Given his great lifespan and the iron certainty of his belief, it was no wonder that Torgathon had risen as far as he had, despite the fact that less than a thousand of his race had followed him into the Church. He had at least a century of life remaining to him. No doubt he would someday be Torgathon Cardinal Tûn, should he squelch enough heresies. The times are like that.

"We have little influence on Arion," the Archbishop was saying. His arms moved as he spoke, four ponderous clubs of mottled green-gray flesh churning the water, and the dirty white cilia around his breathing hole trembled with each word. "A few priests, a few churches, some believers, but no power to speak of. The heretics already outnumber us on this world. I rely on your intellect, your shrewdness. Turn this calamity into an opportunity. This heresy is so palpable that you can easily disprove it. Perhaps some of the deluded will turn to the true way."

"Certainly," I said. "And the nature of this heresy? What must I disprove?" It is a sad indication of my own troubled faith to add that I did not really care. I have dealt with too many heresies. Their beliefs and their questionings echo in my head and trouble my dreams at night. How can I be sure of my own faith? The very edict that had admitted Torgathon into the clergy had caused a half-dozen worlds to repudiate the Bishop of New Rome, and those who had followed that path would find a particularly ugly heresy in the massive naked (save for a damp Roman collar) alien who floated before me, and wielded the authority of the Church in four great webbed hands. Christianity is the greatest single human religion, but that means little. The non-Christians outnumber us five-to-one and there are well over seven hundred Christian sects, some almost as large as the One True Interstellar Catholic Church of Earth and the Thousand Worlds. Even Daryn XXI, powerful as he is, is only one of seven to claim the title of Pope. My own belief was strong once, but I have moved too long among heretics and non-believers, and even my prayers do not make the doubts go away now. So it was that I felt no horror—only a sudden intellectual interest—when the Archbishop told me the nature of the heresy in Arion.

"They have made a saint," he said, "out of Judas Iscariot."

As a senior in the Knights Inquisitor, I command my own starship, which it pleases me to call the *Truth of Christ*. Before the craft was assigned to me it was named the *St. Thomas*, after the apostle, but I did not feel a saint notorious for doubting was an appropriate patron for a ship enlisted in the fight against heresy. I have no duties aboard the *Truth*, which is crewed by six brothers and sisters of the Order of St. Christopher the Far-Travelling, and captained by a young woman I hired away from a merchant trader.

I was therefore able to devote the entire three-week voyage from Vess to Arion to study of the heretical Bible, a copy which had been given to me by the Archbishop's administrative assistant. It was a thick, heavy, handsome book, bound in dark leather, its pages tipped with gold leaf, with many splendid interior illustrations in full color with holographic enhancement. Remarkable work clearly done by someone who loved the all-but-forgotten art of book-making. The paintings reproduced inside— the originals were to be found on the walls of the House of St. Judas on

Arion, I gathered—were masterful, if blasphemous, as much high art as the Tammerwens and RoHallidays that adorn the Great Cathedral of St. John in New Rome.

Inside the book bore an imprimatur indicating that it had been approved by Lukyan Judasson, First Scholar of the Order of St. Judas Iscariot.

It was called *The Way of Cross and Dragon*.

I read it as the *Truth of Christ* slid between the stars, at first taking copious notes to better understand the heresy I must fight, but later simply absorbed by the strange, convoluted, grotesque story it told. The words of text had passion and power and poetry.

Thus it was that I first encountered the striking figure of St. Judas Iscariot, a complex, ambitious, contradictory, and altogether extraordinary human being.

He was born of a whore in the fabled ancient city-state of Babylon on the same day that the savior was born in Bethlehem, and he spent his childhood in the alleys and gutters, selling his own body when he had to, pimping when he was older. As a youth he began to experiment with the dark arts, and before the age of twenty he was a skilled necromancer. That was when he became Judas the Dragon-Tamer, the first and only man to bend to his will the most fearsome of God's creatures, the great winged fire-lizards of Old Earth. The book held a marvelous painting of Judas in some great dank cavern, his eyes aflame as he wielded a glowing lash to keep at bay a mountainous green-gold dragon. Beneath his arm is a woven basket, its lid slightly ajar, and the tiny scaled heads of three dragon chicks are peering from within. A fourth infant dragon is crawling up his sleeve. That was in the first chapter of his life.

In the second, he was Judas the Conquerer, Judas the Dragon-King, Judas of Babylon, the Great Usurper. Astride the greatest of his dragons, with an iron crown on his head and a sword in his hand, he made Babylon the Capital of the greatest empire Old Earth had ever known, a realm that stretched from Spain to India. He reigned from a dragon throne amid the Hanging Gardens he had caused to be constructed, and it was there he sat when he tried Jesus of Nazareth, the troublemaking prophet who had been dragged before him bound and bleeding. Judas was not a patient man, and he made Christ bleed still more before he was through with Him. And when Jesus would not answer his questions, Judas—contemptuous—had Him cast back out into the streets. But first he ordered his guards to cut off Christ's legs. "Healer," he said, "Heal thyself."

Then came the Repentance, the vision in the night, and Judas Iscariot gave up his crown and his dark arts and his riches, to follow the man he had crippled. Despised and taunted by those he had tyrannized, Judas became the Legs of the Lord, and for a year carried Jesus on his back to the far corners of the realm he once ruled. When Jesus did finally heal Himself, then Judas walked at his side, and from that time forth he was Jesus' trusted friend and counselor, the first and foremost of the Twelve. Finally Jesus gave Judas the gift of tongues, recalled and sanctified the dragons that Judas had sent away, and sent his disciple forth on a solitary ministry across the oceans, ''to spread My Word where I cannot go.''

There came a day when the sun went dark at noon, and the ground trembled, and Judas swung his dragon around on ponderous wings and flew back across the raging seas. But when he reached the city of Jerusalem, he found Christ dead on the cross.

In that moment his faith faltered, and for the next three days the Great Wrath of Judas was like a storm across the ancient world. His dragons razed the Temple in Jerusalem, and drove the people forth from the city, and struck as well at the great seats of power in Rome and Babylon. And when he found the others of the Twelve and questioned them and learned of how the one named Simon-called-Peter had three times betrayed the Lord, he strangled Peter with his own hands and fed the corpse to his dragons. Then he sent those dragons forth to start fires throughout the world, funeral pyres for Jesus of Nazareth.

And Jesus rose on the third day, and Judas wept, but his tears could not turn Christ's anger, for in his wrath he had betrayed all of Christ's teachings.

So Jesus called back the dragons, and they came, and everywhere the fires went out. And from their bellies he called forth Peter and made him whole again, and gave him dominion over the Church.

Then the dragons died, and so too did all dragons everywhere, for they were the living sigil of the power and wisdom of Judas Iscariot, who had sinned greatly. And He took from Judas the gift of tongues and power of healing He had given, and even his eyesight, for Judas had acted as a man blind (there was a fine painting of the blinded Judas weeping over the bodies of his dragons). And He told Judas that for long ages he would be remembered only as Betrayer, and people would curse his name, and all that he had been and done would be forgotten.

But then, because Judas had loved Him so, Christ gave him a boon; an extended life, during which he might travel and think on his sins and finally come to forgiveness, and only then die.

And that was the beginning of the last chapter in the life of Judas Iscariot, but it was a very long chapter indeed. Once dragon king, once the friend of Christ, now he became only a blind traveler, outcast and friendless, wandering all the cold roads of the Earth, living even when all the cities and people and things he had known were dead. And Peter, the first Pope and ever his enemy, spread far and wide the tale of how Judas had sold Christ for thirty pieces of silver, until Judas dared not even use his true name. For a time he called himself just Wandering Ju', and afterwards many other names. He lived more than a thousand years, and became a preacher, and a healer, and a lover of animals, and was hunted and persecuted when the Church that Peter had founded became bloated and corrupt. But he had a great deal of time, and at last he found wisdom and a sense of peace, and finally Jesus came to him on a long-postponed deathbed, and they were reconciled, and Judas wept once again. And before he died, Christ promised that he would permit a few to remember who and what Judas had been, and that with the passage of centuries the news would spread, until finally Peter's Lie was displaced and forgotten.

Such was the life of St. Judas Iscariot, as related in *The Way of Cross and Dragon*. His teachings were there as well, and the apocryphal books he had allegedly written.

When I had finished the volume, I lent it to Arla-k-Bau, the captain of the *Truth of Christ*. Arla was a gaunt, pragmatic woman of no particular faith, but I valued her opinion. The others of my crew, the good sisters and brothers of St. Christopher, would only have echoed the Archbishop's religious horror.

"Interesting," Arla said when she returned the book to me.

I chuckled. "Is that all?"

She shrugged. "It makes a nice story. An easier read than your Bible, Damien, and more dramatic as well."

"True," I admitted. "But it's absurd. An unbelievable tangle of doctrine, apocrypha, mythology, and superstition. Entertaining, yes, certainly. Imaginative, even daring. But ridiculous, don't you think? How can you credit dragons? A legless Christ? Peter being pieced together after being devoured by four monsters?"

Arla's grin was taunting. "Is that any sillier than water changing into wine, or Christ walking on the waves, or a man living in the belly of a fish?" Arla-k-Bau liked to jab at me. It had been a scandal when I selected a non-believer as my captain, but she was very good at her job, and I liked her around to keep me sharp. She had a good mind, Arla did, and I valued that more than blind obedience. Perhaps that was a sin in me.

"There is a difference," I said.

"Is there?" she snapped back. Her eyes saw through my masks. "Ah, Damien, admit it. You rather liked this book."

I cleared my throat. "It piqued my interest," I acknowledged. I had to justify myself. "You know the kind of matter I deal with ordinarily. Dreary little doctrinal deviations, obscure quibblings on theology somehow blown all out of proportion, bald-faced political maneuverings designed to set some ambitious planetary bishop up as a new pope, or wring some concession or other from New Rome or Vess. The war is endless, but the battles are dull and dirty. They exhaust me, spiritually, emotionally, physically. Afterwards I feel drained and guilty." I tapped the book's leather cover. "This is different. The heresy must be crushed, of course, but I admit that I am anxious to meet this Lukyan Judasson.''

''The artwork is lovely as well,'' Arla said, flipping through the pages of *The Way of Cross and Dragon* and stopping to study one especially striking plate. Judas weeping over his dragons, I think. I smiled to see that it had affected her as much as me. Then I frowned.

That was the first inkling I had of the difficulties ahead.

So it was that the *Truth of Christ* came to the porcelain city Ammadon on the world of Arion, where the Order of St. Judas Iscariot kept its House.

Arion was a pleasant, gentle world, inhabited for these past three centuries. Its population was under nine million; Ammadon, the only real city, was home to two of those millions. The technological level was medium high, but chiefly imported. Arion had little industry and was not an innovative world, except perhaps artistically. The arts were quite important here, flourishing and vital. Religious freedom was a basic tenet of the society, but Arion was not a religious world either, and the majority of the populace lived devoutly secular lives. The most popular religion was Aestheticism, which hardly counts as a religion at all. There were also Taoists, Erikaners, Old True Christers, and Children of the Dreamer, plus a dozen lesser sects.

And finally there were nine churches of the One True Interstellar Catholic faith. There had been twelve.

The other three were now houses of Arion's fastest-growing faith, the Order of St. Judas Iscariot, which also had a dozen newly built churches of its own.

The Bishop of Arion was a dark, severe man with close-cropped black hair who was not at all happy to see me. ''Damien Har Venis!'' he exclaimed in some wonder when I called on him at his residence. ''We have heard of you, of course, but I never thought to meet or host you. Our numbers are small here—''

''And growing smaller,'' I said, ''a matter of some concern to my Lord Commander, Archbishop Torgathon. Apparently you are less troubled, Excellency, since you did not see fit to report the activities of this sect of Judas worshippers.''

He looked briefly angry at the rebuke, but quickly swallowed his temper. Even a bishop can fear a Knight Inquisitor. ''We are concerned, of course,'' he said. ''We do all we can to combat the heresy. If you have advice that will help us, I will be glad to listen.''

''I am an Inquisitor of the Order Militant of the Knights of Jesus Christ,'' I said bluntly. ''I do not give advice, Excellency. I take action. To that end I was sent to Arion and that is what I shall do. Now, tell me what you know about this heresy, and this First Scholar, this Lukyan Judasson.''

"Of course, Father Damien," the Bishop began. He signaled for a servant to bring us a tray of wine and cheese, and began to summarize the short, but explosive, history of the Judas cult. I listened, polishing my nails on the crimson lapel of my jacket, until the black paint gleamed brilliantly, interrupting from time to time with a question. Before he had half finished, I was determined to vist Lukyan personally. It seemed the best course of action.

And I had wanted to do it all along.

Appearances were important on Arion, I gathered, and I deemed it necessary to impress Lukyan with my self and my station. I wore my best boots, sleek dark hand-made boots of Roman leather that had never seen the inside of Torgathon's receiving chamber, and a severe black suit with deep burgundy lapels and stiff collar. Around my neck was a splendid crucifix of pure gold; my collarpin was a matching golden sword, the sigil of the Knights Inquisitor. Brother Denis painted my nails carefully, all black as ebon, and darkened my eyes as well, and used a fine white powder on my face. When I glanced in the mirror, I frightened even myself. I smiled, but only briefly. It ruined the effect.

I walked to the House of St. Judas Iscariot. The streets of Ammadon were wide and spacious and golden, lined by scarlet trees called whisperwinds whose long, drooping tendrils did indeed seem to whisper secrets to the gentle breeze. Sister Judith came with me. She is a small woman, slight of build even in the cowled coveralls of the Order of St. Christopher. Her face is meek and kind, her eyes wide and youthful and innocent. I find her useful. Four times now she has killed those who attempted to assault me.

The House itself was newly built. Rambling and stately, it rose from amid gardens of small bright flowers and seas of golden grass, and the gardens were surrounded by a high wall. Murals covered both the outer wall around the property and the exterior of the building itself. I recognized a few of them from *The Way of Cross and Dragon,* and stopped briefly to admire them before walking on through the main gate. No one tried to stop us. There were no guards, not even a receptionist. Within the walls, men and women strolled languidly through the flowers, or sat on benches beneath silverwoods and whisperwinds.

Sister Judith and I paused, then made our way directly to the House itself.

We had just started up the steps when a man appeared from within, and stood waiting in the doorway. He was blond, and fat, with a great wiry beard that framed a slow smile, and he wore a flimsy robe that fell to his sandaled feet, and on the robe were dragons, dragons bearing the silhouette of a man holding a cross.

When I reached the top of the steps, he bowed to me. "Father

Damien Har Veris of the Knights Inquisitor," he said. His smile widened. "I greet you in the name of Jesus, and St. Judas. I am Lukyan."

I made a note to myself to find out which of the Bishop's staff was feeding information to the Judas cult, but my composure did not break. I have been a Knight Inquisitor for a long, long time. "Father Lukyan Mo," I said, taking his hand. "I have questions to ask of you." I did not smile.

He did. "I thought you might," he said.

Lukyan's office was large but Spartan. Heretics often have a simplicity that the officers of the true Church seem to have lost. He did have one indulgence, however. Dominating the wall behind his desk/console was the painting I had already fallen in love with: the blinded Judas weeping over his dragons.

Lukyan sat down heavily and motioned me to a second chair. We had left Sister Judith outside in the waiting chamber. "I prefer to stand, Father Lukyan," I said, knowing it gave me an advantage.

"Just Lukyan," he said. "Or Luke, if you prefer. We have little use for hierarchy here."

"You are Father Lukyan Mo, born here on Arion, educated in the seminary on Cathaday, a former priest of the One True Interstellar Catholic Church of Earth and the Thousand Worlds," I said. "I will address you as befits your station, Father. I expect you to reciprocate. Is that understood?"

"Oh, yes," he said amiably.

"I am empowered to strip you of your right to perform the sacraments, to order you shunned and excommunicated for this heresy you have formulated. On certain worlds I could even order your death."

"But not on Arion," Lukyan said quickly. "We're very tolerant here. Besides, we outnumber you." He smiled. "As for the rest, well, I don't perform those sacraments much anyway, you know. Not for years. I'm First Scholar now. A teacher, a thinker. I show others the way, help them find the faith. Excommunicate me if it will make you happy, Father Damien. Happiness is what all of us seek."

"You have given up the faith then, Father Lukyan," I said. I deposited my copy of *The Way of Cross and Dragon* on his desk. "But I see you have found a new one." Now I did smile, but it was all ice, all menace, all mockery. "A more ridiculous creed I have yet to encounter. I suppose you will tell me that you have spoken to God, that he trusted you with this new revelation, so that you might clear the good name, such that it is, of Holy Judas?"

Now Lukyan's smile was very broad indeed. He picked up the book and beamed at me. "Oh, no," he said. "No, I made it all up."

That stopped me. "What?"

"I made it all up," he repeated. He hefted the book fondly. "I drew on many sources, of course, especially the Bible, but I do think of *Cross and Dragon* mostly as my own work. It's rather good, don't you agree? Of course, I could hardly put my name on it, proud as I am of it, but I did include my imprimatur. Did you notice that? It was the closest I dared come to a by-line."

I was only speechless for a moment. Then I grimaced. "You startle me," I admitted. "I expected to find an inventive madman, some poor self-deluded fool firm in his belief that he had spoken to God. I've dealt with such fanatics before. Instead I find a cheerful cynic who has invented a religion for his own profit. I think I prefer the fanatics. You are beneath contempt, Father Lukyan. You will burn in hell for eternity."

"I doubt it," Lukyan said, "but you do mistake me, Father Damien. I am no cynic, nor do I profit from my dear St. Judas. Truthfully, I lived more comfortably as a priest of your own Church. I do this because it is my vocation."

I sat down. "You confuse me," I said. "Explain."

"Now I am going to tell you the Truth," he said. He said it in an odd way, almost as a cant. "I am a liar," he added.

"You want to confuse me with a child's paradoxes," I snapped.

"No, no," he smiled. "A *Liar*. With a capital. It is an organization, Father Damien. A religion, you might call it. A great and powerful faith. And I am the smallest part of it."

"I know of no such church," I said.

"Oh, no, you wouldn't. It's secret. It has to be. You can understand that, can't you? People don't like being lied to."

"I do not like being lied to," I said.

Lukyan looked wounded. "I told you this would be the truth, didn't I? When a Liar says that, you can believe him. How else could we trust each other?"

"There are many of you," I said. I was starting to think that Lukyan was a madman after all, as fanatic as any heretic, but in a more complex way. Here was a heresy within a heresy, but I recognized my duty; to find the truth of things, and set them right.

"Many of us," Lukyan said, smiling. "You would be surprised, Father Damien, really you would. But there are some things I dare not tell you."

"Tell me what you dare, then."

"Happily," said Lukyan Judasson. "We Liars, like all other religions, have several truths we take on faith. Faith is always required. There are some things that cannot be proven. We believe that life is worth living. That is an article of faith. The purpose of life is to live, to resist death, perhaps to defy entropy."

"Go on," I said, interested despite myself.

"We also believe that happiness is a good, something to be sought after."

"The Church does not oppose happiness," I said dryly.

"I wonder," Lukyan said. "But let us not quibble. Whatever the Church's position on happiness, it does preach belief in an afterlife, in a supreme being, and a complex moral code."

"True."

"The Liars believe in no afterlife, no God. We see the universe as it *is*, Father Damien, and these naked truths are cruel ones. We who believe in life, and treasure it, will die. Afterwards there will be nothing, eternal emptiness, blackness, nonexistence. In our living there has been no purpose, no poetry, no meaning. Nor do our deaths possess these qualities. When we are gone, the universe will not long remember us, and shortly it will be as if we had never lived at all. Our worlds and our universe will not long outlive us. Ultimately entropy will consume all, and our puny efforts cannot stay that awful end. it will be gone. It has never been. It has never mattered. The universe itself is doomed, transient, uncaring."

I slid back in my chair, and a shiver went through me as I listened to poor Lukyan's dark words. I found myself fingering my crucifix. "A bleak philosophy," I said, "as well as a false one. I have had that fearful vision myself. I think all of us do, at some point. But it is not so, Father. My faith sustains me against such nihilism. It is a shield against despair."

"Oh, I know that, my friend, my Knight Inquisitor," Lukyan said. "I'm glad to see you understand so well. You are almost one of us already."

I frowned.

"You've touched the heart of it," Lukyan continued. "The truths, the great truths—and most of the lesser ones as well—they are unbearable for most men. We find our shield in faith. Your faith, my faith, any faith. It doesn't matter, so long as we *believe*, really and truly believe, in whatever lie we cling to." He fingered the ragged edges of his great blond beard. "Our psychs have always told us that believers are the happy ones, you know. They may believe in Christ or Buddha or Erika Stormjones, in reincarnation or immortality or nature, in the power of love or the platform of a political faction, but it all comes to the same thing. They believe. They are happy. It is the ones who have seen the truth who despair, and kill themselves. The truths are so vast, the faiths so little, so poorly made, so riddled with error and contradiction. We see around them and through them, and then we feel the weight of darkness on us, and we can no longer be happy."

I am not a slow man. I knew, by then, where Lukyan Judasson was going. "Your Liars invent faiths."

He smiled. "Of all sorts. Not only religions. Think of it. We know truth for the cruel instrument it is. Beauty is infinitely preferable to truth. We invent beauty. Faiths, political movements, high ideals, belief in love and fellowship. All of them are lies. We tell those lies, and others, endless others. We improve on history and myth and religion, make each more beautiful, better, easier to believe in. Our lies are not perfect, of course. The truths are too big. But perhaps someday we will find one great lie that all humanity can use. Until then, a thousand small lies will do.''

''I think I do not care for your Liars very much,'' I said with a cold, even fervor. ''My whole life has been a quest for truth.''

Lukyan was indulgent. ''Father Damien Har Veris, Knight Inquisitor, I know you better than that. You are a Liar yourself. You do good work. You ship from world to world, and on each you destroy the foolish, the rebels, the questioners who would bring down the edifice of the vast lie that you serve.''

''If my lie is so admirable,'' I said, ''then why have you abandoned it?''

''A religion must fit its culture and society, work with them, not against them. If there is conflict, contradiction, then the lie breaks down, and the faith falters. Your Church is good for many worlds, Father, but not for Arion. Life is too kind here, and your faith is stern. Here we love beauty, and your faith offers too little. So we have improved it. We studied this world for a long time. We know its psychological profile. St. Judas will thrive here. He offers drama, and color, and much beauty— the aesthetics are admirable. His is a tragedy with a happy ending, and Arion dotes on such stories. And the dragons are a nice touch. I think your own Church ought to find a way to work in dragons. They are marvelous creatures.''

''Mythical,'' I said.

''Hardly,'' he replied. ''Look it up.'' He grinned at me. ''You see, really, it all comes back to faith. Can you really know what happened three thousand years ago? You have one Judas, I have another. Both of us have books. Is yours true? Can you really believe that? I have only been admitted to the first circle of the order of Liars, so I do not know all our secrets, but I know that we are very old. It would not surprise me to learn that the gospels were written by men very much like me. Perhaps there never was a Judas at all. Or a Jesus.''

''I have faith that is not so,'' I said.

''There are a hundred people in this building who have a deep and very real faith in St. Judas, and the way of cross and dragon,'' Lukyan said. ''Faith is a very good thing. Do you know that the suicide rate on Arion has decreased by almost a third since the Order of St. Judas was founded?''

I remember rising very slowly from my chair. "You are fanatic as any heretic I have ever met, Lukyan Judasson," I told him. "I pity you the loss of your faith."

Lukyan rose with me. "Pity yourself, Damien Har Veris," he said. "I have found a new faith and a new cause, and I am a happy man. You, my dear friend, are tortured and miserable."

"That is a lie!" I am afraid I screamed.

"Come with me," Lukyan said. He touched a panel on his wall, and the great painting of Judas weeping over his dragons slid up out of sight, and there was a stairway leading down into the ground. "Follow me," he said.

In the cellar was a great glass vat full of pale green fluid, and in it a *thing* was floating, a thing very like an ancient embryo, aged and infantile at the same time, naked, with a huge head and a tiny atrophied body. Tubes ran from its arms and legs and genitals, connecting it to the machinery that kept it alive.

When Lukyan turned on the lights, it opened its eyes. They were large and dark and they looked into my soul.

"This is my colleague," Lukyan said, patting the side of the vat, "Jon Azure Cross, a Liar of the fourth circle."

"And a telepath," I said with a sick certaintly. I had led pogroms against other telepaths, children mostly, on other worlds. The Church teaches that the psionic powers are a trap of Satan's. They are not mentioned in the Bible. I have never felt good about those killings.

"Jon read you the moment you entered the compound," Lukyan said, "and notified me. Only a few of us know that he is here. He helps us lie most efficiently. He knows when faith is true, and when it is feigned. I have an implant in my skull. Jon can talk to me at all times. It was he who initially recruited me into the Liars. He knew my faith was hollow. He felt the depth of my despair."

Then the thing in the tank spoke, its metallic voice coming from a speaker-grill in the base of the machine that nurtured it. *And I feel yours, Damien Har Veris, empty priest. Inquisitor, you have asked too many questions. You are sick at heart, and tired, and you do not believe. Join us, Damien. You have been a Liar for a long, long time!"*

For a moment I hesitated, looking deep into myself, wondering what it was I did believe. I searched for my faith, the fire that had once sustained me, the certainty in the teachings of the Church, the presence of Christ within me. I found none of it, none. I was empty inside, burned out, full of questions and pain. But as I was about to answer Jon Azure Cross and the smiling Lukyan Judasson, I found something else, something I *did* believe in, had always believed in.

Truth.

I believed in truth, even when it hurt.

"He is lost to us," said the telepath with the mocking name of Cross.

Lukyan's smile faded. "Oh, really? I had hoped you would be one of us, Damien. You seemed ready."

I was suddenly afraid, and considered sprinting up the stairs to Sister Judith. Lukyan had told me so very much, and now I had rejected them. The telepath felt my fear. *"You cannot hurt us, Damien,"* it said. *"Go in peace. Lukyan told you nothing."*

Lukyan was frowning. "I told him a good deal, Jon," he said.

"Yes. But can he trust the words of such a Liar as you?" The small misshapen mouth of the thing in the vat twitched in a smile, and its great eyes closed, and Lukyan Judasson sighed and led me up the stairs.

It was not until some years later that I realized it was Jon Azure Cross who was lying, and the victim of his lie was Lukyan. I *could* hurt them. I did.

It was almost simple. The Bishop had friends in government and media. With some money in the right places, I made some friends of my own. Then I exposed Cross in his cellar, charging that he had used his psionic powers to tamper with the minds of Lukyan's followers. My friends were receptive to the charges. The guardians conducted a raid, took the telepath Cross into custody, and later tried him.

He was innocent, of course. My charge was nonsense; human telepaths can read minds in close proximity, but seldom anything more. But they are rare, and much feared, and Cross was hideous enough so that it was easy to make him a victim of superstition. In the end, he was acquitted, and he left the city Ammadon and perhaps Arion itself, bound for regions unknown.

But it had never been my intention to convict him. The charge was enough. The cracks began to show in the lie that he and Lukyan had built together. Faith is hard to come by, and easy to lose, and the merest doubt can begin to erode even the strongest foundation of belief.

The Bishop and I labored together to sow further doubts. It was not as easy as I might have thought. The Liars had done their work well. Ammadon, like most civilized cities, had a great pool of knowledge, a computer system that linked the schools and universities and libraries together, and made their combined wisdom available to any who needed it.

But when I checked, I soon discovered that the histories of Rome and Babylon had been subtly reshaped, and there were three listings for Judas Iscariot—one for the betrayer, one for the saint, and one for the conqueror/king of Babylon. His name was also mentioned in connection with the Hanging Gardens, and there is an entry for a so-called "Codex Judas."

And according to the Ammadon library, dragons became extinct on Old Earth around the time of Christ.

We purged all those lies finally, wiped them from the memories of the computers, though we had to cite authorities on a half-dozen non-Christian worlds before the librarians and academics would credit that the differences were anything more than a question of religious preference.

By then the Order of St. Judas had withered in the glare of exposure. Lukyan Judasson had grown gaunt and angry, and at least half of his churches had closed.

The heresy never died completely, of course. There are always those who believe no matter what. And so to this day *The Way of Cross and Dragon* is read on Arion, in the porcelain city Ammadon, amid murmuring whisperwinds.

Arla-k-Bau and the *Truth of Christ* carried me back to Vess a year after my departure, and Archbishop Torgathon finally gave me the rest I had asked for, before sending me out to fight still other heresies. So I had my victory, and the Church continued on much as before, and the Order of St. Judas Isacriot was crushed and diminished. The telepath Jon Azure Cross had been wrong, I thought then. He had sadly underestimated the power of a Knight Inquisitor.

Later, though, I remembered his words.

You cannot hurt us, Damien.

Us?

The Order of St. Judas? Or the Liars?

He lied, I think, deliberately, knowing I would go forth and destroy the way of cross and dragon, knowing too that I could not touch the Liars, would not even dare mention them. How could I? Who would credit it? A grand star-spanning conspiracy as old as history? It reeks of paranoia, and I had no proof at all.

The telepath lied for Lukyan's benefit, so he would let me go. I am cetain of that now. Cross risked much to snare me. Failing, he was willing to sacrifice Lukyan Judasson and his lie, pawns in some greater game.

So I left, and I carried within me the knowledge that I was empty of faith, but for a blind faith in truth. A truth I could no longer find in my Church.

I grew certain of that in my year of rest, which I spent reading and studying on Vess and Cathaday and Celia's World. Finally I returned to the Archbishop's receiving room, and stood again before Torgathon Nine-Klariis Tûn in my very worst pair of boots. "My Lord Commander," I said to him, "I can accept no further assignments. I ask that I be retired from active service."

"For what cause?" Torgathon rumbled splashing feebly.

"I have lost the faith," I said to him, simply.

He regarded me for a long time, his pupilless eyes blinking. At last he said, "Your faith is a matter between you and your confessor. I care only about your results. You have done good work, Damien. You may not retire, and we will not allow you to resign."

The truth will set us free.

But freedom is cold, and empty, and frightening, and lies can often be warm and beautiful.

Last year the Church finally granted me a new and better ship. I named this one *Dragon*.

*Born in Boston, Hilbert Schenck is director of the ocean engineering
program at the University of Rhode Island, where he is involved in
preparing a yearly analysis of fatal scuba accidents; he is also coauthor
of the first book on amateur diving ever published. One of the more
interesting new writers to come along toward the end of the seventies,
Schenck has in recent years been publishing a number of fascinating SF
stories dealing with the sea—what mankind does to it, what it does to
mankind, and the manifold ways in which we may someday utilize it . . .
or attempt to utilize it. Schenck's sea stories have been gathered together
in* Wave Rider *(Pocket Books), an unusually-strong debut collection. A
novel,* At the Eye of the Ocean, *is forthcoming from Simon and Schuster.*

*In the story at hand, one of the best of Schenck's sea stories, he
paints a chilling and all-too-plausible picture of a Balkanizing, desperate, energy-starved America: a picture so black it would be unbearable
if Schenck's world did not also contain the dawning of one other
thing—hope.*

HILBERT SCHENCK
The Battle of the Abaco Reefs

The fall wind blew steadily from the east, dead across Elbow Cay, and the
big, vertical-axis wind machines, running synchronously in the steady
breeze, gentled the island with their hushahushahusha, a giant snoozing
in the lowest frequencies. Susan Peabody toyed with her coffee and half
watched the tiny, jewel-like TV screen at her elbow, thinking of nothing
in particular. Or, really, much in particular such as the department, and
the university, and the screwing, literal and figurative, she had taken
from that bastard. . . . But that was already six months past, and how big a
plum would it have been anyway, in a riotous, unheated Boston? . . .
Susan, a forty-year-old, tall, thin woman, her brown hair cut short and
severe, her thin lips pressed thinner still, thought to herself, hating herself
as she thought it: I have a good face, high color, a straight nose and a
strong chin. I have tits and my legs are long. Oh, for God's sake!

Susan focused on the TV screen, a brilliant spark of color. The 8
A.M. Miami news kicked off with a fire fight between the Pennsylvania
Highway Patrol and a teamster cadre after diesel fuel. In Vermont, they
were shooting wood thieves at the side of the road. Then came the latest
skirmish in the Arizona-California war over the water. . . . At least in

Boston she would have been totally involved in her profession instead of pissing away her life here in paradise. . . .

The scene shifted to London, where Scottish nationalists wrecked two government buildings and killed a number of police. "No longer drunken soccer hooligans, the Scots were well-equipped with Mark Eleven Uzi automatics. . . ." There was a knock on the door. Susan looked down at her drab and torn dressing gown and dashed from her living-room-kitchen combo into her small bedroom to pull on a halter and jean shorts, shouting, "Coming! Coming!" Who in Hell was calling at 8 A.M. in Hopetown, for God's sake?

Susan smoothed her hair and pulled the door open. It was Frank Albury; well, one of the three Frank Alburys, the electronics one. "Hi, Susan," said the portly little man, "Can I talk with you a sec?" He was perhaps thirty-five, a small roll in the gut, and completely nondescript. With an even, round, bland face and thin blond hair, he ran the island C.B. operation. An electronic wizard, Jerry Ravetz had said, but all Frank had ever talked about with Susan was the discovery of Christ and scuba diving. And she shared in this second life, in his love of the water. The first time they went together to the outer reefs where the long, hot waves broke and the massive surge ebbed and flowed over the great coral heads, Susan imagined she entered the magical Lewis story of *Perelandra* and the floating islands on the great-warm sea of never-Venus. Her father, a gentle classics professor, had read her all those books, Narnia, the Langs, *Lord of the Rings, Oz*; and as she rode the long surge of the reef looking down on its society, she flew over fairy kingdoms and the ride was magical.

But Albury watched the fish. Studying the fantastic interlocking detail of their behavior and survival, he understood absolutely that only God could make such an intricate puzzle fit together.

"Hi, Frank. Going scuba?" asked Susan.

Albury shook his head and shrugged. "Sure would like to, Susan, but we got some problems." He looked at her and rubbed his chin. Then he pointed at the TV. "You seen that fellow in Miami, that Abaco independence fellow?"

Susan didn't watch the TV much, but she had noticed an occasional reference on the Miami public station to such a group, one of the many splinter and terrorist gangs looking for fun and trouble in Florida. She smiled. "Is he coming over to run the place, Frank?"

Albury shrugged again. "Maybe. It looks like they got some planes and ships, Susan. From Munoz, the Florida Governor. We figure Munoz has some kind of understanding with Castro to let him go at us and Freetown, and maybe New Providence, while the Cubans work over the islands closest to them." ·

Susan laughed. "Come on, Frank! I realize the U.S. is coming apart at the seams, but an attack on Abaco from the state of Florida? Are they commandeering yachts?"

Albury sat down soberly at her table. "Susan, do you know about the satellite time-lease system?"

"Sure. The Third World rental military satellites open to anyone who can pay the rip-off price. You guys subscribers?"

"The Bahamian government is. We're monitoring Florida ship movements now, at highest resolution, and they've put a fleet to sea. All shallow-draft boats, tank-landing vessels with National Guard tanks, an old destroyer escort, some Coast Guard stuff."

"Coast Guard is federal, U.S. Treasury," said Susan.

"Susan, President Childers isn't minding the store. The governors are all going off on their own. We think Munoz is looking to set up his own Caribbean state and shut off the flow of U.S. northerners. The Abaco energy communes look awful handy."

"The Israelis would never work for Munoz."

Albury looked down at his Bermuda shorts and rubbed his chubby knees. "Munoz doesn't really understand what's going on out here. But he probably figures they'll either work or starve." He looked up. "Susan, there's a meeting of the Abaco Defense Council at ten this morning, and they asked me to come and see if you would attend."

"The WHAT?" laughed Susan. "Abaco Defense Council, those dolts at the customs shed?"

"More than that," said Albury seriously. "We have a command post at Marsh Harbor out at the Wind Commune Headquarters on Eastern Shore. If you could be there at ten, we surely would appreciate it, Susan."

After Frank Albury left, Susan turned to the commercial channels and sought news of the Abaco Independence Movement, but the morning talk and game shows were in full swing. The world was breaking into tiny splinters and these fools were mesmerized by garbage . . . ! Susan shook her head angrily and watched the simpering host lead a young woman through some personal sex questions. . . . She flicked off the set and stared out at the palms and the gentle, sunny morning. Off across the brilliant blue and green Sea of Abaco the squat solar boilers centered in their mirror nests bulked behind the palms and white houses on Man-o-War Cay. The causeways and locks of the tidal-basin control system joined Elbow and Man-o-War by an incomprehensible network of underwater walls and control gates, all operated from a concrete building on tiny Johnnies Cay, a white spider sitting in a huge web of life and energy.

Susan rubbed her hands together and bitterly stared about her small house. Four months, and she knew nothing about this place, these people! Her book on Shastri cycles untouched. Her U.N. duties carried out just as perfunctorily as the locals could hope, from an uninvited snooper checking to see that UNESCO money wasn't decorating casinos or whorehouses.

She had made only a few friends, and most of them among the Israelis, the other arrivés. Face it. Frank Albury was the only Abacoan who called her Susan. That's why they sent him this morning.

She rubbed her hands back and forth across her eyes until the flashes and spots came behind the lids, and she thought about taking the drug. She probably couldn't help them anyway; she hadn't done her homework on Abaco. Yet her only possibility would be to vector for them. She drew back and remembered her lover, intense, brilliant, corrupt Jamie. She had used the drug with him, but he did not believe in Shastri Vector Space. And he had told the committee she was addicted to cocaine. She lost the chairmanship. That bastard . . .! She still couldn't reconcile his tenderness and strength with . . .

Oh, Hell. She was going to dress and ride to the Marsh Harbor ferry. But just before she stepped out the door, she swallowed two small pills and popped the tiny box, not knowing what might happen, or for how long, into her skirt pocket.

Pedaling south the mile to Hopetown Harbor on her bike, Susan saw no one until she arrived at the ferry dock. There, several young Israelis and black Abacoans were wrestling some generator parts off a Wind Commune barge. The Donnie-Rocket glided into the dock right on time and disgorged several wind workers and some school children. Everything seemed very ordinary and peaceful, but the drug was doing its work and Susan vectored on the suppressed excitement among the children.

She waited quietly while they revved up the flywheel on the ferry, listening carefully to the children as they babbled, walking off down the dock.

"I is in D-south tracker, Joan!" said a little black boy excitedly. "Dat's de whole *end* of the system. I is *bound* to get some tracks." The boy looked back, saw Susan staring at him and abruptly and silently ran off the dock. The very incomprehensibleness of his conversation rang alarm bells in Susan's head. What in God's name were they up to? She turned back to watch the repowering of the Donnie-Rocket.

The large island of Abaco and its chain of cays to the north and east were linked and looped together by the ferry system. originally, the Donnies had been I.C.-engined cabin cruisers, twenty to thirty feet in length. Then in the late seventies, the gas-turbined hovercraft, the Donnie-Rockets, had arrived, spectacular, high speed, and kerosene guzzling. Although the relatively new Swiss flywheel boats now ran in total silence, the name, Donnie-Rocket, had stuck with them, for they still went like blazes, up on their stalky foils, forty feet of praying mantis doing thirty-five knots.

The captain of this Donnie-Rocket was skinny, fourteen-year-old

Gerald Beans, black as night with a head like a chestnut burr. He cut off the magnetic clutch and signaled the dock superintendent to hoist the torque bar out of the Donnie's engine compartment. Down below, in a hard vacuum, six tons of steel flywheel spun in perfectly vibration-free gas bearings at over twenty-thousand revolutions per minute. Captain Beans noticed Susan's intense inspection of the Donnie-Rocket's power plant and flashed her a great many large white teeth. "Plenty of crayfish to buy that wheel, Dr. Peabody," he suggested.

But Susan, fully into the drug, suddenly, blindingly, saw how incredibly little she had seen in Abaco. These children and their talk. A fourteen-year-old ferry captain. This incredibly diverse technology. The Israelis, their energy communes, Governor Munoz and Fidel Castro. She was staggered at the vector complexity, and yet the alarm bell in her head was clanging continuously. She suddenly realized she had not thought of Jamie for at least ten minutes, and she smiled, really grinned in fact, at Captain Beans.

The Donnie-Rocket ambled out of Hopetown Harbor as a displacement boat, past the tall, old red-striped lighthouse with its 130-year-old Trinity House lamp and spring-driven occulting gear. Then Captain Beans clutched the propellers into the flywheel more strongly, and they rose up and scooted for Marsh Harbor. The only other passenger, an Israeli computer specialist whom Susan hardly knew, was studying an instruction manual. So Captain Beans turned to Susan. "Did you see that crazy Abaco independence man on TV, Dr. Peabody?"

Susan shook her head. "I didn't watch it last night, Gerald. Is he really nutty?"

Gerald Beans whistled and nodded his head. "Mad as can be, I think. But he's not the real one, I think. Those politicians want us . . . Abaco. All these kilowatts!"

"Yes," said Susan. "We Americans had all the toys, but they've gotten broken and we waited too long to fix them. All we can see to do is steal from somebody else."

"Those folks up north, with the snows. Who are they going to steal from?" asked Captain Beans.

Susan, distracted in her attempts to vector Abaco and its problems, looked at the boy sharply. "They'll steal from each other, I suppose, Gerald. We had it awfully soft for a very long time."

"Then," said Captain Beans inexorably, "why won't Abaco get the same way?" and Susan found she had no answer.

The Donnie-Rocket made a side trip up Sugar Loaf Creek to drop Susan at the big dock of the Wind Commune Headquarters. For the first time she saw a group of young Abacoans with side arms and some Uzi whistle guns on slings. One of them, a customs agent in fact, detached himself and nodded politely. "They've been waiting for you, Dr. Peabody," he said. "Let me show you the way."

She followed the soldier in his short khaki pants and knee socks up a path brilliant with bougainvillaea, the soft coral crunching underfoot. As she walked, Susan watched a big instrument kite leave its launching rack on the top of the building and climb into the sky. The local wind communes in the South Abaco area were fed data from here, and from similar installations on Man-o-War and Hopetown.

On-line computers continuously load-matched the entire system and updated weather predictions. Susan tried to remember who had worked the kites out. The Swedes? The French?

The soldier held open a door and Susan stepped into a large, dim, air-conditioned room with picture-window views of the entire horizon. Around the walls under the almost continuous windows were the various consoles of the wind engineers: instrument boards, video readouts, and interactive computer monitors. The entire center of the room was now filled with a long plain table at which sat perhaps twenty people. Susan looked at her watch. It was just ten. "Sorry," she said to the seated people, "Frank Albury told me . . ." she noticed Albury in a chair. . . . "You told me ten, Frank."

Albury popped to his feet and the other men followed. "You're right on time, Susan. We haven't started." They had, of course, started. They had been talking about her. Susan looked curiously around at the Abaco Defense Council and selected a chair next to Jerry Ravetz, toward which she walked. She was fully vectoring now, and selecting that chair had involved a certain extension of mental activity. She suddenly realized that Ravetz, with whom she was friendly, was perhaps the most important person in the room. Provost of the Abaco Technical College and called Jerry by almost everyone, Ravetz seemed to represent all the Israelis in Abaco in some generalized and unstructured way. And much of the new technology of Abaco, the energy farms, the huge, still-building thermocline system, the tidal impoundments running laminar-flow, low-head turbines, the crayfish farms, all were basically Israeli-engineered. As she mentally projected various vector trees, she began to see how it must have developed. Kilowatts were not the only problem!

"Hi, Jerry," she said firmly.

Ravetz smiled cheerfully. "Hi, Susan, sorry to bother you, but we do seem to have this little . . . ah . . . problem with the State of Florida." Several of the men around her grinned.

"You've got plenty of problems, Jerry," said Susan, and she did not smile. As was often the case of retrospective vectoring, the picture was clearing even as she spoke. "For one thing, you should never have left Fidel out of all this. Who else is Munoz thick with? There's some kind of Washington connection in this, Jerry."

Ravetz, a stocky, crew-cut man in his forties, wearing white tennis shorts and a purple T-shirt, blinked and let his smile slip away, turning to peer more carefully at Susan and her bright, sharp eyes. "It's a little late to get geopolitical, Susan. We may be under attack before dark."

At that moment a tall black man in the same simple khaki uniform as the soldiers walked briskly into the room. He was about forty, lean and muscled, and it was perfectly evident that now he was in charge. Susan looked and looked, then turned to Ravetz. "Who is that, Jerry?"

Ravetz smiled again, "Colonel John Gillam, C. in C. of all Abaco defense forces and presently the acting military governor of Abaco," he whispered.

"Jerry," said Susan rather more loudly than she intended, "that's my garbage man!"

Colonel Gillam turned and smiled frostily the length of the table at Susan. "I do the garbage when things are quiet, Dr. Peabody. It's a way of . . . keeping an eye on things. I'm sure we'll have this Florida business under control in a day or so. Don't worry about the Friday pickup. I'll get your stuff." His voice was like ice. His eyes glinted and his big fat lower lip jutted red and wet at her. Susan flinched at the shock of his hostility. Here was one real hard conch eater, a North American hater. She was at this table over his dead body! He had obviously refused to even be present when they discussed what to tell her.

Jerry Ravetz pulled awkwardly at his T-shirt with its pink, Day-Glo words, "Crayfish Need Love Too," an obscure logo popular with biotechs. "Johnnie," he said quietly, "could we sort of get people introduced and go on?"

John Gillam sat down at the head of the table and pulled a sheet out of his briefcase. "Well, OK, Jerry." He looked around. "Most of you know each other, but maybe some of you don't know who it is you know." He grinned at a young Israeli across from Susan. "Now Merv there is our boat man, kind of our admiral. He bosses the Donnie-Rockets, work boats, and the rest."

The Israeli grinned back. "Just so I don't have to go outside the reefs, John. I'm the Dramamine kid, you know."

"Communication," said Colonel Gillam, "is Frank Albury. You all know him. At ten this morning we put all C.B. on scrambler and took the lid off the broadcast power."

Frank looked around and gave them all a gentle smile. "John," he said softly, "could we have a short prayer before we get into this?"

Colonel Gillam shook his head. "You're the chaplain, Frank. But the time for that is when they're on the screens. OK?"

Several other men were introduced, and Susan suddenly noticed that there were only two other women in the room: Dr. Francis Foot, chief of the Abaco hospital; and Frank's niece, Mary Albury, whose main function seemed to be to select which computer outputs would be displayed and where. Susan looked at Gillam's coal-black face, the flat nose and high, shiny cheekbones. A black honky-hating macho garbage man, just what the crisis doctor ordered!

Colonel Gillam finally turned to Susan and said evenly, "Dr. Susan Peabody is a newcomer. As most of you know, when Professor Hollister of Princeton retired here, we approached him to advise us in our political relations with the U.S. Dr. Hollister had a stroke last month and this, ah, problem required us to bring in someone not familiar with our situation." Gillam paused and looked at some notes. "Dr. Peabody is a professor at Harvard and one of the founding members of the Department of Contemporary Politics, a current academic euphemism for crisis management. Dr. Peabody has come to Abaco as a U.N. Fellow and will make a report to UNESCO on the economic and political effects of our energy program and other developments."

The room suddenly became very quiet, and Susan realized they were waiting for something they had been told by Gillam would happen. The colonel looked at her steadily. "Before we go on, I'd like to ask you a couple of frank questions, Dr. Peabody. If you don't like them, or you don't like this situation, please feel free to go back to Hopetown. OK?"

Susan looked at him as evenly as she could. He radiated anger and resentment at her. She was suddenly standing in for Castro, Governor Munoz and God knows who else. "Shoot, Colonel."

Gillam took a deep breath. "We're probably going to be attacked by American forces today. If you have any doubts about which side you might be on, or if you think you might play U.N. lady bountiful or peace dove, please just go away."

Even the whites of his eyes were brown. He was a most thoroughly colored man. Susan looked steadily into the brown-on-brown eyes. "My tenure with the U.N. is six months, Colonel. They've already forgotten why I'm here. As far as any choice between you or Governor Munoz, I'll take you and the rest here, even though you hate my bloody guts and wish I were dead."

That was vector talk, right down the middle. Colonel Gillam looked at his papers. "I don't hate you, Dr. Peabody. I don't know you."

Susan shook her head. "You can't imagine why we, and I mean Harvard and the State Department and all the big shots who have patronized and snooted you here for years, are now throwing you to Munoz and Castro. Because it's coming apart up there, Colonel! President Childers is yellow to the core and incompetent besides. We counted on more time than the Arabs gave us, than the Arabs could ever give us. Do you know there's a cruise missile battalion in north Florida? Munoz hasn't got much now, but give him some successes, and who knows? Federal troops have gone over to a state before in our history. So hate away, all of you!"

Jerry Ravetz sat up in his chair and cleared his throat. "Johnnie," he said plaintively, "don't we need all the help we can get? There's nobody else here who knows the U.S. situation like Susan. You said yourself, her professional field is crisis management. What do you want, somebody in English lit., for Heaven's sake?"

Colonel Gillam nodded grimly. "Welcome to the Abaco Defense Force, Dr. Peabody," he said evenly. Then, "OK, Frank, let's show everyone last night's TV spec."

Frank Albury nodded to an assistant at one of the consoles and a big flat solid-state screen dropped over the north window and began to flicker. "You mostly saw this before," said Frank.

The TV tape cut into the eleven o'clock news and a black woman who gave a short spiel on the Abaco Independence Movement and introduced its leader, one Basham Kondo, dressed in flowing robes and a busy afro. Basham had hardly gotten into his slurring, high-speed speech about the enslaved blacks of Abaco and the many Alburys and their Yiddish masters from across the sea, when the screen blanked and retracted. "Sorry," said Frank Albury gently, "but the prime minister is coming down on the roof."

The swish of big rotor blades above slowed and then they heard a flurry of footsteps. The far door opened and in swept Prime Minister Sean O'Malley and an entourage of two uniformed and two seersuckered assistants. The old man walked rapidly over to Colonel Gillam and briskly shook his hand. O'Malley was light coffee-colored with a white, kinky poll and a grandfatherly look. Susan suddenly remembered parlor car rides on the New Haven Railroad with her father when she was a very little girl. There was always one porter who was sort of the Old Boss Man, the Chief, and they had all looked exactly like Bahamian Prime Minister Sean O'Malley.

"Colonel," said O'Malley, "don't let us interrupt or slow you up. This is your battle. I'm here if there should be any policy problems." Susan tried to remember what sort of strength the Bahamian navy possessed. Customs and fishery protection vessels certainly, but with what caliber arms? If Florida had DE . . . No, no, there was much more to this, These men weren't fools. Susan vectored continuouly but the tree was too open, too diffuse. She had been all over Abaco. Where could they have the emplacements? The magazines? What about aircraft? Susan looked up startled to see Ravetz and O'Malley bearing down on her.

"Dr. Peabody," said the old man, "Jerry tells me you've agreed to help us and that you're a crisis expert. You couldn't be in a better place!" He shook her hand strongly. "Jerry," he said, "can't we get back to whatever you were doing? I know you have plenty of things to get ready."

Colonel Gillam beckoned for more chairs. "We were watching a replay of last night's extravaganza."

O'Malley's face registered the distaste of a man handed an over-filled diaper. "Well, I've watched it twice, but once more can't hurt."

Everyone adjusted chairs, the screen came down again, and that great lover of freedom and justice, Basham Kondo, told south Florida the way it was. When it ended, Ravetz turned immediately to Susan. "How in the devil can he go on with that Yiddish and Zionist masters baloney? Don't the Jews in Florida listen to TV or vote?"

Susan shrugged. "Demographics. The old old Jews are dying off and the new ones don't come down anymore. Munoz and his Cuban gang disavow the worst stuff, but they know how the Sunbelt is going." She turned and looked directly at Colonel Gillam. "Is that man, that Kondo, an Abacoan, Colonel."

Gillam snorted in disgust. "He worked here as a crayfish harvester but his work record was hopeless. We think he was born on the Berry Islands and his name was Smythe, but it's hard to trace drifters like that. He has perhaps two dozen with him, similar types, misfits from the out islands."

"He wasn't much of a find for Munoz," said Susan thoughtfully, "but I suppose he was the only game in town. Mr. Prime Minister, what steps are you taking in the U.S. about this fleet?"

O'Malley turned to Susan in surprise. "Why, my ambassador to the U.S. is carrying a note of protest to the Security Council this morning . . ."

"Good grief," said Susan impatiently, "I don't mean that Tower of Babel. Why they won't even know where Abaco is, with no casinos, racetracks, or fancy houses. I'm talking about Federal District Court in Miami. Don't you have a law firm there that can get on this for you?" She looked around quickly. "Does anyone have a copy of the Florida state constitution? I'm sure you can nail Munoz on at least a dozen violations of his authority in Dade County. With a federal restraining order, the Coast Guard will have to function. Furthermore, you can get injunctions so that federal marshals and state police must keep his Guard planes on the ground. They couldn't be coming over with a fleet and no air cover. These are simple, traditional thinkers, Mr. Prime Minister. Break this chain anywhere and they'll crawl back into the woodwork!"

The room fell silent as everyone looked at everyone else. Colonel Gillam looked grimly at Susan but said nothing. Finally Prime Minister O'Malley's ancient face broke into a grin. "I'm chagrined, Dr. Peabody, that we did not think of that," he said gracefully, then turned and nodded at an assistant in a seersucker suit. The man rose and hurriedly left the room. Frank Albury also stood up, smiling at everyone. "I'll make sure he gets through on priority to Miami," he said. "We have protected channels through the satellite link." And he dashed out.

For the next hour they watched the successive satellite transmissions of high-magnification video showing the invasion fleet assembling in calm waters off Palm Beach. There were Naval Reserve and Coast Guard vessels from Port Everglades, National Guard tank-landing vessels from Fort Lauderdale and Miami, and a collection of state fishery and patrol craft. A young Abacoan stood up and gave the intelligence appreciation: twenty-nine craft, approximately twelve hundred crewmen and about fifteen hundred troops, tank personnel, and drivers. E.T.A. at present course and speed, assuming a Marsh Harbor destination, 8 P.M.

While they were awaiting an update from the satellite, Prime Minister O'Malley slipped into a chair next to Susan. "Dr. Peabody, at what level of combat do you think the U.S. Federal government might intervene?"

Susan looked sideways at the shrewd old face. "That would depend on who was winning, Dr. O'Malley."

O'Malley looked at her very piercingly, as though seeing her for the first time, and then smiled thinly. "Let's assume we are overwhelmed here and Fidel takes a hand at New Providence, Andros, and points south."

Susan jerked her head around and spoke fiercely, directly at him. "That *must* not happen. You must *never* count on Washington! Don't you understand? That's exactly what they want!"

Her vehemence startled O'Malley. "Who, Dr. Peabody? Who would want that?" he asked softly.

"Munoz's friends, of course. You don't think he got this together without help in Washington, do you? He's being used!"

"But, Fidel?"

"My God, the same! Fidel's a puppet, a decoy. He's their next step. The Bahamas, Abaco, mean nothing to them. Dr. O'Malley, have you ever heard of Shastri cycles . . .? No, no, let's not get into that. This may be blunted." Susan shook her head staring at the old brown man.

"Do you have any idea who these people in Washington are, Dr. Peabody?"

Susan nodded. "Yes, but there is nothing you can do here and now about this, Dr. O'Malley, except stop the war. And if it starts, win as quietly as possible."

Susan was vectoring powerfully. She had never achieved this formidable a high, and the great integrating power of her amplified consciousness created clouds of possibilities, the Shastri vector trees, growing and bunching in the created spaces of her mind. The whole development was transparent to her, Munoz, Castro, the cabal of horrible old men in Washington, made by disaster and uncertainty into monsters more fearsome than the rawest, maddest S.S. camp commandant in the worst days at the end of the last great convulsion of a Shastri cycle, over forty years ago. But through some incredible chance (or mischance, that would only vector clearly after the attack was met), these Florida amateurs had decided to drown a pussy cat that was looking more and more like a hungry tiger. As she waited in an ecstasy of speculation and computation, she thought briefly again of Jamie, naked, his cock wilting that night she had dazzled him with the theory of the Shastri cycle. She realized suddenly that he had never been even close to her in intelligence or ability, and it seemed odd that she had never seen that now-obvious fact.

At that moment, Frank Albury said, "Governor Munoz is on Channel Seven, impromptu news conference on the capital steps." The screen flashed in bright color, and there was Munoz, a short, stocky brown man with a thick mustache and receding hair, waving at some supporters. Around him were his guards and staff, black, brown, and white, as befits the modern Southern governor.

"Governor, is it true the State of Florida is supporting an invasion of the Bahamas?" The question came from off screen.

Munoz passed a hand across his brow. "We're not supporting anything. As I understand it, there may be a volunteer group attempting to liberate certain islands in the Bahamas group. In all fairness, I think . . . "

Another reporter shouted, "Is it true that John Amsler of Amsler, Bigelow and Parke is in Federal District Court right now getting a restraining order on moving those ships into Bahamian waters?"

Munoz shrugged. "That's between the feds and their people. If they can't control discipline on the cutters, that's hardly Florida's problem."

Now there were several reporters shouting at once. "Governor, what if they get an order in Dade County restraining the state and National Guard boats?"

Munoz held up his hand. "Look, let me make a statement. It's simply this. Washington, the federal government, is no longer able to protect or even deal with regional interests. When we had everything, it was easy to resolve these differences. With the price of oil at its present level, it's becoming impossible. Now, the State of Florida has no intention of encouraging a foreign power, a very controversial and bloody-minded foreign power . . . I'm talking about Israel. Let's please get that straight . . . to penetrate to within one hundred miles of the Florida mainland, displacing as it does hundreds of poor blacks and disturbing the only friends who count today, and I obviously mean the Arab nations. The health, safety , and good life of all Floridians is the only thing that motivates me. This administration is . . . "

Suddenly a small young woman popped into camera range, her pad pointing and waving at Munoz. "Then you intend to violate the law, Governor? You intend to defy any court order to ground the Guard jets?"

Munoz shook his head mildly but his magnified eyes were as thick and cold as a snake's. "I have no such intention. This office will obey all federal and state laws and orders of the courts. This office . . . "

A red light over the C.B. speaker rack went on, and all sound in the room went suddenly dead. Then came a cool young voice on a C.B. monitor. ''Attention! Attention, Abaco! This is Argus North. I have twenty-six single-seat bandits leaving the Florida coast. Estimated flight time to Little Abaco, seventeen minutes!''

Susan took an involuntary deep breath. Governor Munoz would evidently obey the court's orders by flying his weapons before the orders arrived.

Colonel Gillam made two long steps to the C.B. center and pressed a protected red button. Priority lights shone all across the monitors and Gillams's voice was multiply projected, still clear and sharp. ''This is Big John. Prepare for air attack. All trackers make final calibrations now. All protection vessels, put to sea at once. Argus North, take direction. Execute!''

''Ten-four, Big John. Trackers all, this is your Argus North. We will number targets consecutively and assign you in groups. Report your calibrations to subdivision leaders as available. I repeat. . . .''

John Gillam turned and grimly nodded at Frank Albury. ''Time for that prayer, Frank,'' he said softly.

Albury stood up and looked out over the room. ''Please bow your heads, whatever you may believe,' he said in his gentle voice. ''Dear Lord, we do not kill and maim our fellow men in Thy name, but because Thy Kingdom has not yet been achieved on this sinful world. Forgive us our pride and our cruelty, for we are imperfect seekers after Thy Truth, and though our sins offend Thy sight, bless us in simple love, we Abacoans and our friends from Thy ancient land of Israel, Amen.''

''This is . . . your Argus North. Our bandits are dividing their forces. We anticipate twelve to attack north from Cherokee Sound. E.T.A. Cherokee, nine minutes.''

Colonel Gillam turned to Frank Albury. ''Picture, Frank!'' The big screen showed a radar presentation, a glowing map of the Abaco chain. ''Project that squadron at twenty-X, Mary,'' said Gillam.

Twelve bright dots, moving far faster than in real time swept across the southern Bight of Abaco and out over Tilloo Cay. ''Argus South, are you tracking?''

''I see the picture, Big John,'' came a new voice. ''Trackers all, Marsh Harbor and south, this is your Argus South. We will number targets consecutively . . .

Susan watched all this intently. By God, they *could* keep a secret here! What in Hell: ''Jerry,'' she started to say . . .

''Urgent! This is Argus North! Enemy in sight! Six bandits on the deck! Numbering consecutively: target one, batteries A and B; target two . . .''

Colonel Gillam peered out the window to the northwest. ''Frank,'' and now he could not conceal the tightness in his voice, "optical blow on these first ones."

The screen flickered and then a projected telescope image showed two large jet aircraft head on, their images made wavery by the intervening hot air layers, growing in size slowly. Suddenly the closer one's wings showed two bright flashes. "He's firing rockets, Johnnie!" Susan could hardly recognize Ravetz's voice, it was dry and tense. Colonel Gillam grinned fiercely.

"This is Big John. All shutters open! Execute!"

Susan looked out at Man-o-War Cay and she seemed to see a glitter, a sudden flash as though lightning had darted across the distant low land. the two jets came at 600 miles an hour southeast down the Sea of Abaco just off the water and heading for Marsh Harbor, a huge, growing roar. In an instant the leading plane cartwheeled and splashed gigantically. His wing man went into a sudden vertical climb, up and up, north of them, and Susan could see without magnification that the plane was glowing red. Smoke began to plume from the entire fuselage, and the pilot ejected, a black bundle. But the bundle smoked too, and when the chute opened, it was no more than a bag of tatters.

Now the C.B. monitors were alive with urgent talk.

"Track! Track! Carol! Hold your target!"

"Harden my focus, Benji!"

"Left, B Battery, left!"

Planes were coming in on several angles now. One of the southern group went directly over them and crashed within a hundred yards of the harbor at Man-o-War. Two more went south on fire, and a third was glowing so brightly that it simply blew apart before ever smoking at all.

Susan turned to Ravetz, her surprise unconcealed. "Solar weapons, Jerry! You're using the mirrors on the energy farms!"

Colonel Gillam turned and his smile was now cruel and twisted. "Not quite what UNESCO had in mind, eh, Dr. Peabody? But on the right day, a nasty toy. You see, even if we don't hold them in the mirror battery's focus long enough to cook them, it's usually long enough to blind them. Of course, if they had brought welding goggles they might stop that, but it's hard to strafe nigger conch-eaters when you're wearing welding goggles!"

"This is Argus South! Batteries M and N, redirect to target eleven. You're tracking too fast, Dawn!"

"I got two already, Argus!" The girl's voice was high and tense, total excitement. "Harden my focus!" she shrieked; then: "Mine's on fire! Mine's burning!"

"Jerry," said Susan thickly. "That's Dawn LaVere! That child is only fifteen! What in Hell are you doing here?"

But now Ravetz looked at her coldly and his voice was low, yet as hard as Gillam's. "Cut the shit, Susan! Don't you see it yet? This is a Shastri community. We're living what you people gave seminars on. You've been too close to it!"

And Susan, watching horrified another ejection at one hundred feet, this time the pilot enclosed in a bright orange tongue of flame, suddenly saw the whole puzzle unfold and, in chagrin put all the pieces into place.

A jet came over Matt Lowes Cay firing cannon at Marsh Harbor, and Gillam raged into the mike. "Argus South! We're being hurt by target sixteen!"

"A-OK, Big John! We're tracking sixteen! Carrie, you're too low! Track! Track!"

The plane continued over the town and crashed into the Bight of Abaco to the west.

Susan turned firmly to Colonel Gillam. "Colonel, stop! Let some of them go home, for God's sake!"

Gillam whirled on her. 'To their fucking subdivisions and their insurance offices? To their darky babysitters and cleaning women!" he shouted.

Susan shrank before his anger, but she stared resolutely back. "Probably a third of those pilots are black, Colonel," she said bitterly. "You're living in another age. I don't give a damn about those men, but if you kill them all, if you win absolutely, it's almost impossible to vector the effect!"

She whirled on Ravetz. "Jerry, you fool! What would Shastri have said? This is a Shastri community? Bullshit! You're all on raving ego trips!" She spun again, frantic. "Mr. O'Malley! I said you must win, but *quietly!* Don't you understand . . .?"

But it was too late.

"Trackers all, this is your Argus North. We have zero . . . repeat zero targets! We are checking the tapes now, hang on . . . Trackers all! We have twenty-six kills! We wiped the sky clean!"

The C.B. monitors lit up like a Christmas tree and a confusion of shouts and cheers burbled out. To the north, several huge meteorological balloons surged upward carrying fluttering Bahamian and Israeli flags. Windpattern smoke rockets flew skyward from Marsh Harbor and Hopetown painting sudden red vertical columns as high as the eye could see, and over it all came the high, sexy, excited voice of Dawn LaVere. "Ohhhh, Big John! I got five! I'm an ace . . . an ACE!"

Susan felt a real chill of panic. She looked around the room at the arrested figures, many of them still unable to believe what they had done, yet already believing and starting to live in a world in which it had happened.

"Well," she said soberly, suddenly remembering with a real pang of love her cheerful, gentle father and one of his favorite Yankeeisms, "You all really pissed on the stove this time!"

Cleaning up after the great battle consisted mainly of locating the pilots' bodies or getting them out of the sunken planes, and this grim business was taken in hand at once by Marv, the Donnie-Rockets, and the biotech scuba teams.

"For," said Colonel Gillam to Susan in as deliberately callous a way as possible, "we wouldn't want any missing-in-action problems, would we? All those wives petitioning your Congress? They're going to get everything back, the charcoaled remains, the dogtags, and the TV tapes showing just how and where we put the sun in their cockpits!"

Susan, sitting slumped in a chair, shook her head. "Come off it, Colonel!" she said with irritation. "Neither the Florida National Guard or the Pentagon is going to want to talk about this very much. Those widows will be an embarrassment to Munoz, all right, but the press will probably represent the pilots as undisciplined and incompetent adventurers. No, no. You're missing the point. Once the power centers hear that an exuberant bunch of thirteen-year-old colored kids and sexy-poos like Dawn can total two squadrons of jets without a single local casualty, they're going to look much closer at Abaco and this Israeli thing. They've been looking and thinking plenty already, and I specifically mean Fidel."

Prime Minister O'Malley, who had watched, wide-eyed and silent, the first great battle of the Abaco reefs, now turned to Ravetz.

"Jerry, I think this is all unbelievable, too miraculous to take in. But I find Dr. Peabody's words more and more disturbing. Could we talk...?"

"Hang on, everybody!" Frank Albury dashed into the room with some tapes. "It looked like the invasion fleet had stopped, but now it's headed our way again."

The cheerful chatter in the room stopped abruptly. "E.T.A., Frank?" said Gillam.

"Hard to say, John, right at this minute. They aren't really up to speed yet."

Susan started. She had completely forgotten the fleet! Hastily she rose and located a ladies' room and went into the toilet to take two more pills. This continuous confrontation with Gillam was wearing her down. She sat, resting and alone, on the cool john and rubbed her eyes. How was it possible that a Shastri community . . . for Ravetz had been absolutely right in so describing Abaco, she saw that with blinding clarity . . . could trigger a Shastri cycle? Or, as Shastri had called it, a spasm, for completed cycles were always accompanied by a multitude of unvectorable changes. Ravetz was right. In the seminars you could always keep things in their compartments; but the moment the insights became more than theoretical, the moment you built a community, weapons, life patterns, tools, ideals, then you rippled the pond; and the more successful and radical the insight, the more ripples there were. Susan gave herself five minutes of luxury, a mental vector investigation of the mirror weapon in all its Shastrian ramifications. Ravetz, or someone in Israel . . . or, what the Hell, Archimedes if you like! . . . had achieved an almost perfect Shastri null-weapon. A weapon so totally integrated into the community that it had no vector strength whatever in most of the critical and dangerous areas. Such as standing armies and their officer corps, almost always more destabilizing than the real and imagined enemies they faced. And all the ideal, extraneous, deadly hardware. Susan wondered how much extra it cost to turn the solar heating mirrors into weapons; they had to move in altitude and azimuth to track the sun anyhow. Ten percent for the control stations, logic chips, and hard wire connections? Probably not even that much. And the beautiful, Shastrian idea that in destroying the weapon, an attacker would be destroying the very reason for his attack; the booming energy wealth of the Bahamas in a world of dry oil wells. And the fact that it could only be used part of the time and only for defense, a fatal flaw no doubt in the tired imaginations of the old incompetents at the Pentagon, was completely in accord with that essential, really primary Shastri vector: self-realization and the necessity for diverse answers in a society.

The greatest enemy in the Shastri canon was traditional systems analysis in which cost, profit, growth, safety, or some other single value dictated a decision. Of course, without the drug they really had to use single-vector analysis; they could not control the vector tree, could not see the cloud of, not end points, but *extensions of now*. Susan suddenly grinned. How it worked! Gerald Beans went to school, but he captained a high-speed foil boat of the most sophisticated sort. Dawn LaVere, with her pouty red mouth, melon breasts, and tanned white flanks that Ravetz had described as simultaneously a treasure and a disaster . . . she with five kills against modern aggressively flown jets. The vector tree always showed that there were several equally good solutions to a problem. This diversity led to wealth and to more diversity, to a social system in which almost everyone could gain somewhere a sense of themselves and their integration into their community. The children were cast in that role by age, but they were also full-fledged and useful members of Abaco society. Doubtless the Israelis had found their tracking reflexes superior to any adults'. Susan had to agree, Shastri would have absolutely approved of that! It totally nulled the whole hero, macho, glory, bravery vector so excrutiatingly dominant in war-beset, single-vector societies, so utterly useless in a Shastri society where heroes were replaced by experts, by persons whose confidence comes from their heads, not their

balls or that mystical"backbone" her New England father made reference to when he really had no idea why someone behaved, or failed to
behave, in a particular way.

But there was still a problem with the children! That most elusive of
all vectors, ethics, the vague, but powerful human-based standards, how
a society thinks about itself. Five dead men, fathers of children like Dawn
LaVere, but prepared to kill Dawn and her black and Israeli friends from
on high, impersonally as pilots always did. Dawn knew she directed the
mirrors because she, and that little boy at the dock—God, twelve?
thirteen? —they were the best in the community at that task. *They* knew
and the *community* knew, that was important. And yet, the children also
know, many would never be able to forget, that they burned those men!
Susan rubbed and rubbed her eyes. Will Dawn love differently, or not be
able to love, because she burned five pilots? Five bastards! Five of the
main fucking reasons why there's burning in the world. . . .

The ladies' room door opened. "Susan, you OK, honey?" It was
Mary Albury.

"OK, Mary. I sort of fell asleep for a sec."

"Oh, don't I know it! This is really too much for everybody. Listen,
honey, the new stuff on the boats is coming in, and Dr. O'Malley
wondered if . . ."

"Be right out, Mary. Thanks." Susan washed her hands and
thought of Frank Albury and decided she would take up the matter of the
children with him.

They were all seated when she returned, watching a blow-up of the
satellite pictures of the fleet, which was apparently steaming at about
eight knots so as to bring it into Abacoan waters well after dark. Susan
saw that Dr. O'Malley was now across the table from her, and as soon as
the pictures ended, he turned to Colonel Gillam. "I think I'd like to hear
Dr. Peabody's appreciation, Colonel," he said a trifle stiffly.

Colonel Gillam inclined his head, and O'Malley turned immediately
to Susan. "Why are they still coming, Dr. Peabody?"

"At what level do you want to discuss that, Dr. O'Malley, the fleet
itself, Munoz, or his helpmeets in Washington?"

"All three, if you please," said O'Malley.

"Well, as to the fleet, I would imagine they left Florida with all
communications, especially receiving stuff; radios and C.B.s, ripped out
and confiscated. The one thing you folks didn't think about, Federal
District Court would be the *first* thing to occur to Munoz's gang. So they
would have perhaps one man per ship with ways of talking either to the
mainland or at least to a central communication vessel. That way, some
judge can't get them on contempt, for failing to obey a court order which
they claim they never got because they had twenty-nine busted radios.

For this, the Coast Guard writes each captain a letter asking him to do better next time. Of course, they've been warned, through whatever hidden radios are left, about the solar weapons. So they're coming in at night.''

O'Malley looked at her and shook his head. "They wouldn't be so stupid as to think we had no other arrows in the quiver? Mister Kondo is doubtless a psychotic, but it defies belief . . .''

Susan shook her head. "Who knows what even Munoz's closest man in the fleet actually has found out? I'm sure the news and TV stations are filled with rumors of death rays and general wild talk . . .'' She looked over at Frank Albury, who grinned and nodded vehemently. "The more important question is, why is Munoz still at this?''

"Exactly!'' said O'Malley in a tense voice.

"Two reasons, I think. First, because he's already in plenty deep. If they could have gotten most of the pilots back, the thing might have dribbled away, a flaming sensation and nuisance, but something that could be handled. But all twenty-six . . . that's what I was trying to tell you . . . absolute victories are . . . absolute. They have nonvectorable elements. Munoz is the gambler suddenly in over his head with one last buck in his pocket.'' Susan looked around the room and even Colonel Gillam sat silent.

"The second pressure is the scary one, the one on Munoz from Washington. He's had to have help all along, and he certainly couldn't keep the fleet coming without both help and, probably, pressure from that same direction. Do you see what that means, Dr. O'Malley?''

The old man nodded at once. "I do. It means they don't care whether they lose the fleet or capture Abaco. That has become irrelevant.''

"Exactly!'' said Susan, and the room became silent for many moments.

"Dr. Peabody, do you use political cocaine?'' said Colonel Gillam. "Specifically, are you on it now?''

Susan flushed involuntarily and turned to face him. "I am, Colonel. I wouldn't dare attempt vector analysis without the drug.''

"Dr. Peabody, I spent three years with the C.I.A., and much of my time was spent working with Shastri vectors,'' said Gillam coldly. "They established that the drug was not only unnecessary but gave erratic results. Crisis experts in Washington vector using computer branching and cluster algorithms.''

Susan curled her lip. "Right! And look at the U.S. political turmoil! The reason, Colonel Gillam, that your beloved C.I.A. could never really work in Shastri vector space is that in 1981, President Carter suddenly eliminated the Drug Enforcement Administration, by then an international scandal, and turned the whole, nutty U.S. drug hunt over to the

C.I.A., thereby making it absolutely impossible for them to make any serious studies of drug-enhanced decision-making.''

Jerry Ravetz ran his hands through his crew cut and pinched his pudgy nose. "Well, this is my fault. I didn't take my pills today, Susan. Believe it or not, the first Shastri null-weapon battle, and I thought it would be so simple I wouldn't need all that vectoring. I wanted to savor it emotionally instead of being endlessly into all that damn thinking.''

"I didn't know you used the political cocaine, too, Jerry," said Colonel Gillam stiffly.

"You never asked, Johnnie, and I didn't offer to tell," said Ravetz quickly. "The point is, Susan was right this noon and she's right now. We're in the initial stages of a Shastri cycle. Somehow the Abaco community has triggered it, chance, something else, I just don't know.''

"Yes," said Gillam angrily, "providing we all believe in this drug-fevered hokum! Jerry, the C.I.A. used Shastri's stuff all the time, but they vectored on a computer.''

Ravetz shook his head firmly. "No way! Johnnie, the C.I.A. showed you a lot of useful stuff, but you can't vector in real time on a computer. It's simply impossible. It takes weeks to write even a rudimentary program, and by then the crisis, decision, or whatever is past.''

"Jerry, this drug, what is it anyway?" asked Sean O'Malley.

"Okay," said Ravetz, turning to look at everyone. "Quickly, here it is for those who don't know the story . . . or have the wrong one. Bar Singh Shastri was an Indian pharmacologist and general all-around genius working in a London hospital on synthesis problems. He got into cocaine as a recreational drug in the early seventies, but it had the same effect on Shastri as on Freud. He gained intellectual power, or at least felt he did, and set about searching for that part of the coca plant that carried the intellectual part of the high. Well, eventually he managed to isolate and synthesize a group of alkaloids that apparently reduce the time delay at the nerve synapses. They do other things as well, but the effect is that the mind can carry many more coherent thoughts simultaneously, in parallel, and can process thoughts more quickly. Short-term memory is also enhanced. Interestingly, even though Shastri was a really top-level scientist, he immediately recognized that his enhanced abilities under the drug would be most extended and useful in a political context. he ran for Parliament and spent three years forming a brilliant political career, then dropped it all and went to Israel, becoming a recluse to study and write. Shastri was far beyond becoming the first Indian prime minister of Britain. He had found a way to reorganize the world using vectoring and the vector tree. Most of you know where the theory leads: null-weapons, multiple, labor-intensive energy communes, decisions based on vectoring a cloud of factors.''

Prime Minister O'Malley rubbed his cheek and shrugged. "Well,

Dr. Peabody, what projection do you . . . ah . . . see? Why do they attack us but not care if they win?''

"A Shastri cycle," said Susan, "can progress in two ways. With primarily external vector interactions, such as Europe in 1914, or with primarily internal vector interactions, such as Germany in 1939. We are in an internal cycle, in which a small, very powerful group in Washington is attempting to escalate a twenty-six plane raid on Abaco into, I'm afraid, an open-ended, transcontinental-level nuclear strike interchange. If you defeat the Florida navy, and especially if you defeat it as decisively as you did the jets, they will attempt, and they obviously have considerable hope of doing it or they wouldn't be taking these risks, to induce Fidel to fall upon you. Or at least make demands upon you."

Susan looked from Ravetz to Prime Minister O'Malley. "The Bahamas government has an agreement with Israel to accept some substantial number of refugees, if the Palestine situation becomes irretrievable. That's correct, isn't it?"

The room now remained very quiet for some time. O'Malley's face flushed darkly, but then the smooth brown calm slowly returned. "You know, Dr. Peabody, that was a very carefully held confidence between our governments that you perceived."

"Yes," said Susan coolly, "but Fidel perceived it too. I won't attempt to guess how many might come, one hundred thousand perhaps? But it would totally transform the Bahamas, this end of the Caribbean. And now Fidel sees that these Israelis, far from dancing the hora and raising yummy crayfish, have the strike of a cobra. No doubt your plans for the Florida navy are equally spectacular, and Fidel can watch them on his own satellite link, and what do you think will happen after that? All of you?"

Susan looked around. She had to vector them too. They must be led to this, inescapably. She looked at her watch. Four-thirty, and the fleet here a little after midnight! She took a deep breath. "Munoz's bosses in Washington, through some ghastly chance, have stumbled into something that could be an all-win situation. If Abaco falls, Munoz will taste blood and go for Freeport. Fidel will have to move or have a far more hostile and expansionist neighbor than yourself, Dr. O'Malley. If, as they now probably expect, Florida goes down to defeat, they throw Munoz to the wolves, who will really be howling at this point, and panic Fidel with now-documented stories of Israeli superiority and hegemony in the Caribbean.

"In either case," and Susan paused and looked around the silent room, "the end result is a move by Cuba against the Bahamas followed by a spasm strike from the U.S. to protect freedom, save Jews, stop Communism, or whatever best serves them. One of the first conclusions Shastri came to when he began to use drug-enhanced analysis was that once the cycle reached a nuclear-explosion level, it could be driven to conclusion. The very fact of a burst over, say, Havana or Miami, would enable a leader to induce other crews and commanders to fire, whatever the dampers or restraints.''

Sean O'Malley nodded. "And so, Dr. Peabody?"

"And so, Dr. O'Malley, we must immediately attempt to get Fidel here, tonight . . . to Abaco . . . and let him watch the big show. And, Jerry, you must decide how to get your government to send Israeli energy communes to Cuba and, I suppose, how to convince them to go.''

"It's impossible!" spat Ravetz in sudden anger. "There's no way to vector that through, Susan. Cut the crap! You know what Cuba's like!''

Susan stared calmly at him. "What's it like, Jerry?"

Ravetz spluttered, "Phony elections, snooping! Secret police! Come on, Susan!''

"Listen," said Susan. "Cuba has softened and Fidel is old. And you Israelis have something big to offer, bigger than anyone else can offer. A transformed society *within* Communism! Shastri showed that multivector planning *requires* a collective approach. Everybody has to give somewhere in this, Jerry. The point is, once Fidel sees a Shastri society at work, he'll be like a child after candy.

"That bastard won't come here!" said Colonel Gillam. "Mr. Prime Minister, I'll resign if . . .''

Sean O'Malley looked darkly at Susan. "Even if I were willing to see the man, what could we offer him? It may be possible in your computer crisis-gaming to call up dictators and have them run over, Dr. Peabody, but in the real world such talks require weeks of preparation . . .''

'Nonsense!'' said Susan fiercely. "Fidel is aware of Shastri concepts. Say that you'll talk with him about sharing all this. Just talk!''

O'Malley, flushed and angry, shook his head. "You don't understand. What do I do? Call him on the C.B.? I tell you . . .''

"Dr.O'Malley," said Susan, "if Frank Albury can get me Major José Martino at the Department of State in Havana on diplomatic channels, that is guarded channels, it may be possible. but you've got to agree. . . .'' She turned and looked at Colonel Gillam, her lips a thin line. "Before you resign, Colonel, you might consider that Fidel will certainly be more fascinated by your efforts than, say, me. The Cuban military forces are . . . crack. If those had been Cuban jets, you probably wouldn't have burned them all and you would have lost some mirrors too!''

"Who is this Major Martino, Dr. Peabody?" asked O'Malley and he suddenly sounded worn and tired.

Susan smiled. "A Shastri scholar.He studied with Shastri the same time I was in Israel. He is close to Fidel, Dr. O'Malley. Nobody is handing the Bahamas to anyone, just remember that. What it really amounts to is you extending your good offices assist in getting energy communes into Cuba. Of course Jerry is right. There are political problems aplenty. But *they won't get smaller!*"

O'Malley squared his shoulders. "All right. Let's try it. Mr. Albury, my Mr. Steen will assist you in putting through the call." Steen, a middle-aged black in seersucker shorts, walked to a communications panel on the west wall and began dialing on a picture phone.

Susan turned and stared coldly at Colonel Gillam. "I've been assuming through all this that there will be a show for Fidel tonight, Colonel, and I don't mean a rifle regiment running ashore on Elbow Cay!"

"That," said Gillam bitterly, "is the one and only certainty in any of this. If the bastards come ashore, they'll be swimming!"

"Susan," called Frank Albury, "Major Martino is on the hook!"

Susan jumped up and ran across the big room, dropping into the seat vacated by Steen. "José, how are you, old friend?" said Susan quickly, looking at the thin officer's image, with his slicked hair and tiny pencil mustache, smiling primly at her.

"Hello, Susan. I knew you were on Abaco and I hoped we would talk." Susan took her deepest breath of the day and held it for a moment.

"José, we may have a chance to socialize but there is now an urgent problem. A Shastri cycle has begun, José."

She watched his brown color fade on the screen, and then he blinked several very long blinks. "Abaco . . . Susan? . . ."

" . . . And Cuba," she finished relentlessly.

"I cannot see it, Susan. I sensed there were deeper problems when you burned the Florida planes, but . . ."

"But you don't have all the vectors, José!" said Susan, looking at him intently. "Cuba is to serve as an excuse for a destabilization strike from the U.S.A. That is all I can say on electronics, but it is true. We are in deadly danger, José."

The little Cuban wiped his forehead and patted his thin hair. "And so . . ." he almost whispered.

"Prime Minister O'Malley has agreed to invite Fidel to Abaco, to watch our defense against the Florida navy. We can talk about it all, José: the cycle, the Israelis, the energy . . . it can be worked out, José!" God, she was sweating in this cold room! She took more deep breaths.

Major Martino nodded. "Hold the channel, Susan. I will ring Fidel. We have been approached . . ." He paused and thought a moment. "Hold the channel!" and the screen went bright and empty.

There seemed to be nothing much to do at that point but have supper, and most of them staggered down to the wind engineers' dining room, one flight below. Ravetz and O'Malley disappeared to some private place, while Colonel Gillam and some of his young staff and engineers ate in a quiet, closed group.

Susan sat down at a table alone with her tray and picked at the fried chicken. She sighed and rubbed her eyes.

"Cheer up, cheer up," said Frank Albury, putting his tray down across from her. "Moses never stepped on the soil of the Promised Land, but he knew his people would, Susan." His soft eyes peered into her shadowed, pinched face.

"Oh, Frank." She gave a deep, shuddery sigh. "This morning before you came I was sitting in a dirty dressing gown feeling sorry for myself. Now suddenly I'm telling everyone how to run the world. These are your islands, your technology, your weapons, and in a few hours I've . . . Oh, Hell, Frank, of course Jerry doesn't want to put Israelis into Cuba, to deal with all that political hassle on top of the whole Shastri and technical thing. And Prime Minister O'Malley, after eight years of stiff-arming Fidel, suddenly has to face him under the worst kinds of pressures and dangers, no agenda, no plans, no data."

She rubbed her cheeks hard. "And Colonel Gillam. The miracle worker, the one man in the world who translates a lot of theoretical, academic hokum into a pure Shastri defense. And by carping and needling him, I've reduced his miracle to crud. He's better, more honest than I am, Frank. He always knew what was right and what needed doing, and he did it with his super toys and his wonder children . . . and, oh, Frank. The children. I can't make them fit. I just can't!" And she wiped her eyes on her napkin and stared at her plate.

Frank Albury rubbed his pink knees and cleared his throat several times. "I'm not sure I can make them fit either, Susan," he said finally. "but David was a young boy. God needed David, not only to kill an enemy of his people, but to teach a lesson, to men, to us."

Susan nodded. "Oh, I know that. I've thought about that. David is very much a Shastrian figure. The small, confident expert facing macho bluster and baloney."

Frank nodded hard. "Susan, the Shastrian society is, at its base, a meritocracy structured to continuously maximize diversity, to maximize the ways in which merit can be achieved. To use adults for tracking aircraft when the children test better would simply admit they were less than full members of the Abaco community."

"Yes, Frank. It's all true. I see it now. But to kill so easily, like a contest or game. To kill with such glee. What if it hardens them, turns them callous, Frank?"

Albury nodded. "And if those troops were to land tonight and rape Dawn LaVere," Frank colored a bit thinking about that, "would she be less hard afterwards because she hadn't killed any of them? Or wouldn't she be both hard and a victim besides?''

A young man dashed up to their table. ''Frank! We've got Castro on the wire! I've sent for the Prime Minister!''

Frank rose at once. ''Coming, Susan?''

Susan shook her head. ''I've meddled enough, Frank. Either Dr. O'Malley sells it or he doesn't, and all I could do is watch and fidget, Frank.''

He nodded looking down at her. ''I know you pray for us all the time and I don't believe a word of it, but . . . don't stop, OK?''

At almost ten that night, three huge Cuban VTOLs settled down out of the dark to crouch on their tails at the Marsh Harbor airport, their jet-prop engines whining shrilly. Susan and Ravetz stood in the floodlit landing area, in front of two dozen Abaco civil police who held back a mass of gaping Marsh Harbor residents, come to catch a glimpse of the terrible old man.

''It's like the three-shell game,'' said Ravetz. ''You never know which one he's in until they open the doors.''

But only in the first, upthrust fuselage did a door slide back and steps swing down, and Susan saw Major Martino start down the ladder. In that instant, Frank Albury was at their elbow. ''Susan! Jerry! We got it off the diplomatic wire ninety seconds ago, and now it's coming over the commercial channels! President Childers has been assassinated! His helicopter was attacked by some kind of missiles, wire-guided or heat-seekers, they don't know which yet, just after he took off from the White House!''

''Oh, my God, Jerry,'' breathed Susan and she began to shiver. ''I've never been so scared, never!''

''Look! said Ravetz tensely. ''They've just gotten the news too!'' Major Martino had been followed down the ladder by the old man himself, white-bearded and wearing an O.D. baseball cap, but then two more Cubans ran down the steps shouting and all four clustered at the bottom of the ladder.

''Jerry,'' said Susan suddenly. ''They mustn't go back! Not now!'' And she ran across the asphalt waving and shouting, ''José! José!''

The dapper thin Cuban turned and watched her come up. ''Ah, Susan, how fine . . .''

''José! You've heard about Childers? Do you see now how it's happening? José, the cycle will diverge. We must all talk!'' The shadowy figure behind Major Martino stepped up beside him and Susan suddenly gulped. Close up, Fidel Castro looked like an aging Ernest Hemingway, the same round beard and shape of face. She blinked and shook her head.

"Dr. Castro! Within an hour, Vice-president Demarest will be sworn in. He is mad, sir! A manic-depressive who can barely be stabilized on lithium!"

The old Cuban looked at her coolly. "Dr. Peabody, José has told me about you and your call this afternoon. But, sane or mad, what is that to us?"

Susan pushed a strand of hair back. "Dr. Castro, have you ever heard of the Last Mile Study?" The old man shook his head. "Sir, the study was kept very secret because of its monstrous conclusions, but basically, Last Mile proved a number of things, all based on defective, single-vector analysis. First, they showed that the U.S. total-war capacity could only slip, was slipping, with time in relation to Russia and the Third World. Second, they claimed that in any all-out nuclear war, and especially a rapidly opening one, the Russians would be revealed as far weaker than believed. Third, that the longer the war continued, the greater would be the U.S.'s relative strength at the end." She paused and swallowed to moisten her dry throat. "The . . . the loss of life in Asia would be . . . beneficial, reducing the population pressure and breaking down super states like India that have become ungovernable. Even in the U.S., the tremendous damage and horror would turn people to the federal government for help, give it back its old clout . . ." She shook her head angrily. "Oh . . . I won't give you any more of that horrible nonsense, Dr. Castro. It's just that President-designate Demarest believes it all, and all his advisors are ready to try it out if they can just get the first one to go off! Cuba, then the Soviets is their sequence."

Major Martino turned to the old Cuban excitedly. "Fidel, that is why they offered . . ." but the old man's narrow and snapping eyes stopped Martino instantly.

"Dr. Peabody," he said, "you urged this meeting tonight to insure that these people could not possibly connect me with this invasion?" Susan nodded. "But that was before this murder. Cannot Demarest do whatever he chooses? To Cuba or anyone else?"

Susan shook her head vehemently. "There has to be a context, Dr. Castro. A logical development. Don't you see that to get even the lowest commander to fire his own missile involves a whole mass of intangibles? What sergeant, no matter how plausible the codes and signals, would fire his missile when he's watching a Lucy rerun on Miami television with no sign of war or sense of trouble?"

Castro pulled his white whiskers and looked at Major Martino. "José?" he asked softly.

Martino nodded. "She is right, Fidel! Now we see many things that we did not see before. We must at once null the political vector between the Bahamas and Cuba. We will force this man Demarest to look elsewhere for his provocations."

"Oh," said Susan, taking long breaths in sudden relief and really smiling at the two men, "I expect Demarest will be dealt with almost immediately, providing our friends here in Abaco can carry out their part tonight."

Castro, Ravetz, and O'Malley left the airport in a staff car and went into private session for an hour, when suddenly all arrived back in the window-room center of the Wind Commune building. It was almost midnight when Frank Albury said, "Hold it everybody," and the big screen slid down. "Here's Channel Two."

The inside of the newsroom behind an open-shirted young black at his desk looked, for once, authentically busy. "Continuing Channel Two's coverage of the incredible Abaco and assassination stories," he said excitedly, "we have learned that Prime Minister Fidel Castro, Cuba's aging patriarch, has made a sensational visit to the island of Abaco, scene this noon of an air battle involving renegades of the Florida Air National Guard and elements of the Abacoan defense forces. Cuban Radio announced that the prime minister wished to demonstrate his solidarity with other island nations who, Dr. Castro was quoted as saying, must now contend with the fall and death throes of the entire Yankee elephant rather than just the tramplings of his large and careless feet, unquote. Channel Two has also learned that the extraordinarily effective Abacoan anti-aircraft defense, which registered a sensational one-hundred percent kill against the Guard jets, was not a laser weapon as first thought but a solar mirror concentration system that can be rapidly tracked. Channel Two also . . ."

The breathless disclosures continued, but the old, white-bearded Cuban sat quietly down next to Susan and whispered, "That was what you wanted, was it not, Dr. Peabody?"

Susan nodded. "Thank you, Dr. Castro, and . . . sir?" He looked at her and nodded. "Shastrian ideas can work in Cuba. I . . ." But he only smiled distantly and held up his hand.

"I know all about that from José, Dr. Peabody. We will see how it all works out."

They continued watching the developing stories on the Miami channels when Ravetz suddenly spoke. "Hush, let's catch this!"

"We have learned," said a frazzled young lady staring down blearily at the prompter readout in front of her, "that Israeli Ambassador Mishka Gur is attempting to see the new president in his Camp David retreat. Sources at the Israeli embassy say that Ambassador Gur is attempting an eleventh-hour appeal to stop the continued Florida-based attacks on the Jewish settlements in the Abaco Island group. Sources at Camp David have refused to comment on the appeal and say that President Demarest is in seclusion with his closest advisors."

"What's that all about, Jerry?" asked Susan, suddenly puzzled, but

Ravetz, his face grim, only shook his head. "Johnnie," he said turning to Colonel Gillam, "we can't win too big tonight. There's no limit on this one!"

Gillam laughed bitterly. "I thought absolute victories were a Shastri no-no, Jerry."

Susan spoke up. "This noon that was true, Colonel, but not now, not with the fleet. The cycle may be damped, but Demarest is still as dangerous as a mad dog. Nothing will help his enemies more than total victory here." Gillam said nothing and Susan noticed that Castro was watching them with quick narrow eyes.

Suddenly, they all turned to stare at the lighted C.B. monitor board. "Attention! Attention, Abaco, this is your Argus North. Our pirates have increased their speed to twenty knots. E.T.A. Man-o-War, entrance-channel buoy, fourteen minutes."

Colonel Gillam jumped up and peered out the north windows. The moon was less than a quarter full and the Sea of Abaco was dark, only an occasional navigation marker winking or glowing along the five-mile channel leading in from Man-o-War to Marsh Harbor. "Infrared, Frank," said Gillam.

The big screen lit with a faint eerie light and in the center was a detailed whitish image of a destroyer escort bow on, with a black bone in her teeth. "She has a missile battery amidships, Jerry," said Colonel Gillam softly. "We mustn't provoke her as long as she . . ." He lifted up the mike. "Man-o-War Traffic Master. This is Big John. Prepare for lamp messages. Send at the DE, the leading vessel."

"Ten-four, Big John. We're waiting."

They were all waiting now. Everyone frozen in the room, watching the infrared, magnified images of the incoming ships. "They're pretty well bunched, Colonel," said a young Abacoan operating the search radar. "Except for the last one. He's hanging back."

"He won't come," said Susan suddenly. "That must be their communications center. They wouldn't want to lose their main radio contact with Florida."

"Imagine," said Ravetz in wonder. "Just plowing in here like that. Of course they have acoustic front-scanning so they can see the channel clear, but after what happened this noon, it just . . ."

The DE was heading directly for the lighted entrance markers at twenty knots. Colonel Gillam picked up the mike. "Traffic Master, this is Big John. Send in plain English the following: Welcome, please identify yourself. Repeat it over and over. Execute."

"Will do, Big John. Commencing message: Welcome, please identify yourself."

A signal lamp flickered at the north end of Elbow Cay, although they could only see it at Marsh Harbor on a video picture of the entrance area.

Immediately the DE began signaling rapidly back from its bridge toward Man-o-War.

"Big John, this is Traffic Master. We are getting return signal lamp traffic as follows: The Abaco Independence Movement reiterates its solidarity with its ... oppressed black brothers of the Abacos ... we emphasize our peaceful intentions to all ..." Colonel Gillam pressed the priority button and silenced Traffic Master.

"Thank you, Traffic Master. Continue sending our message without change. Crawdaddy North?"

A new voice of a young woman came out of the monitor. "This is Crawdaddy North, Big John. We see your targets."

"Crawdaddy North. Is Harmon tracking?"

"Positive, Big John. Harmon is accepting targets."

The great Sea of Abaco, stretching forty miles north and ten south of Marsh Harbor lay in faint moonlight. The small cay towns of Man-o-War and Hopetown were completely black, as was all of Marsh Harbor. Susan peered out of the dark room at the dark water, and far across the flat sea she suddenly had a sense of motion, of activity.

"He's entering the channel now," whispered Gillam. "Here they all come. Crawdaddy North, do we have a wave simulation yet?"

"Hang on, Big John. Here is Harmon's proposed wave now. This is a thirty-X projection."

The big screen suddenly lit up with an outline map of the Sea of Abaco from Treasure Cay south to Cherokee Point. A thin green line starting at Treasure Cay moved south across the image, shifting in shape and thickness until it reached the Marsh Harbor area, where small green ship targets were also moving more slowly in an irregular line. As the green line passed across the ship pips, they winked out, one after another, and the green line continued past Marsh Harbor and disappeared.

Gillam watched the simulation scan closely. "Crawdaddy North. How soon until decision-zero time?"

"Harmon says four minutes, Big John."

"Crawdaddy, I don't like the north end of the wave. See if Harmon can truncate it."

"Will do, Big John.... Stand by, here comes Harmon's new try."

This time the green line did not overlap Man-o-War at all, but passed directly centered over the line of ships. "Crawdaddy North. This is Big John. I like that simulation. Put Harmon in real time and turn him loose."

"Will do, Big John. Harmon has control ... now!"

Susan turned to Ravetz in puzzlement. "Who is Harmon, Jerry?"

"The hydrodynamic computer," said Ravetz with a grin. "The only self-adjusting, boundary-condition simulator in the world. But

212 I HILBERT SCHENCK

Harmon isn't just a thinker. When he gives us what we want, then we let him go ahead and do it.''

Susan looked at Ravetz and then at Gillam. "You're going to pull the plug on them, aren't you Jerry? Empty out the bathtub?''

Ravetz grinned again. "We couldn't keep you guessing very long on this one, Susan.''

"Big John, this is Crawdaddy North. Harmon is dumping now.''

Gillam peered and peered into the night.

"This is Crawdaddy North. The basin is down five feet, and the sinkage is accelerating.''

"That DE should touch anytime now,'' said Gillam tensely to himself.

Susan looked down from the considerable height of the Wind Commune building and gasped. The land beneath her had suddenly increased. The revealed sand and coral bottom stretched out away from the shore and into the night, no water in sight anywhere. "But, Jerry,'' she asked, "how do you get it to come back as a wave instead of just rising and floating them again?''

From way across the water there was a sudden, grinding, crashing sound. Ravetz cocked his head. "The DE wouldn't float again anyway. She's just ripped her bottom out hitting at twenty knots.'' He pointed to the projected map of the Sea of Abaco. "We pump down the tidal impoundment basin north of Treasure Cay, which is also dredged deeper for load-equalization on very low tides. The water surges into it when the gates are opened by Harmon, gaining velocity so that when it strikes the north end of the basin it builds into a south-moving wave. It isn't a wave really, but a bore, like in the Bay of Fundy, maybe twenty-five or thirty feet high.''

Fidel Castro, one liver-spotted hand rubbing his thin white hair, pointed to the screen. "And this, Professor Ravetz, is also a Shastrian weapon. Useful, community integrated, all the other things you have told us about?''

Ravetz nodded. "Quite practical really. With the entire Bight of Abaco, our backside, turned into a solar pond for the thermocline system, approach to our mainland really has to come across the Sea of Abaco.''

"But amphibious vehicles, Professor Ravetz?'' said the old man.

Jerry Ravetz smiled. "Reserve judgment on that question until our defense is ended, Dr. Castro.''

"Big John, this is your Argus North. We believe all vessels numbering twenty-eight are now on the ground. We can see no movement anywhere.''

"Argus North. Light up the sky!''

Immediately a series of pops sounded far to the north and the first parachutes opened sending brilliant white light flooding down from the sky above the Sea of Abaco. Ravetz leaned toward the old man and spoke softly. "We're using the Swedish day-night battlefield system, Dr. Castro. The pyrotechnic projections are programmed to provide a continuous, shadowless carpet of light for as long as we choose. This part of our operation requires much light."

Brighter and brighter still glowed the once-green Sea of Abaco, but now without its water. Out as far as the eye could see were pools and puddles, but no continuous sea at all. And to the north, in its dry center, were the distant ships, an irregular line of beached and heeled craft of all sizes. And in under the high ceiling of flare lights that continued to fly up popping and bursting came three big Bahamian army helicopters. Susan could readily make out what the massively amplified voice said, over and over, booming downward on the little ragged line of doomed ships. "Put on your life jackets. A tidal wave is coming. Do not stay below. Put on . . ."

Susan gave a sidelong glance at the old Cuban Prime Minister. His mouth was open. He was thunderstruck, transfixed by the scene. This was going to work out. Oh, dear God, this was going to work out!

And now Colonel Gillam turned on the room. "We must have absolute quiet now! Please, all of you!" He picked up the mike. "Crawdaddy South, this is Big John. Is Harmon working on Wave Two?"

"All right, Johnnie. He's working but we've hardly assessed Wave One." It was an ancient, cracked, crotchety voice, a voice Susan knew belonged to eighty-year-old Professor Stephen Morheim, of N.Y.U. and the Trondheim Institute for Hydrodynamic Research, long retired to Abaco where he taught physics and calculus to the freshmen of Abaco Technical from a wheel chair.

Gillam leaned forward, tense, his voice low. "Crawdaddy South, we have only three point seven minutes until decision zero on Wave Two."

'Harmon knows that, Johnnie. He's working out the best initial condition within the solution-time restraint. Now you just lay back and . . . " The irritable old voice trailed off and they heard him muttering to himself near the open mike. "Harmon, let's depth-average and get Johnnie something before he craps his pants. Forget those higher terms, Harmon . . . All right, Johnnie," the voice suddenly louder again. "Here's your projection. Fifty-X, since you're in such a raving hurry."

The screen still showed the southern part of the Sea of Abaco, and again they saw a green line projected on the map moving southeast toward Marsh Harbor from Treasure Cay, and as it moved south a second line of green detached itself from the Little Harbor Impoundment and moved north. The two lines came together between Hopetown and Marsh Harbor, and a third, fainter and more irregular line moved northeast over Johnnies Cay and into the Atlantic. But the original line, now very faint and tenuous, continued southeast to Elbow Cay. "This is Big John. Crawdaddy South, that was a simulated seven-foot runup on Elbow!"

"I know it and Harmon knows it. He's correcting, aren't you, Harmon? Let's delay opening on the west end, Harmon, and phase shift the stream function . . . "

Susan leaned close to Ravetz and whispered in his ear. "Does he really . . . talk to Harmon, Jerry?"

Ravetz turned and whispered back. "He claims he does but John thinks it's just his way of thinking, of organizing himself."

"Here comes a better one for you," came the creaky voice. This time there was no discernible wave hitting elbow, the entire result of the collision running northeast out over Johnnies Cay.

"Crawdaddy South. That was perfect! Put Harmon on line, we've only thirty-six seconds!"

"Don't get so danged rushed, Johnnie. Harmon wants to bifurcate the outrun and keep the blockhouse dry. Now you give the boy his chance . . . "

Gillam suddenly turned and thrust his fingers through his kinky hair. "Jesus, God, Jerry. What . . . "

"Here's the wave, Johnny." And this time the green resultant line actually dimmed in the center as it reached Johnnies Cay and left the basin in two strong surges.

Gillam dropped his hands to his sides. "Oh, Hell. They're actually going to do it!"

"Seven seconds, Johnnie, and I'm putting Harmon on line. Three seconds. Gates are opening. This is Crawdaddy South, Johnnie. Your Wave Two is off and moving!" And the old voice was grim and filled with powerful satisfaction.

Castro leaned towards Ravetz. "The second wave is to prevent the first one from doing damage within the sea, Professor Ravetz?"

Ravetz nodded. "The basin turns south at Marsh Harbor. So we have to modify the first bore by cue-balling a second one into it. The control station on Johnnies Cay is designed to go completely under water, but apparently old Professor Morheim and Harmon have the resultant bore splitting and going out on either side. Well, we'll see. . . ."

But Susan now gave a great gasp, for the northern bore was in sight! A great steaming, thundering white wall of water, it stretched almost from one side of the Sea of Abaco to the other, over three miles of blinding foam running like an express train. And it was growing in size rapidly. "It's doing about thirty-eight miles an hour," said Ravetz to the awe-struck old Cuban.

John Gillam stared hungrily at the great bore. "Optical blow on the crest, Frank."

The big screen immediately showed a magnified and vastly foreshortened image of the crest. And riding back and forth along it were great insects, black and stalky in the intense light of the battle field flare carpet.

"The Donnie-Rockets!" breathed Susan.

"Yes," said Ravetz. "Riding the bore to the ships to help pick up survivors. Saving these crews is the biggest systems problem of all, over twenty-five hundred people in the drink at once."

Marv Weinstein, the Admiral of the Abaco Sea, shouted into his C.B. excitedly. "Gerald Beans, Captain Beans! Get back off that crest! You'll skid to the bottom!"

"We riding just great, Marv!" came the high ecstatic voice of Gerald Beans. "Oh my, Johnnie, we Israelites are coming with the Hammer of God!"

"Here's the picture from Gerald's boat," said Frank Albury, and now the big screen showed a blinding color view down the sloping, white, boiling front of the wave to the sea floor. There was no sense of forward progress, just the violent motion, pitching and rolling. The huge, smoking, ever-changing face of the bore fell away in front like a living, steaming sand dune, and as Susan watched, totally transfixed, the first ships came into view, distantly at the top of the screen, small and leaning in hurt attitudes. Now she turned and looked out the window and saw the great white monster itself, gigantic in the brilliant flat light and moving with implacable, terrifying speed. Now, back on the screen was the bore's face and the DE growing suddenly huge beneath them and . . . The bore devoured it! Ate it completely in a second! Susan, shocked, looked again out the window and saw the monstrous, shuffling white confusion of the bore face vanish each ship in turn with no more effort than if they were seed pods or bits of driftwood.

"How bibilical, Jerry!" said Susan gaping. "You've outdone yourself!"

Ravetz shook his head. "This is completely Colonel Gillam's show. Once he grasped the idea of the Shastri null-weapon, he turned this one up. I never believed it would work. I still don't believe it will work!"

The great white bore swept, roaring, past them, the Donnie-Rockets falling back off the crest now to the sea behind that filled the basin from shore to shore with confusion, surge and chop.

But Captain Beans' picture still showed the gleaming lumpy sheet of the face and, now, something in the right corner of the screen! Wave Two!

Marv urgently spoke. "Lay back, Gerald, lay back! We want the picture, not you *in* the picture!"

"Oh, Johnnie, Marv, I hate to leave her. She's such a beauty! But there comes old man Number Two! Don't he look mean, ole man Two!"

The last Donnie-Rocket fell back off the crest and let it roll ahead towards its turbulent destiny at Matt Lowes Cay. The southern bore, not so high but vast enough indeed, had thundered and smoked up past Lubbers Quarters. Now it was abreast of the old striped lighthouse at Hopetown, and then . . . The great meeting of the seas! A tumult in the basin, an endless roar, spume hundreds of feet high! On Gerald's video they saw the boil and literal explosion of waters in breathtaking close-up, but through the east window a grander sight still, for the entire sweep of the horizon was suddenly intruded on, fragmented by a volcano of white waters, tumultuous and blinding under the flare carpet.

Susan felt suddenly dizzy. Is there nothing we cannot try? An ecstasy in the sea itself!

"This is Crawdaddy South, Johnnie. You want to bet ten crays that we won't wet the top of that blockhouse, eh?" The old man was cackling and breathing heavily.

John Gillam grinned, his teeth shining. "I'd rather bet that the sun wouldn't rise tomorrow, you old . . . "

"Well, Johnnie, there goes the run-off. You just watch!" came the dry crackly voice.

And sure enough, the Donnie-Rocket camera showed that the smaller, but still impressive runoff bore did bifurcate, quite magically in fact, and roll by on each side of the Johnnies Cay blockhouse, and although some spray may have touched the roof, no green water did.

The ancient voice really crackled in satisfaction now. "Thought we couldn't optimize in four minutes, eh, Harmon? Why Johnnie was pissing his diapers when I was jumping Navier-Stokes through hoops . . . "

But now the space north and west of them was blackly spattered with heads, and more were popping up every second. The Donnie-Rockets ran slowly into the thickest bunches, and Abaco police and troopers in bathing suits pulled the men aboard with desperate haste.

Fidel Castro, his face white with astonishment and shock under his white beard, suddenly turned to Major Martino. "José, how many guard machines do we have around Abaco?"

Martino looked surprised. "Why, eight, Fidel."

"Colonel Gillam, if we could help, we have eight sea-surface, rotor machines available to you. They might perhaps come down into the larger groups and hold men until the more mobile . . . "

"We accept, Dr. Castro," said Gillam quickly. "This was always the biggest problem. We simply don't have the capacity to do this fast enough."

As Major Martino and Frank Albury contacted the Cuban machines, Susan watched close-ups on several small screens of the moment-by-moment rescues. The scuba teams were down on the wrecks attempting to free those caught below in that precious moment before the sea water irrevocably damaged their lungs.

Now the first of the big Cuban guard machines settled ponderously into an area black with heads. Frank brought the scene into sharp optical close-up, and they saw the first man in white coveralls leap down a ladder onto the huge float and rip his clothing off in a single gesture, diving smoothly into the sea. His target was a head and hand slipping back into the emerald-green waves.

"He got him!" breathed Ravetz. But now more Cubans were in the water, and still others were rigging nets and ropes for the men in the water to grasp. As the next two Cuban machines settled down into the light, their floats were already crowded with brown lean bodies that dove from great heights at struggling figures beneath.

Colonel Gillam turned and looked straight at Fidel Castro. "These men are a credit to your nation, Dr. Castro. Their flexibility is superb!"

The old man nodded, his color almost returned. "Oh, we have learned some things from your Shastri and from José, Colonel." The old man looked again out the window. "But we have still more things to learn, José, do we not?"

"Si, Fidel, si," said Major Martino soberly, but Susan saw his face was now alight with joy.

The continual rescue and transportation of the prisoners to shore occupied every eye, and Susan turned tiredly to Mary Albury. "Oh, Mary, I'll never get back to Hopetown tonight," she said in a soft whisper. "Is there any place I can lay my head?"

Mary smiled, "Sure, honey, the night-duty weather watch bedrooms on the roof. C'mon, I'll take you up. They don't use them much."

They climbed to the roof and found a cozy, breezy bedroom that overlooked the far-flung rescues still going on to the northeast. Susan sat down on the firm bed, looking out at the brilliant light, and hearing the distant excited sounds. Mary Albury looked down at her. "We're part of history now, aren't we, Susan? Really part?"

Susan nodded drowsily. "Oh dear, yes, I really think we are, Mary." And kicking off her shoes she rolled over and fell into a dreamless sleep.

At quarter to nine the next morning, they all reassembled in the window room of the Wind Commune building. Dr. O'Malley, who had watched the night's events from a Bahamian naval vessel, was already seated, as was Fidel Castro and Major Martino. Susan picked a chair as unobtrusively far back as she could and leaned over to Frank Albury at one of his panels, "How did it all come out, Frank?"

He beamed at her. "Over ninety-eight percent saved, Susan. You know, we never got better than about ninety-two percent in the simulations. Having the Cubans really made the difference. That's the answer, put as many swimmers in the water as you can.''

"You mean . . . the next time you do it, Frank?'' asked Susan seriously. Frank Albury giggled, then laughed out loud.

"Well,'' said Jerry Ravetz, "I'm afraid we're not quite out of the woods yet. That 'we' means humanity in general, not just Abaco. President Demarest is to address the nation at nine A.M. We've done all that could possibly be done on Abaco, and with the help of our Cuban friends.'' Jerry nodded at Castro. "But now the final act is elsewhere. To put this quite quickly, we are expecting Demarest to resign the office of President this morning, although not . . . ah, before certain unconditional pardons have occurred, I suspect.''

Susan could not resist leaning forward. "Jerry,'' she said quickly, "what if he won't do it?''

Ravetz shrugged. "He must do it, Susan. Munoz has fled to Nicaragua where his kind can plot endlessly. Demarest's part in this is hours from exposure. And last night was a total disaster for him.''

"But he is mad, Jerry!''

"Channel Seven looks good,'' said Frank suddenly, and they all stared as the big screen descended and flashed the image of the seal on the rostrum. From offstage came the heavy, stagy voice: " . . . the President of the United States.''

"All my fellow citizens . . . '' Susan looked up at the jowly, age-sagged face, newly ruined by defeat and fear. But the eyes were bright, alive, darting about.

"Jerry, he's mad as a hatter. Look at the eyes!'' said Susan quickly.

"Hush,'' said Ravetz. "Hush!'

"I bring you a brief, sad message, my fellow citizens . . . '' His eyes were darting even more, peering every which way, the hands fluttering, the cheek muscles jerking. "Last night a group of brave young Americans were brutally murdered by a cowardly, dirty kike trick . . . '' The screen briefly blurred for several seconds. Then the image skipped and steadied. "But I must now announce to you all, my beloved friends and supporters, that my health will not permit me to continue . . . ''

"That's an electronic dummy, a piece-up!'' hissed Frank Albury. Fidel Castro looked at Frank.

"What is a 'piece-up,' Mr. Albury?''

"Taking snips of video tape with separate words, facial expressions, and gestures and building a completely spurious TV appearance electronically. It's easy to spot if you know the tricks.''

"Turn it off, Frank,'' said Ravetz quietly.

"Off?''

Ravetz nodded and the screen retracted. "All right,'' he said, and took a deep breath. "President Demarest is dead. Whatever I say here, I'll deny absolutely I ever said . . . and I won't say it again. Is that clear?" He looked around the room. "When Demarest became Vice-president or as he was becoming, a person joined his group who gained Demarest's complete trust. That person, who will soon be identified with an extremist Jewish group . . . and you just had a scrap of Demarest on Jews . . . was given a radiation weapon, a no-blast neutron generator. This morning, Demarest was visited by Israeli Ambassador Gur and told that if he did not quit, his part in the Abaco activities would be revealed and the death of those sailors placed on his head." Ravetz paused, then . . . "I'm guessing on some of this, but it must have happened something like this. Demarest balked, so Ambassador Gur played his final ace. if the president did not announce his resignation within the hour, he would be killed, and if he attempted to leave Camp David, he would be killed. Demarest agreed, but he is mad, as you said, Susan, and they were waiting for him with the taped piece-up ready. When that 'kike' popped out, they knew there was only one way to end it safely and they pushed the button."

"And the rest of those at Camp David?" asked Castro quickly.

Ravetz shook his head. "Gone, of course. Sacrificed. Ambassador Gur, other good and brave men, some evil men, some innocent men."

The room was still until Frank leaned forward and said quickly, "It's true. They can't raise Camp David. Phones, TV. Everything's out there."

Susan raised her hand diffidently. "Jerry, could I say one more thing?"

Ravetz shook his head and grinned. "Susan, you've never stopped talking since you got here, and thank God for that!"

"Well," she said looking around at them. "Dr. Castro, Dr. O'Malley, the rest of you, it's just this. The person who damped this Shastri cycle was Colonel John Gillam and no one else. If Munoz had gotten his way here, none of the rest of this would have happened. This was an epic, an historic defense, not only of Abaco and the Bahama Islands, but of Shastrian ideals as well!"

"Hear! Hear!" said Frank Albury loudly, and they all stood and clapped, turning toward Colonel Gillam.

Fidel Castro nodded vigorously, "Dr. Peabody, I will second that. Colonel Gillam, the matchless professionalism, planning and discipline of your action is eclipsed only by the skill and élan of your men." The old man looked around excitedly. "Shastrian ideals can adapt Communism to the new, to the technical present. The sun shines forever, Professor Ravetz! And Cuba too shall have fourteen-year-old men who drive great foil boats to the very rim of the maelstrom!"

So, in the end, it was black, skinny Captain Gerald Beans of Dundas

Town who would change the Caribbean and perhaps the world. Susan stared, transfixed, as the excited old man, his white beard spiky and erect, now not only looking like Hemingway, but talking that same romantic wild stuff about élan and style. Oh, how Shastri would have laughed at that!

Major Martino leaned over and whispered in Susan's ear. "We will make the step, Susan. Someday they will light candles to you in Cuba!"

But Susan looked down at her brown knees and blinked and blinked.

"Oh, José. Oh, I hope not, José," she whispered back.

The Cuban VTOLs took off at noon while all of Abaco buzzed, and met, and organized the victory celebration that night. After some excited C.B. traffic, Elbow Cay was selected as the site, since it had been in the thick of the air battle and stood the greatest risk of run-up during the use of the hydrodynamic weapon. Colored lights were strung in the small revival park in a parade, of sorts, organized before the crayfish barbecue.

The parade never actually ended but metamorphosed into a kind of combination conga line and boogaloo that stretched the length of Hopetown and kept busy every instrument and player in the entire chain of islands.

At the head of the great writhing chain of Abacoans and Israelis, or really in the middle since the head and tail had long since merged, was that ace of aces, Dawn LaVere. Dancing nearby, Susan noticed, was Prime Minister O'Malley, his eyes popping as Dawn's long thighs and tiny ripped jeans shorts flashed like bonefish in the warm fitful light. The extraordinary tightness and brevity of those shorts suggested that they might not come off at all, a possibility Susan smilingly rejected.

She leaned against the fence at the rear of the field where the dancers dropped off momentarily to get food and drink. She was now without the drug and in full possession of the inevitable downer. Her moment, the greatest moment of her life, had just passed, but she had made no more friends, nor was she any more a part of this blooming Shastrian society than she had been yesterday morning.

Susan looked at the gyrating, grinning throng and listened to the blaring music. She sighed and rubbed her eyes and tried to tell herself, as Frank surely would have, that peacemakers were especially blessed. They didn't seem to offer much to a lonely, overeducated, out-of-place woman in her forties, playing a brief, impromptu role in some larger . . .

"Dr. Peabody?" She looked up startled and saw Colonel Gillam, now neatly dressed in Bermuda shorts and a flowered sports shirt, standing before her. "I wanted to thank you for the speech this morning. We . . . ah . . ." he rubbed his shiny black face with a big pink palm. "We both wanted the same things, Dr. Peabody."

Susan sighed deeply. "Yes, we did, and we do, Colonel." she

looked at the shadowed angular face, the high cheeks gleaming in the dim light, the brown eyes large and soft. If you judged a man by his friends— Dawn LaVere, Professor Morheim, Gerald Beans—John Gillam rated tops.

Susan threw her head back and bit her lip. "Colonel, John . . . would you like to try some political cocaine with me?" She looked openly into his face.

He rubbed his chin slowly. "Well, uh . . . Dr. . . . Susan." He smoothed back his kinky short hair several times. "Ah, well look, frankly, you scare the Hell out of me. I'm afraid I'd be sort of like a scout master trying to keep up with Mata Hari."

Two bright tears popped into Susan's eyes and she made no attempt to wipe them away. "Oh? Well, I guess I really asked for that, John. We Peabodys aren't used to . . . Well, look, just forget I said it." And she stared at his face made blurry with the tears.

John Gillam took her hand and smiled, his big lips just parting to show the bright teeth. "I've had my great victories, Susan. I guess I can stand a defeat," and she unashamedly gripped his hand in gratitude for that.

They walked north from Hopetown, hand in hand, leaving the shouts, the happy laughter, and the tinkling music behind. As they paused at her front door and kissed for the first time, the fitful east wind drove the ridge-mounted wind rotors behind them at subtly different speeds and the air throbbed faintly with the beat frequencies. "Shastri's heartbeat, John," she said softly. But now she saw his eyes were holding her and that they had gone fuzzy and soft as his desire for her mounted.

John Gillam suffered no defeat that night. The great subjective time suspension possible with the drug not only drove him to the peak of sensation but held him in a timeless spasm out of which he perceived another Susan, her body in a tight, upward circle of ecstasy, her face rigid yet smooth and lost as a child's. The softness of her arms and her gentle breasts caught John Gillam in a spiraling rush of tender lust. "Oh, how lovely," he breathed again and again. "Oh, Susan," and it seemed impossible that the relief, and yet not-relief could last so blissfully long.

But Susan was riding a hard, upward-curving wave of white passion, a wave that would never break, or else break and break again forever. Her body lusted for John Gillam's strong core, and when she saw his black face, now soft and heavy with desire, her own lust flamed higher. In that wrenching, protracted moment, she remembered her father, the fairy tales, how they lived happily ever after, and she knew that John Gillam and she would live *within this moment* for ever after, and that was better.

And in her final overwhelming submission to utter pleasure, Susan cried out, "Oh, Johnnie! mine's on fire! Mine's burning too!"

When those words were spoken, the Battle of the Abaco Reefs came, as far as any such battle can, to an end. It was not the last battle in the history of the West, but it was one of the most decisive. And as Susan sensed that night, she and John Gillam did live together within that moment, through the rest of their long and useful lives.

HONORABLE MENTIONS—1979

Aldiss, Brian W., "Indifference," *Rooms of Paradise*.
Alterman, Peter S., "Binding energy," *New Dimensions 9*.
Asimov, Isaac, "The Backward Look," *IASFM*, September.
Bear, Greg, "The White Horse Child," *Universe 9*.
Benford, Gregory, "Dark Sanctuary," *Omni*, May.
——, "Time Guide," *Destinies 2*.
——, "Time Shards," *Universe 9*.
Bester, Alfred, "Galatea Galante," *Omni*, April.
Bishop, Michael, "Collaborating," *The Rooms of Paradise*.
——, "Seasons of Belief," *Shadows 2*.
——, "Love's Heresy," *Shayol 3*.
Bova, Ben, " Kinsman," *Omni*, September.
Brantingham, Juleen, "Lobotomy Shoals," *Omni*, February.
Bryant, Edward, "Teethmarks," *F&SF*, June.
Buckley, Bob, "Time's Window," *Analog*, July.
Card, Orson Scott, "The Monkeys Thought 'Twas All in Fun," *Analog*, May.
Cherryh, C.J., "The Dreamstone," *Amazons*.
Chin, M. Lucie, "The Heirs of Joseph Penn," *Galileo 11 & 12*.
Dann, Jack, "Days fo Stone," *Fantastic*, January.
——, "Night Visions," *Shadows 2*.
Davis, Grania, "Jumping the Line," *F&SF*, July.
Delany, Samuel R., "The Tale of Gorik," *ASFAM*, Summer.
Drake, David, "Cultural Conflict," *Destinies 2*.
Earls, Bill, "The Cow in the Cellar," *IASFM*, December.
Effinger, George Alec, "The Pinch-Hitters," *IASFM*, May.
Eisenstein, Phyllis, "The Mountain Fastness," *F&SF*, July.
Ellison, Harlan, "All the Birds Come Home to Roost," *Playboy*, March.
Evans, Beverly, "The Anchoress," *Nightmares*.
Felice, Cynthia, "Only Human Eyes Can Weep," *Galileo 11 & 12*.
Ford, John M., " Stone Crucible," *IASFM*, August.
Gauger, Rick, "The Vacuum-Packed picnic," *Omni*, September.
Garrett, Randall, "The Napoli Express," *IASFM*, April.
Gotschalk, Felix C., "Square Pony Express," *New Dimensions 9*.
Grant, Charles L., " The Peace That Passes Never," *Chrysalis 3*.
Haisty, Robert, "The Madagascar Event," *Omni*, June.
Haldeman, Jack C. II, "Race the Wind," *Omni*, January.
Haldeman, Joe, "Blood Brothers," *Thieves' World*.

————, "No Future in It," *Omni*, April.

————, "The Pilot," *Destinies 2*.

Hansen, Karl, "Dragon's Teeth," *Chrysalis 3*.

Hecht, Jeff, "Crossing the Wastelands," *New Dimensions 9*.

Ing, Dean, "Domino Domine," *Destinies 2*.

Jennings, Gary, "The Relic," *F&SF*, June.

Kelley, James Patrick, "Flight of Fancy," *F&SF*, June.

————, "Not to the Swift," *F&SF*, February.

Kessel, John, "In an Alien World," *Galileo 11 & 12*.

————, "Just Like a Cretin Dog," *F&SF*, January.

Killough, Lee, "Broken Stairways, Walls of Time," *F&SF*, March.

Kingsbury, Donald, "The Moon Goddess and the Son," *Analog*, December.

Klein, T. E. D., "Petey," *Shadows 2*.

Kress, Nancy, "Against a Crooked Stile," *IASFM*, May.

Lee, Tanith, "The Thaw," *IASFM*, June.

LeGuin, Ursula K., "The Pathways of Desire," *New Dimensions 9*.

Leiber, Fritz, "The Button Molder," *Whispers 13 & 14*.

Leman, Bob, "Loob," *F&SF*, April.

Lynn, Elizabeth A., "The White King's Dream," *Shadows 2*.

Maddern, Phillipa C., "Ignorant of Magic," *Rooms of Paradise*.

McCollum, Michael, "Beer Run," *Analog*, July.

McIntyre, Vonda N., "Fireflood," *F&SF*, November.

Minnion, Keith, "On the Midwatch," *IASFM*, November.

Monteleone, Thomas F., "The Dancer in the Darkness," *New Voices 2*.

Morressy, John, "No More Pencils, No More Books," *F&SF*, June.

Niven, Larry, and Barnes, Steve, "The Locusts," *Analog*, June.

————, "The Schumann Computer," *Destinies 2*.

Novitski, Paul David, "Nuclear Fission," *Universe 9*.

————, and Sarowitz, Tony, "Illusions," *IASFM*, June.

Paultz, Peter C., "The Closing Off of Old Doors," *Shadows 2*.

Petrey, Susan C., "Spareen Among the Tartars," *F&SF*, January.

Pohl, Frederik, "Mars Masked," *IASFM*, March.

————, "The Cool War," *IASFM*, August.

Priest, Christopher, "Paley Loitering," *F&SF*, January.

Proctor, Geo. W., and Green, J. C., "The Night of the Piasa," *Nightmares*.

Pronzini, Bill, and Malzberg, Barry N., "Prose Bowl," *F&SF*, July.

Randall, Marta, "The View from Endless Scarp," *F&SF*, July.

Reamy, Tom, "Blue Eyes," *Shayol 3*.

Robinson, Spider, "God Is an Iron," *Omni*, May.

Rothman, Milton, "Prime Crime," *IASFM*, May.

Russ, Joanna, "The Extraordinary Voyages of Amelie Bertrad," *F&SF*, September.

Ryan, Allan, "Goodnight, Thou Child of My Heart," *Chrysalis 4*.

Sarowitz, Tony, "A Passionate State of Mind," *New Dimensions 9*.

Schenck, Hilbert, "Wave Rider," *Chrysalis 5*.

Shea, Michael, "The Angel of Death," *F&SF*, August.

Sheffield, Charles, "Skystalk," *Destinies 4*.

Stern, Donnel, "Reunion," *F&SF*, September.

Thurston, Robert, "The Wanda Lake Number," *Analog*, January.

————, "Vibrations," *Chrysalis 4*.

Tuttle, Lisa, "At a Time Very Near the End," *Shayol 3*.
———, "The Birds of the Moon," *Fantastic*, January.
———, "The Hollow Man," *New Voices 2*.
Utley, Steve, "Abaddon," *Shayol 3*.
Varley, John, "Options," *Universe 9*.
Waldrop, Howard, "Horror We Got," *Shayol 3*.
Wall, Skip, "Furlough," *IASFM*, November.
Watson, Ian, "The Rooms of Paradise," *Rooms of Paradise*.
Weiner, Andrew, "Comedians," *F&SF*, February.
Wilder, Cherry, "The Falldown of Man," *Rooms of Paradise*.
Willis, Connie, "And Come From Miles Around," *Galileo 14*.
———, "Daisy in the Sun," *Galileo 15*.
Wolfe, Gene, " 'Our Neighbour,' by David Copperfield," *Rooms of Paradise*.
———, "The War Beneath the Tree," *Omni*, December.
———, "The Woman Who Loved the Centaur Pholus," *IASFM*, December.
Yarbro, Chelsea Quinn, "Seat Partner," *Nightmares*.
Yolen, Jane, "Angelica," *F&SF*, December.
Zelazny, Roger, "Halfjack," *Omni*, June.
———, "The Last Defender of Camelot," *ASFAM*, Summer.